PLEDGES OF HONOR

GODDESS'S HONOR
BOOK TWO

JOYCE REYNOLDS-WARD

CHAPTER 1

Gods, but it felt good to sit next to a good solid fire burning strong inside a stove after days of bushwhacking in the cold and wet! Katerin Healer leaned back on her stool to take full advantage of the heat playing across her entire body, stretching her feet closer to that warm stove. The border village of Wickmasa was two days west of her usual circuit, but at least she and her horse Mira had reached it.

Safe. Warm. *Finally.*

A rich scent whispering of damp fertile soil and sun-warmed sweet fruit rather than the sage and pine of this village's high mountain meadows teased her nostrils.

"What is that? Starberry?" she asked Wickmasa's healer, Makri, who stirred a small pot that simmered on top of the stove.

"You've a good nose," Makri said. "Starberry wine it is indeed, this year's vintage."

Katerin frowned. *Saubral produce starberry wine.*

"It's not tainted," Makri said quickly. "We don't trade directly with the Saubral. I got this starberry at the Harvest Fair in Nere a month ago. I always like to have a supply for winter. It makes a good cough potion base. I—*we*—don't trade with Saubral."

"I know it makes a good potion base," Katerin said. "I've used it myself."

I just don't like being around it so soon after a Shadowwalker attack.

Especially after she and Mira had escaped that attack two days ago, in a place that should have been safe. Starberry so soon after didn't feel right. Not remembering details that she should be able to remember about Wickmasa definitely felt wrong.

Makri handed a cup to her. "This is starberry with a touch of Dovré's Blessing and winter's mint. I find it helps to settle the spirit after a time like you've just had."

Katerin cautiously inhaled the aromatic scent rising from the cup. She knew the recipe. But if he had gotten the proportions wrong—gods, Dovré's Blessing was rare and often substitutes were sold as the true herb. Such substitutes were at best ineffective and at worst, could kill. Not knowing much about Wickmasa and the competence of this healer Makri didn't help, either. Most border villages couldn't afford to maintain their own healer, depending on circuit healers to pay periodic visits instead. She had never met Makri at any healer's gathering, which gave her even more grounds for caution.

Still, he and the village had given her shelter for the night. Mira hadn't seemed bothered by the place, only grumping about sharing a corral with Makri's horse instead of wandering free. Wickmasa was clearly Keldaran, not part of the Saubral. The longhouse lodge style and the Keldaran banner flying high above the headwoman's house ensured that. The village guards had greeted her in the name of the three Leaders, Heinmyets, Alicira and Inharise.

All good signs. She was just nervous after that Shadowwalker attack.

The drink didn't smell of the poisonous analogs to Dovré's Blessing. Katerin delicately dipped the tip of her little finger into the potion to taste it.

No bitterness but a tiny sour tang that shouldn't be present in a well-prepared potion. Beginner's work, not the work of a skilled potioner. Not poisonous but not the true Blessing, either. Or else the proportions were so low as to be ineffective. She ventured a small sip.

The real thing. The proportions are off, and the winter's mint is souring the Blessing.

Safe enough for tonight, and possibly relaxing, after all.

"Thank you," she said to Makri, who had settled on his chair, leaning against the tripod back. "Thank you for this and for dinner."

"What else could I do?" Makri shrugged with a dancer's grace. "Healer's Code."

"Not all who've studied the Code necessarily follow it. One has to be cautious." Maybe she could find out where he studied. At the least that would ease her mind about the potion.

Makri scowled. "I'm of the Fan. We take our obligations seriously. I didn't study at the Healing House in Dera long, but it was enough to learn my Code and my potions!"

"My apologies if I have offended." Katerin bowed deferentially, then drank a large swallow of starberry to reassure him of her trust. *More prideful than most healers.* "I did not realize that you studied at Dera. I've never seen you at the Healing House."

"I am sorry," Makri said in a low voice. "My studies were cut short through a need to come back here and serve. I am a simple healer. I came to the Fan through my father. He died many years ago. My mother and siblings are Red Chestnut Leaf, and she took me to the Fan kindreds every summer."

He gestured toward a small wooden mask that hung on the longhouse wall. His coming-of-age mask. It had three small fans etched on each cheek. The twisted snarl on the mask repelled Katerin, enough that she had to look away from it.

Small mask, small fans. He was not high in the Fan hierarchy. No wonder he might be a bit defensive, especially if he lost his father at a young age. Fathers were important to the male-dominated Fan. But the nightmarish scowl with dark highlights on the mask bothered her. Fan masks didn't usually have such hideous grimaces. Her own Blue Starry Robe mask sported a serene smile, despite the turmoil that raged deep inside her during the coming-of-age summer she carved it, so soon after leaving Chiyan.

She sought for a new subject, something that would ease the tension. Her rump started to itch. An image of *itchy gray mare* came from Mira, followed by *stupid gelding covered with buffalo dung.*

Katerin stood, sighing. Mira was quirky about her likes and dislikes, though usually she didn't let a lower-ranking daranval like Makri's horse Soisan bother her this much. Daranvelii, the horse breed with extra sensitivity to the Goddess Dovré and an ability to mind-talk to bonded humans as well as between each other, had a strict hierarchy and Mira was close to the top ranks. Her strong abilities made it possible for Katerin to work a circuit alone in safety—*most of the time,* she reminded herself. *Except when a Shadowwalker and his houndriders are where they shouldn't be.*

Perhaps Mira was, like Katerin, more shaken by this last Shadowwalker encounter than she would admit, even though they had worse experiences. Mira's last bondmate had been killed by a Shadowwalker curse. Maybe Mira was just remembering that time.

"You're going out?" Makri asked as Katerin rummaged in her saddlebags for some salve.

"Mira's complaining about an itch. I'd better see to it."

It shouldn't be a problem. I've checked her morning and night to make sure that Shadowwalker hasn't left a mark on her. She's been clear.

Still, Mira worried. Which meant Katerin worried. The Shadowwalker shouldn't have been roaming free that deep in Keldaran territory.

Probably spying.

The Shadowwalker and his two houndriders had been more interested in torturing her pack mule and rifling the goods the mule carried than in following Mira and Katerin, a sign, perhaps, that they were lost and hungry rather than seeking prey. Still, it had been two days of long, hard, furtive riding through rugged canyon country to avoid any possibility of pursuit. She had thought they were heading deeper into Keldara, when they had been heading for the border instead. A beginner's mistake, not one that either she or Mira should have made.

It could have been the work of a Shadowwalker spell. Itchy skin was one sign of those.

"Can't Soisan help her?"

"I need to do this myself. Mira worries."

"Sure grateful Soisan's a lesser daranval."

"It does have its advantages," Katerin agreed as she rummaged through her pack. "My first daranval was one like Soisan. I appreciate Mira's skills."

"She's not your first?" Makri said, disapproval in his voice.

Dear Goddess, he's one of those *Fan.* Odd that he ended up as a Healer if he was as rule-bound as some of the Fan clan hierarchy could be. Most of those Fan were judges. *Maybe he should have gone with Artel the Judge or Terat of the Waters.*

"The Goddess is infinitely flexible," she said instead of the sharp retort she wanted to say. After all, he *had* fed her and was putting her up for the night. She owed him a certain degree of courtesy.

—*Itch, itch, itch,* Mira thought at Katerin. —*Itch touched with worry,* followed by —*gray daranval mare pacing the corral, stupid mud-colored gelding covered with buffalo dung.*

—*Katerin taking care of Mira,* Katerin thought reassuringly as she put a lit candle stub in a tin lamp and tucked the salve in her pocket, picturing scratching Mira's itchy spot and putting salve on it. She shrugged into her heavy winter jacket made from wolf hide and lined with sheepskin, pulled on her deerskin gloves, then slipped out of the lodge.

Winter wasn't far away from these high mountain valleys. Her breath came out in white clouds and small ice crystals formed on the grass. The Hunter's Moon swung high overhead, past the sky's midpoint, suggesting that morning was not far off. Dinner had taken longer than she thought.

Well, she *had* arrived late, and getting settled into Makri's lodge *did* take time.

The village patrol passed by Makri's corral as she fumbled with the rope securing the gate.

"Katerin Healer, visiting Makri Healer, on my way to the Healing House for the winter," she confirmed to the soft-voiced challenge from the woman guard. "Just checking on my daranval."

Mira nickered a soft welcome and moved near the fence as Katerin spoke.

"Good eve," the woman acknowledged, and rejoined her watch partner.

"Good eve," Katerin responded. She closed the gate, tying it shut, scratched Mira's neck, then worked her way back to Mira's hindquarters. She raised the lantern high and opened one flap to look at the rump. Nothing there.

"Darling, it's all in your head," she murmured softly to the mare. "I *don't* see a thing." She put down the tin lamp, unwrapped the leather bag which held the small bentwood salve box, and scooped out a big glob of salve.

Mira swung her head around to watch as Katerin rubbed in the salve.

—Itch, itch, itch. Itch bad. Katerin doing Sight to check on itchy spot.

Katerin laughed. She rubbed in the last of the salve, wiping her fingers clean on Mira's coat, then scratched her way up Mira's spine to her withers. "Dear one, I already did that. But if you insist, I'll do it again."

Mira nudged her softly. *—Itch, itch, itch.* But the intensity of her image had softened.

"It may not work. I've had starberry wine. You know what wine does to my healing senses. And starberry's worst of all."

Mira pressed her forehead hard against Katerin's body. They stood together for a moment, Mira's anxiety overwhelming both of them. Then Katerin took a deep breath. She half-closed her eyes, calling upon Dovré. Healing vision rose around her hands, shimmering with a faint blue glow in the moonlight. Katerin moved her hands over Mira's itchy spots, projecting the glow down, searching even below the hide for a possible fragment of Shadow.

Nothing.

Or was there? Something didn't feel quite right, but it wasn't from Mira's haunches. Katerin pushed harder, and her vision winked out. She growled, and tried again. This time the glow refused to stir. Dovré's Gift was often inconsistent when coupled with wine, especially the Saubral-brewed starberry wine. Starberry had a lovely taste, but gods, it could interfere with her healing senses.

"I'm sorry," she said to Mira. "I can't raise my sight." She scratched Mira's forehead. "I'll check it in the morning, and have Makri look, too. All right?"

—Makri and Soisan covered with buffalo dung, came back to her.

I wish I knew why she's taken such a sudden dislike to them,

Katerin thought, careful to hide that thought from Mira. She continued to rub Mira's nose.

Mira jerked her head away. She snorted, then turned her head, ears pricked, toward the other end of the village. Then she blew hard again, staring off in the direction that had caught her interest. Her nostrils flared wide as her ears swiveled. She snorted a third time, and stomped with her right hind. A war horse's warning signal to her rider, carried over from her previous life as a war mare.

Katerin's fingers closed on Mira's mane as fear clutched at her gut. She leapt on Mira's back. Better to be mounted if trouble was near.

"What is it?" she asked Mira.

—*Stark, mineral-cold Shadowwalker scent. Faint, very faint.*

Katerin shivered as scents poured through her nose as Mira would smell them. Had that Shadowwalker been on their trail after all? If so, the village guards would take care of it first.

Mira flipped up her upper lip, trying to sort out that trace of Shadowwalker. It was old.

No, —*newer Shadowwalker scent.*

Gods. It was so very small, and yet *so near*. Katerin called on her healing vision, straining to look into that shadow world of the gods to find the source of the Shadowwalker essence. Her vision refused to stir.

It's followed us here, she thought, chilled. *Against all odds, that Shadowwalker followed us here.*

And that, too, was wrong. Such persistence wasn't common in Shadowwalkers, unless they had a particular calling from the dark side of the god Staul, the Destroyer. But gods, she didn't think she had done anything to make Staul the Destroyer angry at her. Staul the Balancer held firm here in Keldara, not the Destroyer, not as long as Heinmyets, Alicira, and Inharise lived and ruled.

Soisan walked toward them, head lowered, his ears pinned

back, a shadow dampening the brightness of his silvery poll. The Shadowwalker scent grew stronger as he approached. Mira squealed and lunged at Soisan with her teeth bared. The gelding stood his ground, rearing to meet Mira, the moonlight making his silver-colored hooves shimmer.

Katerin's healing vision returned, flooding her senses as Shadowwalker essence poured forth from Soisan.

He's possessed!

"Get away from him, Mira!" Katerin yelled.

Mira twisted away from Soisan as he lunged at Katerin, jaws open wider than any horse's should be. Mira bolted, kicking at Soisan to keep him away from them, bellowing her rage and fear.

The guards ran toward them, carrying torches.

"*Possessed daranval!*" Katerin screamed. "Soisan's possessed! Get us out of here!"

Someone flung the gate wide open. Mira charged through the opening, Soisan in swift pursuit. Makri burst out of his lodge, running hard toward them.

"Makri!" Katerin pulled the ritual knife from her belt and flipped it toward him. Better for all that Soisan's bondmate killed him before he infected others, horse and human alike.

Makri flinched but caught the consecrated blade's handle. Katerin wheeled Mira around Makri. Makri stepped in front of Soisan and slashed a good, clean slice across Soisan's throat. Katerin kept Mira moving until Soisan collapsed, then pivoted Mira to face him. Makri held the knife at arm's length as dark green goo dripped from it instead of blood, staring at it instead of containing the foul stuff.

It fell to her, then. He hadn't been trained to deal with Shadowwalker possession. Not a village healer's skill.

Katerin muttered a binding chant as the shadow rose from Soisan's throat instead of life's blood. Mira added a deep mareish nicker to right the imbalance caused when one of Dovré's Own succumbed to a Shadowwalker's possession.

Makri's head sagged. He dropped the blade, half-reaching toward Soisan, then stopping. Two of the villagers gently pulled Makri toward his lodge.

"Bring me my bags," Katerin ordered someone.

She leaned on Mira until the guard brought her saddlebags, then searched through them until she found the pouch containing the blue-shaded glimmer dust sacred to the Goddess. She used the dust to make a circle around Soisan before she called down Dovré's cool fire upon Soisan's body.

The ritual ending for a daranval, even one possessed. *Leave no bonded daranval to the earth,* the Goddess had ordered when gifting daranvelii to humans. Otherwise, their spirits roamed restlessly.

The Goddess took Soisan back quickly. When the cool blue fire faded, Katerin collected what she could of the ash and mixed it with protective herbs; sage, cedar, and juniper. She gave two handfuls to a guard to scatter around the village, reserving a handful that she put in a small wooden box that she tucked into one of her pockets, to scatter around Makri's lodge. At least Soisan would contribute to the protection of the village, despite whatever lapse had led to his contamination.

Wickmasa's shaman for the god Artel, Twana, helped Katerin purify herself and Mira, marking their foreheads and shoulders with protective oils while whispering prayers to the Bright Judge. Then she smudged both of them with a mixture of sage and cedar. Katerin took a deep breath of the aromatic smoke. It cleared her mind of the remnants of Makri's starberry potion.

"What about Makri?" Twana asked when they were done.

Katerin glanced toward sunrise's first glow lighting the horizon to the east. A night without rest, and odds were that she should be moving on today.

"It's horrible to have to take the life of one's own bonded daranval, to violate the bond given by the Goddess. But it's the only thing he could have done, with Shadowwalker possession," she said to Twana, trying to avoid a direct answer.

"How could Soisan get possessed without Makri knowing? Could he have consented to it?" Twana gave voice to Katerin's thoughts.

"I don't know," Katerin said. "If you don't know the feel of Shadowwalker possession, you might not recognize a subtle exposure."

"But where would he have been exposed?" Twana asked. "We haven't had any contact with Shadowwalkers here."

"And I shouldn't have been attacked by a Shadowwalker on my healing circuit."

"True." Twana shivered and thrust her hands in her pockets. "The Tyrant Zauril stirs again in quest of his lost daughter." She winced, as if speaking the words hurt.

Twana's words stirred a brief memory. The daughter of Alicira and the Tyrant of Medvara, Rekaré, had disappeared near Wickmasa.

This might be important.

Katerin didn't realize she spoke out loud until Twana raised her eyebrows.

"What might be important?"

Gods, now she couldn't remember. Katerin tried to think back. What had she just thought was important?

"I've forgotten."

Twana's face softened. "Not surprising, after all you've been through."

Her tone was too relieved for the circumstances. Still, there was no time to examine this further at this moment. "Has Makri been checked?"

"I saw to Makri before I came to you. He appears to be without physical hurt. But mentally?" She shook her head.

"Despair has taken him. Worse than is typical for losing a daranval."

"I'd best see to him." The shock of losing one's own bonded daranval, even a lower-level one like Soisan, could be hard, and healer's connections were tighter than most. "Sometimes the Shadowwalker curse touches not just body but also the mind."

That was extremely likely given that no one, not even she or Mira, had noticed Soisan's possession until now.

Katerin glanced again toward the east, gauging the growing light. "He's not alone?"

Twana shook her head. "No. His brother Metkyi is with him, along with others who care for him. Please. Help him. He isn't a master healer, but he's from here, he knows our folk, he knows our needs. More than that, his mother." Her voice caught oddly for a moment. "His mother was from an old Wickmasa family."

"I will try to help him." Katerin went to Mira for strength and reassurance, wishing they could leave now instead of dealing with this.

I'm tired. Tired and too long out on the trail.

The sun broke over the mountains. Katerin pressed her forehead to Mira's. Then she stood up straight, pulled back her shoulders, and walked toward Makri's lodge. As she neared the lodge, she heard voices arguing. A tall young man who resembled Makri ran out the door, then hesitated, turning back toward Katerin, holding himself stiff and straight, his face twisted with distress.

"Healer Katerin?" he asked. Something about the way he stared directly at her with a single-minded focus made her shiver. Memories stirred and flickered away. This must be the brother Twana had mentioned.

"I am she. You are his brother Metkyi?"

The man grimaced. "Yes. Perhaps you can talk sense into him. Where's Twana?"

"She is coming."

"Good. I'm going to hurry her along. He won't listen to me, perhaps he'll listen to you! His thoughts are storm-snared and wind down twisted trails. I can't get him to listen to reason."

"Then I'd better go to him." Katerin turned away from Metkyi.

Things were worse than she thought. Makri sat next to the stove, the materials for ritual suicide arranged around him. He ignored the two young women pleading with him, staring straight ahead. He startled as she strode across the lodge toward him.

Shadowwalker curse indeed.

Whatever had possessed Soisan had touched Makri as well.

I don't know if I can counter this.

He had painted his face with Fan mourning symbols and had already sacrificed a fingertip, sloppily leaving the blood to pool around him instead of cleaning up.

Not usual.

The long obsidian ritual blade rested on its wood stand next to him, along with a dish full of the traditional black dust poison. Makri's broken mask lay in front of him. The scent of starberry overwhelmed Katerin and she wobbled in front of Makri. Starberry with a rotten scent underneath. No question about it this time. Poisonous analog to Dovré's Blessing, making it a curse rather than a blessing.

He's already gone far down the twisted ways.

"Stop this." Katerin did her best to project a confident voice. "Makri, do not succumb to the Shadowwalker." She took Soisan's ashes from her pocket. "Let me mark you with these."

"NO!"

Makri jumped up and slapped her hand, sending the ashes flying around them. The box landed on the broken mask. It burst into flame. Makri broke into a high-pitched, ululating scream. Fire rose around them where the ashes had scattered.

The other women bolted from the lodge, leaving Makri and Katerin to face each other.

This isn't of Dovré or even of Staul. Mira, help me!

Nothing. She could visualize the small gray mare in her mind but a transparent barrier seemed to lie between them.

Something's blocking her. What is it?

She looked around, saw the pot with the starberry wine in it still sitting on the stove.

Get rid of that. The scent is influencing him and it's keeping Mira from me.

She picked it up. Makri wrenched the pot away from Katerin, splashing most of it over his body. The spilled potion burst into flame. She tried to put out the fire but he shoved her across the lodge. Then he seized the dish full of black dust and thrust some in his mouth, pouring the rest over his body. The dust caught fire.

"MIRA!" Katerin screamed.

Oh gods, no, no, no.

Bile rose in her throat, choking Katerin. The starberry wine and part of her dinner came up before she could stop herself. Mira's mind touched hers, giving Katerin the strength to spit out the sour remnants in her mouth. She scrambled back to her feet and grabbed a blanket to smother the flames.

Makri's body tightened and convulsed. He seized the obsidian blade and impaled himself. Flames gushed from his body along with blood as he fell. The fire's heat drove Katerin back.

Metkyi and Twana burst into the lodge. Katerin tried to stand but a coughing fit doubled her over. Metkyi and Twana dragged her out. Metkyi handed Katerin a waterbag and she drank three huge swallows. Her gut settled. She leaned against Mira, and forced herself to watch as fire took Makri's lodge.

"I am so sorry," she said softly. "I tried."

"There was nothing you could do," Metkyi growled. "He chose his course. Damn him." He strode away.

Twana shook her head and followed Metkyi. Katerin watched as flames consumed the lodge, sick to her stomach. She wanted nothing more than to ride away from this place and never come back.

But she had a job to do. She had to make certain that Soisan was an isolated contagion. Her pledges as a healer required it. Her honor as a healer required it.

"My lady healer, the Eldest wants to see you," a guardswoman said to her.

"I will be there," Katerin said.

"Do not tarry long," the guardswoman warned.

"I need to gather my things and find out what may have burned."

"Your bags are over there," the guardswoman gestured to where Soisan had fallen. "I brought them to you."

"I remember now. Thank you."

"And if your tack is not saved, we will give you what you need."

"Thank you," Katerin repeated mechanically. "I will be along shortly."

"I will tell our lady Imnari." The guardswoman bowed and left.

Katerin sighed. "We have work to do," she told Mira. "But first, we have to meet the Council."

Gods, she wasn't looking forward to this meeting. Not after this violation of healer pledges and healer honor.

CHAPTER 2

Katerin stopped ten paces short of the line of elders in front of the Council longhouse and pulled herself up to her full height, remaining tense and tight until Mira's muzzle brushed against her elbow.

"Healer Katerin." The Eldest, a strong-boned woman with long, unbound, silver hair streaming across her shoulders, stepped forward. She wore the headdress of her office, an elaborate crown of eagle feathers whose quill tips were interwoven with fine beadwork and exquisitely braided leather.

"Eldest Imnari." Katerin bowed formally, wishing she wore the formal healer robes that had been packed in one of the saddlebags lost to the Shadowwalker. She looked for clues to tell her more about this Eldest and her attitude toward the Healing House. Imnari's skin bore no clan marks or sign. Golden seed heads were worked into the trimmings of the headdress, but whether that was a clan marker for the Eldest or an honorary sigil for Wickmasa, Katerin didn't know.

"I am Imnari of Harvest Moon Rising," the Eldest said.

"Thank you," Katerin said. "I am Katerin of Blue Starry Robe, originally from Chiyan Village of Waykemin."

Imnari raised her brows, frowning slightly. "Surprising to find one from Chiyan in Keldara."

"I have my reasons for working out of Dera," Katerin said.

"Does Terani the God-Killer still sleep in Waykemin?"

Katerin's throat tightened and she coughed to cover her reaction before answering. "The last I heard, Eldest Imnari, is that she still sleeps."

Imnari gestured to a younger, frowning man standing next to her. He bore a slight resemblance to Makri in the shape of his face and brows. "This is Yetklet," Imnari continued. "Our patrol chief."

"Makri was my sister's son," Yetklet growled.

Katerin's gut clenched. He could claim blooddebt.

"My deepest regrets," she murmured. "I wish I could have convinced Makri to make another choice."

Yetklet waved dismissively. "Makri was a romantic fool," he said. "He should never have trained for a healer. He would have been much more useful as a blacksmith, like his father."

"Dovré's call comes to whom it will, when it will," Katerin said.

"And now my sister's son is gone." Yetklet shook his head. "It's not been that long since Zauril's riders stopped here every summer—"

"Yetklet," Imnari intervened. "We are not here to talk about that."

"At some point we will need to talk about them!"

Katerin caught her breath. Wickmasa had once been a stop on Zauril's annual summer demand for tribute.

Maybe Nere isn't where Soisan's exposure happened.

She tightened the fingers of one hand. What if Soisan had been exposed here in Wickmasa? A memory stirred, then hid itself, to her frustration.

With a jolt, Katerin's attention returned to the Council as

Yetklet started to storm off, then turned back when Imnari growled at him.

"As you wish, Eldest," he muttered, rejoining the other Council members.

Imnari nodded, a faint smile on her lips as he bowed to her. "Thank you, Yetklet. Healer Katerin. This is my Council, except for Twana and Metkyi. Where's Metkyi?"

"With Twana," Yetklet said.

"Ah. Yes. Family honor. Healer Katerin, let me introduce the rest of my Council." Imnari introduced the remaining four members of the Council, three men and one woman. Katerin nodded to them, their faces and names and clans blurring together. Her usual memory for names had deserted her—*the starberry? Something else?*—but at least she could remember their roles. The woman, she noted, was the Gather Chief. One of the men was the Horsemaster, another the leader of the hunters, and the other was the trade chief.

Imnari's the peace chief, then, their negotiator.

Katerin bowed to each as they were introduced.

"And now," Imnari concluded, "to the point, Healer Katerin. Wickmasa needs a healer. We have always felt it best to maintain a healer within the village rather than contract on a circuit."

"That is your choice," Katerin said, keeping her tone neutral.

How can Wickmasa afford to keep a year-round healer?

It looked no more prosperous than any of her client villages. On the other hand—Makri had been of Wickmasa. He would have had housing and clan-rights of his own for access to food, supplies, and services. Faint memories from her history studies years ago stirred, reminding her that Wickmasa had earned its right to have a healer of its own. But the details kept slipping from her memory.

Has someone cast a remembrance spell here? If so, why?

Normally, Katerin remembered the details of village politics and interconnections, a crucial skill on the borders. However, in these days with all but open war with Zauril the Tyrant, some powerful villages might want to be obscure, and so, remembrance spells were cast, to keep all but a handful of outsiders confused about the role of that particular village in the politics of Keldara and Clenda.

What role does Wickmasa play in Keldara's defenses?

As close as it was to the borders with Larij, Clenda and Saubral, that could be a factor. And that closeness to Saubral meant that a representative of the god Staul would guard the village against ravages by followers of his dark side.

Staul the Balancer, she reminded herself, stifling a shudder. *The priest here will follow the Balancer aspect of Staul. Not the Staul the Destroyer that the Shadowwalkers follow.*

Wickmasa most likely was crucial to Keldara's defense in a manner she wouldn't know. And, as such, not only would it have a priest of Staul, it would have its own healer.

"Wickmasa has always had its own Healer," Imnari said. "One of ours is at the Healing House right now."

Katerin relaxed. She would just have to make sure that any Shadowwalker taint was banished. Once she finished, she could be off to the Healing House, her obligations filled, and the Wickmasa student could come home.

"I will certainly make sure that your healer is well prepared when I return to the Healing House for the winter and inform him or her of the need," she told Imnari.

Imnari frowned. "There is a problem. Our healer-to-be left for training a fortnight ago."

"Perhaps you could carry a circuit healer's contract until he or she is ready to serve?"

"A circuit healer's contract will not meet our needs," Imnari said firmly.

"I can't guarantee that the Council can find someone to work here for the next year."

"*You* are here."

"I have contracts I must finish before the Winter Gathering. I have training to do this winter. I have contracts I must meet for the spring."

"Could you not stay here over the winter?" Imnari asked. "By spring, perhaps our Hinet could come back, with the support of a circuit healer. We need to have someone here until Hinet returns."

"The Council will need more information than vague assertions, Eldest."

"I think," Imnari paused, clearly considering her next words, "that you will find that the Council will not need any more knowledge than the simple statement that *Wickmasa has need.* It is a matter of the Gods."

Katerin took a step back and rubbed Mira's poll.

What do I do? What could be so important about Wickmasa? Why would working here for the winter be a matter of the Gods?

A remembrance spell. This place definitely had a remembrance spell operating.

Mira rubbed her left ear against Katerin's hand.

—*Cave opening blocked by a locked door* came from her, a warning of her perception of mixed motives. The clarity of the image emphasized Mira's warning.

Katerin sighed. —*Healing House*, she thought back.

If Mira wouldn't want to return to Wickmasa, then they wouldn't, and would be within their rights to say no.

—*Mira and Katerin in Wickmasa, in shades of red and blue.*

Another warning, but clearly a vote to return. That, plus what little Katerin could pull out of her memory about Wickmasa, clinched her decision.

"Eldest Imnari," she said slowly. "My daranval and I are at Wickmasa's service, at least for the winter."

Imnari smiled. "I do not think you will regret your choice."

I already do.

"I need to finish my business with my other contracted

villages and make my report to the Chief Healer. Then I will be free of my other obligations and can return to Wickmasa."

"We understand this need."

"Before I leave, I need to ensure that there's no other Shadowwalker taint in Wickmasa."

"There is no need for you to seek out any further Shadowwalker problems until you return. Twana and Metkyi can deal with it. I'd prefer you get the matter of stores and your lodging settled today, then deal with your other obligations and return as quickly as you can. Winter storms are coming. It won't be long until winter travel is by caravan only. Shadowwalker taint can wait."

"True," Katerin conceded.

But how many others did Soisan affect? And why is Imnari suddenly so insistent about my leaving quickly?

Between the secrets and Imnari's maneuvering, this definitely looked to be a long winter.

* * *

IMNARI TURNED Katerin over to Myrieke, the Gather Chief, to settle Katerin in for the winter. They retreated to Myrieke's lodge to make the list of the supplies and stores Katerin would need for the winter.

"We can have a lodge ready by the time you return. What design do you want?" Myrieke asked.

"Something big enough for patients but easy for me to keep it warm by myself." Cold. Gods, how cold did these mountain valleys get during the winter? Colder than she was used to, for certain. "I need two rooms, one for my private use, the other for patients."

Myrieke nodded as Katerin spoke, chewing her lower lip. "Yes. Yes. That makes sense. I'll send you two assistants to help you."

"Thank you," Katerin said.

"What about your daranval's lodging? Makri didn't request anything special for Soisan, but I know not all healers feel like he did about their daranvelii."

"A shelter next to my lodge with Mira going free, unless the Horsemaster feels more comfortable with her being corralled. I need a corral for my pack animals."

"We can build a shelter." Myrieke smiled. "And Horsemaster Kwellet will want to talk to you. Wickmasa's healers have always helped with daranval training, though Makri was an exception. Kwellet shouldn't mind Mira going free."

"I can train daranvelii," Katerin said. "After all, it's what I do for the winter at the Healing House."

"Then it is fortuitous that you are here," Myrieke said.

That's what you think, Katerin grumbled to herself. But she said nothing. She would need Myrieke's good will for the winter ahead of her.

CHAPTER 3

Katerin and Mira finally splashed down the mud and snow-mixed path that dropped from the Northern Pass to the Keldara River, late on the fourth day after they had left Wickmasa.

Almost there.

Mira halted to rest at an overlook. Katerin checked Mira's hooves and the leather wraps tightly fastened onto them. She had saved these last magicked wraps for this section of their trip. Surefootedness and speed might save their necks, and those wraps guaranteed surefootedness.

She stepped over to the overlook's edge. Normally, one could see the smoke and lights from Dera and the smaller villages in the Keldara Valley from here. This afternoon, the heavy fog obscured everything. No matter. Fog meant there would be no rain or snow today. They would reach the Healing House and Winter Quarters by dusk.

Katerin checked that her bow and arrows were slung within reach and tapped the hilt of the short sword she carried as a backup to her bow. Then she examined her boots. The magic worked into them was all that kept the boots together. Barely enough magic remained to keep the boots effective and in one piece until they reached the Healing House.

Cutting it pretty tight this year. But down this stretch, through the foothills, and we're there.

As long as the magic held. As long as bandits weren't focusing on this trail and on what little wealth a tired healer and her daranval might carry. As long as another Shadowwalker out of place didn't stumble across her path.

"Let's go." Katerin swung up on Mira.

Mira's thoughts were formlessly grumpy. But grumpy was better than sudden alert. Despite her fatigue, despite the gloom of the dank fog that obscured the ridgetops, every known twist and turn of the trail that followed the Keldara River through the foothills brought relief to Katerin.

Home. They were almost home. They could rest for a couple of days, replenish their medical stores, and buy supplies Katerin had been reluctant to get from Myrieke.

She mentally reviewed her list as they walked, as if she hadn't already thought it through at least five times a day since they left Wickmasa.

Boots and hoof wraps. Medical supplies on Wickmasa's account, not her own. As much magicked clothing as she dared spend credit on, including a winter blanket for Mira. No luxuries, but as much in the way of magicked and healing supplies as she could load on a pack animal. She didn't want Mira carrying a load back to Wickmasa.

The next turn brought them where the Keldara River broke free of the foothills and spilled out onto the open valley, suddenly free from fog. The sun had already set behind the high mountains to the west, but a faint glow lingered on the mountain ridges. Ahead and to her right Katerin spotted the lights of the Healing House and Winter Quarters.

Home.

"Who goes there?" A young, female voice, quavering slightly, challenged them.

Katerin dismounted. "Healer Katerin and Daranval Mira."

Mira added a low whicker, answered by a higher-pitched daranval's squeal.

"Healer Katerin," a deep male voice rumbled. "Greetings, and welcome home. We've been worried about you."

The two sentries moved out from their stations, hidden by screens of magicked fabric. The man, Eldoran, the Head Instructor of the Healing House, strode forward to sweep Katerin up in a big hug.

"Eldoran, you don't know how good it is to see you," she said. She hadn't expected him to be on sentry duty.

Unless he's been watching for me?

Katerin gave Eldoran an extra squeeze. Whatever the reason, she was glad to see the Head Instructor.

"I imagine." Eldoran put Katerin down and eyed Mira's tack. "You're down to the basics. What's happened?"

"I have to go back out."

Eldoran frowned at her. "But your contracts are done—"

"Unfortunately, there's need. Wickmasa's healer is no more, and they want someone there for the winter."

"What happened to Makri?" blurted Eldoran's female companion, dressed in the greens of a first-year apprentice healer.

Eldoran stepped back. "Katerin. This is Hinet, our newest apprentice here at the Healing House. She's—"

"From Wickmasa, arrived a few weeks ago," Katerin finished for him. "I know." She looked at Hinet. "I am sorry. Makri's daranval died, and he suicided."

"Oh no!" Hinet's hands flew to her mouth.

Katerin hugged Hinet. "I am sorry," she whispered. She turned back to Eldoran. "I need to meet with the Council as quickly as it can be arranged. I need to restock. Before I reached

Wickmasa, I was attacked by a Shadowwalker. They killed my mule and stole many of my healing supplies."

"The Council has many end of season obligations." Eldoran flashed a hand sign at Hinet. She stayed behind as Eldoran, Katerin, and their daranvelii strode toward the walls of the Healing House.

"I know. But I was told by the Eldest of Wickmasa that all I would have to say to get Council approval was that 'Wickmasa has need.' Just what in the Goddess's name is that all about?"

Eldoran sighed. "It's a long story."

"Wickmasa has one of the tightest remembrance spells I've ever run into," Katerin continued as they passed through the outer gate. "That has to be lifted if I go back. The place has too many secrets."

Eldoran halted outside the main hostel assigned to incoming healers who had not yet received housing assignments.

"If the Council agrees to your placement I'll lift that spell myself," he said.

Katerin slipped her bags off of Mira and handed her reins to the apprentice healers who came to take her. She caressed the mare's poll, thinking about —*Mira romping with the daranval herd, racing in the meadows.*

—*Mira as part of small band of mares* came back, with added images of —*black and bay mares, friends, Mira, bullying geldings and getting best food and water.*

Katerin laughed, then stepped back and let Mira go with the apprentices, watching wistfully as the gray mare pranced in anticipation of playtime.

Eldoran tapped her on the shoulder. "Better check in and get some grub. The Council will want to talk to you tonight. It *is* Wickmasa and you *are* right, Eldest Imnari only needs to say 'Wickmasa has need.'"

Katerin sighed. "Thanks, Eldoran." She pulled out the sealed letter from Imnari. "This is to the Council from Wickmasa's

Eldest." She handed it to Eldoran. "Or should I deliver it myself?"

"I'll take care of it." Eldoran carefully tucked the letter into his jacket.

"Thanks." Katerin shouldered her bags.

"Be ready at any time," he cautioned. "Wickmasa's status means that the Council will move faster than you expect."

"I'll be ready."

"Good." He bowed, deeper than usual, and left.

Katerin shivered and rubbed her hands on her elbows. Then she turned toward the hostel and heaved another deep sigh.

Wish I were checking in for the winter.

Unless the Goddess had changed her plans, she wasn't going to be at the Healing House for long.

Katerin trudged up the plain wooden steps to the main entrance, considering her timing.

I probably have enough time to get a bunk for the short-term, set up my bed, and eat. If I'm lucky I'll get a drink before I go to Council.

Katerin pulled open the heavy door.

One season ends. Another begins.

A distant bell tolled. Katerin hurried down the hallway. If she were lucky, she would be finished with the procurer in time to eat at the regular evening meal. Making her bed up could wait until she had a good feed.

CHAPTER 4

"*A*hhh." Katerin eyed the platter of roast beef, the mixed roasted root vegetables, and the light, fluffy, warm bread with fresh butter. on the long common table, contemplating another serving.

"Eat up," her friend Senai encouraged. "You've lost weight this season."

"Don't I know it." Katerin shook her head ruefully. "A long and hard circuit. Then that Saubral attack wiped out all my earnings." She drank her beer.

"Hard luck, that. At least you've a winter contract. Where is it?"

"Wickmasa. Up past the Northern Pass, near the Clendan border."

"Never heard of it."

"You're not the only one," Katerin muttered. When the plate of sweet cake came to her, she passed it on without taking any. She was too full to eat the rich cake stuffed with berries.

"I've heard of Wickmasa," Yevtin, one of the other far-ranging circuit healers, chimed in from his seat next to Katerin.

Katerin turned toward Yevtin. "So what do you know about Wickmasa?"

Yevtin ran one hand through his curly dark hair. "I've run into Wickmasa's Makri at the Trading Fairs in Nere. He always seemed to be doing a lot of non-Healer-type trading."

"What do you mean by that?"

Yevtin took a bite of sweet cake and chewed it thoroughly, then dabbed at his mouth and beard with his handrag. Katerin sipped her beer, recognizing the signs of Yevtin preparing to tell one of his tales.

Yevtin swallowed some beer and set his mug down firmly. He leaned closer to Katerin and rested his left elbow on the table, shutting out others from their conversation.

"You have to understand that Makri never talked a lot about village business," he said, keeping his voice low. "The place has a remembrance spell."

"Yes. I know." Katerin leaned closer to Yevtin. Usually Yevtin's tales were loud and boisterous. This time he met her eyes seriously and quietly, his voice near a whisper.

"I'm not subject to those spells anymore," Yevtin continued. "Not after, well, you'll learn. Listen. Makri wasn't like most village healers when they hit Nere. Those other village healers, they're swapping healing tales, and remedies, and all sorts of wild stuff. Figures, since most of them are from the back of beyond."

Katerin nodded, knowing exactly what he meant. "Makri didn't talk?"

"Not about the village. You'd barely know he was from Wickmasa. He wasn't looking for remedies and new herb mixtures, either. No, he was always gathering information on the latest Saubral movements or trade issues."

Katerin pulled back slightly from Yevtin. "That's not a healer concern!"

"Lower your voice, girl," Yevtin cautioned. Senai cast a worried glance over at Katerin.

"It's all right," she told Senai. "Just talking."

Senai nodded.

"What's a healer doing gathering information that should be a war chief's concern?"

Yevtin nodded slowly. "Exactly. He spent time with *questionable* traders."

"Starberry dealers?"

"Starberry and other products from those sources. He wasn't always as careful as he should have been. I had to bail him out of trouble a couple of times. But he was my apprentice when he came to the Healing House, and I thought I should help him."

"Makri *apprenticed*? On a *healing circuit*?"

"There's not a lot of other options for training village healers."

"He didn't strike me as having the savvy to make it through a regular season's circuit."

"He didn't have the skills and flexibility to last on a circuit. As it were, he was doing a poor and way-too-obvious job of intelligence gathering." Yevtin stroked his beard thoughtfully. "I didn't think he was a spy. He was too reckless, too talkative. I thought he might be running some trades for the Fan kindreds, and earning some gold working for smugglers here and there."

"He was one of the last people *I'd* finger for being a smuggler."

"Well. Yes. But the timing was always good for him to be working something for the Fan. He always seemed to be in Nere either before or after a Clan gathering." Yevtin suddenly fell silent.

Katerin looked up. Eldoran glowered at Yevtin.

"Hate to rush you away from dinner," Eldoran said, "but the Council is ready."

"I'm just about done."

"I'll be waiting outside." Eldoran nodded to Yevtin, holding his eyes for a moment, then strode away.

Katerin looked over at Yevtin. "Can you tell me anything else?" she asked.

"Only this. If you're doing business with Wickmasa, my friend, then you need to watch your every move. That place is Gods-haunted in ways you don't want to know about." He waved her away. "Best get going. Council doesn't want to wait these days. Lots of business before winter." His voice lowered. "Maybe more. Later. Private."

Katerin chugged down the rest of her beer and wiped her face. "I'll meet up with you when I'm done," she said to Senai.

"Any idea when you'll be back?"

"Whenever the Council gets done with me."

Senai made a face. "If it's not too late, I'll be by the fire. Otherwise, come talk in my room."

"*Our* room," Katerin corrected. "They bunked me in with you."

"I'll fix your bed if you're not back before I hit the bag."

"Thanks. I'm hoping they won't keep me that long."

"Good luck," Senai said.

Katerin swung her legs free from the bench, stretching before she walked. She ambled out of the dining room and onto the front porch.

Eldoran scowled at Katerin. "Shouldn't be listening to gossip."

Katerin shrugged. "With a place like Wickmasa, it's hard to tell what's gossip and what's fact. As it is, I'm fighting that gods-cursed remembrance spell."

Eldoran nodded abruptly. He stomped down the steps. "You have to be careful about how much you talk," he growled.

Katerin slid to a stop in the mud, the cold glop oozing in through a crack in her left boot.

Boots. Tomorrow. First thing I do.

"Eldoran." Her voice cracked slightly. "By the Goddess's left tit, can you tell me what is going on?"

Eldoran sighed and faced Katerin. "If I knew for certain, I'd tell you. You're the only one who can go to Wickmasa. Not after what Imnari wrote. You're the only healer that Wickmasa will accept."

"And if I don't accept?"

"You're already too deeply involved. It's safer for you to continue than not."

"Damn it, Eldoran, there's too much secrecy! I'll only take so much of 'it's the Goddess' before I want some answers! If the Council wants me there so badly, then give me a reason!"

"A lot is at stake there. Political. Not just with humans, but with the Gods. We need someone there that we can trust. A good observer as well as a good healer."

"Observer? Am I going to be asked to spy?"

"Just observe. Field reports from a village healer. That's all we want. Nothing complicated."

"What kind of field reports?"

"Weather. Illnesses. Anything out of the ordinary."

"Why?"

Eldoran shook his head. "Get through the winter in Wickmasa with as few complications as you can. I promise that you'll have a smaller route next season, perhaps even just a summer route instead of a big spring-summer-fall route like you had this year."

"You can guarantee that?" Katerin stopped again, pulling her arm free and staring at Eldoran. She had no idea he held that much influence in Council.

Or is my Council appearance just a sham, and he's the real negotiator for my services? For being in a rush, he's certainly willing to waste time talking.

Eldoran glanced around to see if anyone else was within earshot. He lowered his voice. "If you can get through this winter without incident in Wickmasa, you'll be able to pick and choose what route and what villages you want. By the Goddess's gold necklace, I swear it to you."

Katerin studied Eldoran's eyes. "What about my credit? I won't earn as much with a shorter route."

Gods, she could replenish her credit; retire to an easier life. This last year had been rough. Pay off the last debts for her training, so that the only thing she owed was for Terani's support. Yes. A good contract would be worth a winter's work.

"Between what Wickmasa's committed itself to, and the raised contract pay for your next summer season, you'll make more next season than you did this one you just finished."

"All right," she said. "I'll cooperate. But I need that remembrance spell lifted, right now."

Eldoran rested both hands on her shoulders. "I told you I'd lift that spell myself. More than that, I'll ride out to Wickmasa with you and a couple of apprentices to make sure that you're set up properly."

"I'm going to hold you to that promise. As for escorts, I'd prefer finished and experienced healers, not apprentices."

Eldoran grimaced. "You drive a hard bargain. I suppose you want Senai and Yevtin?"

"Why not? Senai's my training bond-friend, and Yevtin has a tie to Wickmasa through Makri. Better choices than two apprentices who don't have a clue about magic, healing, and politics."

Eldoran shook his head, but a faint smile twisted his lips. "Healer Katerin, you're a hard bargainer with reasons I can't break apart, even in the name of secrecy and security."

Secrecy and security.

His words confirmed her suspicions. Only the Council spoke in these terms.

"You're negotiating this contract for the Council right now."

"Yes."

"Why?"

"Because Wickmasa is a subject that not even all of the Council is free to discuss," he said. "We'll write up the contract tonight."

"I want a Council steward to check it before I sign."

"And that would be Yevtin, the old busybody."

Katerin grinned at Eldoran. "Exactly."

Eldoran threw up his hands. "All right, Katerin. Just as long as we can get this done tonight, so we can get you outfitted and back on the trail day after tomorrow."

Katerin slipped her hand into his elbow. "Then let's lift this spell and get this contract written, shall we?"

Eldoran shook his head at Katerin. But they walked arm-in-arm the rest of the way to the Council longhouse and Eldoran's office. The desk already had a parchment laid out on it, with writing implements waiting. Her Blue Starry Robe mask and Eldoran's Fan mask lay on the table. Katerin shivered at the fan markings on Eldoran's mask. Even though it lacked the twisted snarl of Makri's mask, the Fan characteristics still haunted her.

What had he done to that mask to make it look that way? Or did it change to reflect who he'd become?

Her own mask had softened and mellowed over the years. Masks could change to reflect changes in their makers, or so she'd heard.

"I want this remembrance spell gone before you sign the contract," Eldoran said. "Yevtin will insist on it."

Katerin nodded. She closed her hands into fists as Eldoran gently pressed his fingertips on both sides of her temples. She whispered the invocation to Dovré after him, and bit her lip as the heel of his hand hit her forehead.

Memories streamed back.

Wickmasa. Closely tied to the Leaders of the Two Nations of Keldara and Clenda. Alicira, the Aireii First Wife of Heinmyets, the Leader of the Two Nations, had ties to Wickmasa. Alicira had diced with the god Staul someplace near Wickmasa to win freedom from Zauril the tyrant from the distant land of Daran. Zauril had abused Alicira and stolen the leadership of Medvara from her.

In Wickmasa, Alicira had negotiated a protective alliance with Heinmyets, the leader of Keldara, and the woman who was now his Second Wife, Inharise, kin to the leaders of Clenda. That alliance protected Alicira and the daughter she had with Zauril, Rekaré, until Rekaré gained her magic at age thirteen.

Rekaré had disappeared near Wickmasa, along with Heinmyets and Inharise's son, Cenarth, while traveling to Medvara to fulfill the treaty with Zauril. Her disappearance was why Keldara and Clenda trembled at the brink of open war with Medvara, and why Zauril's Saubral allies had doubled their raids on Keldara.

Katerin's hands tightened into fists as the implications of what Wickmasa was came clear to her.

Eldoran nodded. "Wickmasa truly has need of you." The lines in his brown face sagged into loose tiredness.

Katerin nodded back. "Now I understand."

Alicira. Heinmyets. Inharise. Rekaré.

She had only met Rekaré once, as a wild child running with her stepbrother and the kidpack that belonged to the Leader's immediate kinfolk. The children were not openly shown in wintertime, when Heinmyets and his wives held court in Dera, the capital of Keldara and Clenda. But Katerin had seen them during a chance encounter during one of her summer trading circuits, years ago.

Heinmyets and family were much less formal in the summer, especially deep in the heart of Clenda. Katerin's throat tightened at the memory of the wild young Aireii horsewoman, she upon whom so much depended. Young and carefree then. Not likely to be so carefree now, if she still lived, and was not a secret captive somewhere.

"Do this," Eldoran said, "and not only are you free from your training debt, but we will clear you from any further obligation to Karnoi and Cirdel's priests for the care of Terani."

Katerin jumped slightly. "How—Eldoran—that—that's more—"

Since she had never known her father, the obligations for Terani's support after she went into the dreamless sleep had been Katerin's alone, and was one reason why she carried such a heavy contract over the years. Others in her training cohort had long ago paid off their training but Katerin always had to send payments to the priests of Waykemin's Healing House to assure the best treatment for Terani.

The mother who had never been a mother. If this contract could finally free her from this obligation, it would be worth it.

"The Council is willing to do it," Eldoran gently rested a hand on her shoulder. "We should have helped you long ago."

"I thank you," she said softly.

"If we can keep from open war throughout the nations of Varen this next year when Rekaré comes into her majority, *I'll* be thanking *you*," Eldoran said. "That's how important your job in Wickmasa will be." He picked up his mask. "Are you ready to swear?"

"I am ready." Katerin picked up her mask. A soft chord sounded deep within herself as she held the mask to her face with one hand and took Eldoran's free hand with her other. The mask's wooden shape stretched, becoming living wood as the Goddess took life within her and within the mask.

"I, Katerin, Healer of Blue Starry Robe, do swear this my vow," she began, her voice clear and firm, much like the voice she heard when the Goddess spoke within her.

Gods, it had been too long since she had taken the mask to herself. She would take it to Wickmasa. After all, she wasn't going to be traveling. She would like to have it nearby.

* * *

"You did *what?*" Senai sat up in her bed, blinking. "You committed me to do *what?*"

"It's just escort duty," Katerin told her. "You, Yevtin, and Eldoran are escorting me to Wickmasa."

"Katerin, I'll have your head."

"Relax." Katerin slid into her bedroll. "You and Yevtin are getting a nice-sized bonus. Yevtin made sure of that when he reviewed the contract."

"So Yevtin's in on it, hmm?"

"I wouldn't do this without a Council representative."

"Smart move." Senai ran her hands through her long dark hair. "So what did the old skinflint drag out of the Council for us?"

"You two are getting ten gold bars. Each."

"*Ten gold bars?* But that's a whole season's worth!"

"Yes. Ten. Seven from the Council. Three from me, at the end of the winter."

"Three from *you?* Katerin, this isn't *just* an escort job, is it."

"No," Katerin said. "It's not."

"Oh, Goddess. What else do I need to do? Flub up some big name's healing contract?"

"Nothing that big. Just keep in touch with me this winter. You'll be writing to Deyatim. She's the shaman of Kinherit. I'll introduce you to her on our way to Wickmasa."

"You'll be writing every moon?"

"No. At the full and new moons. You should be getting two letters with every delivery. I'm told Wickmasa has regular trader caravans in winter."

"Katerin, just what have you gotten yourself into?"

"I—there's more than I can tell. Just don't wait. If you miss two letters from me, bring help."

"It's that bad."

"Possibly."

Senai bounced out of her bed and hugged Katerin. "I'll bring help if I miss one letter."

Katerin leaned her head against Senai's chest. "Thank you, Senai. Thank you."

And I hope you never have to fulfill that promise.

CHAPTER 5

Katerin held her breath as she lit the first fire in her Wickmasa lodge. The tinder and kindling caught the spark from her flint and steel. Katerin fanned it into a strong flame. Only then did she breathe normally, grinning at Eldoran, Senai, and Yevtin, seated on new, non-magicked rugs around the small iron stove used for heating and cooking. She had removed the stove's door so they could enjoy the flames as well as the heat.

"It appears the Goddess looks favorably on this endeavor," Eldoran said.

"At least upon this lodging," Katerin said wryly.

She looked around the lodge, marveling at how quickly Myrieke had put together a comfortable space in nine days. She had several chests to store her personal goods. Her healing supplies and herbs were in the other room. Shelves and hooks on the walls gave her space to store the things she'd use daily on both sides. And, best of all, her mask hung over her personal shrine, located in the corner furthest from the door. It might not be Winter Quarters, but at least she had a few pieces of her winter home here.

"You'll do plenty fine here," Yevtin rumbled. "Wickmasa's not a place where you're going to suffer!"

Katerin stared into the fire, thinking about the bits and pieces about Wickmasa that both Yevtin and Eldoran had let drop on the three-day ride from the Healing House.

Other issues like wars between gods that happen to be carried down into human lives.

"Katerin." Eldoran's voice was quiet. "I'd not fret too much. The likelihood is that you will never get involved in any high politics."

"Don't be another Makri," Yevtin added.

Katerin shivered. Makri, the blacksmith's son, would have done better being consecrated to Artel instead of Dovré. If he had been a blacksmith like his father, he would still be alive.

It almost explained his uncle Yetklet's attitude toward healers and healing. Almost.

But the other Seven Crowned Gods? Karnoi and Cirdel. Katerin shivered again, remembering how they destroyed Terani the God-Killer, even though she was vowed to them. Nitel and Terat were less fearful, though Terani had weakened Nitel in the name of Karnoi and Cirdel.

Staul was a different story. The two-faced Trickster God, Staul the Balancer and the Destroyer, had his followers in the Two Nations as well as in Medvara and amongst the Saubral tribes. Yevtin had seen Makri with followers of Staul, not the Balancer but the Destroyer. It didn't make sense for a healer vowed to Dovré to walk the twisted paths of the Destroyer.

Makri, just what did you get yourself into? And did you drag anyone else into it with you? Who were you working for?

The more she remembered about Wickmasa, the more Katerin worried. Wickmasa had been a regular tribute stop on the pilgrimage that Zauril's representatives made to the high mountains of Clenda each summer to meet with Alicira and demand the surrender of his daughter. All of the villages on the tribute route taken by the Medvaran ambassadors to meet with Alicira in Clenda paid a healthy ransom both going and coming.

Or, rather, Wickmasa *had* been a tribute stop on the pilgrimage route.

Five years ago, Rekaré had reached the age of magical majority, thirteen. The compact between Zauril and Alicira was that at age thirteen, Rekaré would choose between surrendering to Zauril until she reached legal majority at eighteen, or staying with her mother. If Rekaré went to Zauril, she would have kept her ancestral magic, but would not come to full power until sometime in her eighteenth year. That choice also gave her the chance to duel with Zauril for full control of Medvara if she survived to gain her full powers.

Staying with Alicira meant Rekaré yielded her magic to Zauril forever, and lost any claim she might have to rule Medvara.

Then the unexpected third option emerged. Rekaré and Cenarth disappeared the spring before that final summer reckoning, during Rekaré's journey to Medvara. Zauril counted that disappearance as a forfeit and demanded the surrender of Alicira's magic rights. Heinmyets, Alicira and Inharise denied all knowledge of their youths' whereabouts. Alicira continued to maintain her own power instead of losing it to either Rekaré or Zauril, as their agreement required.

If Rekaré managed to remain free of Zauril until her eighteenth birthday, the magic freely reverted to her with no right of challenge from Zauril.

But the *control* of Medvara was an entirely different matter, and no one knew what would happen, or even if young Rekaré had the ability to rule since she had not been at the Medvaran court.

As a result, it was possible that Makri had been subverted by Zauril's partisans in a last, desperate attempt to locate Rekaré.

Makri had lost.

A deep chord sounded from her mask. Katerin jumped, suddenly aware that the flames were taking on shapes.

"Katerin." Eldoran's voice carried a warning note as the shapes faded.

"I've never been able to do that before," she said. "I've never been a fire-watcher or fire-worker, right, Senai?"

"R-right," Senai stammered. "Artel knows, we tried it a couple of times when we were kids. Katerin's never even had a touch of the knack."

"Maybe it's all of us, maybe it's just the power of the group," Katerin said.

"No," Yevtin said. "I had no power go out from me. It's from you, Katerin. All you."

"It's the influence of the Powers around Wickmasa," Eldoran told her. "You should avoid fire-watching from now on."

Is this what happened to Makri?

"Should I be worried that this is a Shadowwalker taint?"

"I would be watchful," Eldoran said.

She hooked the door back onto the stove, shutting the flames safely out of sight.

"Then I probably shouldn't be watching fires."

Senai pulled a small hide purse out of one of her saddlebags. "Here's one antidote. I was going to give this to you at winter solstice."

Katerin pulled knitting needles and assorted skeins of yarn out of the purse. "Senai! Your own tools, and—" She turned the purse over in her hands. "Your own purse. Oh. You shouldn't."

"My fingers are too beat up for me to spend much time knitting," Senai interrupted brusquely. "You've wanted to work with this yarn, now's your chance to master it."

Katerin took a closer look at the markings on the leather that bound the skeins. "Magic-infused yarn? Oh, Senai. This is a princess's gift."

"Something to keep your hands and eyes busy during your long winters."

"But magic yarn?"

"I'll expect a nice pair of mittens with warming charms worked into them. Maybe that'll help my poor smashed fingers."

"Senai, I can't say enough. Thank you."

"Just survive."

"I will," Katerin promised.

Yevtin cleared his throat. "Since we're gifting, it's my turn." He pulled his bag within reach. "Remember the braidwork we did two winters ago? I put together a kit for you, including patterns." He extracted a bag from his bigger one and gave it to her. Inside, Katerin found a small leather-bound book tied shut with a strip of sinew, and thin strings of hide. As she looked up, he added, "That's enough to get you started. You'll have access to leather and hides this winter. One thing I remember about this place, they aren't stingy with good leather to those who show a talent."

"Thank you." Katerin studied her presents. Useful because they not only offered her a means to stay busy, but provided a chance to make things for trade. She wouldn't be dependent only on her healing skills to buy goods and services this winter. "Yevtin, this isn't your own pattern book, is it?"

"Not the original," he said. "A copy."

"But your tradework."

"You'll make things in your style."

"Both of you. This is too much." She smiled at her friends, seeing the worry mixed with satisfaction in their expressions.

"I'm not empty-handed either." Eldoran handed her a wooden box. She eased off the snug-fitting lid to discover inks, pens and a ream of finest Nerean parchment, with a supply of waxed envelopes, all neatly organized in separate compartments. Katerin fitted the lid back onto the box.

"Oh Eldoran. Scribe quality."

He shrugged, a slow smile crossing his lips. "I'm expecting reports from you, so you need supplies."

"I'll keep good records."

"I know you will. And there's more," he added. "This is to keep yourself safe." He gave Katerin a heavy pouch.

She shook out the contents. A clear stone pendant shot through with slender golden rods fell into her hand, mounted in a simple silver bezel. The pendant swung from a silver chain.

"Is this what I think it is?" she asked.

"Yes. The Council approved you to have one of the Eyes of Dovré. Put it on," he commanded.

Katerin slipped it on and tucked the stone next to her skin. A tingle fired through her body.

"Katerin, Healer, Winter Healer of Wickmasa," Eldoran said. "By the wisdom of the Council of Healers, you have been gifted with an Eye of Dovré. You will not need your mask for this vow. Repeat after me."

"I, Katerin, Winter Healer of Wickmasa," she repeated, "do take custody of this Eye of Dovré during my contracted service in the village of Wickmasa. I vow that I will not reveal this possession to any save those now present, or a known member of the Council. I will not seek to use the powers of the Eye for myself, but to protect others and myself should it become necessary. At the end of my service, I will return the Eye to the Council of Healers, or die in the attempt. So do I swear."

The Eye pulsed hot as she finished speaking. Then it faded.

Eldoran turned to Yevtin and Senai. "Do you vow to keep this knowledge of the custody of this Eye of Dovré secret, not to be disclosed to any save myself or a known member of the Council of Healers?"

"We do," they chorused.

Eldoran gave Katerin a tight-lipped smile. "I told you not to worry too much about this service, didn't I? This Eye will give you protection against most Shadowwalkers."

"Thank you."

"Does this ease your mind?"

"It does. It does very much. Thank you, Eldoran."

"Good." Eldoran heaved a heavy sigh. "Now. Let's feast and drink, for tomorrow we'll be leaving."

"Thank you." The Eye was a *presence* that reassured her. Whatever trace the Shadowwalker connection had left in Wickmasa, it was small. Something she could manage without the Eye.

But it spoke to the nature of what *might* lie ahead of her this winter that Eldoran and the Council had thought such protective means to be necessary.

* * *

Leave-taking in the morning was swift. More gifting occurred in the form of Yevtin and Senai's pack mules.

"I can't take them. That's too much!" Katerin protested.

"You can and you will," Yevtin said firmly. "We've only enough goods for the one mule, and we're traveling fast." He snorted. "We left you the slow ones. Use them for leather this winter if things run tight!"

"I can't do that. They're yours."

"They're yours now," said Senai.

"Oh," Katerin sighed, shaking her head. "What am I going to do with friends like you?"

"Accept the gift and make good use of it," Eldoran advised.

"I don't really have a choice, do I?"

"No. You don't. Farewell, Katerin. We'll see you in the spring!"

The others added their farewells. Katerin leaned on Mira's

shoulder, watching as her friends rode away, skirting the main part of Wickmasa village.

Then she turned back to her lodge.

I need to get everything in order before my first patient arrives.

She wondered how long a wait that would be.

CHAPTER 6

Katerin studied the area around her lodge. Mira had a small shed nearby with a small, fenced-off haystack inside. An old but serviceable corral held the mules she now owned.

I'll need more feed this winter.

Two of the mules could go out with the common herd. She didn't need to keep all three mules close.

Gods. What else do I need to think about for village life?

Katerin wracked her brain. Feed. Water. Fuel. Well, perhaps the assistants Myrieke promised could take care of that.

Meanwhile, she had mules to water. Katerin scratched Mira's forehead, thinking about —*herding mules to creek.* A quick flash of —*mules covered in buffalo dung* came from Mira. Katerin kept thinking about —*herding mules.* Mira finally mirrored back the image of —*herding mules to creek in line,* then, —*mules drinking,* then —*mules back in corral.*

"Let's get going," Katerin muttered. She cut a long switch from the willows that lined the creek and returned to the corral. Mira waited just outside the gate while Katerin slowly swung it open.

The mules exploded from the corral. Katerin scrambled to get out of the way. Mira halted their bolt for freedom, her ears pinned and teeth bared as she turned them back toward Katerin. Katerin drove the mules toward Mira. The mules learned quickly after the first mad flurry, though the black one stayed high-headed, snorting and looking around to escape. He tried to bolt on their return, but Mira drove him back into the corral.

Katerin leaned on the corral fence and studied the three mules.

"I didn't come here to train mules," she muttered as the black mule trotted around the corral with his nose high. "And it looks like I need to hobble you before you jump that fence, you beast."

A chuckle came from behind her. "Looks like our new healer is a mule trainer!"

Katerin spun around. Wickmasa's Horsemaster, a big, burly man with a gray-striped dark beard, grinned at her.

"I have standards for my beasts," she told him. "Even my pack animals."

The Horsemaster's grin widened. "That is a good thing to see." He bowed. "Our introduction the other day was hasty, and I fear you might not remember my name. I am Kwellet, the Horsemaster of Wickmasa. Although you may not need much in the way of my services."

"I remember you, Kwellet, and I may yet need your services." Katerin returned his bow. "That black mule could be more than I can handle on my own. May I ask what illness brings you here?"

"Not an illness." Kwellet's smile faded into a slight frown. "I hope that you might be able to help me with joint pains. Makri tried but was not able to ease them. Perhaps you might give it a try?"

"Come into my lodge. I have not yet started today's work fire, but we can talk while I do."

"I would be honored."

They walked toward the lodge. Katerin stopped Kwellet before he entered.

"Let my daranval take your scent."

"Ah. She can smell my aches?"

Katerin nodded.

"Then please have her do so with my blessing.

Katerin brushed her hand against Mira's neck.

—*Sniff, look, tell.*

Mira lowered her head and relaxed her ears as Katerin stepped back. She took small steps toward Kwellet, until she could reach him easily with her nose while standing clear. As she sniffed Kwellet over, she sidestepped carefully around him, stepping, then pausing, then stepping again. She hesitated at his left shoulder, and blew more intently at his left elbow. She nuzzled Kwellet's right knee and ankle.

—*Joints aching. Muscles.*

But, fortunately, not even the slightest whisper of Shadowwalker essence.

"Thank you, Mira. Come on in, Kwellet."

Kwellet limped in behind her and sat on a stool by the fire pit.

"So." Katerin studied how he balanced on the stool. "What have you done to your left arm and right leg to cause these aches and pains?"

"Left arm and right leg?" Kwellet said. "Not every daranval can be that precise."

"Even though Mira started as a war mare, she's a superb healer's mare. So. Your past injuries?"

"I'm a Horsemaster." Kwellet shrugged. "Elbow—got thrown several times. I usually land on that side. Knee and ankle? Wild mare, kicked me last winter."

Katerin nodded. "I want to look at your shoulder and arm. Stand up and take your tunic off, please."

Kwellet grimaced but stood and wrestled the tunic off. He struggled to move his left arm. His chest and shoulders were thick, muscular, hairy, and scarred.

"Turn around," she told Kwellet, examining his shoulder muscles, which appeared to be level and evenly muscled. No withering of his upper arm muscles, at least none that she could detect without a Sight.

"Sit down." She stepped behind Kwellet and raised her Sight, half-closing her eyes as she ran her hands and fingers over his shoulder and upper arm. "Let me work this."

Katerin placed one hand on his shoulder joint and took his elbow in her hand, moving the upper arm slowly. She detected tightness and shortened muscles, with no major restriction of motion. No broken bones. She moved down to his elbow, kneeling at his side as she checked the elbow and wrist, finding much the same there.

"Put your tunic back on," she ordered, watching how stiffly he moved. Yes. Some clothing modifications, a salve, perhaps some massage, and a pain potion would give him relief.

"Let me look at your legs. Back on the stool." Katerin sat on the mat by Kwellet's right foot and slid the pant leg up. She pulled off his boot, easing it over the ankle, noting the stiffness. The knee had little wrong with it, other than a slight inflammation that she could treat with the right potion, but the ankle was something different.

Katerin sighed.

"That sigh doesn't sound good," Kwellet said.

"Your ankle's a mess." Katerin continued to probe with her fingers, feeling where the ligaments and tendons had tightened and pulled the bone out of place, twisting it. "It didn't heal right."

She sighed again, looking at how the foot had been pulled at an angle from where it should be. Then she picked up the boots, comparing the right to the left. There was a telltale outside sag on the right boot.

Kwellet scowled. "Can you fix it?"

"Yes. Not like you were young again, but I can give you relief. I need to make a brace, something that can fit inside a boot. Some massage, and a pain potion. Let me start with manipulation."

She waited for his nod before taking his heel in one hand and the toes in the other. She gingerly rotated his foot, listening and watching for cues that she'd gone too far.

Kwellet took her ministrations stoically, closing his eyes tight and tensing his face. She monitored the tightness of his body, testing, testing, testing.

"Aaah!" he finally cried out. "That's enough!"

Katerin took note of the position. "Anything I'm going to do will hurt at first. But I will be able to ease your pain otherwise."

"It's worth it if it makes my ankle better."

"You might end up regretting giving me that much freedom. You'll have to see me for several days."

"The Gods could impose worse fates than seeing a pretty woman regularly."

Katerin shot him a sharp glance. *Was* he flirting with her?

"It'll hurt," she warned.

"It hurts now. What are we doing?"

She outlined her plan for manipulation and splinting.

Kwellet nodded at her description. "I've done that a time or two for a foal that's lain wrong in the womb and come out crooked-legged. I'm surprised Makri didn't think of it."

"It's not a technique everyone knows." Katerin looked for the right length in her collection of bone braces. "I learned it one year when I was traveling with the Tauri in Clenda."

Kwellet's indrawn breath caught her attention. "You've worked with the Clendan herders?"

"My friend Senai is Tauri. She came into the healers the

same year I did. I ended up spending time with her and her kin during my second apprentice year. A special training. We rode with a horse-trading band."

"Not Heinmyets's family?" There was a note of worry and caution in Kwellet's voice that Katerin didn't quite understand.

"No. Not Heinmyets. Or Inharise's, either, for that matter. Cousin-kin to Inharise, but not close." Katerin smiled fondly at the memory as she measured her strips of bone against Kwellet's ankle. "I learned a lot about daranval and horse care and training that year, as well as healing humans. The old Horsemaster of that band knew a few tricks like this that he applied to human and horse alike."

She picked out sinew strips and magicked cloth and began to weave them together, inserting the bone strips at set intervals.

"Katerin." The note of warning hung strongly in Kwellet's voice.

"What's wrong?" She looked up from her work, startled.

Kwellet looked around, then lowered his voice. "What you just told me?"

"Yes?"

"Whatever you do, don't tell that to anyone else here in Wickmasa."

"Why?"

"Because the secrets of Wickmasa will devour you otherwise."

"What secrets?"

What's left that I don't know?

His hand tightened on hers. "You will learn. Things I can't speak of."

Katerin went back to work, looking at her hands even though she knew this weave innately.

"Secrets. That's all this damned place seems to be about, secrets! Bad enough that it's under a remembrance spell."

"Yes. Exactly. Look at me!"

Katerin looked back up.

"The secrets aren't mine to share, or I would tell you. But listen to me, Katerin Healer. We are wrapped in secrets that too many would kill to obtain. And we will kill to protect them. As will you, in time." He sat back up.

"I am just a healer. A simple healer." She tested the fit of the brace. Katerin slid Kwellet's boot on over the brace. "Stand up. Walk around."

Kwellet limped around the room. At first, his limp seemed more pronounced. Then, as he adjusted to the brace, his limp diminished slightly.

"That's good! So how long will I wear this?"

"Daily for the next seven days. And I want to see you every day for the next two or three. I'll be manipulating your ankle, then adjusting the brace."

"I'll come see you first thing." He winked, and the jolly mood he had been in returned. "Besides, you might need a hand with that black mule of yours."

"I'm sure I will."

"What about the shoulder?"

"I'll prepare a salve and a potion for you to use daily. The injury is too old to fix, but we can ease some of the pain, and if we modify your tunics it'll be easier for you to get them on and off."

"Thank you. With that, Healer Katerin, I must go about my day. Thank you for your very useful assistance. And," he paused. "Remember my words."

"I will," she promised.

After Kwellet left, Katerin put away her scraps.

Dear Goddess, what have I gotten myself into?

CHAPTER 7

Katerin banked the fire so that it would burn slowly but smoothly for most of the morning. She put a water kettle on the stove to steep herbs, the first step in making Kwellet's potion. Voices outside the lodge paired with Mira's warning stomp pulled her away from doing more. She went outside, to find Mira blocking two young women from entering the lodge. Katerin placed a soothing hand on Mira's withers and eased her away from the door.

"Be still," she said quietly to Mira. *More new patients.* "I am Healer Katerin," she said to the young women, recognizing them as the two young women who had been arguing with Makri. "Do you have need of a healer?"

The women—*not women, girls just barely old enough to be women,* she realized—looked at each other and giggled softly. The taller, a slender, dark-haired woman with a smooth, unmarked face, smiled at Katerin.

"My name is Colerei," she said, nodding at her companion, who was shorter, chunkier, and, as Katerin looked closer, younger. "This is Davni. Eldest Imnari said we were to be your assistants."

"Colerei and Davni. So. Have either of you worked with a healer before?"

They looked at each other and giggled nervously.

Then Davni spoke, her voice surprisingly deeper than Colerei's. "Colerei hasn't. But I did some fetch and carry for Hinet when she was Makri's assistant. Hinet's my cousin."

Katerin nodded, studying the girls. "You need to meet my daranval."

Colerei hung back. "She's *mean*. She pinned her ears at us and bared her teeth."

"She pinned her ears at you only because you tried to grab her mane too quickly," Davni shot back at Colerei. She stepped forward. "What do I do to meet her correctly, Healer Katerin?"

"*Katerin* is fine," Katerin said. "Come here, Davni, Colerei. Let her sniff you over."

—*Girls working next to Mira,* Katerin thought.

—*Little dark one alone, grooming Mira, tall one running from mules in corral,* came back.

Katerin turned away from the girls to hide her smirk. Mira would have to learn to accept Colerei.

—*Both girls working next to Mira,* Katerin thought again. —*Sniff, look, tell.*

Mira heaved a deep grunt. —*Both girls working with Mira,* came back to Katerin.

Mira dropped her head, then started with Davni, sniffing her gently from shoulder to toe. Done, she breathed out softly, accepting the girl.

"Scratch behind her ears."

Davni gently rubbed behind Mira's ears. Mira relaxed, and a small smile broke out on Davni's lips.

"She likes me!"

Katerin allowed them a few more moments together before waving Colerei over. The older girl held herself tensely.

"I don't like horses much," she muttered.

"If you listened to Kwellet about how to handle horses properly, you'd be fine, baker girl!" Davni snapped.

"You *like* horses, trader girl!" Colerei screeched, her voice sliding up nervously.

Mira flattened her ears and raised her head, the whites of her eyes showing. Katerin looked closely at Colerei. Tension tightened Colerei's body as Mira swung to face her.

She's afraid. Not much experience with horses, and her nervousness agitates Mira.

Colerei trembled as Mira took one step toward her. Mira was clearly unwilling to move too far away from Davni.

"Davni," Katerin said softly. "Step away and give Colerei a chance."

Davni scowled but obeyed.

"Colerei. Come closer," Katerin commanded.

Colerei obeyed Katerin. Mira examined Colerei more slowly than she had Davni, starting at Colerei's feet. Mira finally finished and blew hard, hard enough to send wisps of Colerei's unbound hair flying. Despite Mira's annoyance with Colerei, she was clear of taint as well.

Just another circumstance where Mira was fussy about inexperienced handlers.

"Colerei," Katerin said softly. "Scratch her poll. Like Davni did."

Colerei's hand darted out as if released from a spring. Mira startled back, and Colerei jumped in the opposite direction.

"She doesn't like me!" Colerei wailed.

"You have to move *slowly*," Katerin told her. "You scared Mira. Try again, but this time, move your hand slowly."

"I—I—"

"You'll do fine," Katerin soothed. "Just come back over here and move slowly."

Colerei lifted her hand in short, jerky increments until it

rested on Mira's neck. She scratched tensely at first, almost too roughly.

Then Colerei relaxed. Her fingers rubbed behind Mira's right ear, and her movements became smooth and softer. Mira lowered her head. Katerin saw the tension ooze out of Colerei's body, with a matching release from Mira.

Davni edged closer. Katerin got two brushes from Mira's shed. Giving the stiffer brush to Davni who, in Katerin's judgment, would have the gentler touch, she gently eased the soft brush into Colerei's hand.

"You want to brush like this." She placed her hand over Colerei's and guided it along Mira's neck until she felt Colerei's hand relax and catch the rhythm of the stroke.

"It's like brushing my hair," Colerei said, the tension gone from her voice.

"Yes. Exactly." Katerin stepped back to watch as the girls groomed Mira.

Mira drooped her head and relaxed her lips and jaw, eyelids drooping. Colerei had the defter touch, Katerin noticed, reacting quickly to Mira's body language despite her lack of experience. Davni had the greater knowledge and skill.

"What does grooming your daranval have to do with healer work?" Colerei finally asked.

"Most healers need a daranval to help with healing."

"Help do what? I didn't think Soisan did anything for Makri."

"Daranvelii help us scan for certain contaminations," Katerin said. "They lend healers strength when we do Sights. They can detect a problem and tell the healer where something is wrong."

"How do they tell you? Daranvelii don't talk," Davni said.

"They send pictures. Mira sends me pictures of where things are wrong. Sometimes she just stops and smells a part of your body for longer than I would expect her to."

"Like when she was sniffing us?" Davni asked.

"Yes. Daranvelii are also our channels to the gods." Katerin scratched Mira's jaw. Mira arched her neck and tilted her head for Katerin to get a better angle. "For a healer, that would be the Lady Dovré. For a shaman or priest, it would be the particular god that they are dedicated to. For leaders, and warriors, and others, it could be Artel, or Karnoi, or Staul."

Colerei shook her head. "How can a daranval be the channel to the gods?"

"If you're called by the god, you'll know it," Katerin told her.

"Was Hinet called?" Davni asked.

"She's at the Healing House and she had a daranval when I saw her. She's been called."

"You have to be called by the god to be a healer?"

"A healer, yes, and a shaman or priest as well. Warriors and leaders are different. Not every leader and warrior is called to a daranval." Katerin decided to change the focus. "I think Mira's well-brushed now."

—*Katerin covered in buffalo dung,* came from Mira, followed by —*girls tending Mira's every need.*

Katerin gave Mira a quick scratch in her other favorite spot under the mane.

"I guess so," Davni said slowly, handing Katerin her brush. "I liked brushing her."

Colerei shrugged and handed the brush over to Katerin. "She's a nice daranval. But what else are we doing?"

"Let me show you where I'll be seeing patients. I need help unpacking and organizing my supplies. After that, we can walk around the village. I need to learn where everything is, and you two are the ones who can show me."

* * *

IT WAS early afternoon when Katerin and the girls finished unpacking and organizing. Katerin had mixed the salve for

Kwellet, then set Colerei to baking bread and organizing the woodpile while Davni did one last sort through the supplies, making lists. Katerin cast a knowing eye at the dough that Colerei was deftly thumping down.

"Colerei. Do you want to go with us? We can wait until you've set the bread to rise."

Colerei shook her head, brushing back a strand of dark hair from her face with her left wrist. "No." She frowned at the ball of dough. "I want to watch it rise and bake, so I know this stove's hot spots. Davni will be a better guide, anyway. She knows more about the trader stuff. She's from trader families. I'm just a cook family girl."

"Davni?" Katerin asked. "You ready?"

"One last thing." Davni blotted the ink and placed her record in the box that now held neat accounts of Katerin's supplies. Then she packed away the writing goods in the lap desk and put the desk on a shelf.

Meanwhile, Katerin had tucked the jar of salve into a small bag, with a magicked rag wrapped around it.

"Did you record this delivery?" she asked Davni.

"I have. Let me show you." Davni pulled the treatment ledger from its protective leather cover, and showed Katerin the neat entry on the page started for Kwellet. Katerin noted the careful, detailed, writing with everything entered in the correct columns.

"You've kept books."

Davni shrugged. "I'm one of my father's scribes."

"Very good. Shall we go?" Katerin turned to Colerei. "If we're not back by the time you're done baking, you may go home for the day."

"That's fine," Colerei said. "I also have handwork with me. I'll wait."

"That's good." Katerin called Mira over as she and Davni left the lodge.

—Sniff, look, tell for Shadowwalker, she thought, adding *—Mira wandering through the village next to Katerin.*

Mira repeated the image back.

The village seemed bigger in the overcast afternoon than it had before.

But then, I haven't seen much of it.

Her first sight of Wickmasa had been at dusk, looking for a place to stay, and she'd been directed to Makri. Yesterday, they reached Wickmasa at dusk as well.

Now, Katerin surveyed it with a critical eye, comparing Wickmasa to other villages she knew.

It was organized into four rows of longhouses in the center, with lodges like Katerin's circling them. Unlike the Healing House and many of Katerin's circuit villages, there was no outer, protective wall. However, Wickmasa was in the bottom of the Wickmasa River valley, where the river emerged from a steep gorge. The valley walls were still high here. The creek Katerin watered her mules in marked the village's northern boundary. The meadows where Wickmasa's livestock and horses grazed were on the plateau above the river, with a path climbing a steep slope to the south of the village. Kwellet's lodge was near the end of that path.

So he's on one edge while I'm on the other.

The longhouses in the center of the village were homes as well as storage for the village's goods.

"We do a lot of trading," Davni told Katerin. "My father and brothers cross into Larij for trade, as well as up into Clenda."

"Not Keldara?" If no one made regular trading forays toward Kinherit, her arrangements for supplies and mail might be a problem.

"Oh, that's a different family. Dikret's family is the one who does the Keldara and Nere trade. Look, there's Colerei's family house." Davni took in a deep breath. "It always smells good here."

They continued on. Myrieke stood outside the main storage longhouse, directing a group of girls and boys unpacking panniers. She waved Katerin over.

"So is your lodge satisfactory?" Myrieke asked.

"It's well done," Katerin assured her. "I'm very happy."

"Had to think about it. The healer, let's see, not the one before Makri, but two healers before him, Siljaren, I think, yes, Siljaren, wanted a lodge setup like yours. I still had the skins for *that* layout." Myrieke smiled. "Old Knost made sure I kept those records. He said I'd need them someday."

Siljaren was here?

Katerin remembered the tales about Siljaren at the Healing House. Was this the same Siljaren, or a local healer of the same name?

Yet another factor to add to the mysteries of Wickmasa. The famous Siljaren had helped Alicira dice with Staul, then cured Alicira of the worst of the curses and compulsions that Zauril had placed on her.

But I had always thought that Siljaren was a circuit healer.

There was nothing in the tales to suggest that Siljaren had been tied to Wickmasa.

Siljaren disappeared. I wonder—

Katerin shook her head. Idle speculation was useless.

"It's a good layout," she told Myrieke. "Thank you."

"It's what I do." Myrieke lowered her voice. "Are the girls being helpful?"

"Yes. Colerei's back at the lodge, tending the fire and baking bread."

"Ah, you found her skill pretty quickly!" Myrieke laughed. "Davni might be our next Healing House apprentice after Hinet. Her father would like to have a trained healer ride with them. He'd prefer a man for a travel healer, but," Myrieke shrugged. "The call comes where it will."

"Yes. The call comes where it will," Katerin repeated. She

bowed to Myrieke. "I need to deliver this salve to Kwellet. Please forgive my rushing off."

Myrieke waved her hands. "Not at all. Hope you can help him. I know he's suffered terribly since Darlna died."

"Darlna?"

"Makri's mother married Kwellet after her second husband Richen died," Myrieke explained. "You're taking him some salve?"

"He came by to see if I could do something for his pains," Katerin said.

"Glad to hear that. He doesn't take care of himself. Anything that gets him feeling better helps. Good afternoon, then."

"Good afternoon," Katerin repeated.

Kwellet and Darlna, Makri's mother. This village is complicated.

CHAPTER 8

Kwellet schooled a horse in the round corral when Katerin and Davni reached his end of the village. He nodded at them, then turned his attention back to the little brown mare bucking around the pen with a saddle on her back. Davni climbed on the fence to watch Kwellet, while Katerin looked around.

Four large corrals had young horses and mules milling about in them. Some of the young horses called to Mira. Kwellet's lodge rose behind the four corrals. Beyond his lodge was a small meadow that followed the river. Katerin spotted one mixed herd of horses and mules grazing together, and a small flock of sheep. Another, larger lodge for Wickmasa's bachelor herders was on the far edge of the meadow.

Katerin joined Davni at the fence. The young mare now trotted around the pen, turning when Kwellet indicated. At last, he motioned for the little mare to stop and face him, then come over. He scratched her forehead, then joined Davni and Katerin, the little mare trailing him.

"What brings me the honor of a visit from two lovely ladies?" he asked.

"I have the salve," Katerin said.

Kwellet grinned. "Just a moment." He checked the cinch on the little mare's saddle, then climbed out of the pen. "She'll do with a little bit of thinking time. Will make a nice riding horse, but she comes from a tough line."

"Tough line?" Katerin asked.

Kwellet pointed toward the meadows. "Bloodline. The herd she's out of has a stud whose babies are hard to get started. They like to buck, but they make strong riding horses once they're trained, and they cross well on daranvelii. The village makes a nice bit of money off of his babies when the Clendan horse-traders come through, looking for stock. They always want some of his get."

Clendan horsetraders? This village gets more visitors than I'd expect, with that remembrance spell.

"When do the horsetraders come by?" Katerin asked.

Kwellet gestured toward his lodge. "Come on in and have some tea with me, you two." He limped toward the lodge. "I'm ready for a bite of something. Oh. The traders come through every spring and winter." He grimaced. "I've been working slower than I like. That little mare should be much farther along than she is, but with this ankle, I've been working more slowly this year."

Kwellet's lodge was a comfortable jumble of horse tack and personal goods. An old, blue-gray dog slept on a hide by the stove, rousing enough to raise his head and thump his tail at Kwellet as he poked at the fire.

Kwellet unearthed some tin cups and made tea, pouring water from a kettle sitting on the stovetop.

"Sit down, sit down," he encouraged them. He came up with flatbread, dried meat, and berries. Katerin took just enough to be polite. She was still full from Colerei's lunch.

"So how is that brace working?" she asked.

"It's making a difference." Kwellet eased himself down carefully and propped up his injured foot. "I still need to stop and rest, but that's not happening as much as it has been. Thank you. And the ankle can take more weight."

"Don't you have an apprentice to help you start some of these young horses?"

Kwellet shook his head. "Not this year. Too much happening with our trade caravans." He sighed. "Just that last little mare to get backed."

"I could give you a hand with her. I'd be helping start daranvelii if I were at the Healing House this winter. It's one thing that Mira and I do."

"Ah. Your daranval is trained to start young ones?"

Katerin nodded. "She was used for starting horses by her previous owners. I'm her third bond. She was a war mare, and has survived two riders."

"How can I pay you back, Katerin? This goes beyond healing work."

"Help me work that black mule. I'm not skilled with mules, and that one is going to be a challenge."

"Trade you a calmer one. I'll take a look at him tomorrow when I come by for my brace adjustment. We can use a big, tough mule like that in the harder runs our traders make. I have a smaller molly mule that may be more to your liking. Your mule's worth more than she is, but we'll figure that out."

"That would be good," Katerin said. "And don't worry about the difference between the two."

"We can straighten out the difference with Myrieke tomorrow."

"Or I could, if you choose not to get Myrieke involved," Davni said.

Kwellet nodded. "That works. So. The salve. Tell me what I need to do with it."

Katerin pulled the bag from her pocket. "This should be good for a month. Put a little on the rag—about this size—" she made an 'o' shape with thumb and forefinger— "and make sure you rub it into your skin good. That should go on your shoulder and upper arm. Use it three times a day."

She handed the bag to Kwellet. He pulled out the jar.

"You can supervise my first use of it." He wrestled out of his tunic, popped the seal on the jar and sniffed appreciatively at the salve. "Smells good."

The salve's strong scent quickly filled the lodge. Katerin watched as he applied it, nodding approvingly as he rubbed his neck, shoulder and upper arm until only a faint, greasy smear remained on the rag. Then he folded the rag, tucked it in the top of the salve jar, and set the jar among others on one of his shelves. He worked the arm back and forth carefully, a smile slowly breaking out on his face.

"Healer Katerin, I swear it feels better already."

"You need to work your arm each time you put it on. Try pushing the arm a little bit further each time." She stood. "Bring the jar back when it's empty and I'll make more."

"This *could* end up being one of your most popular items," Kwellet cautioned as he wrestled his tunic back on. "I'm not the only one in this village with joints that don't work right. We've not had a healer who could make these salves."

"It's not a beginner's skill. I didn't learn this recipe until my third year of training. Most village healers only train for a year or two. I *am* surprised no one here has traded for it. The Healing House has salvemasters who make it."

Kwellet shrugged. "It's not something that that Orelyets would know to trade for."

"Orelyets?" Katerin asked.

"My father," Davni said.

Katerin glanced at her. "It's easy to set up a standard order for that salve. I'll let him know that. Meanwhile, Davni, we should go. Kwellet, thank you for the hospitality."

"Thank *you* for bringing me this salve," he said, bowing low. "I will see you tomorrow morning. I'll bring that mule."

"Very good." They followed Kwellet out of the lodge, and Katerin whistled to Mira, who had been visiting with the little brown mare in the round corral.

"I see your daranval's already been chatting up that mare," Kwellet said wryly.

"I'll come by tomorrow afternoon and we can see how she goes."

"Healer Katerin, I appreciate the assistance."

"Horsemaster Kwellet, if you can relieve me of that knothead of a mule, I'll be in your debt forever."

"Oh, we'll see who owes whom." Kwellet grinned. "I suspect I'll be in debt to you for a good, long time."

"We shall see," Katerin said.

They headed back through the village toward Katerin's lodge. At one point, Davni guided them along the same route they had taken, but Katerin shook her head.

"I want to see the whole village. We haven't gone this way." She pointed toward the other direction, clearly less traveled than the path Davni wanted to take.

Davni frowned. "There's not much to see back here. Mightn't you want to talk to Myrieke about the salve orders?"

"I thought you said your father was the one to talk to. You've not shown me your family's lodge, either."

"Father's—traveling," Davni said slowly, her voice tight. "And you don't really need to see my family's lodge."

"You've shown me where Colerei's family lives. It's only fair that I see where your family lives."

Davni breathed a soft, delicate sigh. "As you wish."

They turned left instead of right, moving toward the Wickmasa River. At first, Katerin thought Davni's reluctance stemmed from the clearly lesser quality of these lodges than the route they'd taken before.

Doesn't make sense. I'd think the head trader's family would live in the finest part of the village.

Davni's steps slowed as they approached a run-down, decrepit lodge. Mira moved closer to Katerin, her lip flipping up as if she were trying to catch a scent. Then she snorted and pressed hard against Katerin. Her senses pounded against Katerin's, flooding Katerin's mind with a daranval's perspective.

Katerin forced herself to keep walking, keep on moving, for both her sake and Mira's, even as her skin crawled and screamed at her to run away. The only thing keeping her from bolting was that the Eye remained quiet on her chest. It wasn't Shadowwalker, but there were other things as dangerous as Shadowwalkers.

Davni's discomfort grew as they passed the lodge, and she looked around uneasily.

"Who lives there?" Katerin asked Davni, softly so she wouldn't be overheard.

Davni shook her head. "Not now," she muttered. "Not now!"

"Davni," a soft voice called from the lodge. "What brings you by this way?"

Davni stiffened, then turned slowly to face the lodge.

"Metkyi," she said quietly, looking down at the ground as a tall man strode out from the lodge.

It took all of Katerin's willpower not to run away.

Is this the Metkyi who was Makri's brother?

He was the same height and shape, but this was nothing like the neatly dressed man she'd seen the other day, and the sense of something roiling underneath her skin wasn't what she'd been feeling then. Bones and skulls of small animals hung from the rough furs he wore and were woven into his wild, unkempt hair. Rotted stumps of teeth jutted from his half-open mouth with one front tooth missing.

And yet there was something about the man that shimmered. If she focused too hard on the awfulness of his hair or teeth or pitted face, he went out of focus.

Illusion. Shapechanger. Staul, Katerin's innermost self screamed. *This is a priest of Staul! Run!*

No. Stay.

Katerin nodded politely at Metkyi. After all, here he would be a priest of Staul of the Balance, not Staul in his incarnation as the Destroyer. And her Eye would be reacting if he served the Destroyer.

Still, Makri's brother is the priest of Staul. Gods. Gods. Why didn't anyone tell me about this? Is this connected to what happened to Makri? Oh Gods, please let this not be connected. Please.

At least she didn't detect any trace of Shadowwalker.

"Do I know you?" he growled.

Why doesn't he recognize me from the other day?

"This is the healer who's replacing Makri for the winter," Davni said.

"And does this healer have a voice for herself?"

Metkyi whirled. He lunged at Mira as if to pet her. Mira squealed and struck at him. Metkyi jumped back, and for a moment Katerin thought she saw fear in his eyes.

"She's a former war mare," Katerin said. "She has little tolerance for liberties."

"Ah. Dovré's Voice *does* speak. Your name?"

"Katerin," she snapped.

Had he gone temporarily mad from the loss of his brother? Priests of Staul were often susceptible to a divine madness, and a brother dying in circumstances like Makri's might be enough to trigger it. Dangerous to be around a priest of Staul in this circumstance.

We need to get out of here. Now. No wonder Davni didn't want to come this way.

"Davni. We need to get back to the lodge." She turned her

back on Metkyi and started to walk away, Mira striding stiff-legged next to her, ready to attack.

Metkyi laughed again, his voice rising nervously. "I'm not done with you, Voice of Dovré!"

Katerin felt the faint twinge of the compulsion those words cast. She stopped, closed her eyes, called on the Eye, and felt the faint warmth as the Eye stirred into life. But still an effect of Staul, not a Shadowwalker touch. At least she knew what to do about this.

She turned slowly. "*I* am done with *you*, Staul's Voice!" she snarled, projecting her annoyance as hard as she could.

Metkyi staggered back, and for a moment Katerin caught a glimpse of a very different-looking man from the gap-toothed, scarred and bedraggled horror, the man she had seen the other day instead. Then the unkempt visage returned.

Shapechanger! Shapechanger gone mad? By Dovré's tits, what have I gotten myself into?

"As you wish, Lady," he said, his voice softer, the horror about him fading. "As you wish." He strode back to the lodge, the glimmer of his façade fading slowly.

Now what was that all about?

At least it wasn't divine madness. He wouldn't be able to walk away like that if it were. She turned to Davni.

Maybe she can tell me something.

"Davni?"

Davni nodded slightly, wetness welling up in her eyes. "That's why I didn't want to come this way."

"I don't understand why we had to come by his lodge if we're going by your family's lodge."

"It's the only way to get to my family's lodge from this direction," Davni stammered. "I-I thought he might be gone. He usually is this time of day." Davni drew a deep, sobbing breath. "He's family. He's not so bad, normally. But I never know. He—

he s-*scares* me in shapechanger mode! I stay away unless he invites me. Safer."

"He's from your family?"

Davni nodded. "Makri and Metkyi—are—were—are my cousins. Darlna was my father's sister. Makri and Metkyi are—were—twins."

Twins. One for Staul, the other for Dovré.

A reflection of the shadowy pairing between the two gods. It made sense. Two dedicated to the god and goddess, and a third —*Twana.*

The village shaman. They're always dedicated to Artel. So how is she related to Makri and Metkyi? Imnari named her as kin to Makri the other day. It fits the pattern—

Katerin shuddered at the thought of that pattern.

That leaves four more of the Seven Crowned Gods. Are there others dedicated to them here?

"Twana?" she asked Davni softly. "Artel's shaman. How is *she* related to Makri and Metkyi?"

"She's their older sister."

"It makes sense," Katerin said grimly.

Twana, Makri, and Metkyi. Three siblings. Artel, Dovré and Staul. To fully fit the prophecy, Twana should have been dedicated to Dovré instead of Makri, but with Makri being a twin, that makes it different. Oh yes, it's all starting to make sense now.

Katerin shivered.

It wasn't her healing skills that brought her to Wickmasa. She was here because she was the daughter of Terani the God-Killer. The Gods wanted her here for their own reasons.

It took all of her willpower not to swing up on Mira's back and ride out of Wickmasa toward Kinherit, toward any other place but this one.

It's not that easy to escape your fate. Healers never walk out on a contract, and with this many gods in Wickmasa, they'd find me one way or another. But Lady Dovré. Me? Why me?

As she expected, there was no answer.

Her fate had been cast years ago, in Chiyan and Waykemin. She had fled to escape it, but here it was, circled back to meet her again. Further flight would only make the eventual reckoning worse.

There is no escaping your fate, the priest of Karnoi and Cirdel had told her when she left Waykemin for the Healing House. *Sooner or later, it will find you.*

Damn him for being right.

CHAPTER 9

Katerin brooded about Wickmasa's connections to the sibling ties of the Gods as she settled in for the night. Colerei and Davni left shortly after their return from the walk around the village, Colerei proudly pointing to the loaves she had tucked into the bread keeper.

An iron pot sat toward the back of the stove on the patient side of the lodge.

"Hunters brought the roast by," Colerei had told Katerin. "Healer's portion. Should be ready by the time the Harvester rides mid-sky tonight. Don't let it overcook!"

Katerin assured Colerei that she wouldn't let that happen. It was almost ready now. But eating would mean leaving the journals she was squinting at, the books she had guarded ever since her mother had passed into the dreamless sleep.

Someone scratched at her door.

"May I enter?" Twana called.

"Just a moment." Katerin closed her books and locked them away.

Always guard this knowledge, her mother had told Katerin

before she collapsed, hiding the transfer from the priest who had betrayed her. *You may need it someday.*

Katerin still obeyed her mother's final waking order.

She hurried to open the door for Twana.

"Good evening." Twana handed a warm bundle to Katerin and carefully looked around the lodge. Her gaze stopped at Katerin's Dovré shrine. "Makri never had a shrine," she said softly, a sad note in her voice.

"Perhaps if your brother had kept a shrine, he'd still be alive."

"You know about him."

"And more. I encountered Metkyi this afternoon. He—well, he was in his shapechanger mode."

"Davni told me. I'll speak to him."

Katerin shook her head. "There's no need. I can take care of myself, Lady of Artel."

"I warned Imnari that you were not an ordinary traveling healer. You know too much about the Shadowwalkers and their ways to be just a simple circuit healer. I knew the Healing House wouldn't send such on circuits to the North."

"Very true." Katerin took a deep breath. "And now I think I almost know too much about Wickmasa and its secrets. But you and Metkyi haven't cut hair for Makri."

"He was a suicide," Twana said softly. "And Staul and Artel didn't ask it of us."

"Nonetheless—" The bundle was almost too warm for Katerin's hands and she wanted to put it down politely. "May I see what you've given me?"

"Yes. Yes. Do." Twana seemed grateful for the change in subject. "Colerei's a good cook, but she's not the best hand for sweets. I took the liberty of preparing a small batch of treats for you as a lodge-gift. They can be eaten hot or cold."

Katerin unwrapped the bundle to find a dozen small pasties, clear blue and red fluids seeping out of them.

"Berry pasties?" she asked, suddenly hungry.

"Huckleberry and strawberry. We've many patches not far from here."

"Huckleberry? I *love* huckleberries. I've not had a good huckleberry pasty for years. The villages on my healing circuits all have good strawberry patches, but not a one of them with good huckleberries."

"We trade huckleberry products. You may be sick of huckleberries by the time winter is over. Dried huckleberries, huckleberry breads, huckleberry syrup, huckleberry preserves, huckleberry wine, we do it all."

"I look forward to getting heartily sick of huckleberries this winter," Katerin said, and meant it. She gestured to a chair. "Sit. Have you eaten yet?"

Twana shook her head.

"Then please eat with me."

"I would be honored."

Katerin brought out plates and utensils, and they dished up chunks of roast and tubers. Afterwards, they each had a pastie.

"I apologize for not having any drink to offer but water and tea as yet," Katerin said.

"No need to worry." Twana grinned and pulled out a small flask. "Huckleberry liquor?"

They laughed. Katerin brought out cups, and Twana poured them each a finger's worth of the liquor. Katerin smacked her lips appreciatively at the rich sweetness.

"Another Wickmasa product?"

"I make this in the summers. It's my side income project." She frowned. "Shaman of Artel doesn't earn much in Wickmasa."

"Still, Wickmasa seems to do well by itself. It manages to support a shaman, a priest, and a healer. Three gods with Voices in one village. Most villages can't afford that level of religious practice."

"No, most villages can't," Twana said. "But Wickmasa is

different." She looked around. "They put you in Siljaren's old site."

"That's the Siljaren of the stories, isn't it?" Katerin asked. "The one who helped Alicira escape from Zauril?"

"Yes. It is the same Siljaren."

"Did you know her?"

"Yes."

"There's more. Darlna, Orelyets, and Yetklet. Orelyets and Yetklet must have been the youngers to your mother. Darlna married Richen, and had you, then Makri and Metkyi. Makri talked about his siblings being Red Chestnut Leaf. You and Metkyi never went to the Fan kindreds?"

"No, we didn't. It wasn't expected." Twana said. "I'm only their half-sister. My mother was married to a trader who was killed in a dispute at the Fair in Nere. Richen took her part against the killer, helped her earn blood payment from him. She married Richen, brought him back to Wickmasa. His price was that at least one of his children would be Fan, and that would be Makri."

"But why *your* family for the gods?"

Twana gave Katerin a sad smile. "Why do the gods choose any family?" she asked in return.

"True." Katerin let that subject drop. After all, *she* had Terani the God-Killer as her family.

Twana looked around the lodge again. "You've arranged things just like Siljaren did. The shrine is even in the same place."

"There is only one spot to put the shrine."

Twana half-smiled and looked down at her hands. "Do you have plans for your evenings?"

"Handwork. Braiding. Books to study. Letters to write. Reports to make to the Healing House. I don't expect to spend the winter idle. I need to make side income for any luxuries I might want."

"That's good. Especially in this lodge. There's something about the way magic flows around this site. I can see why no one has lived here since Siljaren." She rose. "And now that I've brought you my treats and had dinner with you, I need to go. Thank you for sharing the lovely Colerei's preparations. You're lucky she's working for you."

"It was Myrieke's choice." Katerin shrugged. "Stay a while longer. I'll make some tea. You've no reason to rush away, do you?"

Twana hesitated. "I should be getting back."

"Is there something you need to do? Perhaps I can help."

"Brave soul, to be wandering around too late at night."

"Ah, but I have a daranval to keep me company. She'll protect me. She's an old war mare."

"I'd forgotten about that." Twana relaxed. "I'll stay as long as I can get an escort from you and your war mare!"

"We can do that. Is there a problem I need to know about that the Watch doesn't handle?"

Twana frowned. "Let's just say that the darkness holds many things, not all of them congenial. Zauril still holds a grudge against Wickmasa. We don't get big raids and the Shadowwalkers leave us alone, but this lodge is too far out from the main village for my liking!"

"I have a sword, and I've been trained to use it. My bow and Mira are not my only defense against the raiders. Why do you think I can travel alone?"

Twana smiled. "Good! Then you need to know that Yetklet holds weapons practice at midday, every other day, and tomorrow is practice day."

"I'll be there."

"Good," Twana repeated. "Enough of this talk! Let me tell you some family histories."

"Tell me about Davni's family."

Twana smiled. "That one I know well, especially since it's in part the tale of my family."

Katerin poured tea and settled in to listen to Twana's tales.

* * *

IT WAS late by the time Twana finished her family stories and Katerin escorted her home. It was cold enough that Katerin chose to swing up on Mira to stay warm.

Why was Twana so nervous about walking around the village alone at night? The moon was waning from full, but there was still enough light that Katerin felt no need to carry a lantern, much less either her bow or sword. She encountered the Watch three times. Each time she exchanged pleasantries and earned a serene nod back. Plenty of patrols. No concerns about attackers.

Because the place was god-haunted? It might be that. With three representatives of the gods here, with Wickmasa's past history, this was a place of change. But the uneasiness could also be related to Wickmasa's frontier location. That was a more reasonable assumption.

Katerin took a deep breath. *Some people are just nervous about the night.*

A whisper of wings swished past her face. Mira tightened underneath Katerin, quickening her steps. Katerin twisted her fingers into Mira's mane, ice clenching her gut as the shadows around her took shape. She quickly closed her eyes. If she was working figures in moonlight, then what did that mean? Fire-light was one thing. Moonlight was harder and less likely to be worked by those without talent.

Mira remained tense underneath Katerin.

I'm not working shadows.

Not with Mira's reaction.

A faint "rawk" echoed through the trees. Katerin gulped and

swallowed hard as chills tickled down her arms. The raven in the trees croaked again, laughing.

Beneath the trees, a pack of wolves curled up in their beds. Other shapes whispered around the wolves. A pale luminescence grew around the wolves, taking human shapes.

Mira stopped dead in her tracks, every muscle pulled tight. Katerin wrapped her legs around Mira, visualizing the two of them standing like statues.

Stay in place. Stay in place. Don't run from the Hunt.

Dear Goddess, running now would only provoke them. She tried to think of Dovré, tried to awaken the Eye on her chest, but her mind stubbornly remained fixed upon the gathering under the trees.

A tall, silver-maned wolf rose. He shook himself, licked his chops, then sat down, raising his muzzle high as he began his night song.

—*Don't run*, Katerin whispered to herself and to Mira. —*Don't run.*

The pack joined the alpha male's song, a dark-coated female taking the lead. The other shapes remained nebulous, sometimes taking forms that Katerin recognized for the briefest moment before twisting into something else.

The song ended. The big silver wolf barked once, whirled, and trotted off. The dark-maned female shook herself and glanced at Katerin with glowing eyes before galloping after her mate. The iridescent shadows played around the pack as it ran in the other direction, not looking left or right.

Katerin fell forward and wrapped her arms around Mira's neck.

The Hunt is here.

The Hunt had seen her, but chosen not to pursue. This time her mother didn't walk amongst the wolves, shapechanging into one of them. Katerin didn't know if she was relieved that she didn't see Terani amongst the Hunt. Shouldn't she be there?

Not that it mattered. That made five gods who walked here in Wickmasa. Karnoi and Cirdel of the Shadows, the paired god and goddess her mother had served. The only gods Katerin feared.

Now she understood why Twana feared the night.

CHAPTER 10

*M*ira *with ribs sticking through her otherwise slick and glossy coat* roused Katerin the next morning.

—*Mira covered with buffalo dung*, Katerin thought back.

No response from Mira. Katerin quickly splashed water on her face, dressed, then went out to care for her stock, munching on one of Twana's pasties for a quick breakfast.

Her vision of the Hunt seemed minor in broad daylight. After all, neither Karnoi nor his consort Cirdel had *directly* revealed themselves. Neither God nor Goddess had taken human shape. But the appearance was a warning. That meant *five* of the seven crowned gods had taken an interest in this village.

Kwellet rode up on a small brown molly mule, leading a black and white spotted molly mule, just as Katerin was rigging up a rope war bridle on the black mule.

"*Two* mules?" she asked, studying the two closely. Both were well-built, albeit smaller than the black mule. They were close enough in size and conformation to be sisters, with a nice sloping shoulder, short-backed, with horse-like haunches instead of donkey-type haunches.

Kwellet shrugged as he tied the mollies to the corral fence, slipping the bridle off of the brown one he'd been riding and hanging it on the saddle horn, tying her with the halter and lead rope she wore underneath the bridle. "That's what Myrieke told me to do."

"But Kwellet—" Katerin watched the mollies as the other two mules in the corral clustered close. Both mollies were calm but flirtatious as the corralled mules squabbled with each other to establish who had the status to touch noses first. She snapped the rope on the black's nose when he wanted to join his brothers, reminding him that she was in charge.

"Your big mule is just what Orelyets's been looking for. He needs this one to match up with a big, stout harness mule."

"I don't know how well he will do in harness," Katerin muttered.

"Won't really matter," Kwellet said. "By the time he drags a wagon up and down a few hills, he'll be over any attitude he might have. It's more important that he be stout and sound. Orelyets's willing to pay top price for a match. I'll hold him. Go check out your new mules."

"Well, all right," Katerin said. She inspected the spotted mule. The molly accepted Katerin's handling obediently.

"They're both broke to ride as well as pack," Kwellet said. The black mule tried to pull away from Kwellet, only to receive another snap of the rope.

"So how can these two be equal in worth to that black one?" Katerin reexamined the brown mule.

"They're too small for trade caravans. They've been earmarked for the next Trading Fair so that's why I still had them on hand. Never know when you might run across a good winter trade." He grinned at Katerin.

"I should guess so!" Katerin undid both mules.

She led the two mollies away from the corral and whistled Mira over. Mira's tail flagged over her back as she blew at them. Approvingly, Katerin noticed that both mules stood their ground as Mira imperiously swept around them twice in a springy trot, then dropped to a walk, lowering her head and flicking her ears back and forth. Mira sniffed the spotted mule from rear to front, ending with a delicate nostril-to-nostril touch. The spotted mule lowered her head.

Mira repeated her examination of the brown mule, who tossed her head once when Mira nudged her on the withers, but otherwise remained quiet. Mule and daranval stared at each other after the nostril touch, and Mira pinned her ears. Then the mule lowered her head.

Katerin sighed. Good.

—*Mules scrambling after Mira and Katerin on the trail, unroped,* came to her from Mira.

Better than she'd expected. She watered the two mules. Mira joined them. Upon her return to the corral, she saw Kwellet schooling the black mule in a circle around him.

Kwellet caught her eye and nodded. "He'll work for Orelyets. What do you mean to do with those others?"

"I'd like to get rid of them. I don't need four mules. These two will do me just fine."

"I'll put them in with the herd. Orelyets won't need more mules than this one, but by midwinter that could change."

"Thanks. Don't tweak your shoulder with him!" she warned, as the big mule tried to buck away.

"He'll settle down. I've got him. Shall I take your other two now?"

"It would be a help for me."

"Any of them rideable?"

"The brown one," Katerin said.

Kwellet carefully tied the black mule away from the others as Katerin retrieved the halters for the two mules. Kwellet transferred his saddle from the brown molly mule to the big brown jack, leaving the bridle hanging from the saddle horn.

"There. They should stay like this until I'm ready to head back."

"You had this in mind," Katerin accused.

Kwellet laughed. "I wasn't going to walk that big knothead back over to my corrals on foot! Worst case, I'd ride that molly over and have you come get her."

She grinned at him. "So let's work on your brace."

Kwellet followed Katerin into the patient side of her lodge and took up his seat on the stool. She undid the brace and checked the ankle, rotating it carefully while Kwellet grimaced and choked back at least one yelp.

Yes. A very slight improvement, probably not one that Kwellet would notice yet, but an improvement nonetheless. She stiffened the brace and replaced it. Kwellet grunted slightly and she looked up, noticing that his face was pulled tight.

Hurts him more than he'll admit. Bet he overdid yesterday.

She summoned up her courage. Best to ask Kwellet before the girls arrived. "Kwellet, are there any other Gods represented here? Not just Staul, Artel and Dovré, but any others?"

"You saw the Hunt."

"Yes."

"As far as I know, no, no one here has had any of the other Gods calling them. Especially Karnoi and Cirdel, thank the Bright One." Kwellet stretched and stood. "Thank you, Healer Katerin, for helping me. My shoulder and ankle feel much, much better already."

Katerin rose. "You've done plenty for me as well, Horsemaster Kwellet. I was *not* looking forward to making my first supply run to Kinherit with that big mule."

They went outside.

"Will you and Mira be able to help me this afternoon?"

"I will make time for it," Katerin promised.

Kwellet swung up on the brown mule. "Hand me the black's lead," he directed. "Do you know how to tie a pack line tail tie?"

"Yes."

"Tail that other one to the black. That'll slow him down. I assume he's been tailed before."

"He has. Want me to ride over with you?"

"I'd appreciate the additional hand," Kwellet admitted.

"Let me get these girls into the corral." Katerin quickly turned her new mules into the corral and chucked them some hay. Then she swung up on Mira bareback.

"Pretty job of mounting," Kwellet commented. "You've had some training over the years."

"Practice." Katerin guided Mira next to the brown mule, sandwiching the other two between herself and Kwellet. "Mira's made a better horsewoman out of me."

"She's a very fine daranval," Kwellet said.

"She makes me look good."

They rode silently to Kwellet's lodge. After helping him get the mules settled, Katerin headed back home.

Fresh smoke rose from the patient side of her lodge by the time she arrived. Davni was busy currying the little brown mule while the black and white spotted mule watched.

"Patients are here," Davni called out as Katerin slid off of Mira.

"Where?"

"Inside. Colerei's getting them settled."

"Check the waterskins," Katerin directed. "Then come inside."

She threw Mira a flake of hay, then joined Colerei in the tent, where three patients waited, all with various forms of stiff and sore joints.

Word must have gotten out about Kwellet's salve.

* * *

KATERIN STOPPED at midday to join Yetklet's fighting practice. She paired with Twana, running through a medium-level sword drill. Metkyi was also there, pairing off with Yetklet to do a more advanced sword and knife drill.

Katerin was pleased when she finished. It had been far too long since she had a chance to practice, and Twana gave her some pointers. Twana was a more skilled sparring partner than Senai.

If they do this all winter, I'll have no problems with staying in condition for the summer!

Still, Katerin had to rush to make the practice, and when the first bell of the afternoon tolled, marking the end of practice, she rode Mira back to her lodge at a fast trot, waving off Colerei's offer of anything heavier to eat than a quick mug of soup. It was mid-afternoon before she could take a break. The first three scowling men she ministered to soon became a line of men and women with assorted complaints, and a couple of children with tooth problems. No major problems so far, just minor aches and pains.

"Makri just didn't understand these pains," one oldster told Katerin.

At least they'll get their contract's worth out of me this winter, Katerin thought grimly at one point. *I'm going to tell Eldoran to make sure that Hinet knows about pain salves.*

Finally, there were no more patients. Colerei pulled the roast off of the stove and sliced the meat into some bowls, while Davni made tea.

"Is healing always this busy?" Davni asked.

"It can be."

"So what happens if—" Colerei's fingers quickly traced a warding sign, "we get plague?"

"With plague, it never stops," Katerin told them.

Colerei shivered. "I remember last winter," she said in a very quiet voice. "We lost two babies in our lodge, and Grandmother."

"Darlna and some young ones," Davni said.

"I have elixirs pre-mixed to give the sick. Does plague here come on quickly, and hit many people, or does it come on slow?"

The girls eyed each other quizzically, then shrugged.

"I really don't remember," Davni said. "I was too busy."

"Me too," Colerei said. "I'm sure Twana or Myrieke could tell you. Myrieke spent a lot of time helping Makri."

"So did Twana," Davni said. "And Metkyi."

"Metkyi?" Katerin sipped her tea.

"Metkyi was very good with Darlna," Davni said. "Makri was useless to help her, but Metkyi really fought hard to save their mother. Didn't work, of course, and Makri chased him away when she went into her final collapse. But yes, Metkyi did help with Darlna. I do remember that."

Kwellet seemed surprised that Metkyi followed Staul's call rather than Dovré.

It would be worth her time to meet Metkyi on neutral ground. She knew that a priest of Staul helped with the dying, but the sick? Then again, Darlna had been his mother. Maternal ties could make a difference.

I must learn more about Metkyi.

Katerin finished her food. "I'm helping Kwellet with a horse," she told Colerei. "If there's an emergency, that's where I'll be."

Colerei nodded. "I'll make a soup with our leftovers. Should we wait for you to come back?"

"No. Don't wait. Colerei, thank you. Your cooking is very good."

Colerei gave her a quick smile. "It's nothing."

"Better than what I can do," Katerin said.

* * *

SCHOOLING the little mare went well. Katerin ponied her from Mira, then helped Kwellet long-rein her around the corral. The little mare was nervous about the long ropes brushing against her legs, but she didn't kick at them. At one point she startled into a sideways jump when the dogs kicked up a fuss.

"That's enough for today," Kwellet said finally. "Your help is useful, Katerin. I thank you."

"It's a welcome break from my usual work. See you tomorrow." She bowed in farewell.

Rather than take any of the direct routes through the village back to her lodge, Katerin sent Mira up the ridge. It was a clear, crisp, afternoon. She would have enough time to look over the plateau before it got dark. Both she and Mira could use the ride.

Mira responded eagerly when Katerin turned her toward the trail. They chose a narrow track to the top instead of the broader, shallower trail obviously used by Wickmasa's herds. They were rewarded with less mud and occasionally stunning vistas, especially toward the eastern mountains that separated Keldara from Clenda. Snow rested low on those mountains.

Not long before we'll have it here.

She urged Mira into a trot. The top of the ridge spread into a wide, rolling plateau of dried grass where horses, mules, cattle and sheep gathered in small herds. Young riders rode patrol on the edges of those herds.

Katerin rode Mira along the rim of the plateau, drinking in the sun and the sights. Seen from above, Wickmasa was a bigger village than it seemed from within.

They halted at the edge of the gorge. A narrow but well-used track led back down. Katerin turned a suddenly reluctant Mira down it. Mira complied, but switched her tail, snorting warily, her muscles tight and her thoughts suddenly locked down against Katerin's.

A strange crawling sensation swarmed over Katerin's body as they entered a tree-sheltered portion of the trail. Katerin dropped her hand to her knife, tense, wishing she'd brought her sword.

Shadowwalker?

But Mira's reaction was not the one she usually displayed around Shadowwalkers. This warned of magic with the presence of Gods. The Hunt? No, that was different.

The trail opened up into a small clearing. Katerin spotted movement at the far end, and tightened her body in preparation for a response as the creepy-crawlie sensation grew stronger throughout her whole body.

A handsome young man stood up from the log he had been sitting on. With his long gray swallowtail jacket, fitted waistcoat and black breeches, he could have walked out of court in Dera, rather than this clearing. It took Katerin a couple of moments to recognize Metkyi.

"Welcome, Voice of Dovré," he said. "I was hoping to have a better meeting than our last ones. I did not expect anything this auspicious."

CHAPTER 11

"Voice of Staul," Katerin acknowledged, her throat suddenly tight and raspy. "How did you come to expect me here?"

Metkyi shrugged. "I knew that your Goddess would lead you here soon. I didn't expect to see you the first afternoon I sat watch. This is truly auspicious! The gods are with us."

"Why here?"

Metkyi gestured around them. "This clearing is sacred to both Dovré and Staul."

"Oh? How?" Her uneasiness settled.

"Alicira diced with Staul here. Countless other followers of Staul and Dovré have met here in peace, over the seasons, for the good of Wickmasa. Makri wouldn't, but you—come. Dismount. Have tea. We need to talk." He gestured toward his log, and Katerin spotted the faint wisp of a fire.

"You've planned and prayed for this meeting. Why not just come to my lodge? Wouldn't that be more reliable?"

"Your lodge is *your* ground. Here, neither of us are dominant. It is neutral ground, and the Gods will keep it private."

"Why so concerned about privacy?"

Metkyi winced. "You were right to be worried about Shadowwalker influence on the village. Twana told me about your concerns. The Shadowwalker influence is not a direct assault, but tied to what Makri has done. But—there are deep issues, and politics to consider. There are things you need to know that no one else can tell you."

Katerin slid off of Mira and slipped her bridle off, loosening the girth to let Mira graze. "Speak, Voice of Staul."

"Makri wanted more than what he had, and thought he could serve *both* Staul and Dovré. In that pride, bending away from his honor, he may have brought more trouble than—" He shook his head. "For the good of Wickmasa, the two of us must cooperate."

"Agreed. Tell me what I need to know."

Metkyi pointed toward a rock outcropping near the fire. "There are things we must do first. Protections."

She understood. Katerin looked. The outcropping was a rough stone shelter big enough for two small stone statues of Staul and Dovré. Staul's statue had recently freshened garments and a small cake set in front of it, while Dovré's statue wore ragged garments in need of repair.

"I need to fix that," she said.

"Yes," Metkyi said. "You should. And soon."

"Tomorrow. It'll be too late for me to come back tonight."

"Your daranval's hair might be sufficient token until then."

"There's that much need?"

He had tight worry lines around his eyes. "There is."

Don't argue about necessity with a priest of Staul.

Katerin plucked several hairs from Mira's mane, then gathered some from her tail. She found some crumbs, a few leftover herbs, and a strip of leather in her saddlebags. She wrapped the hairs around the statue of Dovré, tightening them in place with the strap of leather, and placed the crumbs and herbs in front of the goddess. She would have left the altar, but she frowned at the statues. Something more was needed.

She plucked several of her own hairs, and added them to the wrapping around Dovré, retying the leather binding, then whispered the words of consecration, promising to return tomorrow with better tokens.

When she turned back to Metkyi, he had two steaming cups of tea ready.

"Well done." He heaved a heavy sigh, then handed Katerin one of the cups.

"I will do better by her tomorrow. This is only temporary."

"Better than it was. At least we now have a balance, such as it is, between us. Later than it should have been, but there's not much to be done about that. It is as it should be."

She sniffed the cup as she raised it to her lips. No magic, a simple herbal blend. Satisfied, she sipped. "Is Staul the Balancer happy?"

Metkyi cocked an eyebrow at Katerin. "How do you think the balance swings?"

"I worry."

"Yes." Metkyi stared down into his tea. "Makri tipped the balance of power in ways he shouldn't have."

"Because he sought power from Dovré and Staul?"

"Not—just them."

"I saw the Hunt. He went to Karnoi and Cirdel," Katerin guessed, her throat growing dry and tighter. She tightened her hands on the cup so that Metkyi could not see them tremble.

"Yes," Metkyi said bitterly. "My brother thought he could be all things to all gods, so he emptied himself out, and you saw where it brought him."

"Oh yes, I did."

Gods. Courting Karnoi and Cirdel while committed to Dovré as a healer was much, much worse than courting Staul. At least the Balancer had a role in healing life. But those gods dedicated to battle and disorder? No ties at all.

"Did anyone else know about this?"

"Twana. We have no speaker for Karnoi and Cirdel here. An opening for Makri to take those roles."

"So it would have fallen to you to exact the justice of the gods upon him," she said. "He spared you that."

"He spared *Twana* that," Metkyi growled. "I would not have done it without her, and I had set aside my own right for justice several times before. Otherwise—" He let the rest of the sentence hang unspoken, but Katerin could easily finish it.

Otherwise, I'd have been the one judged, for moving against the Voice of Dovré without cause.

"Wouldn't it have been better for you to have spoken in this manner yesterday?"

Metkyi flushed slightly. "I was caught unaware, on my own ground. My apologies."

"A bit touchy. Even for a shapeshifter."

"I *am* sorry," Metkyi sighed. "But I hope you understand. There's been times when I needed to take on Staul's form with little warning."

"I do understand." Katerin carefully set down her cup. *Oh yes, I certainly do understand, given the circumstances.* "What should I do if I need to contact you?"

"Send Colerei. Not Davni, unless things truly are dire. Colerei knows my ways."

"Your successor for Staul?"

That doesn't seem right. I think Mira and I would have sensed it.

"No. Not at all. She is the one chosen from the village to make sure I still remember them."

"Forgive me," Katerin said. "My experience with priests of Staul is limited. Just what do you mean by that?"

"It's easy for a shapeshifter of Staul to take different forms. To become lured down the path where walking with the

Shadows is more appealing than real life." Metkyi poked at the fire. "I need to be in contact with the things of this life. Colerei is the village's reminder to not lose myself in the world of the balance, to shift back to the world of the village."

"A potential mate?"

Metkyi shook his head violently. "No. Not at all. Priests of Staul are like you healers! We don't form bonds for long, if at all. We also take contraceptive powders."

"I'm sorry. I didn't know."

"If you've not been around one of us much, you wouldn't know it." Metkyi kept poking at the fire. "You, me, and Twana need to meet here soon."

"Why?"

"To restore the balance. Without the balance, we can't stop what Karnoi and Cirdel intend to do, now that Makri's set them free to act as they will."

Katerin nodded. "Tomorrow afternoon? Or should it be sooner?"

"If tomorrow afternoon is not soon enough, then we truly are staring down the face of the wolf," Metkyi sighed. "I do not sense that significant a shift in the balance. Tomorrow afternoon at four bells?"

"Tomorrow afternoon at four bells," she confirmed. "I thank you for your hospitality, Voice of Staul."

"And I thank you for listening, Voice of Dovré."

Katerin retacked Mira and swung up on her. As she rode back to the village, she would have thought it was only her imagination that suggested that ghostly wolf forms followed them in the woods beside the trail, except for the tension in Mira's movements. Mira relaxed as they descended into the village, and Katerin felt the Hunt ebb away.

I'll come back sooner tomorrow, she promised herself.

She hoped Metkyi was adequately protected against the

Hunt. Even those who walked the Balance were not immune to Karnoi of Battles and Cirdel of Disorder.

* * *

ONCE BACK AT her own lodge, Katerin lit all of her lanterns and candles.

Must remember to order more candles from the Healing House.

Then, finally, she turned to her mother's books.

If Makri had known what I carried—

Katerin pressed her lips together and studied the two books, one with a faded black leather cover, the other with a faded red leather cover. She chose the black leather book, the book of Karnoi.

At first she read the lines slowly, carefully. As the handwriting changed from one priest's scrawl to another's clearer hand, she read faster, until she had finished the last notation in her mother's neat handwriting.

Then she closed the black book firmly. She looked at the red book, shook her head, and locked them carefully away in a trunk. One book was enough for tonight.

Once the books were safely secured, she took her mask off of the wall. She knelt in front of her shrine to Dovré, pressing her forehead to the ground, extending the mask in front of her, holding it tight as she prayed.

Calmness and quiet slowly descended upon her. At last Katerin rose, shaking out cramped legs and arms. She kissed the mask before she hung it back on the wall.

She stirred the fire that had burnt low in the stove and added another log. She replaced her guttering candles with fresh ones. Then she dug out the leather braidwork that Yevtin had given her.

She worked the leather late into the night. The sky showed

early morning when she checked on Mira, then went to bed. Even then, it took her a long time to sleep.

Sleep brought nightmares that she thought had once been banished.

CHAPTER 12

Katerin spent the next morning immersed in her work. Once Colerei and Davni arrived, patients started trickling into the lodge, and when Katerin wasn't working with a patient, she was teaching Davni the foundations of making salves. Still, in brief moments and pauses, she couldn't help but think about her circumstances.

She kept coming back to two questions.

If the Gods want me here, then what else am I supposed to be doing? What else will come my way?

Perhaps simply stopping the Shadowwalker contagion from spreading was why the Gods had brought her to Wickmasa. But Katerin didn't believe that for one moment. She could have left Wickmasa after Makri's death if that were the case, and not returned for the winter.

No, The Gods had something more for her to do. Something tied to her being the daughter of Terani the God-Killer. The Hunt's activity and the concerns shown by both Twana and Metkyi strongly suggested that the Gods weren't done with her yet.

Didn't someone hear me, years ago, when I said I was no heroine?

Katerin sighed at that thought, startling the young man whose strained knee she was tending.

"Is something wrong, Healer Katerin?" he asked.

"No, no, not a problem with your knee at all," she quickly reassured him. "I was thinking about another case. I have to take a moment to fit this brace correctly."

She finished with the brace, gave him a pain potion, fixed him up with a crutch, and had Davni escort him out of the lodge. Katerin sat back. No one else waited for her.

Now was a good time to prepare her offerings for the little Dovré shrine. Katerin rummaged through her goods. She found a fine piece of soft leather she had carried with her for a while, a remnant of nice gloves from years ago. Katerin stroked the leather gently, remembering the craftsman in the Clendan wilderness who had made the gloves for her. The hide had come from a rare albino deer.

When I ran into Heinmyets's summer camp.

High in the mountains of Clenda. Heinmyets was notoriously casual about the placement and predictability of his summer camps, and Katerin had come across this one by accident during her regular circuit that year.

She half-smiled, remembering the tall, heavy-set patriarch. In summer, he looked nothing like the Leader in Dera during the winter. Instead of fullcoat and breeches, he dressed like the simplest roving huntsman, wearing a plain summer tunic, leggings and the tall boots of a mountain rider. His daranval Elantai had been coming into his first strength and power.

Rekaré was just a small child.

Katerin remembered Rekaré as a half-dressed wild thing running with the kidpack of the band, her pale Aireii skin brown from the sun, her long black hair unbound and tangled. Katerin's daranval at the time had been timid, but his timidity only made him more attractive to the wild young horsewoman. It had taken Inharise's intervention to convince young Rekaré that *this* daranval was bonded, not like the unbonded daranvelii that Rekaré and her kidpack snatched rides on.

Katerin shook her head at the memory. This piece of leather would be most appropriate for Dovré, especially in the place where Rekaré had been born.

I wonder where she is now?

Katerin shivered. Of all the secrets she could ever carry, this was one she didn't want.

She put the leather scrap in a pouch that she tied to her belt. She found a fresh seedcake that she added to the pouch.

No. Not enough. It was *sufficient.* But not enough. *Something more.* She rummaged through her bags and chests, looking for that one final piece she needed.

Then she looked in the purse with the magicked yarn that Senai had given her. She pulled the yarn out, once again marveling at its glowing beauty. Katerin spotted a faint gold thread. It came free easily from the others, a short strand not long enough for any working. Wrapped around it was a black string shot through with silver highlights.

Katerin nodded to herself. This was the last piece she needed. She added the strings to the pouch.

* * *

As she hoped, she was first to reach the clearing. Katerin tended to the shrine. She wrapped the leather over the Dovré gently while Mira watched, leaving her offerings from the night before in place. She tied it in place with her yarn, set the seedcake before the Dovré, and stepped back, noticing that the birds and squirrels had been at Metkyi's food offerings from the night before.

A good sign.

Mira blew softly, inspecting Katerin's work. Then she lowered her forehead and nudged Katerin. Katerin absently scratched the diamond star that was fading into Mira's gray coat. Mira relaxed and dropped her head. They stood like that for a few moments.

Then Mira snorted. She hopped back from Katerin and stretched out her neck, listening, ears moving as she turned in the direction of the trail, canting her head one way, then the other, drawing breath slowly and deliberately through her nostrils. She raised her head and Katerin tensed, listening for the loud roller snort, watching for the hind foot stomp.

Mira remained alert but did not react further, her ears flicking back and forth.

Twana or Metkyi?

Whoever it was, Mira knew them. Twana appeared at the head of the trail, wearing a short sword strapped across her back.

So she doesn't go unarmed. Good.

Katerin could not remember seeing Metkyi with a weapon except during practice.

"Metkyi's not here yet?"

"No. No sign that he was here before me."

Twana frowned, scanning the clearing. "That's not usual. Metkyi usually arrives early. You did say four bells, right?"

"He set the time."

"He *should* be here by now. I'm a little late. The watch was ringing four bells when I left my lodge."

"Did you see any sign of trouble on your way up?"

Twana shook her head. "Did you?"

Mira bellowed a warning. She stomped her left hind hard.

Katerin swung up. "Get on! Now!" She seized Twana's wrist and hauled her behind the saddle.

"Hold on to me! *Tight!* When Mira moves, she'll go fast!" Katerin gathered up her reins, picking up information from the vibration of Mira's mouth on the bit. She supported Mira gently, ready for anything.

Mira sprang into a gallop and Twana's arms tightened around Katerin's waist in a stranglehold. Katerin fumbled for her bow and quiver, strung on Mira's right side. She dropped the reins and grabbed an arrow, sliding it up to nock on her string.

I'll get a better nock if we have to stop and shoot.

Mira screamed again as they plunged down the trail, dropping from a gallop to a trot. Katerin struggled to keep balanced so that Twana wouldn't pull them off.

"Plaster yourself to my back!" she growled back at Twana. "Don't fight the motion, just follow my back! And ease up on me!"

Muffled sounds of protest vibrated through her back.

"*Not* a rider!" was the one comment she heard clearly. But Twana moved closer, and her deathgrip eased.

Mira slid to a stop. They heard the growls and howls of a wolf pack, and a hoarse male voice yelling somewhere below the trail.

Metkyi.

"Go!" Katerin shouted to Mira.

Dear Gods, don't let us be too late.

Mira whirled and dropped over the edge of the trail onto a ridge thick with trees and a brush thicket. Her ears flicked once, twice. Mira slipped and slid on the wet dead grass underfoot as she darted through the trees. The ridge narrowed until they had little choice but to turn back or go down one side. Mira hesitated, while Katerin braced herself. Then Mira launched herself down the side, working at an angle sideways along the steep slope.

Twana buried her face in Katerin's back, and her grip tightened briefly, then slacked again. They were halfway down when Katerin felt Mira's balance change slightly.

No. We are not *going down.*

She took a firmer contact with her free hand, steadying Mira and keeping the balance as best as she could with Twana clinging to her. Mira bounded ahead in great leaps, the hillside giving way beneath them, until they were close to the bottom of the little canyon and had reached solid ground.

"Take a breath," Katerin gasped to Mira, who was panting hard.

In response, the mare shook her head, then charged down the canyon, following a narrow game trail that wound along the bottom. More shouting, and the growls of the wolf pack came closer. They thrashed around a corner and thundered into a small clearing, brushy with trees on one side, rocky on the other.

Metkyi was backed up against cliffs and rockfall, a burning firebrand in each hand, in full aspect as Voice of Staul, projecting chills and fear to match his distorted features.

Not that it deterred his attackers. A half-circle of wolves growled and snarled around him. They took turns leaping toward him, then jumping back as he swung a brand. Several broke off from the circle as Mira, Katerin and Twana burst into the clearing.

Twana slid off, unsheathing her sword. Katerin dropped her reins and raised her bow, taking down the first wolf who dared charge them.

Twana chanted, raising her aspect as Voice of Artel. Light flashed off of her sword as she ran toward the wolves.

Katerin sent Mira forward. She focused her thoughts on the Eye of Dovré, and sent a second shot into the pack itself. The arrowhead caught fire as the arrow left her bow. It found its mark in the flank of one of the lesser wolves behind the two leaders snarling at Metkyi. The wolf took off, running down the hillside, ki-yi-yi-ing in pain until it was out of sight.

The whole pack turned from Metkyi. Katerin slid off Mira and slung her quiver over her shoulder. Mira dove with teeth and forefeet at the closest wolf. Katerin sent another arrow flying into the middle of the pack, a satisfying yelp rising as she hit another wolf. Metkyi yelled something she couldn't understand and charged the wolves. They managed to split up the pack, until only the two leaders and a third stood their ground.

Katerin stepped forward. "Go back!" she commanded. "Forms of Karnoi and Cirdel, you have no prey! *Go back!* No battles, no disorder! This is a place of order and quiet!"

The two leaders growled and backed to about twenty strides away from her, then turned and trotted off. The third stood in place. Katerin nocked an arrow. She raised it high and repeated her invocation.

The third wolf did not move. Katerin looked deep into its eyes. Makri's eyes. She released the arrow. It caught flame en route and creased wolf-Makri's back. Howling, wolf-Makri tore off after the others. Katerin nocked another arrow, waiting. Mira screamed a challenge after the fleeing wolves.

A faint, defiant howl came from further down the hillside. They waited until it was clear that the Hunt was gone.

Katerin lowered her bow. The fallen wolves had disappeared. Twana knelt to clean her sword. Metkyi drew a deep, ragged breath. The fires suddenly died from his brands as the aspect of Staul fell away from him and his features slid back to normal. His knees sagged, and he would have fallen, if Katerin had not leapt over Twana to grab him. He held one arm.

"They got me," he gasped, his voice fading. "Arm."

Chills ran through Katerin. "Who? The leaders? That last one—" she refrained from using Makri's name— "or was it another member of the pack?"

"That one," Metkyi mumbled. "The one with Makri's eyes."

"By the Goddess's left tit! Twana. Help me get him up on Mira, *now!*"

Together, they managed to hoist Metkyi onto Mira's back. Mira snorted and flicked an ear. They started down the hillside. Metkyi's body felt cooler under Katerin's hand. She swore again, wishing she could swing up behind him and ride. It would be faster. But they dared not leave Twana, and Mira couldn't carry three adults.

It seemed to be an eternity until they reached Katerin's lodge. Katerin drug Metkyi off of Mira's back. He slumped hard against her. They fell to the ground. Twana pulled Metkyi off of Katerin. They got Metkyi's arms around their shoulders, and helped him into the lodge. Katerin murmured praises to Colerei and Davni for leaving a cot set up and ready for a patient.

"Steady him here," she ordered Twana. She took a moment to add more wood to the stove. Then they eased Metkyi onto the cot, his bitten arm closest to the stove.

"Go tell the Eldest," Katerin ordered Twana. "Don't go alone. Take Mira. Quickly. Who else should be warned that Makri runs with the Hunt?"

"Kwellet. Orelyets. Yetklet."

"Then do that. And have someone bring Davni and Colerei to me. Don't send them alone! Come back. I'll need your help to banish whatever magic's in him."

Twana left. Katerin turned to Metkyi.

"You're sure it was Makri?" she asked as she cut the sleeve free from his coat, the same elegant gray coat he had worn the day before.

"Don't cut—"

"I'll replace it. You can't wear this coat again. It's contaminated by the Hunt and needs to be burned. You're sure that was Makri?"

"I'd know his eyes anywhere."

"Goddess's gold necklace!" Katerin eased the sleeve free, then cut through his shirt.

As she feared, the skin was already beginning to pit and erode away from the bite site.

Cleansing, first.

Katerin dipped hot water into a bowl, then crunched a

handful of aromatic herbs into the water. She found one of the magicked rags and dipped it into the water.

Metkyi bellowed when the rag touched the bite. Katerin lifted the rag quickly, watching. The erosion seemed to have stopped where the rag had touched, so she pressed it against the bite again.

Metkyi's yells faded. "It burns," he groaned through clenched teeth. "Dear Staul, it *burns*, Katerin!"

"It will," she said bleakly. "The magic from the bite is already eating your arm."

There was nothing left of the priest of Staul in Metkyi as he stared at her. Terror widened his eyes and tightened his face. "Am I—is it—will I—"

"I can do more when Mira and Twana get back," she said. "We will use all the power available to us to stop Karnoi and Cirdel's magic. If Staul can help—"

He nodded. "The burning's stopped," he said, in a voice closer to normal.

"Good." She checked the bite. The erosion had halted. "This is going to burn. I'm sorry."

Metkyi nodded. This time he did not yell as she pressed the cloth against his injury. He closed his eyes, his muscles tensing under her hand.

Hurry, Katerin thought. *Hurry, Twana. Colerei. Davni. Hurry.*

She dared not try anything else without help.

CHAPTER 13

*H*elp finally exploded around them. One moment it was just Katerin and Metkyi in the lodge; the next the space was a blur of anxious, worried faces and voices as Davni, Colerei, Twana, and Kwellet burst in. Mira pawed at the door.

"Davni. Throw the door back. All the way. That's right."

Mira gingerly stepped inside, her eyes rolling, ears flicking, tail switching. She approached Metkyi slowly, blowing hard. Katerin breathed deeply, projecting calm. Mira relaxed her head and neck slightly, extending her nose toward Metkyi.

"Davni and Colerei," Katerin directed. "Make sure we have water. Lots of it. Take a firebrand with you. Not just a candle or a lantern, a brand. Don't go alone. No one go alone tonight."

Davni grabbed the empty waterskin.

"Twana. I want you to sit by Metkyi's head."

"What are we doing?" Twana met Katerin's eyes, steady and calm. She wore the vestments of a shaman of Artel.

"The magic is already working on the bite. We need to stop it. Look." Katerin pointed to the bite.

Twana winced. "So what are we doing?"

"An exorcism of Karnoi and Cirdel. They won Makri at the end."

"Karnoi and Cirdel?" Kwellet gasped. "Twana said—but I didn't believe it—"

Katerin glanced at him. "Believe it. He sold himself to them. One wolf had his eyes, and that's the wolf who bit Metkyi."

"What do I do?" Kwellet asked.

"Watch over the girls. Once we're done, if you could wipe Mira down and feed her?"

Kwellet nodded.

"What do I do first?" Twana asked.

"Put any special tokens of Artel you have on the wound," Katerin said. "Metkyi. Do you wear any tokens for Staul?"

"Necklace. Under my clothing." Metkyi said, voice strained. "Quickly, Katerin. I feel their power moving within me. Washing helped, but not enough."

"I understand." She reached under his collar, untied an elaborate necklace made of human and animal teeth, and laid it across the bite, next to Twana's golden orb hanging from a fine golden chain. Katerin recognized both as major sigils of Artel and Staul, matches to the Eye.

The Gods have a lot of power in this village.

Which meant that if Makri had successfully taken Metkyi—

Katerin pulled out the Eye and laid it across the top of the orb and tooth necklaces.

"Mira. To me," she said.

The gray mare delicately moved between the cot and the fire. Her muzzle brushed Katerin's neck, her breath warm and soothing. Katerin closed her eyes and called upon Mira. They became *MiraandKaterin.*

MiraandKaterin reached out a hand. *They* felt the soft warmth of Twana's hand, and then the weight of Metkyi's uninjured hand. *They* put *their* free hand on the wound, on top of the Eye of Dovré, channeling *their* power into the wound, going *themselves* into it.

Their crystalline foe snarled through Metkyi's veins, quicksilver-like, darting and dodging as *they* pursued it, leaving its mark wherever it went. *They* dared not stop the pursuit to fix the damage until either it beat them to the heart or they stopped it. If it beat them to Metkyi's heart—

They cornered it in Metkyi's lungs. Pushed until it had no choice but to join with them. *They* retraced *their* steps, stopping on *their* way to mend what damage they could.

Then *they* were outside the wound. *MiraandKaterin* separated from Twana and Metkyi, took the Eye back, and hung it around *their* neck. Katerin carefully separated from Mira, making sure that she took on all of the *thing* they had captured and left none in her daranval. She fought back the rising tide of bile inside her.

"Kwellet. Mira. Care for her as if she's run for miles," she choked. "Davni. Colerei. Bring wooden bowls." She fought back bile, even as Metkyi and Twana were also visibly struggling not to vomit, hands clasped over their mouths. "When we're done, burn the bowls and everything in them. Don't touch any of it. Use gloves. Burn the gloves."

Once the bowl was safely in her hands Katerin allowed herself to vomit. When she was done, she set the bowl down, then stepped away from Metkyi's cot, staggering a few steps before she fell.

"What do we do?" Colerei whimpered.

"Get Kwellet to help you burn the bowls," Katerin whispered. "One of you watch him so he's not alone. Don't let any of that stuff get on you." Aching, her head throbbing and pounding, Katerin dragged herself over to Twana and Metkyi. She eased the bowls from their hands and set them next to hers.

"Katerin." Kwellet's voice rang loud in the lodge, louder-seeming than it probably was. "Mira first, or the bowls?"

"Bowls. Burn near her. She needs to watch too."

"Understood."

She turned to Metkyi. His eyes were closed and his forehead was clammy to her touch, his face pale.

"Better?" she whispered.

"Sick," he groaned. "But it's gone. Just sick."

"Try to sleep," she said. "Rest."

"Cold."

"I'll get covering for you." His open wound still looked awful, but it no longer had that awful bleached white and blue.

Must get it bandaged.

Katerin crawled over to Twana, who had fallen in front of Metkyi's cot.

"Tired," Twana murmured to her inquiry. "And sick. Gods, Katerin. I've never chased down a piece of the Gods inside someone before."

"Hope you never have to do that again. Stay tonight. I'll have the girls fix bedrolls. And purification. Must purify the lodge. Purify us. Stay awake until we're done."

"Gods, Katerin. I've never worked with a Voice of Dovré as powerful as you are—"

"It's nothing," Katerin said sharply. "Nothing." Her heart raced entirely separately from her reaction to the exorcism.

Just a legacy of being Terani's daughter, and whomever my father was.

She rocked back on her heels. Her mind was draining, emptying from exhaustion, and she couldn't risk that yet. She used Metkyi's cot to steady herself as she rose, staggering to the basket that held bandages.

Then she cleansed Metkyi's wound again, bleakly wondering if he would lose use of the arm. Even as a simple, non-possessed wound it looked bad. The Makri wolf had taken a big bite out of the muscle. She was careful to wrap it so that what pieces of flesh she could somehow fit together adhered.

Can't stitch it tonight. Not until my hands are steadier.

She put the bowl and washcloth where Kwellet would find them.

Covering. She found a blanket for Metkyi and cut off the rest of his jacket. He moaned softly as she worked, but did not protest further. Then she worked off his boots, and tucked the blanket around him.

Purification. She needed purification materials for a smudge.

She lurched, step by weary step, to her purification box. Katerin pulled out a long bundle of sage, juniper and cedar, and twined southern myrtle tree leaves from her herb stores into the bundle, murmuring a prayer to Dovré as she worked. Twana's voice slowly joined hers in a counterpoint chant. Then Metkyi's voice, weak and thin, made a third.

Katerin lit the smudge. When it was burning well, she passed it over Metkyi, waving it several times over his arm as well as over his body. She passed it over Twana from head to feet, front and back. Twana passed the bundle over Katerin. Katerin took it back. They processed slowly around the lodge, waving the smudge, chanting. When they had finished, Katerin mounted it in an iron sconce next to the door.

Finished. Rest. They staggered back by the stove. Katerin collapsed onto her treatment stool, resting her elbows on her knees, holding her throbbing head in her hands. She remained like that until Colerei's hands brushed her shoulders.

"Bedrolls," she told Colerei through her hands. "For all of us. In here with Metkyi. No one goes anywhere tonight."

"No bedroll for me," Kwellet said. "I'll stand watch."

"Not alone," Katerin said.

"We'll take turns," Davni said.

Katerin watched dully as Davni and Colerei laid out the

bedrolls, then darkened the lanterns. She shook her head when they would have guided her to the bedroll first, and gestured to Twana. Only when Twana was settled did she let herself relax.

"Headache preparation," she whispered to Colerei, one last memory of things to do stirring. "Must give to all three of us. Now."

"I will," Colerei said soothingly.

"Have more ready for us for the morning."

"I will," Colerei repeated.

It seemed an eternity until Colerei held the cup to Katerin's lips, steadying her trembling hands. Katerin gulped the mixture. Only then did she allow herself to yield to the spiral of exhaustion pulling at her.

But even then, rest evaded her.

She was not sure when sleep finally won. She was vaguely aware of the wind rising outside. It seemed louder than the usual evening breeze.

Storm blowing in?

She was too tired to care.

When she finally slept, the battles controlled Katerin's dreams. Gusts of wind roaring in the trees punctuated her restless dreams, and the distant sound of cracking branches stirred her into wakefulness. Finally, a small gray daranval's image stepped in, thoughts tinged with annoyance and piles of buffalo dung. Mira paced out a defensive perimeter, and Katerin calmed.

* * *

THE FAINT GLOW of dawn lit the lodge when Katerin woke. She listened to Metkyi's snore and Twana's smooth breathing. Then she could identify the light, soft breathing of the girls. *Both* girls.

Damn it, did they leave Kwellet alone?

She heard a faint chuckle from outside, then the soft, deep rumble of several men speaking quietly.

No. He got help. Good.

She lay still for a few more breaths, letting her awareness circle through her body. Her head hurt, and her shoulders and legs were sore. Had any piece of those gods remained inside her?

The Mira figure stirred, the daranval image sending reassurance.

Katerin slowly sat up. She saw the small waterskin next to her bedroll, and picked it up, grateful for the drink. The bitter taste of the headache preparation rolled across her tongue with the water. When she had finished drinking, Katerin slowly slid out of her bedroll, careful not to disturb Twana. She quietly knelt beside Metkyi. His face was pale, but his snores and breathing rhythm were normal.

Must ask the girls if they gave him some pain potion. I forgot to tell them.

She gently rested the back of her hand against his forehead. He was cool to the touch, but not so cool as to worry her. As she moved her hand away, his eyes flickered open.

"Katerin?" he husked.

"Yes," she whispered. "Sleep. Rest."

"Starting to hurt. Girls gave me something last night."

Katerin looked under the cot and saw the glass bottle of pain potion, along with the serving spoon. Her hands trembled slightly as she poured some potion for him, noting the level inside. They'd given him one dose.

She helped Metkyi sit up as she held the spoon to his mouth. She marked the level of potion in the bottle with the chalk hanging on a string from it so she could track how much he was taking. Then she found the matching waterskin to the one that had been lying by her bed. He groaned wordlessly.

"You need this too," she said.

"Need to go out," he whispered when he was done.

Katerin helped Metkyi up. The door was a struggle, but one of the men outside caught it. Orelyets took Metkyi, guiding him to the latrine. Katerin waited by the door. Clouds rode low over the valley.

Storm coming in. Dazedly, she wondered if it was rain or snow. It felt cold enough to be snow. Tree branches lay scattered around the lodge. *I didn't dream the wind.*

A fire crackled by Mira's shed. Kwellet lay wrapped in a blanket by the fire, while Yetklet stood nearby. Mira stood halfway inside her shed. She nickered softly at Katerin.

Metkyi and Orelyets slowly made their way to Katerin. Katerin guided Metkyi back inside and settled him on the cot. His eyes closed as she tucked the blanket around him.

"Thank you," he breathed. "Thank you for everything."

"It was what had to be done."

"Without you, without your ability, we couldn't have done it."

"It took all three of us," Katerin said.

"You're a *very* strong Voice. You know that?"

"I have the support of a strong daranval," she said.

Metkyi shook his head. "More than that. The Goddess walks strong in you. Almost as strong as—" his voice trailed off. "Sorry. Tired."

"Rest," she whispered. "Sleep." Katerin squeezed his good hand gently. It wasn't long before his breathing resumed the slow rhythm of sleep, this time without the slight jerk from pain. She became aware of Colerei standing next to her and led the girl outside. "You two did well," she told Colerei in a low voice.

"It was hard to remember everything," Colerei said. "We were scared."

"Better to be scared but do what you need to slowly and

carefully than to let the fear stampede you into doing the wrong thing. You girls did the right thing."

"We just kept reminding ourselves of what you'd told us. And Davni found a list that you had her make, what to do in case of possession by the Gods." Colerei stopped. "Was that it? What happened?"

"Yes," Katerin confirmed.

Colerei shivered. "It was also easier once Orelyets and Yetklet got here. Orelyets helped us remember."

Orelyets. Why Orelyets?

On the other hand, if anyone here would have seen possession before, it would have been a trading chief.

"You did well," Katerin repeated to Colerei as they joined the others around the fire. "You did very well."

Orelyets looked sharply at her. "You trained these girls to do the right thing."

"Only a few days worth of training," Katerin said. "They came to me with the most important things they needed, good sense and the knowledge to ask for help."

Orelyets flashed her a grin. "I'm glad to hear that. My daughter speaks highly of you."

"And of you."

"How is Metkyi?" Yetklet asked.

"He survived. He does not have any of the Gods inside him, at least none other than the one to whom he's pledged."

"Will he be all right?"

"The arm muscle is ripped up. I'll stitch it later. But he has no fever, and he took no possession."

Yetklet nodded. "How long do you think it'll take for him to recover?"

"He'll stay in my lodge for several days. I need to make sure that wound doesn't go bad."

"I'll need his help before I go on my next trade trip." Orelyets looked at the sky. "Though, from the looks of the weather, that will be a few days longer."

"That bad?" Katerin studied the clouds.

"The first big storm of the season," Orelyets said. "It's calmed now, but the first winds were strong."

Small white flakes began to drift down around them. Katerin shivered, not from the cold but from worry.

Winter storms were the Hunt's favorite pursuit time.

CHAPTER 14

"So tell me why, after all these years of leaving us alone, the Hunt has chosen to attack Metkyi," Imnari said during the mid-morning Council meeting, raising her voice to be heard above the howl of the storm outside.

The rest of the Council eyed Katerin and Twana, waiting for a response.

"Makri was walking with Karnoi and Cirdel before he passed," Twana said. "He was seeking power. Dovré was not enough for him."

Orelyets coughed and shifted on his seat. "Makri had been gathering information for me when we went on trips," he said. "Things that perhaps only one walking with the Gods could learn from our sources."

"Why not Twana or Metkyi?" Imnari demanded.

Katerin pulled her shawl closer about her. She had changed into heavier clothing as a response to the rising wind As an afterthought before coming to this meeting, she had grabbed her big woolen winter shawl. Now she was glad for it.

"I need to know," Imnari repeated, her voice sharper.

"We needed to know for—" Orelyets stopped, staring hard at Katerin. "You know what I guard, Eldest! This one—"

"Will need to know the full truth soon enough," Imnari snapped. "Hasn't she proven herself to you?"

"It is not my job to decide," Orelyets growled in a low, hard voice. "I do not have the permission nor do I have the authority to make that decision. I vowed my honor to the God!"

Imnari sighed hard, leaning back in her chair. "So that is what is at stake here," she said. "But *why*, Orelyets? Why Makri? Why not Metkyi? Why not Twana? In the name of the Seven Crowned Gods, *why*?"

"Makri was the one the god wanted," Orelyets said in the same low, hard voice. "Not Twana. Not Metkyi. Makri."

"He failed." Imnari snapped. "Now we're all at risk. Do you think this storm is a coincidence?"

A wolf howled nearby.

The circle fell silent as a closer call answered it.

"We have no more time," Imnari said grimly. "Orelyets. Yetklet. I have no further time for discussion. I need you out *there*." She flung one hand toward the door. "Pull together what fighters you can; what protection you can."

"I hear and obey." Orelyets bowed sharply toward Imnari. He caught Yetklet's eye and Yetklet nodded, dropping his own quick bow before following his brother.

Twana rose. "They'll need me outside."

"Mira and I should be there as well," Katerin said.

Imnari shook her head. "No. Sit, both of you," she commanded. "You're in no shape to fight the Hunt."

"My daranval is war-trained. I've fought Saubral Shadowwalkers," Katerin insisted.

"You are my healer. I have greater need for you, and you, too, Twana." Imnari turned her gaze to the shaman. "I don't delude myself that those men are going to win any fight against the Hunt in this storm. At best, they'll keep those *things* at bay so that we'll not lose anyone else. No. Long-term victory is going to come from you, Twana, and you, Katerin, as well as Metkyi. We have too much at stake for you two to go on an errand those men can handle. *Should* handle."

"But—"

"You two have already served me in battle, and right now you're too tired to think effectively. Sit!"

Katerin dropped back onto her stool. "Eldest, what's so much at stake that your trading chief dares not reveal it to me?" she asked.

Imnari sighed, shaking her head. "If *he* can't say, Healer Katerin, then I lack the authority to tell you this."

"If you trust me so little, then perhaps I should go back to the Healing House and send you someone you *can* trust!" Katerin snapped.

"Healer Katerin, it's not a matter of trust. I lack the authority."

"Then let me go out and battle against those wolves!"

"No," Imnari said.

"But my daranval—"

"You'll get the battle you seek against the Hunt," Imnari said. "Either as Healer or as fighter. I have a greater need of your healing and your magics. We won't catch the Hunt in this storm. I need you three to be in accord. With my village under attack by Karnoi and Cirdel, I certainly don't need to have any discord going on between Dovré, Artel and Staul!"

"There will be no discord," Katerin promised.

"No discord," Twana echoed.

"Good. Keep yourselves safe. Without your protection, Wickmasa will suffer."

"We will keep Wickmasa safe," Katerin and Twana promised before they left.

Katerin picked up her sword at the lodge door, then went outside, still simmering. Why didn't Imnari trust her?

Wickmasa and its secrets.

Mira waited for them, haunches turned into the wind, head drooped low, ice dripping from her forelock, tail and mane. Katerin took a deep breath, then turned into the wind to walk back to her lodge, ice and snow painfully lashing the uncovered parts of her face.

Twana matched Katerin stride for stride as they slogged through the snow. Mira provided some shelter, but even so, the wind was too harsh to speak, and walking in the ankle-deep snow against the wind while listening for the wolves took all of Katerin's effort.

Twana turned toward the lodge as they came to Katerin's home, but Katerin turned toward Mira's shed. Twana followed Katerin into the shelter. Katerin broke as much ice free from Mira's blanket and mane as she could, and pulled down more hay.

"I'll send the girls out with water," she promised the daranval before leaving. "Warm water, and a mash."

The girls startled up as Katerin and Twana entered the lodge, Metkyi still sleeping soundly.

"You're all ice!" Colerei exclaimed.

"The storm worsens," Twana said.

Katerin unwrapped her shawl. The light sheet of ice covering her clothing crackled off. Davni muttered and fussed as she helped Katerin, then Twana, break free from the chunks of ice.

"How's he been doing?" Katerin asked, keeping her voice low as Davni brought her a steaming cup of tea.

"Sleeping. We had to give him more pain potion while you were at the meeting," Davni said. "He stirred and shouted when the wolves first howled. They were *right outside* the lodge, until the men chased them away."

"Did he wake?"

"No. The wolves went away and he settled back into sleep."

Katerin checked Metkyi. Paler than before. When she rested the back of her hand on his forehead, he stirred restlessly. The forehead was warmer. She hissed through her teeth and checked the wound. As she feared, given his restlessness and the new warmth, the skin around the stitches was turning red.

"Colerei. I need you to prepare a poultice for me." Katerin gave directions quietly while she got a bowl and cleansing cloth. While Colerei worked, Katerin cleansed, then stitched the wound. Metkyi opened his eyes slightly.

"It's all right. Rest," she told him.

Metkyi grunted and stirred, then closed his eyes.

"Is this bad?" Twana asked.

"Could be," Katerin said.

"Did we not get it all last night?"

"Yes. This is normal for this kind of wound." Katerin decided not to mention the worry his rousing for the wolves had caused her. Even though they had pulled the essence of the Gods out of Metkyi last night, that still didn't mean that a connection had not been made between Metkyi and Makri in wolf form.

They are twins, with a twin's claim on each other.

They had to kill the Makri wolf before Metkyi could be safe from it.

To be secure, she decided on a third potion besides the draught for fever and the potion for pain. It was specific to Dovré and would normally not be given to any but those vowed to Dovré. But in an emergency like this, she could administer it to others.

Protection against possession, the potion was called. The ingredients were rare, expensive, and not a part of Katerin's typical stores. She had added them to her supplies while packing as an afterthought, not knowing what was awaiting her here in Wickmasa.

I have enough for the three of us.

She would have to send a request for more to the Healing

House. That thought reminded her that reports and Senai's letter needed to be sent with the next caravan.

Colerei brought the poultice to Katerin, and she applied it to Metkyi's wound. Then she set about putting together the *protection against possession.*

Twana joined Katerin at her compounding bench.

"Is there anything I can do to help?" she asked. "I feel so useless."

"We'll have things to be doing soon." Katerin stirred the liquid, eyed the consistency, and murmured a blessing from the Goddess over it. *I suppose this will have to do.* "Take this. I don't know how well it will work with a shaman of Artel." She dipped a spoon into the mix and handed it to Twana.

Twana took it gingerly and delicately sipped it down, making a face at the bitterness.

"What *is* this?"

"*Protection against possession.* Not perfect, but it might help."

"Maybe we should be giving it to the hunters—"

"I don't have enough ingredients to make it for the whole village! Besides," Katerin added, in a quieter tone, "we're the ones most at risk. This is designed to protect those who walk with the Gods. Like us."

"But still—"

"Who will the Hunt want more, us, especially Metkyi, or random people from the village?" Katerin estimated the amount left. There would be enough for Colerei and Davni as well. She dipped her spoon into the mix and took her dose, then handed the bowl to Twana. "Here. Make sure that Metkyi, Colerei, and Davni get some. One spoonful. Then bring it back."

That dose would last them two days.

Katerin's next job was to mix a mash for Mira. At least Kwellet had taken her mules back to run with the herd this morning. On their own, with the herd, they'd find shelter from the storm.

Unless the Hunt—

She shook her head. The mules would be better off with the herd rather than trapped in a corral.

"Davni. Help me take this out to Mira."

Davni got her shawl. Katerin handed Davni the steaming mash while she filled a skin of hot water. Twana opened the door for them, and they went out, bracing themselves against the wind.

Mira nickered a welcome as they slipped inside her shed. She dropped her nose into the mash while Katerin broke the ice on her water trough and poured the water into it. Then Katerin pulled off her gloves and slipped her hand under the blanket to check Mira's temperature and comfort level. If Mira got too cold, she would bring the mare inside the lodge.

Mira's thick coat was dry under the blanket.

"Are we in danger?" Davni's voice trembled. "I've never known the Hunt to do this."

"We could be," Katerin said. "Bad choices were made that left people open to Karnoi and Cirdel. Now we have to deal with those choices."

Davni shivered. "So what are we going to do?"

"Stay safe during the storm. That's the best we can do."

"And after?"

"That will depend on what the Eldest decides." Katerin frowned. "When Metkyi wakes, I want you and Colerei to go over to my side of the lodge. We're having a meeting of those who walk with the Gods. Unless you want to be a part of something like that—"

"No. No," Davni said quickly, and left.

Katerin hid a smile. But a quick thought occurred to her.

Of the Seven Crowned Gods, only five had made an appearance in Wickmasa to date.

What was to stop the remaining two from coming? Who was

to say that those Gods didn't have voices for them, lurking hidden amongst the villagers?

Gods, I wish I hadn't thought that.

It would be one thing to deal with three, even five gods using those experienced in having the Gods ride them. But all Seven Crowned Gods in one place? Katerin shivered. No good could come of such a thing. Finding their own speakers for Nitel and Terat to ally with them against Karnoi and Cirdel might be their only hope.

And who will lead them? Who else but the daughter of Terani the God-Killer?

I'm going to end up like her.

CHAPTER 15

The storm was raging harder than ever by the time Metkyi woke. To Katerin's relief, his pallor had faded and he sat up without help. Metkyi felt his injured arm with his good hand, wincing as he poked at the bandage, then tried to move the arm.

He groaned and dropped his hand. "I'm not going to be able to use this for a while, am I?"

"No. That wolf bit you good. Even without the God." Katerin checked the bandages.

"I'm surprised the Hunt cornered you like that." Twana squatted on her heels next to Metkyi's cot.

"So am I," Metkyi said. "They followed me close the night before, but didn't give chase. This time, thanks be to the God, I had my firebrands. There was just enough time to spark them up. Without them, the Hunt would have taken me."

"The Hunt started pursuit?" Katerin asked.

Metkyi snorted. "I was raised in Wickmasa, where the Hunt runs every winter, Katerin! I know better than to flee at the simple *appearance* of the Hunt. I've lived with them since childhood. No. I had no choice. No chance. They came at me from the front."

Katerin dropped her hands from Metkyi's arm. "Which wolf was in the lead?"

"The Makri wolf." Metkyi grimaced. "I thought it was just a typical manifestation of the Hunt. I stopped and waited, expecting them to just go on by, like they normally do. But they didn't." He stopped, gasping for breath.

"Slow down and take your time," Katerin said. "No need to rush the telling." She jerked her head toward the outside. "We're not going anywhere." A blast of wind-blown ice pellets against the top of the lodge accented her words.

"Hurts. Suddenly. Sorry." Metkyi moved his free hand toward his injury and stopped short, wincing.

"I'll fix that." Katerin poured a dose of pain potion for Metkyi.

"I was standing there, when they came at me, that Makri wolf in the lead," Metkyi continued, his voice low. "I thought they were passing by, but the Makri wolf came right at me, tried to get my throat. I knocked him away, the rest of the pack hung back. They didn't all rush me."

"You were his chosen prey," Twana said. "Makri wouldn't have led the pack unless—"

"Unless the Gods wanted a sacrifice," Katerin said. "Where were Karnoi and Cirdel?"

"They watched with the rest of the pack. I tried to hold my ground against Makri. He kept going for my throat while I worked on lighting my brands. I was focused on them when he got his teeth on me. I knocked him to the side so that he missed my throat, but he worried my arm. Got my brands lit at the same time or I'd be dead, no, *worse*, now. Once Makri got my arm, they moved in. Tried to hold my ground, but I had to run. They circled around trying to hamstring me, backing me down the hillside. I hoped to stay on my feet to hold them off until one of you heard me. Knew I could keep them away for a while."

"You fought well, brother. It could have gotten much, much worse."

"And it will, if we don't do something. We have to kill that wolf," Katerin said. "Then perhaps the rest of the Hunt will leave us alone."

"No," Twana said. "Once the whole Hunt starts, they won't stop until they have their prey. We have to figure out how to drive them away or how to kill them all. I don't know how to kill a god, even in wolf form. Especially Karnoi and Cirdel."

"The other Gods could intervene," Katerin said. "Our intervention with Metkyi was an act of the other Gods."

Metkyi groaned, resting his forehead on his good hand. "Karnoi and Cirdel aren't going to listen to our gods, ladies. If they respected Staul's rights, I wouldn't have this injury."

Katerin paced slowly around the fire.

Is Metkyi the Hunt's only prey?

The Hunt always had an order of victims. Just because someone wasn't attacked didn't mean that person wasn't prey. It just wasn't that person's time. That had been emphasized in the reading she'd done in her mother's books.

Rational enough to assume that all three of them were the Hunt's target. The Hunt had been glad enough to turn on them when they came to save Metkyi, perhaps only because they were intervening, but she didn't think so.

If I didn't typically magic my arrows we'd have had a harder time of it.

She only magicked her arrows as an old habit from fighting Shadowwalkers.

Sword. Magic it, and carry it along with my bow. Only way to protect myself, like from the Shadowwalkers.

Except that the Hunt was worse than any Shadowwalker.

She would have to go back to her mother's books. She'd

barely glimpsed an answer there, but she hadn't read both of them. Terani the God-Killer had gone up against a god.

I am Terani's daughter. This is why I am here.

Katerin looked up. *My old life is gone. Forever.*

"There are other Gods besides ours," she said, her voice low and bleak.

"We have no speakers for them!" Twana said.

"Have Nitel and Terat ever needed speakers in a time of need?"

Twana shook her head. "No. No. But Katerin, if we do that—"

"We must do it. We don't have much of a choice."

Twana closed her eyes and shivered. "I could wish for anything else. All seven Gods here. I wish we had Voices for Nitel and Terat. Someone who's ridden with them before."

"There is no one else," Metkyi said. "Not here. Perhaps we can get Yetklet and Orelyets to take them on. They've the strength. It'll have to be that way. We have no choice. Makri won't want to stop with just me. You'll be next, sister, and I can't imagine him not wanting to eliminate Katerin. Or the Eldest. Or Orelyets. Yetklet. Others."

"The entire village." Twana rubbed her hands together.

"Did he have the power to change shape yet?" Katerin asked Metkyi.

Metkyi shook his head. "But if he gets me, he has that power."

If Makri killed Metkyi, then he would assume Metkyi's shapechanging powers.

How far can he go? She didn't know what Metkyi was capable of doing. *Illusion only, or can he change form?*

"Are you a full shapechanger?" she asked.

Metkyi shook his head. "I can alter my appearance but it is not a true change of form. I am still myself."

A small whisper of hope.

"Makri could take other forms," Twana said. "He's not under the same rules as Metkyi. Doesn't need to mirror Metkyi's strengths. Rule of the Hunt. He possesses Metkyi, he could take on human form and no one but us could tell. *If* he gets Metkyi."

"We can't let them capture their prey this time. We have to stop the Hunt." *Which will change me forever.* Katerin paused, trying to find words for what she wanted to say. "Then there's whatever that secret is that no one will tell me. The reason why Makri went dancing on the knife's edge of power."

"They did not tell her in Council?" Metkyi asked Twana, his voice gruffer and sharper than before.

"Orelyets said he lacked the authority to do so."

"No one told you before you came here?" he asked Katerin.

Katerin shrugged in frustration. "If they did, I certainly don't remember!"

Metkyi shoved the hair out of his eyes impatiently with his good hand, scowling at Katerin.

"Orelyets might not have the authority, but I do. I thought you already knew, or I'd have told you yesterday." He swallowed hard. "The secret that Wickmasa holds, Katerin Healer, Voice of Dovré, the secret that all of us are vowed to protect, is tied to Alicira's dicing with Staul. If you betray us, you betray not just Wickmasa, but Clenda, Keldara, and Medvara."

"Pretty big secret," Katerin said sourly. "You sure I can be trusted with it?"

"It *is* a big secret," Metkyi said sharply.

"The only thing that could be that big would be the whereabouts of Rekaré and Cenarth! And surely Wickmasa wouldn't be—" Her voice trailed off as realization flooded over her. "Oh. *Now* I understand."

"You knew it without knowing," Metkyi suddenly grinned at her. "Out of your own mouth." He nodded at Twana. "Sister, am I still the best at telling without telling?"

"You have no equal," Twana agreed.

"No one can say I broke confidence," Metkyi said.

"Oh, by the Seven Crowned Gods. Rekaré and Cenarth," Katerin said. "That's who Wickmasa guards. Am I the only one in Wickmasa who *doesn't* know?"

"The secret is truly a secret, limited to the Council, Twana, myself, and now you," Metkyi said. "As the Voice of Staul, I am the primary guardian. I am tied to her. She draws strength from me in need when we are close to each other. We renew this connection every winter. Makri thought that he should be the connection to sustain the magic that helps keep Rekaré hidden, not me."

Now the entire book of Wickmasa's secrets lay open to Katerin. She gazed down at her hands.

I'm not going to be able to go back. No more circuit healing.

"How long has Wickmasa guarded this knowledge?" she asked.

"From the beginning," Metkyi said. "I was bonded to Rekaré as her protector when she was twelve and I was twenty. I would have gone with her to Medvare-the-city as a silent guard to her safety. It was felt that she needed a priest of Staul of the Balance, to protect her against Zauril."

"Do you know where they are right now?"

Metkyi shook his head. "They are part of a trading team made up of members of Heinmyets's band under Orelyets's supposed command."

"Tell me more," she said in a low voice. "Tell me how it started."

"There's not a lot to tell," Metkyi said. "At thirteen, rather than meet her fate, Rekaré chose a third path. She had been on her way to submit to Zauril until her majority, where she planned to contest him for all of her mother's power."

"Everyone knows that. What happened to change that plan?"

"There was a betrayal. An injury to their party near Wickmasa. Alame, Alicira's uncle, was the party leader. The Hunt injured him and scattered their escort. Rekaré and Cenarth fought off the Hunt and brought him to us."

Thirteen-year-old and fifteen-year-old against the Hunt. Unlikely odds for success.

"How could they have done that?"

"We *are* talking about Alicira's daughter and the son of Hein-myets and Inharise," Twana said. "Rekaré came partially into her magic while fighting off the Hunt. Cenarth possesses his own resources. And though he was injured, Alame of the Aireii was also not without power."

Alame. The uncle who helped Alicira get free of Zauril. The one no one thinks about. Could he have gotten Rekaré free, too?

Alame.

Her mother had made several references to meeting him in her books. Something about the way Terani wrote about Alame touched a chord deep inside Katerin.

"Rekaré wasn't supposed to have power at that point," Katerin said, puzzled. "She only was supposed to keep the option of retaining her power. Zauril was supposed to have all of it—" Her voice trailed off as she suddenly understood.

The Gods never intended for that bargain to be carried out. But which God or Gods made this plan?

"Exactly," Metkyi said. "The Gods have another plan. Which is why Zauril constantly seeks to change it back. Especially now. This summer Rekaré turns eighteen. Since he's never seen her himself, he has no idea of how strong she really is. He won't know until she rides into Medvare-the-city."

"The Hunt was meant to take out Alame and Cenarth, and leave Rekaré helpless in Zauril's hands," Twana said. "That's what Alame feared. He confided in me as Artel's Voice, in case something else happened to him."

"I was newly sworn to Staul. Makri was away at the Healing House."

"Our healer was old and failing. So the vows were made

between me and Metkyi, in our service to Artel and Staul, to support hiding Rekaré and Cenarth."

"And Makri?" Katerin asked.

"He did not swear," Metkyi said. "I spoke as his twin. Jeralte passed shortly after, and Makri took his place, but never would vow. We need you to swear as Dovré's Voice, to protect Rekaré this coming year."

"I will swear without reservation," Katerin said.

"Best to do it now. We all bear our tokens of power," Twana said.

"Then let it be done," Katerin said. "After that, the Hunt."

"I don't know if our threefold power can beat the Hunt this time," Metkyi said. "None of us bears the power of Rekaré, Cenarth and Alame, either singly or together."

"You are not the only ones who carry secrets." Katerin took a deep breath. *This changes everything.* "I am the daughter of Terani of Waykemin."

Metkyi's face brightened. "You are Terani's daughter? *The* Terani? She who—"

"Yes. I am Terani the God-Killer's daughter. You wanted to know why I am so strong. Do you wonder now?"

Metkyi shook his head, but a slow smile spread across his face. "Who could have known that Terani's daughter would have vowed to Dovré?"

"Much less come to Wickmasa," Twana said, her voice lighter. "The Gods walk with us, indeed. Katerin Healer, daughter of Terani the God-Killer, this is welcome news."

Perhaps for you. But for me, it's the end of a life I'd always wanted.

CHAPTER 16

Katerin stared at the black and red books lying in front of her. She had retreated to her portion of the lodge. This gave her time not only to review her mother's journals but to think.

Politics. Worse yet, politics between the gods, not human politics. Karnoi and Cirdel had taken the threads running through human lives into their hands to play for power.

And that I don't feel capable of managing.

For once, Katerin wished that she could channel what remained of her mother and find out what it meant to banish a God. Terani had banished Nitel in Karnoi and Cirdel's names. But with that power came a price. Terani lay in honor in distant Waykemin, with no more mind than a baby. Even less mind than a baby, for at some point one expected a baby to wake and cry for her needs.

It had been years since Terani had wakened.

Will that be my fate? Facing down two Gods instead of one could be much worse. *I have the support of Metkyi and Twana.*

Against their brother, who had cultivated support from Staul as well as being vowed to Dovré. Who had obviously won favor and support from Karnoi and Cirdel against Staul and Dovré. And it boded worse for her that this was a battle among human siblings as well as divine.

Katerin rested her head in her hands.

I'm the odd one out. The vulnerable one. The one most likely to end up like her. Oh Gods, I never wanted to have something like this come to me.

She rubbed her eyes hard, working up her courage to face the books again, then jumped as a hand touched her shoulder.

Twana held a steaming cup of tea. "I thought you might want this."

"Thanks." Katerin wrapped her hands around the cup, letting the warmth ease its way into them.

Twana hovered on the other side of the stove, deliberately looking away from the books. Katerin half-wished she would go, half-wished she would stay.

"So how fares the reading?" Twana asked finally.

"I'm having a hard time getting started. I keep thinking about my mother."

"Katerin, I'm afraid."

Katerin snorted. "*You're* afraid? Twana, have you seen what banishing a god does to someone?"

Twana shook her head.

"My mother lives without a mind, locked in sleep until she dies," Katerin said bitterly. "And that was with the support of two Gods against one. I'm facing *her* patrons. What do they know about *me*? What will they use against me?"

"We have Staul, Dovré, and Artel. Three gods against two."

"The two who are now the strongest of the Seven Crowned Gods, thanks to my mother. Who *still* rewarded her by letting her go into the dreamless sleep. Not that you or Metkyi will meet that fate."

"What do you mean?"

"The two of you are connected. This is a war of siblings, divine and human. I'm the one likely to get hurt."

Twana shook her head. "Three of us with three gods. Katerin, that has to improve the odds in our favor. Our gods are more reliable than Karnoi and Cirdel."

"We hope. The odds might improve even more, if we can raise Nitel and Terat with skilled Voices. I just don't know, Twana. I just don't know. He has Karnoi and Cirdel behind him." Katerin sighed. "Perhaps we should call for assistance."

"We won't have time to get help once this storm's gone, because we'll need to act fast, and only a fool would try to travel in this weather." Twana looked thoughtful. "I'll talk to Metkyi. He might be able to find a way."

Katerin buried her head in her hands. "I just don't know if we'll have the strength to deal with them."

Twana squeezed Katerin's shoulder. "Don't lose hope. If Metkyi has the strength, he can call upon his bond with Rekaré. Her caravan has those who have spoken for Nitel and Terat."

"They can't reach us through this storm."

"You might be surprised." Twana's grip tightened for a moment on Katerin's shoulder, then eased. "I'll talk to Metkyi now."

Katerin looked at the books. At last she picked up the black book.

Lady Dovré, give me the strength I need to deal with this.

She expected no response.

Then the Eye warmed slightly against her chest and the faint image of a gray daranval mare flickered in her brain.

I am not alone.

Katerin began to read, comforted by the gentle warmth against her chest and the faint touch of Mira's mind.

* * *

THE STORM SHOWED no signs of abating by dusk.

"Three day storm." Metkyi peered outside after Katerin and Davni came back from caring for Mira. "This is just the first day. Tomorrow will be worse."

"How could it get worse?" Katerin shook the ice off of her shawl. "Bad enough already. Snow's halfway up to my knees, and it's not all snow, there's a lot of ice to it."

"I've seen storms where you'd get that much snow in a quarter of a day. Tomorrow this will turn to ice. Can't you feel that it's getting a little bit warmer?"

"Yes," Katerin said.

"Yes. Ice tomorrow, then snow again the third day. That's the pattern. If I could get my books, I could be more precise." He scowled. "I need to be recording."

"I have writing materials. But why record this weather?"

Metkyi gave her a quizzical look. "It's one of the things Staul's priesthood is called to do. Part of tracking the patterns of the God's reasoning."

"I've never thought of Staul as a weather god."

"Mostly we follow it as a marker to the End of Days. Which, fortunately, seem to be far off." Metkyi tapped his injured arm. "But *this* is going to make writing difficult."

"Maybe we should try the sling again." Katerin frowned. Their first attempt at a sling had caused Metkyi more fussing and pain.

He's not a patient man.

"If we must. I hate the feel of it."

"You'll heal faster. Sit down." Katerin decided to make a slightly different sling. When she was finished, Metkyi grumbled and growled, and worked his arm, wincing as he moved.

"Guess it's better than nothing," he finally said.

"Katerin, don't take this personally," Twana said. "Metkyi's always been difficult when he's sick or hurt."

"A good healer doesn't take note of the grumps and growls of an injured patient," Katerin said smoothly.

Ice pellets rattled against the lodge, and she frowned, thinking of Mira. "You're sure it's going to get worse tomorrow?"

"If he says it will get worse, then it will," Twana answered. "Metkyi *knows* the weather."

"It'll start tonight," Metkyi said. "Sorry, Katerin. I feel this change coming. This is going to be a bad one."

"God-fueled?" Twana asked.

Katerin didn't listen to Metkyi's answer.

I don't want to leave Mira outside. Not with the weather getting worse.

She went to her side of the lodge to rearrange it for Mira. Davni followed her.

"What are you doing?"

"I'm going to bring Mira inside," Katerin said.

"A horse? Inside?" Colerei joined them.

"It won't be the first time. She'll ask to go out to relieve herself. I'll feel better if she's close to us."

"I've never heard of any such thing," Colerei pronounced.

"What are you planning, Katerin?" Twana asked.

"I'll bring Mira in here," Katerin said.

"It's a good idea," Metkyi agreed, sticking his head through the doorway. "I'll feel better with a daranval in the lodge."

"*You* go rest," Katerin ordered.

"I've done enough resting," Metkyi grumbled. "I'm doing nothing *but* resting."

"We'll have more important things to do soon enough. Save your strength."

Metkyi growled, but went back to his cot.

Once the dividers and furniture were rearranged, Katerin looked around the space. They would need to bring in enough hay and oats to keep Mira for two, perhaps three days. She needed to rig up a drinking trough or keep refilling the big bowl.

Twana wordlessly grabbed her sword and stepped out with them to stand guard when it was time to bring Mira inside. Katerin was unaware of Metkyi's presence until the flame of one of his firebrands gave them just enough light to work by.

Damn fool.

But it was too stormy to argue with him. She saddled Mira and hung the bridle from the saddle horn, then tied the bag of grain on the saddle. Next, Katerin tied hay on top of the grain. Then she and the girls grabbed as much hay as each of them could carry. Only then did they head out of the shed, Mira following Katerin.

Once inside the lodge, she had the girls stow the hay and grain against one wall while she unsaddled Mira and stacked the tack by another wall. Mira whuffled at the stove, stuck her nose into the big bowl of water and drank, then pressed her forehead quickly against Katerin's torso before turning to her hay, sending images of a happy, satisfied daranval.

The others retreated to the other side of the lodge, but Katerin lingered. She pulled off Mira's blanket, then scratched Mira's neck as Mira continued with her ritual of eating hay, turning to the water to drink, then eating more hay. At last Mira finished eating, and looked expectantly at the door. Katerin threw the blanket back on and let her outside.

Mira returned, covered with snow and ice. Katerin brushed away as much of the snow and ice as she could before pulling off Mira's blanket, the chunks of ice sizzling as she flicked them onto the stove. Katerin gave Mira one last scratch, then reluctantly returned to the other side.

The others had retreated to their bedrolls, lined up along the edge of the lodge. Katerin blinked at the warmth.

Someone's stoked the fire up quite a bit.

Metkyi sat on the edge of his cot, huddled in several blankets, leaning in as close as he dared to the stove. Katerin wondered if he built it up or if Twana or the girls had. She sat next to him and felt his forehead. Cool, no fever. But going out in that storm could have caused more problems.

"Foolish of you to go out," she said, keeping her voice in a soft whisper.

"Twana wouldn't leave me, and I figured you'd get done more quickly if I were on watch. No one should be out in this weather for long, and besides, I got one brand started."

"At the cost of more energy for yourself," she scolded. "You shouldn't have done it. Look at you now!"

"Just cold. I always chill easily." He shivered and pulled the blankets even closer around him.

"Too easily. You should be warmed up and asleep by now."

Metkyi shook his head. "I've reacted to cold like this ever since I took on Staul. It's the nature of the priesthood. I'll get warm soon enough. It takes time."

She couldn't answer that, and chose not to, instead easing the blankets away from his wound to check it. He could *say* that this was of the God, and that very well could be the case, but she wanted to make sure the wound wasn't brewing infection.

Katerin frowned as she unwrapped the bandages. The edges around the wound were hardening slightly, a bluish edge forming around the stitches, the skin unnaturally white around that. No red streaks led away from it, but when she saw the hard blue edges, she would have preferred to see the redness instead.

More magic. Makri's doing, or just Metkyi's reaction to the use of magic to get that piece of the God out of him?

Magic complicated wounds. If the wound was on a voice of a God, well, she had to watch for magic reactions as well as fever.

"I need to clean your wound," she whispered to Metkyi. "There's a small magic working on it. Nothing to worry about," she added as his eyes widened.

"You and your washing," Metkyi growled. But a faint smile touched his lips.

Katerin prepared a simple infusion. When she had cleaned the wound using a scrap of magicked cloth, she carefully folded the cloth, including some of the leaves she had used, and wrung it as dry as she could, then pressed it against the wound before wrapping it again.

There. That will protect it.

"Thank you," Metkyi murmured. "It does hurt less." His hand closed on Katerin's, and suddenly she was aware of him, not as a priest of Staul, but as an attractive and intelligent man.

Her breath caught slightly as their eyes met. His hand slid from hers and moved onto her back, pulling her closer to him. She found herself straddling his thigh, her heart pounding, willing and wanting as their lips joined.

Should this be happening? one part of her wondered while another responded to his caresses, breathing faster, her legs tightening around the lean and powerful thigh underneath her, thinking of what she'd seen of this man's body.

And then Metkyi gasped, not from passion but pain. They stopped.

"Your shoulder?"

He nodded.

"We probably shouldn't do any more. The gods, your shoulder, you need to rest—" She realized she was babbling like an inexperienced girl but had to add one more thing. "The others—"

He chuckled softly and pulled her close again.

"I'm sure your daranval needs checking," he whispered. "Unless you think she would object to us."

"If she did, we'd need to stop."

"She won't." The confidence in his voice made her tremble, then go warm all over, like a young girl with her first lover. "Ask the Goddess. Ask *her*." He punctuated his breathy statement with small kisses and nuzzles to her ears and neck.

Katerin leaned her forehead against Metkyi's good shoulder. An inquiry to Mira only got a sleepy approval.

Her daranval approved. That was enough. And it would be nice to have a connection with someone, some sort of a tie, before facing what lay ahead.

"Twana told me of your worries about being vulnerable and unconnected. Unprotected," Metkyi said. "A bond between us will protect you. We'll all be stronger."

"You're sure?" she whispered back.

"Yes. And Gods, Katerin, I've wanted you, if you want me—"

Yes. Katerin met Metkyi's lips with her own. He wrapped her in his blankets, the firmness in his touch making her tremble. Then they stood, his good arm around her waist.

Mira grunted but didn't move from her place by the stove as they joined her. Katerin helped Metkyi to the floor, then wrapped the blankets around them, being careful of his wound, all the time aware of *him*, of the intensity in his caresses, of the thinness of his body as they parted garments and pressed flesh against flesh.

Bright light exploded inside her head, and the Goddess was there. Katerin had enough time to wonder *is this us or the Gods in us?* before she was swept up in the unthinking glow, the warmth, the arousal as they joined.

Time stopped.

They shuddered together one last time, and were finished. Slowly, the glamour of the Gods faded away. Metkyi slid off of her and onto his good side, moaning in pain as one movement tweaked his shoulder.

"It's all right," he whispered. "Hit it wrong. And you?"

"All right," she murmured back. "Was it the Gods?"

"Part. Only part, for me."

"The Gods were only part for me, too."

Metkyi chuckled softly. "Good. That means it's stronger and not just a bond of convenience."

"I'd have never thought it." Katerin shook her head. "I've heard of connections between Staul and Dovré, but I thought they were rare."

"Not that rare. You've always been a traveler, haven't you?"

"Yes. Always on the edge. Always on the frontier, especially after I got Mira. The help of a war-trained daranval lets me go places few others can safely travel without being in a group. But she's my second daranval."

"What happened to your first?"

"Killed. A Saubral attack on the group I was traveling with, near Nere." Katerin shivered, remembering the despair his death had plunged her into, how close she came to walking the path Makri had chosen. Mira snorted and began to rouse.

"Shh," Metkyi said. "No need to say more. Mira's picking up on your mood. *I* can feel it in you." He stroked her face. "Story for another time."

"You know a lot about daranvelii," she whispered.

He nodded. "War mounts. You can't live here without knowing at least a little. Mira's nothing like Soisan. She looks to be of Heinmyets's breeding. The refinement of her head, general build. Probably a very well-bred daranval, but too old to be of his Elantai."

"You've seen them?"

"Umhmm. Yearly. Trading circuit. Not the time to talk about this. So what were we talking about?"

"Traveling. The Gods. Staul and Dovré's connections not being that rare."

"Ah." He wrapped himself around Katerin. "Gods, but you're warm. Curling up to you is like curling around the fire. Feels good."

"I'm surprised you're still so cold."

"I'm *always* cold. It's of the God. So," he continued. "You didn't get a lot of exposure to God stories."

"If they didn't involve Karnoi or Cirdel, no."

He chuckled. "We get further into the storytelling season, you'll have to come listen at children's nights. Then you'll hear that Staul and Dovré have a long history together as lovers and fighters against a common cause."

"I knew they had some affinities. I'll be eager to hear the stories. Who tells them?"

"Sometimes Twana, sometimes Imnari, sometimes Myrieke. Sometimes even me." His voice started to fade slightly.

"You all right?"

"Just sleepy."

"We should go back."

"This is comfortable."

She didn't argue. Katerin finally felt Metkyi's body warm as his breath slowed into sleep.

This is going to complicate things.

But she wasn't about to move away from the comfort.

CHAPTER 17

Something's not right.

Katerin went from sleep to wakefulness as Mira snorted loudly and stomped, sending mixed images of the Hunt and Makri and Shadowwalkers. Metkyi startled and reached for his clothing. The same urgency infused Katerin and she grabbed for her things, not certain yet what had roused Mira.

She slipped out of Metkyi's blankets and went to Mira. Metkyi joined her a heartbeat later, his good hand resting on her shoulder.

"We need weapons and outer clothing," he said. "I'll get them and wake the others."

"Get my sword as well as my bow. " Katerin kept her attention focused on Mira. The mare fidgeted, snorting repeatedly and stomping.

That should be enough to wake anyone.

Any minute she expected Mira to bolt outside.

She heard Metkyi talking on the other side, but no one answering.

Metkyi returned. "They won't wake." He handed Katerin her things. "I tried."

She pulled on her heavy outer clothing, slung her quiver across her back, braced her bow, and strapped her sword to her side. "Whatever this is—"

"Is of the Gods. We're the ones to face it." His hand closed on her shoulder. "Katerin—*be careful!*"

A low howl rose just outside the door. Mira lunged toward the door. Katerin pulled the door aside before Mira crashed through it. She plunged into the storm after her daranval, Metkyi behind her. Light flared. Katerin was grateful for Metkyi's firebrand as she pulled out an arrow, whispering the chant to awake the magic in the arrow. Wind-whipped snow lashed her face, mixed with ice.

This is not a good time to fight!

The Makri wolf ducked away from Mira's hooves and teeth. The rest of the Hunt surrounded them in a half-circle, their tongues lolling as they watched.

Mira stopped.

"Mira. To me!" Katerin commanded.

The Makri wolf ducked at Mira's forefeet. Mira charged at him.

Katerin jumped toward Mira, ignoring Metkyi's yells. She couldn't get separated from Mira.

Cursing, Metkyi stumbled toward them. "They'll circle us now," he growled.

"I *know*. Can't leave Mira." Katerin twisted her fingers in Mira's mane, trying to pull her back. Mira dragged Katerin with her.

"He's magicked her!" Metkyi dove toward the Makri wolf, swinging his brand with his good hand. The wolf stepped back. "Katerin, try—"

Mira ignored her. Katerin pushed on her thoughts, but there was a crystalline wall between them.

The Makri wolf leapt at Metkyi. Katerin didn't have time to disentangle her fingers from Mira's mane before she was pulled along as Mira charged at the wolf. Mira's hooves and teeth briefly connected and he cringed away, yelping. Then Katerin was flung free of Mira, crashing into Metkyi. They fell into the snow.

She struggled to her feet and pulled Metkyi up. Katerin staggered over to Mira. If she mounted, Mira couldn't spill her as easily, and she would have both hands free to shoot.

But that leaves Metkyi alone on the ground.

Mira could carry both of them. And hopefully he wouldn't impair their balance. If she could just keep Mira still long enough!

The encounter with Mira's hooves and teeth seemed to have injured the Makri wolf. He stood before the Karnoi and Cirdel wolves, his head lowered as they licked him.

Katerin pushed at Mira's mind. Mira responded with a wordless grumble.

Good. Now.

She swung up on Mira's back.

"Metkyi!"

He shook his head. "I can't—"

She sidestepped Mira over to him. "Don't argue. Get up!"

"Katerin, my arm, and how are we going to—"

"We'll make it work. Give me your brand!"

He hesitated.

"Give me your brand! We don't have any time!"

Metkyi handed Katerin his brand. Clinging tightly with her legs and holding Metkyi's brand and her bow in one hand, she leaned over as far as she dared and offered the other arm, pointing the burning brand away from them. Mira crouched slightly. Metkyi grabbed Katerin's arm and jumped up behind her. He settled firmly against her back, lightly using his injured arm to steady himself as he balanced against her.

"My brand," he said.

She passed it back to him and adjusted her bow.

"Now what are we going to do?" he asked.

"Stay on Mira the best way we can."

"I'll stick on," Metkyi said. "Can you manage fighting without a saddle?"

"I have before."

"What's the plan?"

"We have to take out that Makri wolf. They aren't attacking us directly yet. What happens when he's gone, I don't know. Maybe then we face the full Hunt."

"After dark. With ice coming. Twana out in a God-caused stupor. By Staul, Katerin, she's never like that. Never. She's a light sleeper, always has been. Gods, Katerin, we're in trouble."

The Makri wolf whirled away from Karnoi and Cirdel. He howled. The Hunt answered. Katerin tightened her free hand on Mira's mane, clinging tight to her bow with the other, willing herself to become one with the mare.

This time the Makri wolf did not directly approach Mira from the front, but sidled off to their left, away from Katerin's bow and Metkyi's brand. Mira spun to face him and Katerin tensed, worrying about the pack behind them.

"Metkyi!"

"Got it," he growled, half-turning and keeping his injured arm on her waist to steady himself. "*You* try to get a shot at him!"

She urged Mira to spin a little ahead of Makri but the wolf doubled back before she could take aim. Katerin pressed her lips tight, waiting for Mira to place her in the best spot.

The opening happened. She chanted her invocation as she shot. Behind her, Metkyi growled something.

The arrowhead burst into flame but flew wide of its mark. It struck another wolf. Katerin drew a second arrow, nocked, targeted a different member of the Hunt, and fired, striking her target. The circle broke, the Hunt moving farther back as she drew her third arrow.

"Go forward," Metkyi said. "Push them. Maybe we can send them away, rather than continue fighting. We can't win a fight. Not like this. Not without Twana. We need her!"

Katerin sent Mira forward at a slow walk, not toward Makri but toward Karnoi and Cirdel. Metkyi twisted behind her, his brand at the ready, his injured arm lightly holding her waist.

The Makri wolf yipped. Mira veered toward him.

He's a distraction.

She urged Mira forward, focusing on Karnoi and Cirdel, trusting to Metkyi to keep Makri away from them. Mira pinned her ears and dropped her head, snaking it slightly as she broke into a trot.

Here it comes.

Katerin tightened her legs on Mira. She raised her bow high, aiming at the Gods, fighting the icy fear that crawled through her.

They sat, lolling their tongues as Mira approached.

"The rest are closing in on us!" Metkyi shouted. "Katerin—"

Karnoi and Cirdel yipped. Then they broke, one running on each side past Mira. Katerin risked a shot, and missed. Two wolves dived at Mira's hinds and she jumped. The rest of the pack closed in around them.

We have no choice but to run now.

Katerin grabbed Mira's mane with both hands, somehow managing to hang onto her bow, and leaned forward, urging her ahead. Mira launched into huge, leaping bounds, then managed to find her stride despite the deep drifts, soon skimming over the top of the snow, expending energy and magic in the swift daranval magic gallop.

Daranval. Oh my sweet daranval.

Katerin sent as much strength and power as she dared to Mira. Their only hope now was to outride the pursuers behind them. She had little hope of escape. At some point they would need to stop and fight. Magical strength poured into her from

Metkyi, and she recklessly fed it through to Mira. She ignored the wind and snow and ice whipping hard against them, concentrating only on keeping Mira going, wherever it would be that their fate would meet them.

At least she had Metkyi with her. Perhaps Staul and Dovré together might be enough to stop the Hunt at some point. But she didn't dare think too much about that, didn't dare concentrate on anything but the powerful muscles of the brave daranval running hard under her. Wherever they were headed, it was away from the village.

The clearing?

They were running uphill now. She couldn't see in the dark and the storm around them. But she was grateful that she had taken care of the tokens for Dovré at the clearing.

Now if we only had Twana with us—

Perhaps it was fated that they didn't have Artel with them.

Mira moved more slowly and Katerin felt her falter, then steady.

Can't go much further. She's tiring.

"We're close to the clearing," Metkyi said. "I thought that was where we were headed. But we've nothing to survive the storm. Even if we manage to defeat them."

"I know."

Getting back will be iffy. Mira's going to be useless. But still— maybe—maybe we can do it.

Or not. At the least, perhaps she and Metkyi could wound the Gods, if not kill them.

I didn't even last the season.

But the secret of Rekaré and Cenarth would remain safe. She might have been tempted to write it to Senai, would have definitely written of it to Eldoran, in elaborate cipher.

And who knew? They might still survive this disaster.

The terrain flattened out and Mira picked up speed. But her pace was jerky and tight and she slipped on the ice once more, jerking hard as she recovered. Soon she had to stop, or collapse under them.

Then it'll be time to fight.

Mira paused, rocking back on her haunches. Then she launched herself up, over a snow-covered obstacle.

The logs around the shrine? Yes.

Strength ebbed from Mira's muscles as they rose into the air.

"She's going down!" Katerin yelled. She managed to pull herself and Metkyi clear as Mira somersaulted into the snow.

Oh my sweet daranval, you've given yourself for us—

But she had no time for Mira. Katerin sprang to her feet, pulling Metkyi with her. They stood back-to-back next to the writhing Mira, Metkyi raising his brand high as Katerin raised her bow.

"This is it!" he yelled, and she could hear exultation as well as fear in his voice. "Fight well, oh Voice of Dovré!"

"Fight well, Voice of Staul!" she yelled back.

Then the Hunt was upon them. She leapt to the top of the log, fired, then nocked another arrow, not caring which wolf she shot at. Metkyi joined her on the log, then hopped down among the wolves in front of her, swinging his brand wide and yelling, driving the wolves back, his brand occasionally contacting a wolf and sending it yelping, keeping them away from Katerin.

Katerin blinked after her fifth arrow. The Hunt *was* lessening in number as her arrows and Metkyi's brand made contact. But the three she most wanted hung back, too far back for her to shoot clearly in this storm. Katerin pulled another arrow, fumbling in the quiver to count how many she had left.

Two, after this one.

"Metkyi. I'm almost out of arrows!"

He nodded, not looking back at her. "If I try to pick any up, will that help?"

"Don't try it."

Arrows were too far away for him to safely retrieve. Perhaps they could gather them together, and perhaps she was dreaming to think she would survive the next few breaths. Even with her sword, they were no match for the Hunt. She sent the next arrow skimming across the top of two wolves before it found its mark in a third.

Two arrows left. If only those three wolves weren't so far away!

She nocked, aimed, shot. Pulled her last arrow out and tossed her quiver behind her, flinching at Mira's deep groans.

Sweet daranval, if I had the time, I'd cut your throat and spare you this.

But now it was too late.

Katerin aimed, fired, hit her mark. Then she dropped her bow behind the log and jumped down to join Metkyi, pulling her sword free. Together, they faced the wolves.

We can only keep them away for so long.

Hopefully Mira would be dead by the time the Hunt was finished with her and Metkyi. At the least, that would spare her daranval the final indignity of the tearing, rending death at the fangs of the Hunt. Katerin growled at the approaching wolves.

The Hunt paused. Torches blossomed into light around them.

Help!

Twana must have wakened after they left, and somehow figured out where they were.

Metkyi raised his voice in a chant, and Katerin joined in, intertwining the songs of Staul and Dovré in two-part harmony. A third, bass voice joined in, counterpointing with a melody of Artel. Katerin startled, but dared not let her voice falter as a sudden surge of power washed through her when a fourth, high soprano added to her Dovré part. Two others chimed in with Artel parts, two more chanted for Nitel and Terat.

The Hunt milled between Metkyi and Katerin and the

unknowns. Then Karnoi sounded a trembling call, and whirled away. The Hunt followed, tails tucked tight between their legs.

The song came to a slow conclusion. Katerin stood stupidly, blinking.

I thought we were going to die for certain. Or did we really die and this is just a dream?

Mira's moans brought her back. She sheathed her sword and started to turn to her daranval, then stopped as a tall man strode toward them.

"My Lord Alame," Metkyi murmured, quenching his brand as he sank to his knees. "Lady Rekaré. Cenarth." His good hand grabbed at Katerin and pulled her down.

"My daranval," she gabbled, frozen into place by something she couldn't quite explain. "I need to help Mira! Metkyi, I can't —Mira! My daranval!"

"Voice of Staul." Alame nodded at Metkyi.

Katerin wanted to flinch away from Alame's thin, fair face, the intensity of his recent use of magic threatening to blind her. Alame. *The* Alame, uncle to Alicira. Power still radiated from him. It called to her but she didn't know why.

How did they know we were here? Oh. Twana said Metkyi could call them. He must have done it.

Now if they could just save Mira.

"My daranval," she repeated. "She's in need."

"Where is she, Voice of Dovré?" Alame asked.

"Back there—behind us—by the shrine." Now she could move. Katerin scrambled over the log, tears flooding her eyes. "Mira. Mira!"

Mira rocked back and forth as she lay on her left side. Katerin knelt behind her, resting her forehead on Mira's neck, sending forth all of her strength to aid Mira. She felt Metkyi's hands on her shoulders and almost shook them off until she realized that he, too, was sending Mira his magic.

Mira's mind spiraled away from Katerin's, circling into death.

Katerin gulped, sobbing, feeling the tears turn to ice on her cheeks.

My daranval. My sweet, sweet daranval. You gave yourself for us. Oh my Mira, I wish you hadn't paid this price—

Hands pulled her and Metkyi back, and she struck out blindly, crying out in rage that they would separate her from Mira at this point.

"Voice of Dovré. Be still." Alame's voice froze her. "We can help your daranval, but you need to move."

She silently obeyed. Metkyi guided her away from Mira. He wrapped his good arm around Katerin.

What can Alame do that I can't?

She buried her head into Metkyi's chest, trembling with exhaustion and sorrow.

"Hush," Metkyi whispered. "He will save her. I've seen him do it. He's Aireii."

"But she's—but she's—"

"Staul is not coming for her."

The confidence in his voice sent small prickles up and down Katerin's spine and she lifted her head to look into Metkyi's eyes. He met her eyes firmly, not flinching away, not taking on his full aspect as Voice of Staul, but still speaking with the God's authority.

"Staul is not coming for her. Or, thanks be to the Merciful Ones, for us as well. Artel is strong in Alame, Katerin. Trust that if Alame says he can help, he will."

Alame knelt next to Mira, taking her head into his hands.

"Child of Dovré," he commanded. "This is not your time. Rise!"

Mira's eyes remained closed and she groaned, rolling around and tossing her head in Alame's hands.

Katerin doubted Metkyi's confidence. She had seen enough dying horses and daranvelii to know Mira's condition.

Maybe if Alame had reached us sooner.

Priests of Staul were not infallible. What if the God felt it best for Metkyi to believe that Alame could help, even if he couldn't?

"Child of Dovré," Alame repeated. "Heed my words!" He gave Mira's head a shake. Mira grunted again, her eyes still closed. This time her body remained still.

"Child of Dovré," Alame repeated a third time. "Rise!" With a graceful motion, he was on his feet. Mira grunted, gathering her legs under her, attempting to stand, but fell.

"Rekaré! Cenarth!" Alame snapped. Two of the torch bearers jumped across the log, one a tall, burly, broad-shouldered man whose dark hair hung in a braid and the other a tall, lithe woman with twin dark braids. "She needs help getting up."

The woman nodded. Katerin shuddered as even more power washed through her, wanting to touch the magic radiating from Rekaré but deeply, suddenly afraid of it.

Rekaré noticed Metkyi and Katerin. "You'll need to get back further," she told them, her voice the clear high soprano that had sung the Dovré part. "You'll be in the daranvelii's way."

Katerin managed to move.

Rekaré and Cenarth.

Neither looked like she would have expected, although Cenarth clearly resembled Heinmyets and the feel of the magic radiating from him was as strong as his father's. Rekaré was nowhere near as fragile and delicate-appearing as her half-sister Cirenna.

Two daranvelii, one golden, the other a red bay, neatly hopped over the log. They took up positions on either side of Mira, nuzzling her gently and talking to her in soft whickers.

Mira answered their whickers with a stronger nicker,

throwing her head high, grunting urgently. Rekaré and Cenarth stood behind her back.

"Child of Dovré—" Alame said a fourth time.

Mira flailed around, getting her forelegs under her and lifting her forehand off of the ground. Rekaré and Cenarth knelt next to her as Mira scrambled with her hind legs. The daranvelii nickered encouragement and pressed in close, the golden one's body lending support to Rekaré and Cenarth as Cenarth grabbed Mira's haunches and Rekaré lifted her barrel. They struggled for a moment, and then Mira was up. She dropped her head to the ground, breathing hard. Rekaré and Cenarth slipped away, letting the daranvelii press in next to Mira to support her.

Katerin knelt in front of Mira's head, stroking Mira's face as she murmured wordless encouragement. Mira's eyes closed and she swayed slightly. But the spiral of death was broken. Tired though Mira was, she would survive.

Katerin looked up at Alame. "How can I thank you?"

Alame shook his head slightly, a faint smile twitching at the corner of his lips even as his shoulders slumped.

"Voice of Dovré, there was a need and I answered it. Metkyi, what brings you out here? Why aren't you safe inside your lodges?"

"It's a long story," Metkyi said. "We were fortunate that you were close enough to hear my call yesterday."

"Not as close as it seems," Rekaré said. "We left all but this core of fighters, riding through the storm all night."

"I thank you," Katerin said. "If not for you, then the Hunt—"

"We can speak more later, then." Alame looked around. "This mare won't have the strength to go any farther tonight. We need to set up camp." He whistled, and the torch bearers came closer. He began to issue orders.

Katerin gratefully ignored Alame, turning back to Mira and

stroking her head gently, murmuring soft praises to her daranval. Metkyi crouched next to Katerin, chill growing in his body.

He needs shelter as well.

She balanced herself between Mira and Metkyi, continuing to rub Mira's forehead as she held Metkyi close. Cenarth reappeared, brushing the ice and snow off of Mira and tossing a blanket over her back, tweaking it gently as it settled.

"Thank you," Katerin whispered.

She wasn't sure how long it was before someone thrust a steaming bowl of oats at her.

"See if she'll eat this," Rekaré ordered, before rejoining the flurry of people setting up camp.

It took little encouragement for Mira to stick her nose into the warm meal with the aroma of healing herbs rising from it. The mare ate slowly at first, then more quickly as she gained strength. By the time she had licked the wooden bowl clean, she was standing steadily on all four feet, the trembling gone.

Another person brought them warm drink.

"Come with me," this person said. "You need to get out of the storm."

"My daranval—"

The other woman smiled at Katerin. "She will be all right. She has eaten, she has Basnen and Quartel with her, and she has a blanket. Soon she'll be under a tent as well and out of this. Come. It is time for you two to get warm and dry."

The woman led them to a small tent which already had an open fire burning inside on packed snow, smoke wisping through a small opening at the top. Gentle hands helped them pull off their icy coats so that they could crawl into a leather and fur bedroll. Someone gave them the same warm mash Mira had eaten.

Metkyi was still cold as she slid closer to him after they finished eating. They spooned together and Katerin gradually grew warm enough to ease into sleep, Metkyi's smooth, quiet breath tickling her ear.

She had enough time to think of one quiet, grateful prayer to Dovré before she let sleep take her.

CHAPTER 18

The cold air from Metkyi's tossing and turning woke Katerin.

"Metkyi. Metkyi. It's all right," she whispered.

It was still dark, so they hadn't slept long. She opened her eyes wider, listening to the faint roar of the wind. Surely there had to be ice and snow with that wind, but she couldn't hear it battering the tent.

Metkyi stopped thrashing. "Katerin?"

"Shh," she murmured. "It's all right. We're safe. You were dreaming."

"Was I ever. And my arm hurts. The storm is worse. We're almost buried in here. Can't you see it?"

"No. Not really."

"Look along the sides. See how they're pushing in? You can see the snow line there."

"Are we safe?"

"Safer than we'd be with almost anyone else camping out in this weather."

"I hope Mira's all right." She risked a faint inquiry, and got the faintest of stirs.

"I doubt they'd let anything happen to Mira. Not after what it took to save her."

"I'm just amazed they showed up when they did."

"I called on my bond to Rekaré once the storm started," Metkyi said. "I took a chance they were close enough to hear." He worked his arm. "I wish this would stop hurting."

"I don't have any pain potion with me. Maybe someone else does. I could ask."

"Wait. It's not that bad. I'd just as soon not rouse anyone. I dreamed that help never came," he whispered. "Karnoi and Cirdel took you, and I felt Makri's teeth at my throat."

Katerin felt his forehead. Warm. She pressed above and below the bandage, frowning as it felt warmer.

Not that I can do anything about it right now.

Lighting something to see by would be horribly unfair to those who had gone without sleep to answer a distress call.

And if they hadn't heard the call?

What if Metkyi's dream had been the reality?

His lips found hers. This time their passion was entirely human, although she sensed faint traces of the Goddess in her responding to the God in him.

Just as she was on the edge of sleep, he stirred once.

"Thank you," he murmured. "I can go back to sleep now." His hand gently cupped one of her breasts.

For the first time, his body felt naturally warm against hers.

* * *

THE TENT WAS BRIGHTER when she woke the second time. Others were moving; someone stirred a pot at the edge of the fire.

Katerin half-rose as Metkyi grunted next to her.

"Don't get up." Cenarth looked up from stirring the pot.

Even with the fire it was cold enough that she saw the clouds from his breath. "Not unless you have to. It's bad out there."

"Three-day storm," Metkyi rumbled from behind her. "This is the third day. Going to be the worst one, too."

A low chuckle came from a bedroll across the fire from them.

"I'll hold you to that, Metkyi," Alame said.

"The daranvelii?" Katerin asked.

"They're fine," Rekaré said. "I took mash out. They're in shelter with a low fire. Your Mira is doing well this morning. If this is a three-day storm, like Metkyi says, then she'll be fine for a slow walk back to Wickmasa tomorrow."

"So what are *we* going to do today?" Katerin asked.

"Stay in our beds and talk," Alame said. "Tell stories. Rest. Save our energy. Heritklet and Manek are on watch?"

"With the daranvelii," Cenarth said. "Safest place. It's a nasty storm. Daranvelii will sense trouble before humans."

"How are you two faring?" The silver-haired woman who had given Katerin and Metkyi the hot drink and food last night rose up from behind Alame.

"Well enough, Siljaren," Metkyi said. "Katerin's done a good job with my shoulder."

"Siljaren?" Katerin asked. "You're *the* Siljaren?"

Siljaren rolled her eyes. "I see my fame's preceded me."

"But I thought you were dead!"

Siljaren shrugged. "Easier for Zauril to think, wouldn't you say? Better than telling the truth and attracting even more attention to Alicira, and now Rekaré."

Katerin sank back down in the bedroll. "I'm confused."

Alame chuckled again. "You've secrets of your own, Terani's daughter."

She wasn't surprised that he knew. "I guess I have. Siljaren, after we eat, I'd like to borrow your healing kit, check Metkyi's wound. If you would help?"

"But of course. My kit's not much."

"Better than what I have. I didn't grab anything when we ran out of my lodge. I didn't think we were going anywhere."

"I've learned to keep something quick to grab every time I leave my tent. If you're going to play with the Gods, you need to take precautions."

And there it was, plainly spoken.

"I didn't expect to be playing with Gods. I didn't expect anything like this. There's still a lot I don't understand."

"We have all day to talk." Rekaré crawled out of her bedroll to take bowls from Cenarth and carry them to Katerin and Metkyi. "But eat now. Keep your stomachs full."

"Thank you," Katerin said.

She eased out of the bedroll slightly to eat, and gasped at the chill inside the tent, even with the fire. She slid back down into the bedroll with Metkyi, copying Metkyi's awkward stomach position. She curled her hands around the hot bowl, lowering her face close to the steaming grains to let the heat caress, closing her eyes to savor the small warmth. She had known it was cold in the tent, thanks to the white breath clouds, even with a fire, but *this* cold?

At last her meal cooled enough to eat. They ate quietly. Rekaré and Cenarth finished eating, then Cenarth stoked the fire while Rekaré took their bowls.

Siljaren slid out of her bedroll and bundled up. Katerin pulled on her own jacket and wrapped Metkyi's around his body, baring his injured arm. Rekaré silently brought Katerin a small bowl of warm water and a rag. Katerin began cleaning Metkyi's wound.

"Try this." Siljaren crunched some dried leaves into the faintly steaming water, stirring them around with her forefinger.

Katerin nodded. The aroma from these leaves was faintly

pungent, with a sweet undernote. She dipped the rag into the water and wrung it out. Metkyi flinched once as she worked.

"Use this as the bandage." Siljaren handed Katerin a poultice with more of the pungent leaves tucked inside it.

"Thank you."

"If you still had your kit, you would have been fine. This is what I have, and I always sling it over my shoulder when I go out, even if it's just across the village." Siljaren dropped a soft pouch about the size of two palms side-by-side into Katerin's lap.

"May I?" she asked.

"Of course."

Katerin untied the latch and opened the flap. Inside were neat twists of bandage material, wrappings and sinews for bandages, small vials of fluid, labeled neatly in a code Katerin recognized as standard Council sigils, and small bundles of herbs and leaves identified by standard Council writing.

A basic kit. More basic than her own travel kit, but lightweight, easy to grab.

"When you get back to Wickmasa, it's a good idea to prep one of those. Keep it close by you, always. I'll help you set it up."

"Thank you," Katerin murmured.

She slid back into the bedroll. Rekaré brought them steaming cups of tea, and Katerin wrapped her hands around her cup, turning on her side, then tucked herself against Metkyi as she sipped her tea. Rekaré and Cenarth crawled back into their bedroll and pulled their blankets over their heads. Alame and Siljaren talked in low voices.

"So," Katerin finally said to Metkyi. "We just sit here and wait?"

"Pretty much. Down in the village we'd be working on handwork or such, but here?" he shrugged. "Hunker down and wait for the storm to blow past."

"I'm glad we found help."

"We were doomed otherwise. Even if we won the fight against the Hunt, we had no shelter. Mira was in no shape to bring us back."

"How did the Hunt get her so wound up? She's usually not so easily provoked."

"The Gods got involved."

"But shouldn't a daranval with war experience be less susceptible to magic?"

"Not really," Alame said. Katerin startled, not aware that he and Siljaren had stopped talking. "Why don't you two tell us what's been going on in Wickmasa? We've heard some disturbing things. We were on our way when Metkyi called, which was why we were here, just when you needed us. But how did all of this happen?"

"You first," Metkyi said to Katerin. She told of Soisan's contamination, then Makri's suicide.

Alame and Siljaren listened intently, and Rekaré and Cenarth roused enough to throw their covers back and listen.

Metkyi picked up the account after Katerin.

Alame shook his head as they finished. "The Gods force our choices."

"The Gods, or Zauril's workings," Siljaren said. "Remember, it was like this when you rescued Alicira."

"Forcing when these events happen instead of waiting on the Gods would be easier," Rekaré said. "We need to be bolder in our actions."

"I'd prefer to wait until you come into your full magic in the summer," Alame said, his voice sharpening.

"That's a time my father knows and a place he expects me to be. He'll be ready for me then. I need to strike before he's ready."

"It's a gamble."

She shrugged. "All life is a gamble. Right, Voice of Staul?"

"Some things are more of a gamble than others," Metkyi said.

"My life's been shaped by the fall of chips since before I was born," Rekaré said. "It's time to act."

"Winter is not a good time," Alame argued.

"Summer is the height of his magic. Winter is mine. There's no reason for me to wait for the traditional time. I'll be just as strong now."

"If we strike too soon—"

"If we strike too late it will be just as bad!" She gestured toward Metkyi and Katerin. "Do you think the Gods brought them across our path for nothing? Especially *her*, in Makri's place? Uncle, we have Terani's daughter available to us as the Voice of Dovré. We have brother and sister as the Voices of Staul and Artel. That is not power to take lightly! We risk offending the Goddess if we don't use the gifts she has thrown in our path!"

"Ah, but is it the Goddess or is it something else?"

Rekaré tossed her long braids back over her shoulders. "We ignore the gift at our own peril."

"I will take your thoughts into consideration."

"Don't take too long," she warned. "Time is crucial."

"Are you *really* talking about a march on Medvara? In this weather?" Katerin found it hard to imagine. "Where are you going to be able to get a force to storm Zauril and still leave enough warriors here to help the villages through the winter?"

"That's going to be an issue at any time," Rekaré said. "No. I'm not taking Zauril on by force. He *expects* my army at his gates."

"Then what are you going to do?"

"Something romantically foolish," Alame growled.

"Nothing quite like that!" Rekaré shook her head. "We'll ride into Medvare-the-city as a small trading party. I'll reveal myself once we're inside his palace."

"He won't let you keep your daranval or your companions."

"I'm not going to wait until summer," Rekaré insisted.

"There's too much of a risk to wait. We have to move before he is ready!"

"Enough!" Siljaren interjected. "You aren't going to change each other's minds this morning!"

Alame grimaced. "You're right. Dealing with the Hunt needs to come first."

"Especially since this time we have a human incarnated as the leader of the Hunt's attacks," Siljaren said. "Katerin. Do you remember any of your mother's stories? Anything about her encounter with Nitel and Terat?"

"I have her journals, back at my lodge."

"Good," Alame said. "She wrote of her preparations?"

Katerin hesitated. "Somewhat. But she also used a code for some parts that I can't decipher."

"I may know what she used," Alame said. "If not, it can be easy to piece together. I studied with her. I should know some of her codes."

"Perhaps." Katerin shivered, and not from the cold. "But there are a number of prophecies scattered throughout those books."

"Prophecies?"

"Descriptions of events that hadn't happened yet, with outlines of at least two separate outcomes." Katerin stared down at her hands.

"Incomplete, then." Alame's voice held a tinge of regret. "I'd have hoped for more."

"I doubt that she could have done more," Siljaren said. "Especially speaking through Karnoi and Cirdel. Katerin, does she write about this particular manifestation of the Hunt?"

"At first I didn't think so. Not when I read it two days ago."

"But now?"

"Now? Yes."

"I think this is a subject best left alone right now," Siljaren said. "Especially with this storm." She slid back under the covers, tugging at Alame.

Metkyi pulled Katerin close. She buried her head into his chest, not wanting to talk as the memories from her youth in Waykemin flooded back.

I was born to this. I have no other alternative.

CHAPTER 19

The storm stopped sometime in the middle of the night. The sudden silence roused Katerin, enough to note the darkness. Cold was the next harbinger of the storm's fading at dawn, shivering her awake long before Cenarth and Rekaré came in from watch duty.

Alame half-rose and Cenarth knelt by him. "We need to walk," he said. "Snow's too deep to ride. It's iced over since the storm stopped. I'll make snowshoes."

"How's Mira?" Katerin asked.

"She'll make it into Wickmasa," Rekaré answered.

"Wickmasa will send out searchers," Alame said.

"Should we wait?" Siljaren asked.

Alame shook his head. "No. Waiting can only bring us to the attention of the Hunt or those Saubral raiders we were chasing before Metkyi called us. I'm not inclined to face either until we have the rest of the troop with us."

Katerin helped Siljaren pack the bedrolls and strap them on one of the mules their rescuers had brought with them. Meanwhile the others took down the tents and the small shelter for Mira and the other daranvelii.

How could a mule easily keep up with daranvelii on a forced march?

She studied the mule closer, and decided that it must be one of the rare daranval/donkey crosses.

Mira was clearly thinner from what Katerin could see of her under the blanket, but showed no other harm from their adventure.

She'll go back inside, Katerin decided. A little more pampering would not hurt.

As the others loaded the second mule with the tents, Alame trudged over to Mira. He carefully inspected Mira from poll to hock, running his hands over her body and down each leg, lifting each hoof to inspect it for foundering.

"You're lucky," he said finally. "She's taken no lasting harm."

"By the Goddess's good grace. I'll bring her inside my lodge once we're back in Wickmasa," Katerin said. "A day or two more to recover would not be a bad idea."

"She's a well-bred mare. Any idea of her lineage?"

Katerin shook her head. "I found her in a high-country trader's herd. All he knew is that she was a war mare who had been through two warriors before he sold her to me. She managed to bring her last one to safety before he died, and he was able to share a few things with the trader about her history before he passed, but not much."

"She looks to be one of Heinmyets's breeding," Alame said. "Not Elantai, too old to be one of his get, but possibly by the same sire as Elantai. She could be the full sister to my Findel. Same red gone to gray, same build."

Katerin looked at the other daranvelii. "I don't see a gray with your daranvelii."

Alame shook his head. "He died. I ride that black one now, a son of Elantai."

"I didn't think she was that old," Katerin murmured.

"She's not. Findel was the first foal of his dam. As I recall, she had a filly last, the spring before she died of old age." Alame squinted at Mira. "Mira's about the right age to be that filly foal, around twelve winters or so. Not old at all for a daranval." He studied her. "You have a little of Terani's look, but not all. Who was your father?"

A flush rose on Katerin's cheeks. "No one knows. She never told me."

"How old are you?" Alame asked.

"Twenty-seven. A summer birth."

"Twenty-seven. You were born after the winter I studied with—" Alame began.

Anything more he would have said was cut short by a call from Rekaré. Alame patted Mira's neck one more time, then trudged off.

Cenarth joined them with two pairs of snowshoes roughly crafted from pine branches. He helped Metkyi while Katerin tied on hers.

"Let's go!" Alame called.

Heritklet and his daranval broke trail. The rest of their party followed. Katerin put Metkyi ahead of her. They were at the end of the line, followed only by Alame and Siljaren with their daranvelii.

Even with snowshoes, it was slow, tedious going. The leaders rotated through, skipping only Mira. The path was difficult for Mira, and during the rest breaks while the leaders changed she dropped her head as low as possible, breathing hard.

Metkyi was in little better shape than Mira. When they stopped, he sagged into a squat, head between his knees.

"I want you back in my lodge when we get back to the village," she told him during one break. "Not by yourself. Not yet."

Metkyi only nodded. The fact that he seemed too tired to speak added to Katerin's worries.

But he rose back up quickly at the end of their break, and moved with more energy.

They had gone for two more short stretches when Katerin heard distant voices. Rekaré and Cenarth snapped alert, unslung weapons and grew visibly tense. Alame and Siljaren came up beside them, Alame to Katerin's left, Siljaren to her right. Both had their weapons out, peering intensely ahead.

Katerin tensed. She would have thought that voices meant help from Wickmasa, but the reaction of her companions suggested otherwise. She hoped it was nothing more than caution. Cenarth and Rekaré moved back by Metkyi and Katerin, weapons ready. Heritklet and Manek moved closer but still remained in the lead.

They're planning to protect us, if need be.

Her fingers tightened on Mira's mane. They would have to make a stand here.

Then Metkyi sagged against Mira, pointing with his good hand. "From the village. Look! Kwellet and Orelyets are in the lead."

Katerin looked past Metkyi. A group of ten riders rode behind Kwellet and Orelyets. Cenarth and Rekaré rode forward to meet the riders from Wickmasa. Metkyi continued to lean on Mira, his face gray with fatigue and pain.

Twana broke loose from the Wickmasa group. She paused to talk briefly to Rekaré and Cenarth, then rode forward, sliding off of her horse and stumbling through the snow to join Katerin and Metkyi.

"We thought you were lost!" she exclaimed. "What happened?"

"The Hunt happened," Metkyi said. "They lured Mira out and we followed. They gave chase, and, well, if we'd not met up with Rekaré and her riders—"

Twana nodded. "We have extra horses, and a sled if needed."

"Give that to Metkyi," Katerin said. "I need to stay with Mira. She's played out."

Twana nodded. "I'll send Kwellet to help you."

She took Metkyi, and Katerin heaved a sigh of relief. Now she only needed to worry about Mira. She scratched Mira's poll. Mira blew gently on Katerin's leg before dropping her head back down to the snow, breathing hard.

Kwellet rode over. He slid off of the young brown mare and checked Mira.

"Once Twana and your assistants told us what had happened, we knew we needed to come looking once the storm was over," he said as he checked Mira. "We would have been fodder for the Hunt if we came out during the storm. I'm just glad we found you three alive instead of dead. The Gods work in mysterious ways. Let me get you a horse so you don't need to walk."

"But Mira—"

"If we need to support her, horse bodies are stronger than human bodies. I don't think it's that bad. And I brought her some grain. We feared the worst but planned for the best."

Kwellet fumbled in the pockets of his saddlebag. He offered Mira a nosebag. She eagerly plunged her head into it. He left the brown mare and strode off toward the Wickmasa party. A few minutes later he returned with a chunky spotted gelding that had a ratty tail and sparse mane.

"This one's nothing fancy, but he's steady. He'll take you the rest of the way, and help hold Mira up if need be. Ho, there, Mira! About done with the grain?" He rattled the nosebag.

Mira raised her head and Kwellet slipped the nosebag off, peering inside.

"She's gobbled it all down," he told Katerin. "Good."

Mira continued to hold her head up, and Katerin was pleased to see a brighter look in her eyes than before.

Wonder what else Kwellet snuck into that mix besides grain.

She slipped off her snowshoes, tying them to the spotted gelding's saddle in case she needed them again, then resumed rubbing Mira's withers and back.

Orelyets gave the call to mount. Katerin swung up onto the spotted gelding, pushing him close to Mira's barrel. With the larger group, they traveled three and four abreast and Mira seemed to find it easier going, although she jostled against the horses a couple of times for support.

Even so, the last rays of sunlight were fading as they rode into Wickmasa. Katerin was never quite so glad to see a winter home as she was her lodge, lit up with lanterns and the glow of the fires on both sides. She slid off of the spotted gelding, thanked Kwellet for his help and handed the reins to him, then guided Mira inside.

Mira looked around, whuffing softly, then went to the water trough. Someone had managed to bring in a larger trough while they were gone.

Colerei and Davni slipped in and gave Katerin a hug.

"Should we stay?" Colerei asked.

"No need," Katerin said. "Stay safe with your families." The girls gave her another hug each, then left. Katerin switched Cenarth's blanket for Mira's regular one.

After Mira drank, she plunged her nose into the hay. Then she heaved a huge sigh, and slowly lowered herself to the ground, her nose still in the hay.

Katerin sat by the stove, watching Mira nose around in the hay.

"Everything all right?" Siljaren stood in the doorway between the two sides of the lodge. "Dinner's ready."

"Yes." Katerin gave Mira one last pat and followed Siljaren to the other side, breathing in the delicious smells of dinner. She gathered a plateful of food, and sat on her pallet to eat.

Metkyi joined her. He looked tired, but his color had improved since they arrived, back to its typical caramel shade.

Not walking that last stretch was helpful.

She noted the pile of books and manuscripts next to the pallet.

"What's all that?" she asked, nodding toward the pile.

"Colerei brought notes and records from my lodge. I had Orelyets send that message ahead. I need to record the weather and the Hunt's behavior."

"You have written records of the Hunt?"

"*I* do. Not all of my predecessors were concerned with the Hunt's behavior." Metkyi shrugged. "Then again, before Alicira gamed with Staul, it wasn't really a concern." He patted the pile. "But you might want to look at some of these. There's tales of past alliances between Dovré and Staul, Staul and Artel, Staul and everyone but Karnoi and Cirdel."

"I'd like that." Katerin frowned, thinking of her own collection of books and manuscripts. "Do you know if Orelyets is sending out a trade party soon?"

"Tomorrow, I think."

"I need to send some letters to the Healing House. They should know about the Hunt's behavior, and Makri's change."

The others did not seem to be in a talkative mood, and turned in to their bedrolls quickly. The only other one awake was Metkyi, who was writing.

Katerin crossed back to her side of the lodge. Mira lay sprawled on her side, deeply asleep. She stirred briefly but settled as Katerin sent her a quick, wordless reassurance. Katerin gathered up her own writing materials as well as her mother's books and went back.

She used the lap desk to support her paper and the vial for her ink. She wrote a chronicle to Eldoran; carefully omitting all references to Rekaré, and frowned. How to explain their escape from the Hunt? She pondered the question for a moment, then decided.

Some matters need to be discussed face-to-face, she wrote finally. *Rest assured that all is well.*

When she'd finished the letter to Eldoran, she wrote a brief note to Senai.

She looked up to see that Metkyi had finished writing and carefully put away his materials. He was leaning against a backrest, staring thoughtfully into the fire.

"Want to inspect my letters before I seal them to make sure I'm not telling anything I shouldn't?" she asked.

He shook his head wearily. "I trust your judgment." He glanced over at the leather bag that held Terani's journals. "*They're* in there?"

"Yes. I'd just as soon not bring them out tonight."

"Me neither." He sighed. "Rearnex will arrive tomorrow with the rest of Rekaré's party."

"Just who is this Rearnex? I've been hearing a lot about him."

"One of Inharise and Cenarth's cousins. He's always been the support person for Cenarth. Not quite as magically strong as Alame, not quite to Cenarth what Alame is to Rekaré, but close. A powerful person among the Clendans. Once he gets here, we go after the Hunt as soon as possible. They know the Hunt's methods." He tossed his long forelock back from his eyes. "But it still won't be easy."

"And then?"

"Then Rekaré will push for what she wants."

"You think she can challenge Zauril this winter?"

"She can. She will. She desperately wants to finish this. And —" He stopped.

"And?" she prompted.

"Both of us will end up being a part of it. I know I will, because of my bond to Rekaré, and that brings you in, with your bond to me. If Rekaré wins that argument with Alame, then you and I are going to Medvara."

"I hear it's warmer there than here."

"Rain isn't much better than snow. I've been on the other side of the mountains."

"I've never seen the Chellana, except for where the Kitskan runs into it, in the Larijian plateau country up north."

"It's a sight, especially when it plows through the Medvi Mountains," Metkyi said. "You've seen the big canyon of the Kitskan, right?"

"Yes. The southern end." She had crossed the upper part of the big Kitskan canyon when she'd first come to the Healing House. It took three days to wind down into the bottom of the canyon, cross the swift-flowing river, then climb back out. The caravan had lost two horses to the spring floods. She had learned to appreciate a surefooted mule on that trip.

"The Kitskan is smaller. The Chellana is much, much bigger than any part of the Kitskan."

Katerin absorbed that idea, strange as it seemed. "Then again, we might end up staying here."

"What will happen will happen."

They leaned together, staring into the fire. At some point, her eyes closed and she slumped into sleep. She roused briefly when Metkyi gently shook her awake enough to climb into their bed.

CHAPTER 20

Morning brought a whirlwind of chores. But at least a full lodge meant more hands to help. Most of the morning work had been finished by the time Colerei and Davni arrived with supplies.

"Father said he needs your Healing House orders and letters right away," Davni said. "The caravan leaves soon."

Katerin gathered up her letters. "Did you make a list of our needs?"

"Yes." Davni gave Katerin the list. Katerin added a few things, then handed it back to Davni, along with her letters.

After the girls left, Katerin stood with Mira, scratching her neck and withers. Metkyi joined her shortly afterwards, resting his hand softly on her shoulder. The contact gave her an odd jolt, sending tingles throughout her body.

"Alame wants you," he said. "He wants to look at the journals, to get ready to fight the Hunt."

"Twana? Don't we need her here as well?"

"He asked the girls to bring her."

Katerin buried her head in Metkyi's chest, taking a deep

breath, drawing in the spicy, musky scent that was Metkyi. He kissed the top of her head.

"Let's get this over with."

They went back together. Alame looked up from the manuscript he was reading, a pair of small spectacles perched on his nose.

"Excellent details, Metkyi. I've been reading your records of when I was attacked by the Hunt, when I was taking Rekaré to Medvare-the-city."

"Thank you." Metkyi dropped heavily onto the stool next to Alame. "I didn't know what to edit out. So I put it all in."

"You did a good job. So. Katerin. Those journals of your mother's?"

Katerin knelt by her bags, fumbling with the latches to the bag that carried the journals. She handed the books to Alame.

"Thank you," he said. "You should read this." He gave her the journal he had been reading.

Katerin reluctantly took it. Metkyi silently pointed to the place where the description began. Metkyi's script was easy to read, larger than her mother's tight scrawl.

She startled at the point where a wolf other than the ones that were Karnoi and Cirdel's avatars led the attack.

"That lead wolf—"

"We never knew for sure who it was," Metkyi said.

"I had some ideas," Alame said.

"Since you banished the Hunt then, maybe that method will work now."

"It will not work twice. If *that* wolf was who I think it was, that one was used against her will. We freed her from unwilling bondage. In this one, Makri is a willing accomplice."

"How do you know that?" Katerin asked.

Alame grimaced. "The previous one was my sister. Alicira's mother. Killed years ago, when Zauril conquered Medvara. Consumed by Karnoi and Cirdel."

"Oh." Katerin said no more, conscious of Alame's intent study of her face while she read. Then he turned to her mother's journals, and she was relieved to be free from his gaze.

An outbreak of plague had followed the banishing of the Hunt that year. Katerin grunted to catch Metkyi's attention and pointed to that passage.

"This concerns me. Could there have been a connection?"

"I don't know. Siljaren?"

Siljaren looked away from Twana. "Yes."

"The plague after we banished the Hunt last time. Could there have been a connection between those two events?"

Siljaren frowned thoughtfully. "I'm not sure. The trading party that came in shortly afterwards had several members sickening. I always thought that was the source, not the Hunt."

"I remember that year. It was a bad year for the winter plague in many places," Katerin said. "But it seemed to come on late and fast. Many of us had to go out from the Healing House to help the winter healers."

"We did not call upon the Gods for help, at least not other than Staul and Dovré," Alame said. "From Terani's notes, it seems that we should have done more."

"You're saying that you unleashed a plague across the Two Nations by banishing the Hunt?" Katerin asked.

"The wrath of the Gods," Alame said. "Even though I think it was their will for us not to go to Medvare-the-city that winter, yes. I think there was a connection."

"How do we stop that from happening?"

Alame sighed deeply. "A price must be paid when one takes on Gods like we did then, like your mother did. You know that, you of all people."

Katerin nodded, thinking of Terani's motionless, mindless, still breathing body.

"But will it be too high a price?" she asked softly.

"Until it is time, we will not know," Alame answered. "We can only prepare for the worst."

Katerin bit her lip and resumed her reading, despite the distracting worries now dancing through her mind.

One thought kept coming back.

Who better to sacrifice than the daughter of one who had already made the sacrifice herself?

To what degree did that assumption play into Alame and Rekaré's calculations?

Gods, she hoped she was wrong.

* * *

REARNEX and the remainder of Rekaré's party arrived around midday. The day had turned warmer and they moved to an outside fire, to enjoy the sun while it lasted. Mira basked in the sun with the other daranvelii, occasionally pawing for grass and romping in the snow.

Move her out tonight.

The daranvelii raised their heads. Rekaré's golden Basnen snorted, and stomped. The other daranvelii gathered around her, wary. Then Basnen nickered a welcome.

"Rearnex is here," Rekaré said.

She whistled Basnen over. The others followed, Mira tagging along. Rekaré swung up on Basnen, and the others followed her lead, all except Katerin and Metkyi. Katerin called Mira back when she followed the others. Mira gazed after her new companions, a hint of wistfulness threading its way into Katerin's mind.

"You're not going?" Metkyi asked, as the village dogs barked at the newcomers.

"Are you?" she asked in return.

He shrugged. "We'll see them soon enough."

Katerin shivered. Metkyi tucked his robes around her.

"I'm not cold." Nonetheless, she didn't pull away.

"I didn't think you were. It'll be all right. Any harm we'll take will come later. We're not going to fall to the Hunt." But the confidence in his voice bore an edge.

"You're sure?"

"The game will be in Medvare-the-city. The main battle will be in Medvare-the-city. This foray of Makri's is but a tiny piece of this battle of the Gods, a distraction to test our determination and will. We're meant to be in the main game."

"But the sacrifice—"

"Will be paid in Medvare-the-city. I'm sure of it."

"What if Makri's meant to interfere with Rekaré's plans?"

"It could be. But I tell you this, Voice of Dovré, banishing the Hunt is not the main game. I tell you this as Staul's Voice."

"I'm not sure I like this being a plaything of the Gods."

Metkyi laughed suddenly, softly, easing his hold on her to stroke her cheek. "I think you've been in that role since you were born."

They leaned on each other by the fire, until one of Imnari's assistants came to tell them of a meeting with Rearnex, Alame, and Rekaré.

* * *

When they joined the group sitting around the fire outside of Imnari's lodge, Alame was speaking of strategies, drawing patterns in the snow while Rearnex and Twana looked over his shoulder. He looked up as Katerin and Metkyi joined them.

"We ride tonight," he said. "You three will lead us, as Voices for Artel, Staul and Dovré."

"Will that be enough?" Katerin asked. "We had talked about the need for finding a way to raise Nitel and Terat as well."

"That will be covered," Alame said, pressing his lips together tightly. He exchanged a long look with Siljaren. "Two of us have had experience with Nitel and Terat." The tone of his last words reflected the dread rising in Katerin's gut.

"That's not a choice I'd have you two make," Rearnex said. "How am I going to explain to Alicira and Heinmyets if this goes wrong?"

"I will do any explaining," Alame said.

"If you survive," Katerin said.

A rueful smile twisted Alame's lips. "I'll survive. I know my fate. I already live on borrowed time."

He glanced over at Siljaren, and his look sent chills up and down Katerin's spine, reminding her that Alame was royal Aireii of the House of Miteal, born knowing magic, power, and sacrifice.

Miteal, born of the Gods. Miteal, descended from Dovré herself. Miteal, the outcast rulers of the Empire-over-Sea, exiled for reasons for which Alicira's betrayal and exile from Medvara was only the faintest shadow.

Katerin swallowed hard and was glad she lacked the easy magic in her blood. Her magic only came as part of her contract with the Goddess. Even if it came to her easily, it wasn't the same as being born to magic.

It still didn't make the choices ahead of her any simpler, but at least she didn't have that constant intensity pounding through her. The bleakness in Alame's face and the age that suddenly showed in it told Katerin that he didn't expect to survive much longer.

She thought of the discussion by her fire last night and shivered, suddenly seeing an imperfect vision of a possible future. His fate lay ahead of them, on the road to Medvare-the-city.

If they didn't fail this test.

Katerin drew a deep breath. "Tell us what we need to do."

CHAPTER 21

Unnatural stillness hung over Wickmasa that night. Katerin rode Mira while Metkyi and Twana were on unbonded daranvelii borrowed from Rearnex. They wore ceremonial blanket coats over their winter clothing, and tall hats dedicated to their Gods. The hats and coats had been reconsecrated that afternoon.

Behind them rode Alame and Siljaren, arrayed with the coats and hats dedicated to Nitel and Terat. Further behind Alame and Siljaren came Rearnex, Rekaré, Cenarth, and the remainder of Rekaré's guard.

Fresh arrows rattled in Katerin's quiver. Her bow was strung and ready, and her sword had been freshly dedicated to Dovré. Metkyi carried one flaming firebrand, along with a consecrated sword strapped to his belt. She hadn't the faintest idea how he could manage to use both with his crippled shoulder, but he insisted.

Katerin centered her attention on Mira.

—Sniff. Look. Tell.

The command echoed like a drumbeat through their bodies. Bonded. Smelling the same things. Seeing the same things.

—Wolf. The scent whispered that the pack and Makri were nearby.

—We'll find him. And when we do, he'll meet my sword.

She would spare Metkyi and Twana the agony of killing Makri if it were at all possible. He *had* once been their beloved sibling. Best they not carry this on their spirits.

—Wolf. Fresh scent, whispered across their nostrils by the tiniest wisp of wind. Mira changed trails.

"Katerin?" Metkyi asked, worry in his voice.

"Mira is leading us," she answered with a calm she did not feel. "Let the others know. She has a scent."

He reined back his daranval. Twana fell behind, leaving Katerin and Mira in the lead.

Dear Gods and Goddesses, walk with us this evening. The scent grew stronger. *We are but your tools.* Icy fear choked her stomach.

Then Metkyi's daranval pulled up alongside her.

"You all right?" he asked softly.

She nodded brusquely, afraid to say any more. His Aspect began to flare as Metkyi searched for Makri and the Hunt in his own way. He wasn't waiting for Mira.

—Strong scent. Mira quickened into her ground-eating, smooth, traveling jog, almost ready to break into a canter.

—Katerin and Mira ride together. Without words, she showed her plan to Mira.

—Buffalo dung covering the Hunt. Mira snorted and picked up a slow canter.

Katerin bent low over Mira's neck, urging her to faster speed, ignoring the surprised shouts from Metkyi and the other riders behind them as Mira took off in the daranval fast gait. Mira needed no encouragement to fly along, the pursuer instead of the pursued. They burst into the small hollow where the Hunt was hidden, sending the lesser wolves scattering.

The Hunt surrounded Katerin and Mira. Katerin ignored them, focusing hard on Makri.

Him first, then the gods.

Mira dove at Makri, sending him scrambling behind Karnoi and Cirdel as Katerin dismounted, pulling her sword. Karnoi and Cirdel moved forward, stiff-legged. Mira drove them away, ignoring the other wolves snapping at her heels, except for firing off a hind hoof when they pressed too closely. Karnoi and Cirdel formed a protective cordon around Makri.

"Come on, oathbreaker!" Katerin screamed at Makri. "Face your fate!"

The Makri wolf growled at her.

"Oathbreaker!" she taunted. "Coward! Fool! Hiding behind these gods. When will you betray *them*?"

The Makri wolf launched himself into the air, leaping at Katerin. She slashed him with her sword, drawing blood along his ribs. He fell back, whimpering as Mira caught him with a forefoot.

Katerin sensed Karnoi and Cirdel creeping up behind her. She turned to face them, drawing on the full power of Dovré's Aspect, counting on Mira to keep Makri away.

"You. Will. Not. Interfere!" she screamed.

The Goddess rose fully in her. Metkyi roared, his voice amplified by the Aspect of Staul. He stood across from her, Makri facing him. Katerin turned and leaped on Makri, wrapping her legs around his body. This time he would not escape her.

Makri clawed free and snapped at Katerin, his fangs sliding off of the blanket coat. Katerin jumped on him again, throwing him on his back.

Makri almost squirmed free. Katerin knocked him to the ground a third time, cuffing his head hard before she could pinion him under her knees. She raised her sword high, breathing an incantation. He broke loose, knocking her backward, snapping at her throat. The hot slickness of his saliva dripped on her neck as his teeth clapped together just short of her throat. Then Metkyi hauled Makri back by his scruff, screaming in a voice that was a mixture of pain and the God in him.

Katerin leaped once more, letting the Goddess completely take her as she landed on Makri's side, pinning him with her knees. It was the Goddess, not Katerin, that thrust the sword into its mark.

Jolt. She quivered, screaming, her voice a mixture of Goddess and human as she held the sword in place. Her eyes nearly popped out of her face as pain raced through her body. She dared not let go. Dared not move. *Could* not move or let go.

The wolf under her writhed in death throes. She kept her sword in place, even as the pain rose higher. Agony centered in her chest; burning, growing, searing, almost as if the sword were in her own heart.

Gods, could she take any more pain? Every breath was a sharp, fiery knife to her chest.

Then Makri lay still under her. Katerin kept her hands in place on the sword's hilt. It wasn't over yet. Not from what her mother had written.

And now I die.

Two dark shadows rose from the Makri wolf, lashing at her, slapping her face.

Karnoi and Cirdel. Makri bargained with the Hunt and hid himself with them, knowing suicide had no cost. Oh Gods, can I do this?

—Do not show weakness or fear, a melodious voice whispered inside her head. *—I cannot protect you otherwise. Hold strong. Endure. I will bring help.*

The Goddess. Katerin closed her eyes against the pain stabbing at her. It raced up and down her body, but warmth flowed from the Eye on her chest, supporting and strengthening her against the agony that finally faded as other hands tightened on hers.

Gone. At last.

Is this all?

She opened her eyes to see Twana, Metkyi, Alame and Rekaré. Light played in and around their faces. Otherworldly shapes lingered around them.

The Five are here.

"Have we prevailed, kin?" the Goddess whispered through her.

—They are gone, one voice answered. Alame nodded crisply at her, then charged away. Rekaré and Twana followed him.

The wolf under her felt colder than a recently dead body should feel. Katerin's hands cramped on the short sword's hilt. Wetness soaked through her deerskin gloves—blood, but whether it was his or hers, she wasn't certain.

"Katerin. KATERIN!" She was dimly aware of Metkyi.

"Staul," she whispered, in a voice not her own.

The Aspect of Staul grew stronger. "Dovré. You must leave her. It is time."

"I will have my vengeance," she whispered.

"You have had that. He is gone. *They* are gone. You must leave this flesh." He placed his hand on hers.

A sharp separation pierced her. Then Katerin was fully herself, aching all over. She collapsed into Metkyi's arms as the Aspect of Staul left him.

"You fool!" he yelled. "Whatever possessed you to do it yourself? Did you know what you risked?"

"I did it, didn't I?"

"He was *mine*. I should have been the one to kill him!"

"You were his brother," she said tiredly. "And it was Dovré who was owed the vengeance. Not Staul. Not Artel. Not you or Twana. *Dovré. Me.*" She staggered to her feet, yanked her sword free of the Makri wolf's body, perfunctorily wiped it clean on the body, shoved the sword in its scabbard, and looked around for Mira.

Metkyi grabbed her by the wrist.

"Let me go!" she snapped. "You'll be thankful I was the one who took the shadow of your brother!" She yanked her wrist free and stumbled away.

Katerin reached Mira and leaned hard against her shoulder. Slowly, her awareness of the fight raging around them came to the surface. She was not done yet. Groaning softly, she unhooked her bow from the saddle, slung the quiver over her shoulder, and clambered up on Mira, grateful that the mare stood steady.

The rest of the battle was a dim shadow. She remembered shooting arrows, hitting some targets and missing others, until at last there seemed to be no more wolves, just still bodies lying around the hollow, illuminated by Metkyi's firebrand and other torches as riders milled around.

Katerin drew a deep breath. Somehow she managed to unstring her bow and sling it on her saddle. Somehow she got her quiver off of her back to hang it on the saddle horn. Now all she had to do was cling to Mira's neck with both hands while the world turned into a roaring circle around her.

This is how my mother felt. What happened to Terani.

Now that what she feared was here, it seemed silly to have been so afraid. This was her fate.

Alame rode up to Katerin. "We've gotten them all." He peered closely at Katerin.

"Yes," she answered.

Alame's face was remote and far away. Her own voice seemed distant from her body, as if she were listening to someone else speak.

"Katerin. Are you all right?"

She stared at him.

"*Siljaren!*" Alame bellowed. "To me! Katerin, you can't be—not like *her*—" his voice trailed off in a groan.

Katerin rested her head on Mira's neck, leaning her chest on the saddle horn. She didn't know why Alame was raising such a fuss, but she wished he'd stop. She was tired.

Gentle but firm hands pulled Katerin up. Siljaren took Katerin's jaw in her hand and looked into her eyes. She dropped her hand, snapping her fingers, saying something to someone Katerin couldn't see, then held a flask to Katerin's lips.

"Drink," she commanded.

Katerin swallowed the fiery liquid.

Slowly, her surroundings grew clearer.

"We need to get her back to the village." Siljaren turned her head and spoke over her shoulder to Alame. "It's not the possession. She didn't take hurt from that, but she's drained. Dovré rode her hard. Good thing for us that Katerin took on the Goddess as much as she did, saved us from dealing with Karnoi and Cirdel. But she needs warmth and rest."

"How could she have done that?" Alame asked. "She's not vowed to that level of magic. She shouldn't have that much skill!"

"I don't know, but we need to take care of her!"

Katerin slumped in the saddle, kept awake by Siljaren's hand on her shoulder.

"Can you ride?" Siljaren asked Katerin.

"I think so." Katerin's tongue felt thick, fumbling with the words that seemed hard to form. "Dark. So dark."

More words she couldn't follow. Someone tried to ease Katerin off of Mira, and she cried out, grabbing hard at Mira's neck. Metkyi's voice echoed the loudest in her ears, arguing with Alame, though she couldn't make out the words.

"Steady, Mira." Metkyi's voice. "Katerin. I'm not taking you off of Mira. I'm moving your foot out of the stirrup so I can ride with you and keep you from falling. Understand?"

She nodded.

"Don't fight me," he said.

She grunted. His hand guided her foot out of the stirrup, moving it slightly forward. He muttered to someone behind him, and then the weight of his foot in the stirrup, his leg against hers, his arm across her leg and arm as he grabbed mane. He growled, then was behind her, scooting around until he was centered on Mira's back. His good arm reached around to ease the reins from her fingers, and his other hand rested on her waist.

"We're ready to go," he said. "I'll make sure she stays on."

Then they were walking slowly. She relaxed against Metkyi, letting her body sag against his. Mira's rhythmic walk eased her into a dim sleep, full of visions where it seemed that the Gods rode along with them, Dovré in the arms in Staul, like she was in Metkyi's arms.

I've seen that scene before. The memory returned unbidden. The stained-glass window in the chapel in Waykemin that had been built for Terani. *How did they know?*

Mira stopped.

"We're here," Metkyi said. "I'm going to get off, and then Alame and I will help you. All right?"

"Mira—" she began.

"Kwellet will take care of her." Metkyi slid off. Alame pulled her off of Mira, Metkyi's hand steadying her. It took Katerin a few wavering moments to stand on her trembling legs. She stroked Mira's neck, then leaned her forehead against Mira's cheek.

"Good girl," she murmured. Then hands guided her away from Mira. Alame and Metkyi bracketed her, half-carrying her into the lodge. Davni and Colerei eased her out of the ceremonial robe and her outer clothing. They sat her down and washed the blood off of her hands.

"Injured." She started to rise, suddenly remembering that she wasn't the only one hurt.

"Sh, sh," Colerei said. "Siljaren is taking care of them."

Katerin sat, letting the daze sweep over her again. The girls wrapped her in a blanket and left her to sit by the stove. She remembered the first night she had seen her mother sit like this next to the stove, staring off into nowhere.

Is this how it starts?

Voices, one male, one female. Something shoved into her hands. Warm. Wooden bowl. The smell of a warm meat and grain stew wafted up to her nose, and Katerin realized that she wanted to eat, but couldn't force her hand to move to grasp the spoon.

Someone held a spoon to her lips, and she opened them to accept the warm meat and grain mix. Several spoonfuls later, and the world became clearer and less fuzzy. She moved one hand to take the spoon.

"No," Metkyi said. "Hold the bowl. I'll do the work. Just swallow. Think about eating."

She could do that. The bowl grew lighter in her hands, until she heard him scraping the bowl with the spoon.

"That's all." He took the bowl from her hands.

Siljaren moved into her line of sight. "Better?" she asked.

"Yes," Katerin said, surprised that she could speak more easily. "What happened?"

"The Goddess drained you to kill Makri and drive Karnoi and Cirdel away. It was almost too much for one person." Siljaren shook her head ruefully. "You had me worried."

"That I'd end up like my mother?"

"Yes."

Katerin shivered. "It seemed the right thing to do."

"Anyone other than you would have ended up like your mother. You're very strong in magic, Katerin Healer. Did your mother ever tell you who your father was?"

Katerin shrugged. "No, she never told me. Do any of us who are Voices know who the father is when we bear children? You know how it is. We come together with someone for a season, sometimes more than one person. We take powders so we don't bear children, unless the gods will it. How many Voices are there with children?"

"Very few. Just an idle thought, Katerin, nothing more. You are a strong Voice. I tell you this now, I don't know anyone not born of either the Miteal or of the shaman class of the Tauri who could have done what you did without sacrificing themselves."

"Maybe it's because I'm Terani's daughter."

"Perhaps." Siljaren sounded unconvinced. "Rest and regain your strength. There will be time enough to work."

Katerin allowed Siljaren to guide her into bed.

"Katerin." Alame knelt beside her bed, one hand stroking her cheek softly. Tired as she was, she found that odd, but couldn't summon the strength to say anything. "How are you feeling?"

"Tired," she whispered.

His hand closed on hers. "You frightened me. You looked like your mother out there."

"You knew her."

"It was a long time ago." Alame's voice wavered. "Before you were born."

The door between the two rooms rustled. Then Metkyi sat on the bed beside her, his good hand stroking her cheek.

"I'll leave you two alone." Alame patted Katerin's shoulder and left the room.

"Siljaren says you're feeling better."

"I am," she said.

"You looked like you were dying." His voice was tight. "Like one of those I'm called to ease on their final trail. I didn't want to face that, didn't want to be your guide to the next world. Gods, Katerin."

"I don't want to fight about this again," she whispered. "Not tonight."

"I'm not going to fight with you. I know what you did, and why you did it. I was as much in the God's grip as you were." He drew a deep breath. "But the cost, by all the Gods, I wasn't sure of the cost." His hand closed gently around hers as he raised it to his lips. She shivered at the brush of his lips on the back of her hand.

"We made it. We survived."

"*You* survived. I wasn't sure you would for a while. My Sight failed." His voice caught. "You are too close to me! I couldn't see what would happen! I can't see true for you now. Oh Gods, Katerin. You're too close for me to see what happens to you."

"I didn't know."

"Ah, Katerin, Katerin. This feels like the first time I can really talk to you as a man, not as the Voice of Staul. When I saw you almost falling off of Mira, when I held you in my arms, such as they are right now. I shouldn't. We shouldn't. I don't even know if, apart from the Gods, if you're at all—" He broke off. "But you're not feeling well. I should leave right now."

"Metkyi. Stop." She studied his features in the light from the fire. Metkyi was nowhere near as handsome as his brother had been, and the Gods only knew how arrogant and demanding he was capable of being. He was not a patient man. But, after the past few days, there was little question as to how she felt about him.

"Katerin?"

"Stay. I don't know how much of this is the Gods in us. We can't bind ourselves to each other. But. For a season, at least, we can take comfort as a couple, as long as our Gods choose to walk together."

"You're sure? It's not just the Gods?"

"We're going to disagree," she said. "You know we will. But, for a season at least, let's allow ourselves a taste of what the others around us can choose to enjoy for a lifetime, and pretend that we can be like them."

The smile on his face was enough to light up the lodge by itself. "I don't want you feeling sorry for me."

"Oh, shut up and get into bed. This bed feels pretty damned big without you in it next to me. We can argue in the morning."

Metkyi chuckled. He sat on the side of the bed, pulling off his boots, then his outer clothing. He slid under the covers with the smooth, economical grace she was starting to learn was a part of his every motion.

"Ah, Katerin Healer," he breathed as he spooned against her back, easing his injured arm onto her side, burying his face for a moment into her shoulder. "Katerin." He settled against her. "Night."

"Night," she said back, stretching into him. With his body curled next to hers, their breathing settling into a matching rhythm, it was easy to slide into sleep.

CHAPTER 22

Did I really say what I thought I did last night? Katerin paused before going outside the next morning. *Did I really propose a seasonal union to Metkyi? Where in the Goddess's name did THAT come from?*

Exhaustion. The aftereffects of the Goddess riding her.

And yet it felt right. Just thinking about Metkyi made her smile. She gave herself another moment to savor that feeling, then took a deep breath. Her legs wobbled and she grabbed at the doorframe. *Need to slow down.* She staggered toward the outside fire.

Metkyi hurried toward her, sliding his arm around her.

"You look tired," he said.

"I *am* tired. Shouldn't be, after a night's sleep."

"Comes from the Gods riding us. We're all on rest today. Siljaren's orders."

Metkyi seated her on a stump by the fire, then served her more of last night's gruel. This time Katerin sniffed it over carefully, trying to identify the ingredients. Siljaren had slipped in a few regenerative powders, she decided finally, things to help those who heavily used magic recover.

She looked up after she finished about half the bowl. At first she didn't recognize Rekaré sitting across the fire from her. Rekaré smiled back grimly.

"The aftereffects of the Gods riding us aren't pretty," she said. "You had Dovré. I had Nitel."

Nitel. Why her for Nitel?

Katerin caught her breath.

Rekaré as Nitel.

No. Dovré should be there. Katerin reached up to her own face. Metkyi stopped her.

"Don't," he said.

"Am I—" It was only now that she noticed how drawn he looked, his face the desiccated dry brown of desert dust in high summer.

"We all look like that," he said. "The Gods exact a price. You and Rekaré more than others since you faced off more directly with the Gods."

"Makri wasn't a God."

"No. But Karnoi and Cirdel gave him a lot of power. And Nitel had her vengeance on them while Dovré was busy with Makri." His hand caressed her cheek. "Eat. It will help."

That explains a lot.

Rekaré must have exiled Karnoi and Cirdel from Keldara.

She finished eating. Katerin leaned against Metkyi, staring tiredly into the fire. He pulled her to her feet.

"Let's go inside. You need more rest."

Once inside, they lay together on the bed, not bothering to crawl under the covers.

"What happens now?" she asked.

Metkyi rolled onto his good side, propping his head on his hand. "I don't know. I meant what I said last night, but neither of us are free to do what we will."

"No." She rolled onto her back, staring up into the pointed ceiling, studying the stovepipe. "The Gods seem to be looking favorably on us as a pair, at least for a season. But for the long term? I can't see it. We have pledges and vows to keep."

"I know." Metkyi dropped onto his back. "And, until now, the God's been enough for me. You've got the Healing House."

"Even that can be lonely. I've had to pull long circuits over the past few years to pay my mother's debts. You have your family and the village."

"A village that's known me from infancy. A family that's cursed with three children gone over to the service of the Gods. Not always a good thing."

"I'm sorry." Katerin turned onto her side, wrapping her free arm around his chest. "It would be nice to have companionship in this lodge during the winter. Metkyi, priest of Staul, would you be part of my hearth this season?"

"Katerin Healer, I would be honored to join your hearth for this season." He kissed her, then smiled.

* * *

THAT AFTERNOON they recruited Colerei to help move some of Metkyi's things to Katerin's lodge.

"Do you have a token of Dovré you could spare?" Metkyi asked while they waited for Colerei to bring one of Katerin's mules from the herds.

"Yes, but why?"

Metkyi nervously brushed back a clump of hair that fell into his eyes. "You'll see," he said as Colerei and the brown mule came into sight. "I—it's hard to explain. The words—" he shook his head. "If you could find it, and perhaps wrap some hair around it?"

Katerin ducked back into the lodge. She found the small worry stone she frequently carried in her pocket, and pulled some hair to wrap around it. She showed it to Metkyi.

"That will work. Thank you."

The token's purpose became clear once they reached Metkyi's lodge. Uneasiness stirred through Katerin's gut as they came within ten strides of his lodge, crawling up to tighten her throat as prickly tingles ran up and down her arms.

"Wait here." Metkyi took her token, then went inside.

She waited impatiently outside with Colerei, fidgeting as the prickling *shouldn't be here* sensation grew stronger. Then the feeling was gone. Metkyi came back out and took Katerin by the hand.

"Now," he said. He shook his head at Colerei. "Not yet." He led Katerin into the lodge.

The lodge was darker than her own, illuminated by only the faint light from two candles on the far side from the door. Something stinky smoldered in the stove. Katerin wrinkled her nose at the foul-smelling thing as Metkyi led her over to his version of her shrine. Her worry stone sat next to a carved black stone which was clearly Metkyi's token, while a third token, a polished white stone with Artel's emblems carved into it, was placed farther away. She didn't see Metkyi's mask over the shrine.

Probably in the chief's lodge.

"If you could bless it?" he asked, nodding toward the shrine and the tokens.

Probably should do the same in my lodge.

She pressed her fingers on both the Staul token and her own Dovré token, murmuring a few soft words. Light flared around her fingers, causing both tokens to glow softly for a moment. Then they faded back to what they had been.

"Wha—I've never done *that* before."

"I'd say that the Gods appear to approve of our bond."

"I *guess*. But this?"

"I don't know. But you are now welcome to my lodge. I couldn't let you in before. My workings wouldn't let you in safely, not until I got rid of *that*." He nodded at the stove.

"It stinks! What is it?"

"Protection. I didn't trust Makri not to sneak into my lodge. I made a poppet, to repel all powers but those of Staul. That's why Davni didn't like it here. She's not vowed, but she's close enough to the Goddess."

He lit a lantern, revealing skulls and feathers strewn around the trunks and shelves lining the walls, as well as furs and different types of rocks that ranged from plain black lava to glittering crystal chunks. Some crystals were colorless, while others shone in hues of pink, red, orange, and even a couple of purples. Some stones had matrices of green or threads of bluish green running through them.

Katerin spotted one double-lobed stone that had chips of a dark, polished green embedded in a dark gray country rock. She picked it up from where it had been sitting next to a collection of bird skulls, a stuffed eagle, and sinew-wrapped feather quills. The rock fit snugly in one hand, point against the base of her fingers, the two lobes bracketing the base of her thumb. She turned it over and over, marveling at the different shades of the green chips. The stone felt smooth and warm to her touch, as if it were alive.

Metkyi chuckled. "I knew you'd find that one." His hand closed her fingers over it. "We'll take it to your lodge."

"What is it?"

"I found it by the Kitskan River. When I picked it up I heard the God talking to me."

"I'm surprised you don't have it on your shrine."

"It's been safer away from it. But it will be my gift to your shrine. It belongs there."

Katerin placed the stone in her pouch.

Metkyi pointed out the things to load, several small trunks, a couple of bags.

They loaded the mule and Colerei led it off. Metkyi held Katerin back.

"She can unpack the mule; she doesn't need us for that. Katerin, I need you to look at something and I didn't want to do it at your lodge. Or with others around." His face turned solemn. "I need you to look at my wound again."

Katerin eased his jacket off. "Does it feel worse?"

He shook his head, looking away from her into the distance, scowling. "No. It feels as if nothing happened. Like I can move it easily again, and use it right."

"I haven't done anything."

"No. I know you haven't. Katerin, I think Rekaré did it."

"What?" Katerin stopped unbuttoning his shirt. "*How?*"

"*I don't know.* Katerin, look. *Please.*"

Dread tightened her throat as she finished unbuttoning his shirt and eased the sleeve off of his injured arm. Katerin unwrapped the bandage carefully. She gasped at what she saw.

"What is it?" Metkyi asked sharply.

The wound was gone. No, that wasn't right. She could see faint marks where the wound had been, the slightest trace of a scar along the edges where teeth had once torn skin. But the skin was unbroken, paler in color than the skin around the injury, and the stitches were gone.

"How. Did. This. Happen?" Gods, it felt like she had to force her words through layers of magicked cotton batting stuffed into her mouth. "Why is it Rekaré's doing?"

Metkyi cleared his throat and looked down at his feet. "Right before we engaged the Makri wolf, Rekaré touched me." He pointed to his shoulder. "*There.*" He shivered. "Said something in magic-speak that I couldn't understand. It burned. Then it stopped hurting." He shook his head. "I don't know. I've slowly been able to move it more and more. This morning it's like I didn't get hurt at all."

"The marks are still there." Katerin ran her fingers over where the wound had been. A small tingle followed by a sharp jab zapped her fingertips. "Ow!"

"Are you all right?"

Katerin looked at her fingers, pulling up her healing vision. No hurt there. She looked closely at Metkyi's wound. No trace of Shadowwalker dark reds or blacks. Just a faint blend of purple and blue where the wound had been.

"I'm all right." She studied Metkyi's wound closer. Purple was the shade of Nitel, blue that of Dovré. Both shades twined together along the wound site.

Magical healing. Not anything I can do. Not anything anyone here can do—except Rekaré. And Alame. Magic. Aireii magic. Dear Gods, this Aireii magic is stirring again, after ages of being quiet.

Or had it ever stopped?

"Katerin, do you know what happened?"

"Magic. Aireii magic."

"Which means Alame or Rekaré. Alame's not had this form of power, not the healing magics, so," he sighed. "Rekaré. And this isn't an easy magic. Gods. There's always been a possibility that she could come into her magic easily and sooner than planned. That does happen with Aireii magicians."

Aireii magic.

She hadn't been around Aireii magicians before.

"She's not supposed to be dedicated to Nitel," Metkyi said. "I don't know who she's supposed to serve. Katerin, this is—" He waved his good arm nervously. "If Rekaré's coming into her power this quickly, this strong, then she's more than what any of us suspected. She may be the one prophesied to reconquer Daran and restore the Miteal as rulers of the Empire."

Katerin looked down. "What does that make us in the prophecy?"

"I don't know. I'm afraid to reread it."

"I reread it several days ago." Her dull tone matched his. Their eyes met. Metkyi pulled Katerin close, wrapping both arms around her and rocking her gently until they heard

Colerei and the mule outside. Then Metkyi stroked Katerin's hair.

"At least if we have to walk in something out of the old stories, we have each other," he whispered.

"At least we have that," she echoed.

By all the Gods, I hope we're wrong about our places in the old prophecy.

* * *

WHEN THEY RETURNED to Katerin's lodge, she installed Metkyi's heartstone on her shrine. There was no corresponding flare of light to match the one at Metkyi's shrine when he blessed it; nonetheless she felt the same faint stirrings of power.

She expected more disapproval when it became obvious that Metkyi was moving in with her. If not from Alame and others of Rekaré's party, then at least from villagers, especially the elders of the village who might prefer their healer remain unbonded.

Instead, Alame raised one eyebrow and made a single wry comment. Siljaren poked her head into Katerin's side of the lodge and looked around.

"Works well for a winter's match," was her first comment. She drew Katerin aside. "You've put up tokens on your shrines?"

"The stone on mine, and I left a token on his."

"Good." Siljaren nodded approvingly. "Staul and Dovré can work together well, especially with two Voices as strong as you and Metkyi, but it's a good idea to take precautions. Tokens on your shrines are the best way."

Katerin contemplated asking Siljaren about Metkyi's healed arm, and decided against it. A curious reluctance to talk curbed her tongue.

More magic?

Siljaren grinned at Katerin. "You two are a good match, your

Gods aside. I know there's been concern about Metkyi in the village. When he and Makri started arguing, well, no one wanted to take sides, and he became even more isolated."

"Did they like Makri better?"

Siljaren shook her head. "No, but Metkyi felt it was only fair to not force people to take sides." She scowled. "Sometimes I think our Councils put too much pressure on our dedication to our service. Having a partner makes you more human."

"I'm still not sure how I'm going to explain this to the Healing House."

Siljaren shrugged. "Why should you?"

"I guess you're right." Katerin glanced over to the other side of the lodge. "How fare our injured?"

"Not as badly as I feared," Siljaren said, lowering her voice. "Rekaré's been helping while the girls bring in water."

Rekaré.

Katerin almost spoke of Metkyi's healing and her fears after she learned that Nitel had ridden Rekaré, but the look in Siljaren's eyes, the direct, knowing focus, combined with the curious reluctance to speak of it shushed her.

She knows.

"I did not know we lacked for water stores," she said instead.

Siljaren laughed. "Tonight's a good night to have baths."

Katerin nodded. "Makes sense. Purification after what we've been through. Ritual baths, then. Women on my side?"

"Nothing that formal, Katerin! Especially for our newly matched pair! We've *assumed* you two would want your privacy."

"No, no, that will be fine," Katerin hurried to agree with her, a blush rising high in her face.

"Things should be ready two bells after we've eaten the evening meal."

"Thank you."

Siljaren lightly rested one hand on Katerin's. "No. Thank *you* for what you've already done, Banisher of Shadows." She squeezed Katerin's hand gently, then left, leaving Katerin to stare after her.

Banisher of Shadows.

A title from the old stories. The thought gave her chills.

Then Metkyi called, and she went to see what he needed.

But the restless worry stirred faintly within her, even as they accepted Imnari's bond-gift of fine Medvaran wine.

Banisher of Shadows. The destiny of the one who had originally borne that title had not been gentle. *I hope that fate does not repeat itself.*

* * *

LATER THAT EVENING, Katerin and Metkyi retreated to her side of the lodge. A big metal tub barely large enough for one of them to sit in alone awaited them, while a big kettle of water steamed on the stove.

Katerin busied herself with lighting candles while Metkyi adjusted the fire. When she had lit every lantern and candle possible, there was nothing to do but stare across the space at Metkyi, kneeling by the stove and poking at the logs inside.

She shook herself.

It's not our first time together. And we're not virgins.

But she had never been part of a seasonal bond; the closest being the occasional relationship as part of the friendships at the Healing House. Certainly nothing like this, with no one like Metkyi.

She crossed the room to him. He wrapped his arm around her legs. She eased down to her knees. He slipped his arm around her shoulder and held her tight. They leaned against each other, listening to the fire crackle, watching the steam rise from the kettle.

"So how shall we do this?" he finally asked. "You can go first."

"I'd like to wash my hair. Then my body."

"Would you like some help?" He ran his fingers through her hair, then bent over to kiss her, their lips lingering together.

"Yes," she breathed into his mouth. "And I'll help you, if you'd like."

"I would very much like that." He broke off the kiss, devouring her with his eyes. She could lose herself in the blackness of his dark eyes, the way they followed her every move. She reached up and stroked his cheeks with both hands, bringing him back to her for another kiss.

"I'll prepare the water," he said softly.

She nodded, unable to speak for the tingling warmth that ran through her. Metkyi kissed Katerin again, then dipped hot water into the tub. Katerin pulled off her tunic. Metkyi stopped long enough to shed his upper clothing. He paused, smiled at her and she startled, realizing she had more clothing yet to go.

She was pleasantly surprised by how warm the lodge really was by the time she finished undressing and unbraided her hair. Katerin retrieved her bath soap and came back to the tub, acutely aware of Metkyi's eyes on her.

She dunked her head and hair into the tub, then vigorously soaped it. Metkyi poured the warm water carefully over her head to rinse. When all the soap was gone, she wrung as much of the water out of her hair as she could, and sat in the tub quietly for a moment, knees tucked to her chin. It was better than the morning plunge into the icy creek, but not as good as the big soaking tubs of the Healing House.

What I'd give for a good soak.

Katerin finished washing. When she stepped out, Metkyi wrapped her in a drying cloth. Katerin helped him wash his hair, though it was nothing like hers for length and thickness. Then she sat cross-legged on the bed and combed her hair.

"Let me." Metkyi took her comb. Katerin enjoyed the warmth of the fire and the softness of the fur underneath her as he untangled her hair.

At last he was done, and pulled her to him.

"*Now*," he breathed, running his hands over her, the fiery sensation of his touch causing Katerin to breathe quickly and tremble slightly.

"Yes," she answered, going into his arms, her passion rising to match his. "Oh, yes."

When they were done, they crawled underneath the covers and curled up together.

If only this could last forever.

The next morning Siljaren and Katerin dawdled by the outside fire, savoring the first rays of sunlight before they went to work.

"Why is Davni running?" Siljaren squinted toward the main part of the village.

Katerin looked up just as Davni arrived.

"There's a cough going around the village," Davni gasped.

No. Oh no. Did we release a curse?

"When did it start?" Katerin turned for the lodge, Siljaren a stride behind her.

"Mother heard about the worst cases just this morning at the women's meeting. Several started last night."

"How old are the patients?" Katerin asked.

"Two to six years, mostly."

Katerin nodded. "Any adults?"

"Two or three. But six households. Maybe more."

Katerin caught Siljaren's eye. "Will you take care of things here?"

"I will. Katerin," Siljaren added, "this cough hits Wickmasa after the first storms of winter. I don't think it's tied to banishing Karnoi and Cirdel. Not this quickly."

"How severe does it get?"

"Nothing like the plague," Siljaren reassured her.

Katerin nodded. She checked her healing bag for the liquids and powders she needed against the cough.

If it was the cough, and not something else.

"Let's go," she said to Davni.

Goddess, let this be a minor outbreak.

* * *

To her relief, that was the case. While five of the six households had sickness in their families, the sick ones responded well to Katerin's elixirs.

The sixth was different. This lodge was shabby, small, and crowded. It was neat and well-kept, but from the looks of the furnishings and the clothing the woman wore, this family was one of Wickmasa's poorest. The victims here were the eldest, the family patriarch, a frail old man who was so thin that Katerin could see his bones outlined through his faded dark skin, and a tiny baby.

"I've tried and tried," the young mother, Sarsaji, thin and drawn herself, said. "She won't eat, Healer."

Katerin glanced around the lodge. It looked as if the only residents were Sarsaji and her two patients. "Do you have any help?" she asked.

The mother shook her head.

"Davni," Katerin said. "Have Colerei bring a small kettle of warm gruel. Tell Siljaren the situation."

Davni nodded and left.

"Why are you alone?" Katerin asked point-blank, as she dosed the patriarch. He coughed it back up.

"Worthless woman!" the patriarch snarled. "No one wants to help one like her!"

Sarsaji flushed.

"That's enough!" Katerin snapped. "Now. Take this medicine." She poured another dose, keeping her hand steady.

The patriarch stuck his lower lip out at her. "I *won't* take any of that poison stuff! You ask Makri! *He* knew better than to give me that crap!"

"Makri's dead! I'm his replacement."

"Stupid women. He was a fool, too. Still not taking that poison crap!"

Katerin sighed. The old man was clearly not in his right mind and hadn't been for some time. She sent a wordless plea to Mira.

When elixirs fail, that's when the daranval strength can help.

"Let my daranval in," she said to Sarsaji.

"No, no, *no!*" the patriarch objected.

"*Let my daranval in,*" Katerin said firmly.

"No daranval!"

"For your baby's sake," Katerin added. "Not for *him.*"

Sarsaji had barely pulled aside the door before Mira shouldered her way in.

Must have been waiting right at the door.

The patriarch cringed away from Mira. Katerin reached out to touch the mare, forming a question about the old man.

—*No life in him.* Mira projected a cloying, grasping grayness. *What is this?*

Not the shadowy form of a Shadowwalker. This felt like something long dead.

Mira pushed toward the old man, her ears pinned. The old man scooted away until he was pressed up against the lodge wall.

"Mira! No!" Katerin grabbed her mane to pull her away.

We can't help him. Not if he was supposed to be dead. *How can that be?* Katerin shuddered. This was Metkyi's province. Not hers.

She pointed Mira toward the baby. *Her,* perhaps they could save. But as Katerin stroked the feverish, coughing child, she couldn't sense the child's life force either. She picked up the child, far too light for a babe of this age.

I'm going to lose both of these patients.

She met Sarsaji's despairing eyes.

"*He* dominates everything," she whispered, half-choking back a sob. "He just won't let it happen!"

"Where's your husband?" Katerin lifted the baby up to Mira, letting the daranval sniff the child over.

"Lojyet went out on a long trading circuit shortly after Naket was born. He's one of the caravan guards. Things were fine when he left. *He* hadn't started in on me."

Mira nuzzled the baby. The baby hiccuped, and her breathing momentarily eased as Mira blew gently on Naket's face.

"Do you have any other kin to help?"

Sarsaji shook her head. "I'm from Kinherit. No other kin there, he's my grandfather, and I had to bring him with me when I married Lojyet."

"Lojyet's kin?"

Before she could answer, Metkyi strode in, followed by Colerei, his eyes focused on the old man.

"Begone, you vulture of Staul!" the old man commanded in a quavering voice.

"No." Metkyi stood tall and stern.

The old man howled and flung himself at Metkyi, baring surprisingly long teeth. Metkyi grabbed him by the throat, holding the writhing, snarling figure at bay. Mira lunged toward the old man. Katerin tried to reach for Mira but the baby in her arms hindered her.

"*No,*" Metkyi repeated. Mira stopped, ears pinned back hard.

He began to chant. The old man still struggled, swiping and kicking at Metkyi.

The baby began coughing again. Katerin laid Naket down and fumbled in her bag. Too many of her potions were too strong for so small a baby. But she had to stop the coughing. The baby's lips and the skin around her nose turned blue even as Katerin tried to work the mildest of her potions down the child's throat, stroking the throat to encourage swallowing. Naket coughed the first dose up. Katerin called on Mira as she worked with the baby. Mira nuzzled the baby, exhaling hard against the child's chest.

Not even a daranval's breath can make a difference.

Katerin kept trying, determined not to stop until Naket either breathed freely or was blue and cold.

Finally, she was able to get the baby to swallow some of the elixir. She picked Naket up again, watching the baby's breathing while resting one finger on her neck to track her pulse. Mira kept one nostril on the baby, ears flicking between Katerin and Metkyi. After a few moments Naket breathed more evenly. A few more moments, and the rattling in her throat subsided.

A barrier fell. At last Katerin could touch the life force in the baby.

It's not your time yet. Not your time.

A hand touched her shoulder and she half-jumped, looking up at Metkyi's tight, grim face.

"It's done," he said sharply. "It should be easier for you now." His hand closed on her shoulder, almost a caress, and then he strode out of the lodge.

Katerin stared after him. Then she handed Naket over to her wide-eyed, trembling mother. The old man lay still on his bed again, not breathing.

"He's gone," she told Sarsaji.

Sarsaji's face momentarily twisted. Then she sighed as she looked at the patriarch's body. "He looks like he did a month ago," she said. "Before he first got the cough." She shook her head. "He got the cough, and Makri came to see him. But Makri didn't seem right. And then my baby started fading."

More Makri problems. Was that when Soisan's possession had bled over into him?

"I brought warm food," Colerei said. Katerin, startled, looked around. Colerei had started a large kettle of hot water and warmed some gruel. Katerin sent Mira out.

"You didn't need to do this." Sarsaji started to cry.

"Yes, we did," Colerei said softly but firmly, putting her arm around Sarsaji's shoulder. Katerin realized they were age mates. "You're tired, your baby is sick, your man's caravan is overdue. You need help."

"I don't need help." But Sarsaji's voice trailed away unconvincingly as she sat down abruptly. Without Colerei's help she would have fallen.

Katerin checked the baby. She mixed up more elixir and caught Colerei's eye. Colerei nodded.

"Explain this to her, please."

"I'm going to be here for a while."

"That's good." Katerin left the lodge. She swung up on Mira, wondering where Metkyi had gone. To his lodge? She thought about going there, then decided against it.

Halfway back to her lodge, she changed her mind. She couldn't explain why she turned Mira toward Metkyi's lodge, nor why she kept on riding even when a warding, tingling sensation pushed against her.

He knows I'm here. She rode Mira up to his lodge door and dismounted, wondering if she should announce herself. *No. He'll either ignore it or tell me to go away.*

As she pushed the door open, Metkyi doubled over a stone bowl, vomiting black bile. Katerin rushed toward him, but he held up one hand.

"*Stay back,*" he gasped.

Metkyi vomited several more times, then sat back on his heels, breathing hard. He reached to one side, picked up a cloth and wiped his mouth, and heaved a deep breath, shuddering all over. Then he dropped the cloth in the stone bowl and reached for his firebrand. With a flick of a finger, the brand caught flame. Metkyi chanted, then plunged the brand into the bowl. The stuff in the bowl, wet as it was, caught fire.

Metkyi heaved another deep sigh as the fire in the bowl faded. The flame in his brand went out. He tried to get up and fell back on his heels. Katerin started forward again, only to be waved back.

"Not yet." His voice was faint. He rocked onto his hands and knees, shaking his head. Then, slowly, he rose to his knees. He took another deep breath, then another. Metkyi gathered his feet under him, at last heaving himself up, wavering on his feet.

Slowly, he staggered over to the stand where he kept his fire-brands and put the brand away. He hung his ceremonial hat and clutched at the rack for a moment when it seemed he would fall. Metkyi leaned his head against the rack for several breaths, then straightened up.

He slowly worked his way out of his heavy ceremonial robes. Katerin wanted to run over and help him, but she held back, aching with misery as she saw how exhausted he was. Finally, he was free of his ceremonials.

Metkyi turned toward Katerin, half-smiling. "Katerin." His knees buckled.

This time she had nothing holding her back. She ran to Metkyi and took him into her arms. He was cool and clammy to her touch, shaking hard.

"Food," he gasped. "Oatcakes. The chest. Next to my shrine."

Katerin found oatcakes in the top of the chest, grabbed one, and raced back to Metkyi's side. He took a careful bite, chewing it thoroughly. She slipped the waterskin from around her shoulder and gave some to Metkyi. He drank in slow gulps.

After he finished the oatcake he sagged against Katerin. "Thank you. That sending was a bad one."

"I was surprised to see you. What did you do?"

"My duty and calling. Davni told us what was happening."

"I couldn't feel his life force. Or the baby's."

"He had been dead in all but name for several weeks. He would have eaten up the baby's life, and then Sarsaji's, just to stay alive. Possessed. Not like Soisan. But a creation of Makri's, all the same. I should have seen it."

"I've never seen this before. Is it a Wickmasa thing?"

"No. He gave his soul to Makri to cling to life. I don't think there are any others like him here. I should have thought about this. I'll talk to the Women's Council to be certain. It's not common." He shuddered. "This was a very bad one."

"Gods. You do this often?"

"Not all that often. Usually, I simply help release souls on the final path. They just need a friendly hand, a helpful voice, someone there when they say farewell to this existence and move on to the next."

"What happens to those who don't have your help?" Katerin thought of her mother.

Would one such as Metkyi have released her early on?

"A harder passage, for many."

"Oh Gods, Metkyi. And you vomit like this every time?"

"Not every time." He gave her a tired smile. "He had a lot of grayness."

"I never realized this was part of what you do."

"Does it change things between us?" He looked solemnly at her, his face suddenly an impassive, blank mask.

"No. No. Well, no, that's wrong." She took his hand and held it tight. "I don't understand how you do this all by yourself, without the help of a bondmate."

The tired smile returned to his lips. "I don't understand how you do your work all alone either, Katerin."

"We do it this way because that's the way the Gods tell us it should be."

He shrugged. "And there it is."

They sat in silence. At last, Metkyi shook himself.

"Much longer and I'm going to be asleep. I think we'd both be more comfortable back in your lodge, don't you?"

"Most certainly." She helped Metkyi to his feet.

"Ride back?" Katerin asked Metkyi.

"Only if you do."

"I plan to."

"Then yes."

She swung up bareback and offered Metkyi her arm. He shook his head and swung up with only slightly less grace than she had.

They rode back to her lodge in companionable silence.

CHAPTER 24

aterin promptly put Metkyi to bed. "It's not been that long since you were hurt, and you still need the rest."

"But you had the Hunt."

"You had the injury. Rest," she ordered. Metkyi complied, although he propped himself up and watched as she worked around the lodge. The faint tones of an argument between Rekaré and Alame echoed from the other side.

She brought their dinner over to the bed. She was too tired to talk, and Metkyi clearly felt the same way, but she wished there was something they could do to avoid hearing the argument.

Then someone scratched on the door flap between the two lodge sections.

"May I come in?" Siljaren asked.

Katerin and Metkyi raised eyebrows at each other.

"Of course," Katerin said.

Siljaren slipped in. "They won't miss me."

"What's going on?"

Siljaren rolled her eyes. "The usual. Alame wants to wait

until spring. Rekaré wants to move now, says she's certain that's what her mother wants."

"Do we know what Alicira wants?"

"Vengeance," Siljaren said. "But the how and when of it?" She shrugged. "We won't know without asking. Alame feels we need to consult Alicira. I can't think of any better way for Rekaré to shout *I am here* than to meet with her mother." She frowned. "Meeting with Heinmyets and Inharise alone won't work, either."

Katerin and Metkyi exchanged glances. *Us?* his lips formed without making a sound. Katerin nodded.

"Could someone else be an intermediary?" Katerin asked. "If so, maybe Metkyi and I could go."

Siljaren shook her head. "Anyone that goes to see Heinmyets, Alicira or Inharise is going to be watched. You'd just lead them back here. We already have contacts."

"But if there is a way we can help?" Metkyi said.

Siljaren frowned. "I'd ask. But I don't have any control over what we do."

"Sit down. Have you eaten?"

"Yes. Your Colerei left some food for us."

"Sit down anyway," Metkyi said. "No use for you to get worried, is there?"

Siljaren dropped onto a stool. "I suppose not. Alame needs to let Rekaré follow her instincts. That's how she's managed to avoid her father so far." She scowled. "Then again, if I were in charge, we would be on our way to Medvare-the-city, and in a lot more trouble. I just want to get this over with. I worry that Zauril's people will find us."

"Perhaps some Larijian brandy is called for, to ease everyone's nerves." Metkyi padded over to one of his trunks. He rummaged around, unearthing three small, stemmed glasses. "Ah! There it is." He pulled out an intricately twisted, blue glass bottle. "Have to be careful with this," he muttered. "It packs a bit of firepower."

"Larijian brandy?" Katerin frowned at him. "That's nothing like starberry, is it?"

Metkyi shook his head. "Nothing at all. But it's an elixir of the Gods, I promise you. And after the day we've had, I think we've all earned it." He poured a thimbleful of a pale green liquid into the three glasses. He handed one each to Siljaren and Katerin, then raised his glass.

"Sip it," he cautioned them. "Now. A toast. To survival."

"To survival," Katerin echoed. She cautiously sipped the liquid. Its sweet, fiery overtones reminded her of the sagebrush blossoms and juniper berries of Larij. It was not a liquor to be gulped, but it gave her a pleasant, comfortable glow.

"That's fine stuff," Siljaren said. "Thank you for sharing, Metkyi. How did you come by this?"

"Trade with Larij, about the time Rekaré broke off her trip to Medvare-the-city." Metkyi lifted his glass to the light, studying the fine engraving on it. "A few of us ended up visiting Alicira's old allies in Larij. I took advantage of the trip to get some supplies. This is the last of it."

"An auspicious libation," Siljaren said.

Katerin heard another scratch on the door flap. "Come in," she said.

Alame entered. "There you are," he said to Siljaren. "It's safe now. We've come to a decision."

Siljaren held up one hand to stop him from saying more. "Wait," she told him, and drained her glass, handing it back to Metkyi. "Pour some for Alame."

"Gladly." Metkyi filled the glass with the same careful amount he'd poured before.

Alame took the glass gingerly. "And this is?"

"Larijian brandy," Metkyi said. "I got it when Rekaré decided it was time to disappear."

"Ah. A very good vintage, then." Alame sipped from his glass. "A *very* good vintage." He tossed the rest of it back sharply, and broke into a coughing fit.

Siljaren pounded him on the back. "You weren't supposed to do that!"

Metkyi shook his head ruefully and got up to dig out a fourth glass while Alame finished coughing. He poured more brandy, a more generous serving this time.

"Are you trying to get us drunk, man?" Alame demanded.

"After what I think you're going to tell us, I'd say it's the best course."

"All right." Alame took a deep breath. "Rearnex leaves tomorrow, with two support riders. The rest of us start preparing to leave for Medvare-the-city."

Katerin and Metkyi's eyes met again. "Who's going with Rekaré?" Katerin asked.

"Our troop," Alame said. "Some others from Heinmyets. Our troop isn't big enough to support a winter trip across the mountains, much less a passage down the Chellana. Especially if we plan to challenge Zauril in Medvare proper."

"How long before you leave?" Katerin asked.

"*We* leave in ten to fourteen days, depending on how quickly Rearnex gets back here." Alame fixed Katerin with a steady gaze. "And you and Metkyi will be among us. I've already discussed this with Imnari. Twana stays, but I need strong Voices with us. You and Metkyi have proven yourselves for Dovré and Staul. Your bonding makes you an even stronger combination of the Voices of the Gods. It might just make the difference between success and failure."

"But the Healing House," Katerin started to object.

Alame waved her to silence. "Rearnex is taking Rekaré's formal request for your services to them. Neither the Council nor Eldoran will deny Rekaré."

"Then it's done." Katerin eyed the small glass in her hand,

tempted to swig the brandy as Alame had done. Wisdom prevailed, and she simply held the small glass.

"For better or worse, you two will be a part of history."

Katerin stifled a shiver. Then Metkyi's hand was on her shoulder, steadying her.

At least I won't be alone.

Alame raised his glass high. "To Rekaré the Uniter, Queen of the Three Nations!"

"To Rekaré," they echoed, and sipped the brandy. No sooner had they finished then the flap was thrown back, and Rekaré entered the room, followed by Cenarth.

She seemed different in the way she carried herself, no longer just a part of the troop she rode with, but the leader. Alame bowed to his great-niece gracefully, his fist on his chest, with no sign of any disagreement he might have had with her. A faint aura glowed around Rekaré.

She has come into her magic, indeed.

"Oh, that's not necessary," Rekaré growled. "I'm not even revealed, much less crowned! Until then I'm just plain Rekaré."

Metkyi shook his head. "No, Lady. You've changed. You've assumed your power."

"Even though you're not revealed and crowned yet, you *are* a Queen, great-niece," Alame said gravely. "And, as such, it's better to treat you as one."

"I thank you for your support," Rekaré said. "But I depend on you for advice and strength, and it's easier for me to do that as just plain Rekaré." She took Cenarth's hand. "I can't do this without you. All four of you." Her voice trailed off as she looked at Cenarth and for a moment Katerin thought she saw the glimmer of wetness in the corner of Rekaré's eyes. Then she blinked and it was gone.

She's really not that old, Katerin realized with a start. *Not even eighteen.*

"Would you give this to Rearnex?" Rekaré handed a sealed

packet to Alame. "It's the request to the Healing House for Katerin's services." She turned to Katerin. "I need your strength. Yours and Metkyi's, together."

"We will be with you," Metkyi said.

"Thank you," Rekaré said. She turned to leave.

"Lady?" Metkyi said.

"Yes?" Rekaré stopped.

"Thank you for healing my arm."

"Your arm is healed?" Siljaren asked.

"Completely," Katerin said. "With only the slightest sign that the injury ever existed," she added.

Alame and Siljaren exchanged worried looks.

"You're certain, Metkyi? That it was Rekaré's doing and not Makri's death?" Alame asked.

"I did it," Rekaré said, her voice brittle. "We need him to be whole. I felt my power move within me while carrying Nitel during that battle with the Hunt. It was a test of what I could do. If I made a poor choice, let it be on my head."

"No," Alame said. "Not a poor choice. Not at all." He swallowed hard. "Great-niece, you've grown up, and I apologize for not seeing that." He kissed Rekaré on the cheek. "You are a true daughter of the House of Miteal. I am honored to be in your service."

"Thank you," Rekaré breathed.

Alame and Siljaren left, along with Cenarth and Rekaré.

"Well," Metkyi said, his voice unsteady. "It seems that we have a part to play in history."

"I've been too close to history already."

Metkyi wrapped his arms around her. "It'll be all right," he whispered. "It will be all right."

Katerin buried her face in his chest, remembering Terani and the faraway look in her eyes before she fell into that final sleep.

How can I tell you, Metkyi, what I know of history and being history's child?

"Katerin." Metkyi slipped two fingers under her chin and lifted her face free of his chest. "It will be *all right.*"

She gazed at him desperately. He didn't understand. He hadn't heard the prophecies that she had before fleeing to the sanctuary of the Healing House. It would not be all right now. It would never be all right.

Metkyi bent his head to kiss her and she kissed him back, willing herself to lose her doubts and fears in his lips. Perhaps this fate would avoid them. Prophecies had been proven wrong before. Perhaps this was another one that had been changed by the intervention of the gods.

But still she shivered as his kiss deepened in passion.

Medvare-the-city. The prophecy said I would meet my fate in Medvare.

Until now, she never really thought she'd see the place.

CHAPTER 25

"Riders coming in! A lot of them!" Davni called out as she burst into the lodge the next afternoon.

Katerin looked up from mending a set of reins. She had traded Kwellet leatherwork and braidwork for horses and tack for Metkyi to use on the trip to Medvara. She was deep into repairing a horsehair romal rein that had frayed at the bit ends, using hairs she'd pulled from Mira's tail.

Nothing like daranval hair to strengthen a set of reins.

"It's good weather. Why shouldn't there be riders coming in?" Colerei asked as she stirred a batch of salve. "Katerin, is this simmering like it should?"

Katerin put down the reins and went to check. Colerei's cooking skills were also useful for most of the salve-making process. She only needed a little bit of magical help at the right moments. Hopefully they would have time to make enough to hold the village in stock for a while before she had to leave.

"This many riders?" Davni handed Katerin the two baskets of goods from Myrieke. Katerin fingered through the supplies, clothing in one basket, dried food in the other. "It's not traders."

"How many?" Metkyi asked.

"A big troop. Banners. Flags. Rekaré, Cenarth and Alame rode out to meet them. Left a meeting with Imnari when the first report from the scouts came in. Scouts said that the fellow from Rekaré's troop who just left is riding with them."

Metkyi and Katerin exchanged a quick glance.

"Rearnex took off before daylight," Metkyi said. "But there's no way he would make it to Dera in one day. It can't be anyone from Alicira."

"Unless they were already riding out." Katerin put the reins down and gathered her sword and go-bag. "Let's see what's happening," she said to Metkyi.

"I'll need time to saddle a horse," he said.

She shook her head as they went outside. "No need. Mira can carry us both."

"She doesn't mind?"

"Unless she starts sending me images of you covered with buffalo dung, it's all right."

Metkyi burst out laughing. "So as long as buffalo dung doesn't come into the picture, it's all right?"

"She has a *very* specific way of expressing her displeasure." Katerin jumped on Mira's back, then offered Metkyi an arm. "For a short ride like this, I'd just as soon ride bareback without tack. Easy to do with Mira."

"I've not wanted the bond of a daranval before. After seeing you and Mira, I wish I had one to ride to Medvara."

Medvara.

The reminder silenced Katerin. She focused on Mira as the mare continued climbing, breathing easily, no apparent effect on her peryormance from the other day. She had been trying to think of this as just another trip.

"You're awfully quiet," Metkyi said as Mira topped out on the trail.

Katerin couldn't think of anything to say.

"Katerin?" Metkyi repeated. "What's wrong?"

"Too many prophecies."

"Prophecies about what?"

"Medvare-the-city. Myself. My fate."

"Katerin, how detailed are the prophesies?"

Katerin took a deep breath. "They were among the last things my mother said before she went into the deathless sleep. The priests took them very seriously."

Metkyi's arms tightened on her waist. "Have any of them come true?"

"Some have. Some haven't."

"Then these prophesies about you might not be true. You may have stepped off of the path of fate."

"Or just changed rivers in fate's flow."

"Not everything that looks like a prophecy is locked into the future. Things change. How old were you when she went into the dreamless sleep?"

"Eight, nine, something like that. I was a child of the village in Chiyan for several years. Then I found my calling and went to the Healing House. Her minders were more than happy to see me go by then. I was a reminder that my mother was not perfect, had conceived and birthed a child she wasn't supposed to have."

"Your father?"

"No one knows. You know how it is. It was the same for her as it is for us, we take our powders, we sleep with people, but we don't bond."

"No one came forward to claim you after she went into the dreamless sleep?"

"I think by that point no man was willing to acknowledge the possibility of being tied to Terani the God-Killer. You know how it is. We don't have children."

Metkyi sighed. "If a child happens, it's as much her fault for allowing it if the village doesn't support it. I know that discussion. I've heard it in other villages. Wickmasa's tolerant, though we've not dealt with that issue for years. What you must have gone through!"

"Some blamed me for her fading into the dreamless sleep."

"Fools. The magic doesn't work that way. She never gave you a clue about who your father might have been? No one tried to find out?"

"Nothing. I was just an inconvenience."

"I'm sorry. I would have hoped your father might have come forward."

"He may not have known about me. My mother didn't take partners from within Chiyan village, and rarely for more than just a few days with someone visiting Waykemin. Priests, most of the time. Voices. Rarely someone not touched by the gods."

"I'm sorry," Metkyi repeated. "It doesn't sound like that pleasant a childhood."

"I was happy to leave Waykemin and go to the Healing House. But now I'm worried. What if being her daughter means that I'm likely to be sacrificed to the dreamless sleep?"

"You survived banishing Karnoi and Cirdel."

"My fate is supposed to meet me in Medvare-the-city. I haven't been there yet. But I will be there soon."

He stroked her waist. "Katerin, I'm with you. I promise you, upon my pledges and honor as a Voice of Staul, that I will do everything I can to keep you from the dreamless sleep."

"But what if you can't change my fate?"

"Just because your mother succumbed to the dreamless sleep doesn't mean that's the fate intended for you."

"I've seen fate's games played far too close to me to trust myself to its whims."

"You'll get your chance at a normal, quiet life," Metkyi said confidently. "That's *my* prediction." He straightened up. "I think I see them." He pointed off toward the northwest, and Katerin tried to forget the sudden memory of how he had cried out *I can't see true for you now.*

"That's not the direction anyone would be taking from Dera, is it?"

"No. It's not. Maybe Davni was wrong when she said the scouts thought Rearnex was with this troop."

"Rekaré and the others would have come back by now if that were the case," Katerin said.

"You're right. So. Let's see what we have coming."

Katerin urged Mira into an easy canter. Mira skimmed across the top of the snow like she had the night they were pursued, only with a better rhythm, settling into a gliding three-beat gait, snorting with each stride as she cantered at a pace that only the fastest horse could match.

The troop approaching Wickmasa came into sharper focus after only a few moments.

"Big group, all right. Doesn't look like they're too worried about secrecy."

Katerin nodded, focusing on Mira and what impressions she could get from her mare's senses. Mira's mind was strangely blank. Still, despite the quiet, nothing about the troop seemed to trigger her defensive reflexes. That told Katerin that whoever approached rode at least one daranval higher in the daranval hierarchy than Mira.

As they approached the troop, several riders intercepted them. Mira probed ahead, daranval mind to daranval mind, shutting out human links. The other riders came up slowly, openly displaying lances and swords. If Katerin had any doubts about who was riding with that troop, they were gone now.

Mira's responses seemed to have satisfied the other daran-velii. They fell into position surrounding Mira, the riders nodding to Katerin but not speaking. She recognized their garb as the traveling attire of the royal guard that accompanied Heinmyets, Alicira and Inharise, especially in Keldara. In Clenda, source of Heinmyets's and Inharise's power, they frequently rode out only with the closest clansmen and women to protect them. Not so here, especially with the borders so close by.

Except that it almost looks like they've come from one of the borders instead of from Dera. Maybe Larij?

Rekaré's Basnen pranced next to a golden daranval who carried herself with an elegant grace that made Basnen seem lesser simply by the quietness of her carriage. The daranval's rider was a thin, pale woman with gold and silver strands of hair peeking out from under her headscarf. The woman's fine, delicate features were clearly the pattern Rekaré's had been molded from.

Alicira, abused and exiled sorceress, who had gambled with Staul and won.

Next to Alicira, on the other side from Rekaré, strode a powerful black daranval stallion with silver mane and tail, carrying himself pridefully, as if he were fully aware that there was no other daranval in the Two Nations that could touch him for speed and strength. Rather than exhaust himself with an unnecessary display, Elantai moved with minimal effort, flowing along with his neck arched slightly, giving the impression he was ready to break free at any moment should there be a need.

And his proud tall rider, with dark skin, black hair, with black eyes that could make miscreants cringe, was none other than Heinmyets, who defied Gods and Zauril alike to win Alicira as his First Wife. Heinmyets, Leader of Keldara and Clenda.

On his other hand, less showy, but no less elegant and powerful in her own way, ambled a brown daranval mare, compact yet strong, with a white blaze that zigzagged down her nose like a bolt of summer lightning in the mountains. Her slender rider sat tall, her black hair bound in a long braid that brushed the back of her daranval. Inharise of Clenda, Heinmyets's Second Wife, and equal partner with Alicira and Heinmyets in the ruling of Clenda and Keldara. Some said she was the secret power that helped Alicira keep Zauril at bay. Few made the mistake of thinking that because she was Second Wife, she was lesser than Alicira. She was a power in her own right in Clenda, and her marriage to Heinmyets and Alicira made her no less powerful in Keldara.

Cenarth rode by her side.

They stopped five daranval lengths away. Rekaré waved Katerin closer. She gave Katerin and Metkyi a thin, quick smile, turning her daranval so that she stood next to Mira.

"So who are these riders?" Heinmyets asked Rekaré, the authority in his deep, quiet voice sending chills through Katerin.

"This is the daranval Mira, bearing Katerin, winter Healer for Wickmasa, and Metkyi, priest of Staul for Wickmasa. They led the battle against the Hunt."

Heinmyets sidestepped Elantai over to Katerin and Metkyi.

"It's not often I hear Rekaré speak so well of a Voice of Staul," Heinmyets told Metkyi as they shook hands.

Metkyi bowed, one arm braced around Katerin to keep from falling. "Thank you. I feel that my Lord Staul is fearsome enough without needing to add to it with my own bad behavior."

Heinmyets laughed. "Well spoken, Metkyi!" He took Katerin's hand. "Healer Katerin. My dear, we've heard much about you." He studied her carefully, then raised her hand to his lips and lightly kissed it, sending tingles up and down Katerin's spine.

"Terani's daughter needs no introduction," Alicira added. "And it seems you're walking in her footsteps."

"Not completely so, I hope," Katerin said. "I'd prefer not to experience the dreamless sleep."

"Understandable," Inharise said.

"Ride with us," Heinmyets said.

They reined in next to the royals. Alicira and Rekaré spoke together quietly, with occasional comments from Heinmyets. From what Katerin heard, it sounded as if mother, stepfather and daughter had seen each other regularly during the five years it had been since Rekaré had officially disappeared.

Is this another Wickmasa secret?

"So, Healer Katerin, how are you finding Wickmasa?" Alicira asked.

"Complex."

"Wickmasa can be an *interesting* place to stay. What brought you to this village?"

Katerin retold the story of the ambush by Saubral raiders, then Makri's death.

Alicira shook her head at the ending of Katerin's story. "A waste. Dovré needs every healer these days."

"Unfortunately, he was more interested in power," Metkyi said.

Alicira peered closely at Metkyi. "You're his brother, right?"

"Yes." Metkyi pulled himself up a bit straighter. "He wanted my strength from Staul as well as what he'd earned from Dovré." One hand tightened slightly on Katerin's waist, then released. "Makri had always sought power. Even when we were young. Our half-sister is the Voice of Artel. She and I get along well. When he was called to Dovré, she and I hoped," his voice caught. "We hoped that his calling meant a change of heart, that Makri was changing his ways. Instead, it seems to have been more seeking after power."

"I am sorry to hear that. One does not always hear of such behavior in someone called to follow any of the gods. It was a true calling?"

"As true as my own." The pain deepened in Metkyi's voice. "At least at first, it was a true calling, my lady. I wish I knew why he changed."

Heinmyets caught that last comment. "We can't always

predict betrayal." He exchanged knowing glances with Alicira, and Katerin felt the same sharp surge of magic that happened when Mira spoke to other daranvelii.

Just how much power do these three have?

Mindspeech between humans was not very common, certainly not as common as mindspeech between daranvelii, or human and daranval. It was usually limited to the most powerful and gifted of those with the ability to wield magics.

So why haven't they dealt with Zauril themselves?

The world went silent around her. Katerin looked up from Mira's withers to see them studying her.

They can hear my thoughts.

"I did not mean—" she began. "I did not know I could—"

"No offense taken," Alicira said. "And in answer, I'm banned from direct conflict with Zauril. As he is from me. That was part of the long compromise."

"I am sorry," Katerin murmured.

"Katerin, daughter of Terani the God-Killer, you've the right to wonder such things. You more than most."

Katerin nodded, looking down at Mira's neck again, trying hard to control her thoughts. Silence ruled the rest of their ride. As they drew near to Wickmasa, several outriders rode ahead.

"Katerin. Metkyi." Heinmyets said. "We would like you to join us at dinner tonight. We will be discussing plans and strategies with Rekaré. You need to be there."

"We will be there."

"Good. Meanwhile, several persons from the Healing House would like to speak with you." Heinmyets waved unseen riders forward.

"Thank you." Katerin sidepassed Mira out of the way. Alame and Siljaren rode in the second tier, along with Rearnex and his co-riders. And in the third tier, Katerin was not surprised to see Eldoran, Yevtin, and Senai.

Isn't that the way my doom unfolds?

Of course they would be here.

Eldoran raised a brow as he took in Metkyi seated behind Katerin on Mira. "Do you have room for us in your lodge?"

"We can make room."

Eldoran nodded. " It's been a long, hard ride these past two days."

"Two days?" Katerin whirled Mira around. "I didn't think it was possible to ride out from the Healing House that quickly, especially in the weather we've had."

"We never made it back to the Healing House. We were already with the Leaders and their party," Eldoran said. "Things have been moving very quickly."

"So it seems."

"We especially need to know more about what Makri was doing."

"I can tell you some of that," Metkyi said.

Eldoran shot a sharp glance at Metkyi. "And you are?"

"Metkyi. I was Makri's twin brother. I'm the Voice of Staul for Wickmasa. I'm also Katerin's winter bondmate."

Katerin hid a smile at his defiant tone. "Metkyi and I worked together against the Hunt."

"We might want to stop by the shrine first," Metkyi said.

"I think that's a very good idea," Eldoran said. "I've heard of Wickmasa's shrine, but never seen it."

"Will we have enough time?" Katerin asked.

"The parts that matter can be dealt with there."

"Lead us on, then," Eldoran said.

Katerin urged Mira into a faster jog, worrying about Eldoran's opinion of her bond with Metkyi. He could make it rough for her with the Council next spring if he disapproved.

It's a winter bond, she told herself firmly. *No more and no less than what anyone else does for winter.*

Except that most other healers didn't choose a priest of Staul to be their winter consort.

CHAPTER 26

Once they arrived at the shrine, Metkyi quickly snapped up a flame where the old fire had been. Then he took Katerin's hand, gesturing to the others to circle around the small fire.

"I ask us to keep in mind the old Wickmasa traditions of the long friendship between Staul and Dovré, traditions which *have been forgotten* in other places," Metkyi said.

Eldoran winced. Katerin squeezed Metkyi's hand in warning, long enough to make him look, then follow her quick glance toward Eldoran. He nodded.

"Despite this forgetting," Metkyi continued, "I ask us to remember and renew these old traditions of friendship between Staul and Dovré. I call upon our patrons to look upon this discussion with favor, and help us to walk in the correct paths. May our hearts be ever straight, without confusion. I so will it."

"I so will it," Katerin and the others echoed.

"Lord and Lady, help us to gain understanding," Eldoran said, his voice falling into a practiced cadence that Katerin recognized from Healing House rituals. "Help us to have patience and find what has been hidden. I so will it."

"I so will it," Metkyi led the others in this response.

"Help us to mend what has been done wrong if we can do so. Help us to help our sister and her chosen bondmate to do your wishes," Yevtin added. "I so will it."

"Guide us in your paths, oh Lady and Lord," Senai said. "Help us to understand and to act as is needed. I so will it."

Metkyi glanced at Katerin. She shook her head. What had been said was enough. She squeezed his hand gently, and he nodded.

"And so it will be," Metkyi concluded.

They dropped hands.

"The shrine?" Eldoran asked.

"We cleared the snow away from it before we left," Metkyi said. "This way."

Katerin hung behind as they walked to the shrine. Senai joined her.

"So," she whispered. "You and this priest of Staul. How did that happen?"

"It's a long story. Maybe later. But the Gods were involved. We've been dealing with the Hunt."

"I've heard." Senai made a face. "Glad it's been you and not me. But him. Easy on the eyes, but a bit pushy and overbearing. Why him?"

"I don't know, but it feels right. He gets pushy and over-bearing when he's nervous." They stopped further away from the shrine than Yevtin, Metkyi and Eldoran. "It's more than the Gods between us. Senai, after the Hunt chased us out here, I was sure that we were going to die, and Mira had collapsed. It just happened."

Maybe not quite in that order.

But if she and Metkyi hadn't been together that night, what would have happened?

Senai shook her head ruefully. "Ah, well, just remember your old friend once in a while, will you?"

"It's only for a season!"

"Things can change when the Gods get involved. Unpredictably so."

"Neither of us are free for anything more than a season."

"Rules change when the Gods get involved."

Katerin changed the subject. "Why were you already meeting with the Leaders?"

"We were summoned." Senai kept a wary eye on the men as they inspected the shrine. "They were on the border, and met us halfway. The daranvelii told us to be there."

"What's that about?"

"The daranvelii are talking to each other over the distances again." Senai frowned. "Mine seems to know things I wouldn't expect him to know. Eldoran said the calling for the original meeting with the Leaders came from his daranval."

Katerin moved closer to the men, troubled. Daranvelii didn't talk across the distances very often, and when they did, it meant trouble.

"Katerin!" Metkyi called. "I need you to look at this."

She slogged through the snow to join Metkyi. He pointed at the snow around the shrine. Wolf tracks circled the shrine. It looked as if one of the wolves had tried to jump an unseen barrier.

"I'm no tracker," she said.

"After your years on a healing circuit, you know more than most of us," Eldoran said.

"Not a paw print within a body's length of the shrine, in all directions. What do you make of that?" Metkyi's voice was tight and controlled, worry in his eyes.

"I'll ask Mira." She waved Mira over.

—*Sniff. Look. Tell.*

Mira moved toward the shrine, then jumped back, snorting, followed by an angry squeal.

—*Makri's image shadowed by wolf body.*

"Makri?" Metkyi asked.

"Yes."

"How old?"

"Older than the day we banished his shadow," Katerin said.

"I want you to look at the shrine," Metkyi said, urgency in his voice again.

Why are they so spooked?

Katerin stepped past Eldoran.

The statues had changed. When she last left them, the Dovré and Staul images faced each other. There had been at least two hands worth of space between the two. Now, the two statues were fused together, back-to-back.

"That is not the way they looked when I left them." She tried and failed to keep a quaver out of her voice. "Can they be separated?"

Metkyi shook his head. "They're as tightly tied together as if they've been carved out of the same piece of stone. Which they might have been." Fear tightened his face.

"The gods have spoken clearly. You two belong together." Eldoran looked at the stone figures, then back at Metkyi. "What happened in Wickmasa before Katerin came? Why did Makri turn to Karnoi and Cirdel?"

"I'll tell you what I know," Metkyi said.

They settled around the fire, then Metkyi described Makri's behavior of the past year. The trips, the subtle jostling for power within the village counsel. The sense that *things weren't right* around his brother. Their clashes when Metkyi came to oversee the deaths of some of Makri's patients.

"Was he trying to keep them from dying, and you were hurrying them?" Eldoran asked.

"No! I don't do things that way," Metkyi cried out, genuine anguish in his voice. "It's not easy for me to ease someone into death, even the willing." He reached for Katerin's hand, his hand tightening on hers convulsively. "I pay afterwards. Katerin can tell you. She's seen it." His voice trailed away and he stared into the fire.

"He's right," Katerin said, shivering as she remembered yesterday.

"I'm sorry," Eldoran said. "But it had to be asked, so that I could tell it true."

The Council. He's asking this for the Council.

Metkyi continued to hold Katerin's hand as he described how he had caught Makri with tokens of Staul the Destroyer, tokens he'd not seen before. The discovery led to Metkyi's actions to protect himself. His consultations with Twana, and their fears that they couldn't safely share the information they held about Rekaré's latest locations and plans with Makri. The growing suspicion and doubt even in the village, aimed at Metkyi instead of Makri. Metkyi's fears that Makri would depose him and take on Staul's power for himself.

It was dusk when Metkyi finished talking. The fire had burned down to ashes.

At last Eldoran looked up. "We are in your debt, Metkyi. Without your vigilance, things would have been much worse. The Council should have listened to you, Yevtin. Myself included. We should have been investigating what was happening here in Wickmasa. Metkyi, I wish that you and your sister had tried to tell us about Makri. That would have given Yevtin's warnings about Makri's behavior more weight."

"You might have listened to Twana, but she didn't see the more damning things that I did. Would you have listened to a priest of Staul making accusations against your healer? Especially one that was rumored to be scheming against his brother because he wanted to draw all power to himself?" Metkyi stared at Eldoran. "After all, isn't that what a priest of Staul is supposed to be like?" he added bitterly.

Eldoran was the first to look away, glancing down at his hands before meeting Metkyi's eyes again with a rueful smile.

"Every word you just said was true, Voice of Staul," Eldoran acknowledged. "Every word. We were fortunate that Katerin and Mira were diverted here by that Saubral attack."

"It was an action of the Gods that brought Katerin here," Metkyi said.

"I agree." Eldoran glanced toward the west. "Let's go. We need to meet with the Leaders soon."

Katerin helped Metkyi kick apart the coals, then swung up on Mira, sidepassing her over to one of the logs so that Metkyi could mount more easily.

As they rode down the trail, Metkyi's grip on her waist transmitted his tension. When they returned to the lodge, she took a moment while they were rearranging Mira's shed to take his hands.

"Are you still worried they'll separate us?" she asked.

"No, my love," Metkyi said. "I'm more worried about what lies ahead of us."

"And yet you were the one warning me not to get too worried earlier."

"A lot can happen between here and Medvare-the-city," he said, his face solemn.

That, more than anything else, struck a chill deep inside her.

Katerin had expected a formal Keldaran Court dinner like the ones she sometimes attended as a representative of the Healing House, with multiple courses, elaborate preparations and fancy dress. Instead, the dinner resembled a gathering of Tauri chieftains.

Heinmyets's hunters had brought in an elk, and the village contributed root vegetables, bread, and some fine pastries made with huckleberry preserves. The group sat around the big table in Imnari's lodge, chatting about horses, daranvelii, and trade routes, before retreating to the council lodge next door. Hein-myets gave them time to settle while Imnari handed around cups of steaming cider.

"So. Rekaré. You are convinced it is your time to act."

"Yes, father," Rekaré didn't flinch away from Heinmyets's steady gaze. "I've come into my magic, a season and a half before Zauril expects."

"You're certain?" Alicira leaned forward. Even though it was warm in the council lodge, she draped a heavy shawl around her slender shoulders. Her face was thinner and more hollow-cheeked than it had been the last time Katerin had seen her in Dera. Her skin glowed palely in the light of the fire. It seemed to Katerin for a moment as if a flame blazed inside her.

She doesn't have many years left.

"I'm positive, Mother. I know what this means to you. I wouldn't chance it if I weren't certain."

"A winter challenge will not be easy," Heinmyets cautioned.

"I know that," Rekaré said. "But my magic is that of winter, not summer like his. I *will* be at my strength."

"We could argue about the timing for most of the night," Inharise said. "Let's discuss what we *can* do."

"A voice of wisdom." Heinmyets smiled at his Second Wife.

Alicira sat up taller and smiled at Inharise as well. "It's diffi-cult to ease the control over a child. I've been struggling with this ever since you went on your own path, Rekaré. As has your Secondmother, over Cenarth."

"I appreciate what you've done, all three of you," Rekaré knelt at her mother's feet. "Five years that you worked so hard to hide me from him. Mother, I know the cost. And I am grateful to you for stepping back and letting me make this choice." She leaned her forehead against Alicira's hand for a moment, then kissed it.

"I remember too well what was done to me by *my* parents, daughter." Alicira slipped her hand out of Rekaré's and cupped

Rekaré's cheek, stroking it with her thumb. "I wanted to spare you that, even though my deepest desire was to hide you far away. It wasn't what you wanted; it wasn't how we raised you. I have died many deaths from worrying about you this past five years. I never knew from season to season if you could avoid Zauril's searches. I knew it was a risk. But I also knew that the risk would make you a stronger and better magician, which it has."

"Thank you," Rekaré rose, bowed to her mother, and returned to her place next to Cenarth.

"You agree with her?" Heinmyets asked Alicira.

Alicira and Inharise exchanged glances.

"*Both* of us agree with Rekaré," Inharise said. "It's time. She's right."

"So, First Wife, what do you recommend to our daughter?" Heinmyets and Alicira's eyes met. Then Heinmyets nodded.

Alicira rose slowly and carefully from her seat. She tightened the shawl around her and, once again, Katerin had the impression of a solitary flame intensely consuming the fuel that fed it.

"I met with my old friend and ally in the Mershaunten of Larij's court, Orlanden en Selail, during our recent trip to the spa at Wixtnal," she said. "Orlanden speaks for the former Mershaunten's youngest son, Haran, who has always been a friend to us, to *me*, from before my exile."

"I remember you speaking of Haran but not of Orlanden," Rekaré said.

"Orlanden had remained hidden," Alicira said. "Politics of Larij. He helped your uncle Alame and my brother Delian extract me from Zauril's clutches. Were it not for Orlanden and, through him, Haran, I would have never won free of Zauril."

"Can we still trust him?" Cenarth asked. "If he's been hidden, how do we know he still speaks for Haran, or that Haran even looks at you with favor? What can a younger son do for us?"

"Ah, they can do more than you think." Alicira began to pace, slowly at first, then sped up in cadence with her words, ticking points off on her long, slender fingers. "Orlanden is hidden from most outsiders because of his role in Haran's household. The former Mershaunten did not want to admit that his youngest son has Orlanden for a life companion in preference to any woman. He was even willing to contemplate the possibility of a marriage between Haran and myself, the daughter of an unreliable ally, to do away with the rumors, until Zauril claimed me." She started coughing and stopped pacing as the coughing racked her body, doubling over with each hack.

Siljaren and Inharise hurried to Alicira's side. Siljaren offered a flask while Inharise steadied Alicira.

"While Haran and Orlanden were forbidden to give direct help to your mother," Heinmyets continued, watching Alicira, frowning, "they managed to help her escape from Medvara to Keldara." He sighed with relief as Alicira stopped coughing and Siljaren and Inharise helped her ease back into her seat. "Her brother Delian had found a place with my riders when he was exiled, and we had discussed a marriage to protect your mother, should things have gone wrong in Medvara."

"Which they did," Alicira said, her voice faint.

"Yes," Heinmyets said. "But Medvara's loss was my gain, and I have never regretted it."

"Nor have I," Alicira said. "Although I do wish my parents had chosen the easier path, and spared us this mess."

Inharise rested a hand on her shoulder. "Who knows what would have come instead, if they granted an easy consent? It was a rough road, sister-wife, but one that might not have been so sweet had it not been for the choices of those others."

Alicira briefly leaned her head against Inharise's arm.

"Things might have been different, true, but not always better. Thank you for reminding me of that." She straightened up. "Rekaré. I recommend that you start by going to Larij. Cross the Great River, and follow it down to Chellni on the Larijian side, then cross back over. Orlanden and Haran can give you protection in Larij, especially if you ride quickly." Her voice faltered.

"I understand, Mother. And at Chellni?"

"There will be people there who have been waiting for you for many years. Exiles, who will know the quiet passages into Medvare-the-city."

"How will we know them?" Cenarth asked. "And they us?"

"We will give you tokens and passwords to share with them," Inharise said. "We've been building this support in Chellni for many years."

"But how? Oh," Rekaré said. "The Fairs in Chellni. The races."

"Exactly," Heinmyets said. "You will know your supporters when you get there, just as they will know you. You will arrive in time for Midwinter Fair. What better way to hide you than as part of a group of horse and daranval traders?"

"Wouldn't that draw more attention to us?" Alame asked.

Midwinter Fair in Chellni.

Katerin ignored the discussion for a moment. She had been to the great fairs in Nere, but the Midwinter Fair in Chellni was known as the greatest of all, for racing, for gaming, for trading. She had never been part of the delegations the Healing House sent to Chellni, although she had hopes of going this year, until she came to Wickmasa.

She heard her name, and jumped slightly. Eldoran was speaking. "Katerin, Yevtin, Senai and I will be the delegation from the Healing House. It won't be the first time we've had a small group ride in with traders and riders from Clenda."

"Will I be part of your delegation, or will I be one of the riders?" Siljaren asked.

"Neither," Alame said. "You need to stay with Alicira."

Siljaren frowned at him. "No. I want to be there."

Alame shook his head. "It's not the path for you. You're known in Chellni."

"I want to go," Siljaren insisted.

"I honor your wish." Alame looked down for a moment, then back up. "But I ask you, dearest, please spare me. Knowing what possibly awaits me. I ask you, please. Let me know that you are safe. My one request of you."

Siljaren drew a ragged breath. "How can I refuse what you ask?"

"I ask this of you now," Alame said. "Much as it pains me. Much as it pains you. Please, dearest. Be safe, and keep Alicira safe."

Siljaren nodded. "I will stay," she said.

I'm not the only one who fears what may happen in Medvare-the-city.

"All right," Rekaré said. "If we're to do this, best be done quickly. How soon can we have my party prepared and ready to go?"

"Our people will need to reprovision," Heinmyets said. "Give us four days, so that we can put together a credible team of racers and stock to trade."

"Good," Rekaré said. "What about food?"

"Myrieke has started to prepare a trading group to go to Chellni," Imnari said. "We can meet further needs easily within four days."

"Then it will be so," Rekaré said. "I will meet with those who will be our guides to plan our route. Katerin, you and Eldoran need to prepare our Healing contingent. Rearnex and Alame, you will ensure that we have a credible party for trading purposes, while giving me enough support to slip into Medvare-the-city to challenge Zauril." She drew herself up even taller. "We have four days before we ride. Make good use of your time. Go, now, and prepare."

They walked into the cold, still night. Metkyi slid one arm

around Katerin and they walked together, silent, locked in their thoughts. When they were almost at the lodge, Metkyi finally spoke.

"It's really happening. We're going to Medvare-the-city."

"Yes," Katerin said.

They paused to check in on Mira and the other daranvelii, then went into the lodge, each lost in their thoughts as they went about their evening tasks, until at last they turned to each other in bed.

Whatever dreams she had that night left no traces in Katerin's memory.

CHAPTER 27

Four days later, Katerin and Mira waited as dark slowly faded away to crisp, cold morning while the caravan assembled in the big meadow next to Kwellet's lodge. Mira felt tight under Katerin.

—*Ride. Ride far?* came to Katerin from Mira.

—*Ride far.* Katerin pictured them riding as a group. Mira pricked up her ears and snorted, her breath coming out in big white clouds. She shifted her weight from foot to foot eagerly. Her wordless joy at being on the move again flowed through Katerin. Katerin laughed and patted Mira's neck.

Has it only been fourteen days since we settled in Wickmasa?

Not that long. She had stayed longer during her circuits, at larger villages.

I should be more nervous about this. What's going to happen at Medvare-the-city?

Despite their goal it felt good to contemplate traveling again, with an eager daranval underneath her. Before Medvare-the-city there would be travel. New country. Movement. Differences.

Katerin leaned over and hugged Mira's neck. Mira sent back

an image of them leading the entire caravan, Mira prancing, holding her head high and flagging her tail proudly. Katerin sat back up and laughed.

Metkyi rode up on a brown mare. Mira touched noses with the brown mare, who lowered her head.

"Ready?" he asked, half-grinning. He seemed more relaxed than he had been for days.

He likes traveling too.

"I'm always ready to travel," she said. "Why else would I be a circuit healer?"

Metkyi's grin widened. "Spoken like a true daughter of Wickmasa. Even if it is just for the winter. Ah! I'm ready to go. I've been locked up in the village for too long. No matter how this turns out, Katerin, the traveling will be sweet with you at my side!"

"Flatterer!" she laughed, deliberately trying to push away the worry that came to mind when she thought of Medvara.

"But true," he said. "We should have a good first day's travel. Weather looks good."

"Ride out!" Orelyets called, and took up the lead.

Katerin and Metkyi took their places as part of Rekaré's core group in the middle of the caravan. And, just like that, they were off, riders, a single wagon, and, behind them, a herd of loose horses and daranvelii.

Mira settled into her long-striding travel walk. Orelyets kept them going at a steady walk-trot pace, with breaks where riders slipped off to walk next to their horses. A festive atmosphere soon sprung up amongst the riders, joking and singing. Katerin joined in as she recognized the tunes. Most of them she knew from past campfires and other villages, but there were some songs which she didn't know that seemed to be from Wickmasa. On those, she hummed along, following the words as Metkyi sang them. His singing voice rang solid and deep, sending tingles through her. At times they took each other's hands as they walked along.

Sweet travel, indeed. She couldn't remember when a trip had started out so pleasantly.

"Is this typical for a Wickmasa caravan?" she asked.

The grin which hadn't seemed to leave Metkyi's face expanded. "Yes. First day with Orelyets anyway, when the weather is nice. Orelyets runs a good caravan."

By mid-afternoon a crisp, cold wind had set in, chilling Katerin to the bone. The joking and singing fell off though the traveling mode remained festive. Mira's mind was a pleasant singsong underlying Katerin's, the familiar routine of travel. Occasional images of villages and corrals with buffalo dung piled in them popped up, but otherwise Mira's thoughts were about the smooth swing of legs and feet, the rhythmic stride that carried them along the trail, the presence of good horses, daranvelii, and friendly people, looking at new things, but mostly moving, moving, moving.

They stopped in a high mountain meadow to set up camp well before the early winter dusk fell. The wind still blew hard. It took all hands to get the small tents set up around the wagon. Then Metkyi and Katerin helped gather wood and kindled the camp's main fires.

"Good ride for a first day," Alame said when they had finished the travel chores and eaten dinner. "We might have gone farther, but that's hard with such a large group."

"Better for the young stock," Cenarth said.

Katerin let the others around the fire chat about the day's travels. Metkyi wandered off to talk to some of the drovers from Wickmasa. The fire felt good on her chilled body.

Doesn't take long to get out of the traveling mode. At least Mira's still in better shape than I am.

She did wish there was a way to get warmer before going to bed.

Metkyi came back and jostled her elbow. "Some of us are going to a hot spring. Interested?"

"Is it safe?"

"We won't be the only ones there. I checked. Orelyets has a group set up to go to the springs, and we're in it. That is, if you're interested."

"I am."

"Then let's go. Bring your bow. I've already got a bag packed."

"You were pretty sure of me going."

He shrugged. "I would have gone anyway. It's worth it."

They slipped away from the fire, stopping to pick up Katerin's bow and quiver from the tent before joining a small group of Wickmasa drovers and Kwellet at the edge of the camp.

"This spring is that big?" she asked.

Metkyi shook his head. "No. We'll take turns guarding each other. Five in at a time, five guarding."

After a short walk down the side of the canyon, going single file for the last steep, icy stretch, they reached a small pool on a ledge above the Wickmasa River, now a creek below them. While five riders quickly lit a fire, then took up a watchful stance, Katerin, Metkyi, Kwellet, and two women she didn't know from the drovers tied up their hair, undressed, and slid into the steaming pool. It was about waist deep, with a shallow bench that allowed Katerin to sit with the water up to her chin and remain warm. The water was pleasantly warm and the firm mineralized soil lacked the muddy clay of other hot springs Katerin had used over the years.

Metkyi wrapped an arm around Katerin and they leaned into each other, letting the warmth seep into their bones. Until now, Katerin hadn't realized how cold she'd been all day. The warm water eased the bite of the cold and made her relax. She could almost fall asleep.

"So is this the place *she* was talking about, where we'll meet our advisor?" she asked Metkyi.

"No. The place *she's* talking about has the pools under cover. Quite the fancy place."

"Huh," Katerin said. "So it's in Larij, proper?"

"Over the river. About a day's ride over, actually. Two days more from here, in good weather."

"I wouldn't know. I've never been this far north and west."

"Never?" he asked.

"Wickmasa's the furthest west I've ever been."

"And here I thought that I was nowhere near as traveled as you."

"Most of my traveling after I came to the House has been on my healing circuit. Winters, I've not had the wherewithal to travel without being paid by the House, and I've not had a lot of time. Healing House responsibilities."

"So this is new to you."

"Yes."

He was silent for a moment. "I'm glad I'm seeing it with you," he whispered.

Katerin smiled. They sat quietly for a time longer, Katerin's eyelids drooping.

Then Metkyi gently shook her. "Our time to get out. Stay in until I call. I'll get the clothes."

As he and the others got out, the water sloshed around and the level dropped slightly so that Katerin's shoulders were exposed. The cold woke her with a start.

"I'm ready," Metkyi said. She moved quickly into the cloth he held. The cold on her warm body roused her even more, and she hurried to get dressed, then pick up her bow and stand guard.

The others didn't seem to linger as long in the pool as they had. The walk back was cold, but failed to completely chill Katerin again. As they got back to camp, and headed toward their group's campfire, another group heading for the spring passed them. Orelyets stopped Metkyi and Katerin just before the fire.

"You two have the watch shift just before dawn," he told them. "Every two days, starting tomorrow morning."

"We'll be there," Metkyi said.

"You're the last before wakeup call, so you won't need to wake up your successors." Orelyets trudged on.

They stopped by the fire. No one else seemed to be in a talkative mood, so they warmed themselves further, then said their good nights and went to their tent.

Tired as she was, Katerin roused enough to respond to Metkyi's caresses. When they were done, she drowsed off in his arms.

Scratching on their tent door woke her.

"It's time," Kwellet said.

"We'll be there," Metkyi answered.

They dressed quickly. Katerin grabbed her sword and bow, and she noted that Metkyi had his short sword tucked into his belt as well as his firebrands.

They climbed out of their tent and into the dark. Kwellet handed Metkyi a non-magical torch.

"Not much going on," Kwellet whispered. "Herd's quiet, drovers have their own night watches running. Few coyotes howling earlier, no sign of wolves."

"I've had enough of wolves for one winter," Katerin said.

Kwellet laughed, keeping his voice soft. "Agreed. Even *normal* wolves, not the Hunt. But it looks good right now, for watch as well as weather. No sign of clouds in the sky. Cold as Nitel's heart out here, but clear. We might just get another good travel day out of this weather break."

"I'd be surprised if we get even that," Metkyi said.

"As long as there's enough clear weather to get over the pass today without a storm, I'll be happy," Kwellet said.

"As will be my uncle."

Kwellet trudged away. Katerin and Metkyi walked the circuit of the camp. They nodded at the night watch near the horse herd. Katerin took a second to look for Mira's light gray form, over to the side with the rest of the daranvelii.

Darkness faded away in small increments. The dulling of the weaker stars signaled the change, until only the brightest remained. A coyote lifted a voice in song over on a neighboring ridge as the sky paled further, followed by others of its kind. Red-gold light spread from the eastern edge of the horizon, sparkling on the faint wisps of clouds beginning to ease in from the southwest. As the light expanded, the drovers snarled and cajoled while they scattered feed for the horses, mules and daranvelii.

Metkyi stared at the clouds to the west, frowning. "With any luck, we'll be over the top and halfway down before it starts. Another storm. Maybe as big as the last one. Looks bigger than Orelyets and I figured when we planned this stretch. I'd better let him know."

She nodded. "Caravan planning's one of your duties?"

"Staul of the Balance also considers the weather. It's easier when I'm along, but Orelyets always asks me about the weather before he sends out a caravan." He paused. "Looks like Orelyets is stirring. Once he's up, we'll be off duty. I'll check in with him."

"Then I'll start packing."

Metkyi shook his head. "Not this morning. That'll be taken care of for us. We're in the second breakfast group. Get something to eat, then tack up. It's a privilege for being on night duty. Tomorrow we'll have to pack up right away and be on third group breakfast, but not on our duty morning."

Katerin nodded. They waited near Orelyets's tent. Katerin saw light and shadows of moving figures inside the back of the cook tent. Her stomach rumbled. "Sorry."

"Go. Get your food. I'll be right there."

"You sure?"

He jerked his chin toward the tent. "There's Orelyets coming out now. I'll be quick."

"All right."

Katerin trudged over to the cook tent. The drovers were finishing off their breakfast around a fire in front of the tent. She went inside and got a tin plate filled with pancakes and breakfast steak as well as a cup of tea, then joined the drovers around the fire, setting her tin cup on the ground. Soon Metkyi joined her.

"All good. We might catch a bit of weather but we should be over the top before the worst of it. We're going to pull out of here faster than planned, though. Luckily Orelyets planned for this possibility." he said. "I'm not surprised."

"Rolling out faster?" one of the drovers asked, kneeling to pick up his cup.

Metkyi nodded, gulping down a pancake. "He's gone to get the main camp up."

"Better get moving then," the drover grunted, flicking his last drops of tea into the fire. "Kenat! Take the dishes and give the cook crew a hand." He handed his plate and cup to a younger man who silently gathered plates and cups from the drovers as they filed off, following the first drover.

"We'd probably better get going, hmm?" she asked Metkyi.

"We've enough time to drink tea. They'll still have to clear the stove coals. Can't rush the kitchen."

They finished their tea and handed their plates off to Kenat. Katerin followed Metkyi to where their tack had been neatly piled, along with the bags from their tent. She made sure that her saddlebags carried what she'd need for the day, then nodded at the packer waiting to load her bigger bags. She slung her saddlebags over her shoulder and gathered up her saddle and bridle.

Mira met her after about thirty strides, snorting a morning

welcome. Katerin pulled a brush out of one saddlebag, quickly grooming Mira's back and belly before throwing the saddle on. Rekaré and Cenarth trudged by, their daranvelii already tacked. Shortly after, Senai dropped her tack and bags to saddle her daranval near Katerin and Mira.

"I've heard about these Wickmasa winter caravans, but never experienced them. It's interesting. The winter trips to Nere aren't anything like this," Senai said.

Metkyi stopped his horse next to Mira. "No other caravan is like this. Orelyets has a good system for winter travel."

"You've been to Chellni?" Senai asked.

"Two Midwinter Fairs," Metkyi said, half-frowning as he checked his gelding's cinch. "It's part of growing up in Wickmasa. All of us go along with at least two big caravans as help, no matter what our callings are." He shrugged. "We're traders. Taking kids along is how we identify who's going to travel as adults. We'd have more than drover and packer kids along on this trip, usually."

"Is it because of the dangers we're going to run into?" Katerin asked.

"The drover kids wouldn't be along if that were the case. No. We've inexperienced adults on this caravan, so no kids. I'm with you two, while Kwellet is with Yevtin and Eldoran." He pointed his chin toward where Yevtin and Eldoran were tacking up.

"I didn't notice that level of supervision yesterday," Senai said.

"We didn't have a storm blowing in yesterday," Metkyi said grimly. "We have to make it through the pass and down as far as we can get toward the Great River before the worst of the storm hits."

The call to move out sounded. Katerin swung onto Mira's back.

"So we both ride with you?" she asked.

"I'd advise it," Metkyi said, brushing her free hand with his fingertips, then looking over at Senai. "Things could get rough today. Stay close, Senai."

Senai nodded.

And with that, they were off.

* * *

By early afternoon, they had barely crested the high mountain pass above the timberline, and were making their way down the sparsely forested, steep northern slopes that plunged sharply toward the plains below. Yesterday's sun was gone, obscured by high clouds.

The wind came up strongly, and with it, a faint scattering of light, dusty snowflakes. Metkyi glanced at the sky.

"Now it begins," he said.

The passage down the far side of the pass was rougher than the climb had been, with fewer trees to break the wind. Several riders went back to help rope the wagon down the steep, narrow pitches. Riders who weren't helping with the wagon took the herd of loose horses, daranvelii and mules ahead of the main body of the caravan. Rekaré, Alame and Cenarth rode with the loose stock while Kwellet and Metkyi rode behind the herd with Katerin, Senai, Eldoran and Yevtin. Katerin wondered at the placement of the loose stock, then realized they were trampling a path.

Several times they halted as the wagon was eased down over the steepest of pitches.

The wagon holds us back.

Yet without it, they would need more pack stock and would not eat as well.

The world grew grayer as snow fell harder, driven by a stiff wind that swirled around them. Katerin adjusted her hat and scarf so that only her eyes were unprotected as the wind drove icy pellets into her face. It became difficult to see the trail.

Kwellet rode ahead of their group to guide them while Metkyi trailed behind, keeping them together. Katerin wasted no time in talking when Metkyi came alongside during his periodic check-ins with Kwellet. He always managed to sidestep the spotted gelding he was riding close and brush his hand against hers quickly before riding on.

The wind had a knife-edge to it as snow billowed in great clouds around them, so thick she could only see one horse's length ahead. Katerin could no longer tell what was earth and what was snow. Her head spun and she grabbed at Mira's mane to steady herself.

Should we even be out in this storm?

Then Metkyi rode by, sidling close to her.

"Not much farther!" he yelled. "We'll hold for the night in the trees!"

Katerin nodded. The cold and wind made it hard for her to breathe, even through the scarf covering her face. Metkyi seemed to sense her mood for he rode close, one hand steadying her shoulder. With him there, she could orient herself, even in the whirling world of white where she couldn't tell what snow was on the ground and what snow was in the air.

They had to stop for the wagon. Kwellet gathered them close, pressing their horses and daranvelii tightly together until their bodies touched one another. Metkyi reached over and brushed Katerin's eyelashes.

"Get the ice off," he told her, doing the same for himself. "Do it for your scarf, too."

At last they got the signal to move on as the wagon plunged almost into their midst. They kept closer together and it was easier to see the ground without getting dizzy.

They finally entered a stringer of trees. The brush and tall pine trunks gave Katerin a much-needed relief from the dizzying whiteness around them. The wind roared high in the treetops, but down low amongst the trunks it lacked the power it had in the open. They wound along the trail, and plunged into a small clearing where the loose stock gathered in a heavy timbered pen. Tents were already set up, three big long tents this time instead of the smaller tents.

"Big tents tonight," Metkyi said as they untacked and groomed before turning Mira and the spotted gelding over to the drovers. "Less work, easier to keep warm, and there's always a stock of poles at this site, handy for the big ones."

"Is that why we didn't have them last night?" Katerin asked.

Metkyi nodded. "These big tents need a ridgepole and side poles, at the minimum. Not possible to carry the poles. Orelyets always plans to use them as we come off the mountain on this side, and we have other pole caches."

He tossed back the flap door of the tent, letting her slip inside before him. The circle of people around the fire in the middle of the tent widened to let them in, and they clustered close, shivering. Metkyi put one arm around Katerin and they stood together.

Food that night was a stew, followed by warm water. After they ate, Metkyi led Katerin to their bedroll.

"It'll be warmer here than to stay up longer."

Katerin crept into the bedroll. Metkyi joined her, and they shivered until the combined heat of their bodies warmed the bedroll. She could hear the murmurs of others talking, but sleep seemed more important at the moment than anything else.

Wonder if we'll move on in the morning.

Metkyi stirred, as if he had read her mind. "We'll be here one night," he said. "We need to keep on moving. Tomorrow will be a long enough ride as it is."

"I was just wondering if we'd hold tight like we did with Rekaré and Cenarth in that storm."

"It'll get better tomorrow. This isn't a nasty storm like that one."

Katerin shook her head. "That whiteout on the pass was nasty."

"We're also higher up in the mountains. More exposed. You'll see tomorrow. Go to sleep now." His arms tightened around her.

I could get used to this, she thought as she settled comfortably into his embrace, and then reprimanded herself. *This is only for the season.*

But by all the Gods, it certainly seemed very sweet.

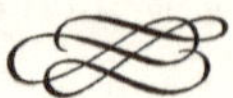

CHAPTER 28

Metkyi's prediction proved to be correct. The next day's snow came in a lighter pattern of flurries, then nothing, then flurries. They pressed on for another long day of riding.

That night they slept in the smaller tents again. The fourth day, they came to the Great River, the Chellana, and crossed it on a ferry, which took most of the day.

Katerin was surprised at the many groups waiting to cross on both sides of the river. At least one other party of their size waited to cross from the other side. Rekaré kept to the middle of their group, and buried her head deep inside her hood. Her features blurred the few times Katerin directly saw her face, masculine in shape and darker-skinned than Rekaré's normal shade, looking more like Metkyi.

"Our last day before the springs of Wixtnal," Metkyi said as they got on the ferry.

"I'm surprised at how many people are traveling in this weather," she said. They hadn't experienced the storms of the second day, but the snow still came down in a steady pattern of flurries with sunbreaks.

"Many people follow the River up and down its length this time of year. Besides Midwinter Fair, there's a lot of trading and visiting going on. People here are farmers. They have more time to visit in the winter, catch up on visiting and trading."

"Even with the weather?"

"It's not so bad, once you're off the mountains. It isn't always snowy at Chellni, and if it does snow, it doesn't stick around all winter. We're more likely to run into rain."

Katerin shook her head at that thought. She had rarely seen a winter without snow.

This night they slept in the big tents. The group in their tent was still their small core of Rekaré's followers, with the addition of Kwellet, his drovers, and the children.

"How long will we be staying at Wixtnal?" one of the children, a ten-year-old girl, finally got bold enough to ask.

"Two days," Rekaré said, breaking off the quiet conversation she'd been having with Cenarth. "Long enough to catch our breath, do some trading, and head out again."

"Oh." The girl sank back against another girl, and they returned to the whispering and giggling they had been doing while playing a stick game on the bedroll.

"What trading will we be doing?" Katerin asked Metkyi.

"Supplies and more trade goods for Chellni. We'll be taking advantage of the facilities at Wixtnal. Tomorrow night we'll get to sleep inside. Sound good?"

"Sounds promising. Maybe they'll have some baths that won't cost too dear?"

Metkyi laughed. "Sleeping inside *and* baths and soaks, my dear. That's part of what we'll be trading for when we get there. Once we leave Wixtnal and head for Chellni, we'll be pushing hard across the plains. The good news is that we probably won't run into a lot of weather. But we'll need to be riding pretty hard if we want a good spot at Midwinter. Wickmasa and Clendan horses and daranvelii are prized, but we need to be visible to make our best trades."

"So is Chellni Fair like Nere, with built stalls and such that a trader keeps from year to year?"

Metkyi shook his head. "No, it's a free-for-all. The Midsummer Fair is even bigger, though. Bigger races."

"There *are* races at Midwinter," Rekaré said thoughtfully, grinning at Cenarth.

"Not for you!" Alame said. "No better way of announcing your presence to Zauril! Too many people remember you taking Elantai to beat Zauril's man your twelfth summer."

"That was quite the race!" Kwellet laughed. He looked over at the children, listening intently to the adults. "But don't be getting any ideas! No racing for any of us. We'll attract too much attention."

"How are we going to set up?" Katerin asked.

"We'll use these big tents as our base camp," Kwellet said. "Once the word's out that Wickmasa's at Midwinter Fair, we will be getting a regular procession of buyers."

"We'll talk more strategy as we get closer," Rekaré said.

"Zauril's agents may be watching," Alame cautioned. "Once we're identified as the group from Wickmasa, we have to assume that we're being watched."

"All the better that we get there soon as possible, so that we select a place where we control most of the ground," Kwellet said. "So enjoy your time at Wixtnal, all of you. Carefully. We ride hard once we leave."

I thought we were riding hard when we crossed the mountains.

She wondered just what Kwellet meant by riding hard. Crossing the mountains had been hard enough. If the run across the plains would be harder, she had a hard time trying to imagine how that could be.

* * *

SHE HAD a taste of what that was going to be like the next morning. Rekaré and Cenarth seemed to vanish from amongst them before sunup, and Katerin couldn't see either of them as they left their campsite.

Instead of making their way amongst mountain trails, they followed a clearly marked road, at a stiff travel pace, alternating canter with long distances at a brisk trot.

During one of their rest breaks, Katerin suddenly noticed that Rekaré was back among them, talking urgently to Orelyets.

"Rekaré and Cenarth look like they're back. Any idea where they've been?" she quietly asked Metkyi.

"They rode out while we were at breakfast. We will see more of that once we leave Wixtnal. They'll come in later and leave earlier. That way, if anyone's watching our party, they won't be seen."

"But wouldn't they be noticed leaving alone, and be at more risk of an ambush?"

"Possibly. But it's a pattern they've found to work when traveling with a caravan. I don't think they ride on too far ahead. I don't know. I've not been among the riders who go out with them."

The order to mount up cut off any further conversation.

THE SKIES slowly cleared as they rode. At lunch break, the sun peeked through thin clouds. By this time the road had climbed from the creek bed it had been following to wind up and down the rolling hills of the plains.

"See that furthest ridge?" Metkyi asked during one of their rare walk breaks.

Katerin squinted toward the West. She could barely see a dark line at horizon's edge. "Barely. Why?"

"When we turn and make for Chellni after leaving Wixtnal,

the point of that ridge is our destination. We'll cross the Great River there and proceed down to Chellni itself. The ridge is on the other side of the Dry Line."

"The Dry Line?"

"Where the rain fades out. It rains much more on the other side of the Medvi Mountains."

"It doesn't seem to be that far away."

"Farther than it seems. We'll be a good five days riding, and nothing like this. I've seen Orelyets do it in four, four and a half days."

"I'll be sore by then," Katerin grumbled. "As if I'm not already."

Metkyi grinned at her. "Keep riding. We're almost to Wixtnal now. We've made good time today."

Then the order came to trot again, and Katerin focused on easing her aching muscles by alternating half-seat and posting.

At least Mira's holding up well.

If anything, Mira seemed to be more energized by the speed of their travel than tired by it. She was using her ordinary horse gaits, not the peculiar ground-covering quick glide of the daranval. Katerin suspected that if they needed to do that, the quick speed of the daranvelii would leave the ordinary horses far behind them.

Now I know why warriors ride daranvelii.

Orelyets rode back and swung his daranval around to match Metkyi's brown mare.

"Katerin, Metkyi. I'm sending a small group on ahead with Cenarth and Rekaré, to make arrangements at Wixtnal. You two ride with them."

"Understand." Metkyi urged his mare into a canter as Orelyets turned his daranval and headed further back. Mira broke into a slow canter as they followed Metkyi along the column. They dropped back to a trot alongside Cenarth and Rekaré.

Kwellet galloped up. "Ready?" he asked. At their nods, he urged his daranval ahead. "Let's ride!"

Unlike the fixed pace of the larger group, Katerin found the gallop of the advance party to be pleasant. Kwellet kept them slow enough that Metkyi's brown mare could keep up with the daranvelii. They paused at the top of a hill, and Metkyi nodded at the small town below, clustered around a stand of trees.

"The springs of Wixtnal," he said.

Katerin couldn't see anything special about Wixtnal, at least not from a distance, except that the valley around the small creek lacked snow. Even the snow on the crest of the rolling hills around Wixtnal was light.

They walked the rest of the way into Wixtnal, letting their mounts catch their breath and cool out. Wixtnal's buildings were mostly wooden frame cabins and two-story big wooden storefronts on river stone foundations, more like the Healing House and the buildings of Dera than the longhouses of Wick-masa. Some were small, obviously personal residences, and others were larger, with businesses lining several busy streets. One huge building dominated the center of the village. As they came into the main part of the village, Rekaré pulled up the hood of her jacket and huddled deep inside it. Her shape changed slightly, appearing shorter and thicker than she normally was.

Shapechanging skills?

Rekaré's own, or borrowed from Metkyi?

Kwellet entered one of the smaller buildings and came back out with a smaller, stocky man who, though dressed in what seemed to be the local attire of Wixtnal, moved stiffly in the leather clothing.

"We have two buildings for our party," Kwellet told Cenarth. "Go with our host. I'll take care of our animals.

"Should I help you?" Metkyi asked.

Kwellet shook his head. "No. Leave the horses and I'll take

them to stabling. Stay with Re—stay with the others. Both of you." He gave both Katerin and Metkyi a pointed look.

Metkyi nodded. Katerin dismounted, pulling her bags off of Mira's saddle and stopping to scratch her brow before slipping her a treat. Then she moved to cover Rekaré's side. The small man watched them, waiting, nervous tension radiating from his entire body.

"We can go now, yes?" he asked finally.

"Yes." Cenarth's voice held an edge Katerin hadn't heard before.

They gathered less attention as a party on foot than they had mounted. There were only a couple of groups of finely dressed young women bold enough to openly gawk at the other parties around them. These groups were accompanied by several older women who joined their charges in staring briefly at others. Katerin found that a disapproving scowl made the matrons draw themselves up huffily and herd their charges away.

A very interesting place.

She had never seen that many of the Larijian rich, especially their women, in one place before. Larij had its own Healing House, so their House rarely sent healers there.

They reached two medium-sized buildings. The small stocky man led them up the steps of the smaller of the two and unlocked the door.

"These are your quarters for the next two days." He bowed, handing the keys to Cenarth. "And these are the keys to the other building, for the rest of your party."

The door opened into a large, central room that ran the length of the building, narrowing about halfway through to a hallway with several rooms off of it. The main room had an iron stove and comfortable couches and chairs aligned around the stove. A table for ten stood close to one window, next to shelves that contained drinking glasses and cups.

"Thank you," Cenarth said. "We appreciate your guidance. What else do we need to know?"

The man glanced at Katerin, then stepped in front of Rekaré. Cenarth bristled and Metkyi tensed. The small man ignored them, his entire focus on Rekaré.

"Lady Rekaré," he said quietly as he dropped to one knee. "My name is Orlanden en Selail, and I am at your service."

Cenarth lunged forward but Rekaré stopped him with one outthrust arm, not even looking at Cenarth as she straightened up, flung back her hood, and glowered down at the small stocky man.

"How do I know you are who you claim to be?" she demanded.

Orlanden palmed her something small. Katerin thought she saw a flash of blue before Rekaré's hand wrapped around it. Then Rekaré opened her hand slightly. She studied what was in her palm for a moment, then nodded.

"She trusts you that much." She slipped the ring onto her finger, then pulled Orlanden up.

Orlanden blinked four times at Rekaré before speaking. "I got her out of Zauril's clutches in Medvare-the-city. I may have saved her initially, but I owe her as much favor as she owes me. More, even, for what she has done to help Haran over the years."

"I understand," Rekaré said. "Do you advise I move around openly, or remain hidden?"

"It would be wise." Orlanden measured out each word precisely. "It would be *very* wise for you not to move around openly. Even though your masking illusion is good, there are those here who could break through it if they tried."

"Thank you for that advice." Rekaré scowled. "So I'm to skulk here like I'm afraid of my own shadow?"

"No, not at all. Care is simply advised. You have your own private soaking spring in the back of this house," Orlanden said.

"You will not need to go out to the public soaking pool. No, the problem is that we have visitors who don't match where they say they come from. If you go out, be careful of the matrons around town. Not all are what they seem."

"Spies?" Cenarth asked.

"Possibly. Three months ago, Zauril sent a delegation to the Mershaunten, demanding that he turn over all information we have on Rekaré's doings since she disappeared, right after Haran's brother was newly announced as Mershaunten. We're more in favor with his brother than we ever were with his father, so the Mershaunten refused to do anything to help Zauril. As a result, we've had more spies roving through the country."

"Should we recross the river and go down the other side?" Rekaré frowned at the news.

Orlanden shook his head. "As I told your mother, the Saubral are stirring even greater than before, and the Medvaran army has become more aggressive in the Medvi Mountains and across the Chellana. By summer it will be open warfare, if not before. So far the Mershaunten has seen no need to support Zauril. We will try to keep it that way."

"I *knew* it was a good idea to move against Zauril now," Rekaré said.

"I agree," Orlanden said. "I have a small group of men to lend you, but more on that later. All is in readiness for your stay here, including simple food stores. I would suggest you send someone to the common house to collect your meals when it is time." He sighed. "Would that we could speak further but now is not good."

"And we will meet when? Tonight? Tomorrow?"

"Tomorrow," Orlanden said. "I have other obligations tonight. It would draw too much attention if I were not there."

"Tomorrow," Rekaré repeated. She took Orlanden's hands in

hers. "I am sorry for my impatience. I had hopes of doing more here—alas, it is not to be."

"Understandable. We will do our best to keep your stay here pleasant, but safety is advised."

Rekaré sighed. "Safety. I have had far too many discussions of safety—but never mind. That should not be your concern. Rather I would speak of good things. I have heard much of you, Orlanden en Selail. It is a pleasure to meet you at last."

"I've long wanted to meet you, Rekaré en Miteal," Orlanden answered. "I saw you as a small child. You have grown into a woman worthy of your mother's courage." He pulled his hands free and bowed low, his right fist on his chest. "I am honored to finally make your acquaintance. We will speak further tomorrow. Rest, and enjoy the hospitality of Wixtnal."

"We will," Rekaré said.

Orlanden left. Rekaré sighed, and looked around the room. "It is a comfortable place. A comfortable and *effective* prison."

"You wouldn't think of going out?" Cenarth asked.

Rekaré shook her head. "Orlanden is correct, deny it though I will. Much as I'd like to see how much Wixtnal's changed since we were last here, I think it's best if you and I stay in."

"There will be other times." His voice softened and Katerin felt uncomfortable as he stroked her cheek.

We need to give them some privacy.

She started to walk away, but Rekaré's voice stopped her.

"Metkyi. Katerin. Do you have a preference for rooms? Metkyi, I know you've been here, but Katerin?"

"I've never been here before," Katerin said. "I'll let you choose what you prefer."

A faint smile twitched Rekaré's lips. "Indulge me, and make the choice yourself."

Katerin glanced quickly at Metkyi.

"Let's look," he suggested.

"What do *you* prefer?" Katerin asked Metkyi.

"One down by the pool," Metkyi said. "Even with the robes they give you to wear to and from the spring, it's better to be close. Warmer. There'll be a slight smell from the spring, but I think the extra warmth makes it worthwhile."

"Show me."

A grin widened Metkyi's lips. "I thought you'd never ask." The room he led Katerin to was slightly smaller than the rooms closer to the front. But it was warmer, with only the faintest whiff of sulphur.

"It's really warm back here."

Metkyi grinned even wider. "The advantage of the room next to the pool. Do you like this room?"

"Yes."

"Then let's choose it." He slipped his bags from his shoulder. "I'll be right back. Don't go too far."

"What's going on?" she asked, but he had already left.

Katerin sat in one of the low chairs and pulled off her boots, then sagged against the chair back, slowly unbuttoning her jacket. Done for the day. Hard to believe it. She worked her toes deep inside her socks, letting the heat sink into her bones.

Metkyi returned with a bowl of nuts and dried fruit, a bottle of amber liquid, and two glasses. He set them on the dresser.

"I thought we'd fortify ourselves for the wait until the evening meal's ready. Rekaré and Cenarth told us to go ahead and use the baths." He grinned wickedly at her. "This'll be our last easy time for a while. Let's take advantage of it."

"If I wasn't so tired—" She grinned back at him, and held up her hands. He pulled her out of the chair and held her close, his lips seeking hers as he eased her jacket off.

She kissed him back as her hands worked with his clothes.

"Tired? Doesn't seem that way now," he chuckled into her mouth.

"The promise of a hot bath and soak, a little food and liquor, sleeping in a real bed, all that does wonders for my energy," she murmured back between soft kisses.

"Speaking of that bath, we'd better go," he said. "Once everyone gets here—"

"Understood." She stepped back. "Undress here or there?"

"There. Bath first, then soak. Then, after that—"

Her breath caught as she met his gaze.

"Yes," she said. "After that—"

Our last easy time for a while. I fully plan to take advantage of it!

She picked up her robe and followed Metkyi into the spring room.

CHAPTER 29

As Katerin had begun to suspect, *easy* was a relative term in an Orelyets caravan. She and Metkyi ended up trading goods in Wixtnal. None of the woolen goods they dealt were the magicked wear. Without it being spoken she realized those goods were being saved for Chellni. For Wixtnal, they traded fancy caps, scarves and gloves woven to attract the eyes of various wealthy ladies, but nothing she would choose to keep warm. Pretty things, not practical things.

At their third stop, she noticed something in the swarm of people. "Let's walk slowly," she said, trying to watch behind them.

Metkyi frowned, adjusting his heavier load. "I'd like to get our errands finished. I was thinking that after we get these things back to Orelyets, we could look around on our own."

Katerin tightened her lips as she confirmed what she suspected.

"We're being followed. Doesn't matter how fast we go now, I've figured out who it is."

"Who is it?" he asked without looking back.

"The woman from the first shop. Green jacket, brown skirt.

Should be with a group of girls. I remembered her jacket from yesterday; she was with one of those groups who stared at us."

"Damn. We need to hurry back and tell someone."

"Orelyets?"

"I'm thinking our *other* leader. You keep an eye on that person. This could be trouble."

As if we needed any more.

* * *

DESPITE THE SPY, Metkyi made careful bargains. The green-jacketed woman followed them to two more shops, sometimes stopping to gossip while Katerin tried to watch her. At least Wixtnal made regular use of windows and glass, more so than any other place Katerin had been. If she hadn't been so worried about the spy, she would have been enthralled by the sight of so much glass in the windows.

The spy seemed to have a number of friends.

Is this place safe for Rekaré?

Katerin fretted as the woman visited with several other matrons. With this group the woman didn't even bother to try to hide her interest in their activities.

Maybe she's just a gossip. But gossips made the best spies, didn't they? *Besides, what would make Metkyi and me interesting?*

Nothing except our ties to Rekaré.

Metkyi broke into Katerin's reverie. "I'm done. Let's go."

Katerin nodded. "She's been talking to a lot of other people."

"Just our luck, she's probably someone prominent from the Mershaunten's court. Wouldn't surprise me one bit. Not *here*." He took her arm as they stepped out of the store. "Instead of hurrying back, let's act like we genuinely were traders with a caravan. Bore her."

"I like that idea."

"Good. A bite to eat, and then we'll shop for ourselves."

"For what?"

"You'll see. Meanwhile, let's play up being newly bonded." He shifted his bags to one arm and slid his free arm around her back, pulling her close.

Katerin had to smile. "You're enjoying this."

"There's nothing else we can do. I don't want to head back to our lodgings with her on our tail."

Katerin leaned into Metkyi and relaxed into the role of newly bonded woman. They stopped at a street vendor and bought hot meat pastries, stepping a few feet away to eat them while Green Jacket fidgeted on the other side of the street, unable to find a good cover for lingering in front of a disreputable-looking, noisy saloon.

With his back to Green Jacket, Metkyi had the freedom to smirk at Katerin. "She's still there?"

"Yes."

"Good."

When they were finished, Metkyi put his arm around Katerin again. He took her inside a shop they hadn't visited while selling goods.

"I'd planned to visit this one after we took our purchases back to Orelyets. I'm not sure we'll get the chance to come back out, so I want to do this now."

Katerin raised a brow at him. "What are you buying here?"

"What are *we* buying," he corrected. "Do you like these?" He pointed to the dealer's case filled with rings and pendants. Some of the pendants were mounted on sturdy necklaces, others on simple chains.

Two necklaces caught Katerin's eye. One had a pale green stone set in a fine silver pendant that hung from a detailed, fancy-worked silver chain, with a matching ring. The other was a similar piece with purple, black and white stones.

"That purple set, I guess," she said finally.

"May I, Jeral?" Metkyi asked the dealer.

Jeral laughed. "I've only seen you drool over that one how many times, Metkyi? About time you brought someone in to try it out for you. Put that on her and see how it looks."

Metkyi delicately fastened the necklace around Katerin's neck. It was heavier than she expected, and as she looked down she saw that other gems beside the big, heavy purple stone were worked into the silver pendant; clear purple stones, freshwater pearls, and smaller versions of the original.

He took her left hand and slid the ring onto her fourth finger.

"It fits," Jeral announced. "Now how lucky is that, Metkyi?"

Metkyi smiled but didn't answer him. "You like it?"

"Yes, but—" It had to be expensive.

"Then it is yours. Jeral, do I owe you anything for this above what I have on account?"

"Not one thing," Jeral said, beaming at them. "We're even now."

"It's a pleasure doing business with you," Metkyi said.

"But—" Katerin started to say as Metkyi took her hand and led her out. "Metkyi, you can't."

They stopped outside the shop. "It's a bond gift," he said. "I owe you that."

"I have nothing for you. Really, Metkyi, it's too much."

"You've given me yourself. That's enough. I only wish I could do more for you. But Jeral's owed me for years, and now we're even."

"I can't do anything like it for you. I don't have anything—"

"You have who you are and what you've done for me, Katerin, and there's nothing I can ever do for you to equal that."

Metkyi kissed her. As he pulled back, he held his hand over the pendant. His eyes unfocused for a moment and he muttered a few words. The necklace momentarily warmed, like the Eye, then cooled, leaving her tingling.

"What is this?"

Metkyi's eyes refocused. "A gift." He blinked and twitched his head in one quick shake. "We need to get back to the others. Let's see if we can get rid of that old harridan first, shall we?"

"How are we going to do that?"

"I doubt Her Ladyship will want to traipse through the stables. Besides, we should check on our mounts and drop off our goods. Better at the barn than hauling them to the house, then back to the barn."

"Yes," Katerin agreed.

They strode off toward the edge of town. Green Jacket bravely wobbled after them, until Metkyi took a hard right and marched them between cattle pens.

"This is a short cut to the horse barns," Metkyi said.

"She'll know we went this way to get away from her."

"I don't really care. If we've been identified as part of our leader's party, then they know enough to connect us. Maybe we can confuse her into thinking we're not that closely tied."

"But what if someone else follows us?"

"Then they do. Look, there's the barn. Let's see if we can find Kwellet. Maybe he can send one of the kids with a message. You see her at all behind us?"

Katerin looked back, half-expecting to see Green Jacket struggling between the corrals. "No. No sign of anyone else interested in us. Yet."

"Figured she wouldn't try to follow us too far off the board-walks with the kind of heels she had on those boots."

Mira nickered as they walked into the barn.

—*Girls currying Mira, warm mash, good sweet hay, pushy bay stallion flirting over the stall door before getting yanked away* came to Katerin. Mira crowded the stall door, whickering softly as Katerin slid the door back.

"I'll look for Kwellet," Metkyi said.

He slipped in the stall after Katerin, though, and took a moment to scratch Mira's forehead and poll. Mira nuzzled

Metkyi gently, blowing soft breaths against his body, her mind quiet and calm. Katerin watched their interaction as she leaned against Mira's withers. She never had a partner before, at least not a seasonal bondmate, and she had heard how temperamental daranvelii could be about sharing their bondmates with human bondmates.

Mira, at least, did not appear to be one such. Either that or her past experiences as a war mare had taught her the tolerance that other daranvelii lacked.

Or she genuinely likes Metkyi.

For his part, Metkyi seemed to relax as he only did when he was completely alone with Katerin. Katerin could faintly sense his mind stirring, the same sort of contented thought pictures drifting from him as from Mira.

Metkyi straightened up. "I need to find Kwellet. You'll be here?"

"Yes."

Metkyi kissed her, then gave Mira's poll one last rub.

Katerin retrieved her grooming equipment. She checked the condition of Mira's hooves, pleased to note that someone had freshly rasped them and beveled the edges, taking off the roughs she had acquired scrambling over the rocks, even with magicked boots. Then she combed out Mira's mane and tail and braided the tail. No telling how hard this next section of the ride would be, and at some point she might want to tuck Mira's long silver tail up into a tight mud braid to keep it clean.

Someone knocked at the stall door.

"Come in," Katerin said softly, slightly annoyed by the interruption.

Senai slid in. "Good grief, but you two have stirred up more of a commotion. You were really followed?"

"Yes."

"What'd she look like?"

"Chunky matron with gray-streaked brown hair tucked

under a brown hat. Green jacket, brown skirt." Katerin frowned, thinking further. "She was wearing fine boots, green, again, with some sort of pattern worked into them. Couldn't tell the pattern, she was too far away, and they had high heels."

"Hmm. You weren't the only one she was watching, then. We got followed for a little while, too. But I guess Yevtin and I were more boring than you two."

"Where did she pick us up?" Katerin put away the comb for the mane and tail and brought out the stiff brush.

"I don't know. From what Metkyi said, once you two appeared in the trading section, she left us and glommed on to you two. Sounds like she followed you further than she did us."

"We left her on the other side of the cattle pens."

Senai laughed at that. Then she looked closer at Katerin.

"That's a beautiful necklace, Katerin. Wickmasa pays better than I think."

"I didn't buy it. Metkyi did. He said something about the trader owing him a favor."

"By the Goddess, Katerin, that must have been a huge favor!"

"That's not all." Katerin rotated the stone of the ring from the inside of her palm, where she'd turned it to protect it while she cared for Mira, and extended her hand for Senai to examine.

Senai shook her head as she peered at the necklace, then the ring. "By the Goddess, Katerin," she repeated. "That must have been some huge favor. This is much more than just a seasonal bondmating gift." Her voice went softer. "This is something you give to someone you want to bond to for life."

Katerin bit her lip. "I know that. And—he put a magic on it. He didn't say anything and I didn't either, but—"

"He means that much to you? Enough to leave the Goddess?"

"No, not that. He wouldn't ask that of me, no more than I could ask him to leave his God. But oh Senai, at first I thought it was no more than the Gods moving in us. Now I'm not so sure."

"What are you going to do?"

"I don't know. I just know that he means more to me than just a casual winter's relationship." She gulped. "But Senai, Medvare-the-city. My mother. What she said, just before she went into the dreamless sleep."

"I know, my friend. I *know*. You've told me about it several times."

"I'm not making any long-term plans until after Medvare-the-city. I can't."

"I understand. I think." Senai hugged Katerin. "And until then, if you can squeeze every bit of happiness out of life that you can, who am I to judge?" She slipped out of the stall, leaving Katerin alone with Mira and her own thoughts and worries.

* * *

As it turned out, she didn't have long to wonder what the reaction would be to Green Jacket. She and Metkyi had returned to their lodgings, delivered the payment for what they had sold, taken yet another long soak followed by quiet love-making, and had wandered out of the room ready for dinner to be met by a serious-looking council around the main table.

"How soon can you two be ready to ride?" Cenarth asked Metkyi as Katerin blinked at the urgency in his voice.

Metkyi exchanged a glance with Katerin. "We'd need to eat and change into travel clothing. Are our things even back from the wash? How soon would we need to leave?"

"Your things are ready," Rekaré said, her tone bleak. "It's not so dire that we need to leave right this moment, but in the middle of the night?" She glanced over to Alame, who nodded.

"The woman who's been following you is the wife of one of the minor Larijian trading functionaries who conducts business in Medvara's name," Alame said. "She sent out a report today, after you two dumped her near the cattle pens." He allowed himself a faint smile. "Fortunately, Orlanden has his own spies. *That* message got intercepted, praise be to the Gods. But he warns us that there probably are others, slower ones, that he might not be able to stop."

"So we need to leave tonight," Metkyi said.

"*Rekaré and Cenarth* need to leave tonight," Alame corrected. "I'm putting together a small party to ride with them. We'll go on ahead, leaving fast, then slow down after we get a good day's lead on the road, waiting for the main party to catch up. You and Metkyi need to be with them because Metkyi's giving Rekaré support and you're giving Metkyi support."

"But Metkyi doesn't have a daranval," Katerin objected. "How is he going to get away if we need to ride quickly?"

Alame scowled at her, and Katerin caught her breath, fearing what he would say. She half-expected Alame to say *He won't.*

"You can trail an unbonded daranval," Kwellet said. "I have a young mare who'll do that. One of our traders, but this is a higher need than trade."

"I don't have the credits," Metkyi said. "Not for a daranval."

"This one's on Keldara's account," Rekaré said tersely. "If I need you to keep up with us, the price of a young Wickmasa daranval is well worth it."

"She's been started?" Cenarth asked.

"Yes, she's been backed. Not a lot of training on her, but enough to accept Metkyi, especially if he has the opportunity to handle her before he tries to ride her."

Katerin frowned but said no more.

"So when will we be leaving?" Metkyi asked.

"Around midnight. You best eat and get some rest," Alame said.

"There's food on the sideboard," Rekaré said, her tone still bleak.

Katerin followed Metkyi over to the sideboard and dished

up. They ate quietly, then returned to their room. Their travel clothing sat on the bed, neatly folded. Metkyi laughed sharply.

"I guess this is it. Oh Katerin—" He reached out for her and they held each other. Then they broke apart and stripped off their town clothing to pack it away.

Katerin started to undo her necklace.

"Don't put it away. It won't fall off."

"You sure? It'll attract attention. And I'm afraid of losing it."

"It won't come loose. Jeral's work is stronger than that. And as for bandits, wear something over it," he said. "Just wear it. As a favor to me. Along with your Eye. It's not much, but I put a small protection on it. A favor of Staul. It won't harm you or your ties to the Goddess, but—it's a protection. I hope you don't mind."

Katerin smiled. "I wondered."

"I didn't have time to tell you." He sighed. "It needed to be done right then, without much talk, and I hoped you wouldn't be offended."

"That's all right." Katerin put the necklace over the high-necked inner softshirt that kept her warm while riding. The softshirt kept the necklace and the Eye from rubbing together.

They finished packing and laid out their outer clothing and riding boots, ready to be pulled on. Metkyi blew out the lantern.

"Let's get some sleep, if we can," he said.

They curled together in the bed. Katerin could tell from the tension in Metkyi's body that he was no more sleepy than she was. But she remained quiet, unwilling to stir the peace of the moment.

They must have finally fallen asleep. A scratch on the door startled Katerin, then Metkyi awake.

"It's time," Cenarth said.

Metkyi rolled over and took Katerin's face in his hands. He kissed her, long and slow and lingeringly.

"Now it truly begins," he said, as he pulled away.

CHAPTER 30

a faint silver moon half-obscured by clouds dominated the midnight sky as they gathered outside the stables. The moon spilled enough light that they didn't need lanterns to see. Katerin secured her bow on the saddle and checked her sword. After she mounted, Kwellet handed Katerin the lead to the young daranval, a small bay mare whose color faded to black in the darkness.

A very nice young daranval. Kwellet's not stinting.

The little mare was fully tacked, wearing a rope hackamore. The hackamore's rein was tucked over the horn of her saddle, a continuous rein that tied off at the knot under her jaw, although the rein extended further and was the rope Katerin held.

"She will follow Mira just fine," Kwellet said. "Have Metkyi handle her every time you stop, just in case. Won't be enough to bond until he actually rides her, and that'll depend on how they get along. Lightweight for him for the long term, but a daranval's a daranval and she's the best for your needs."

"Thank you," Katerin breathed.

"The Lady ride with you." And with that, Kwellet was gone, leaving six riders in the stableyard, herself and Metkyi, Rekaré and Cenarth, Alame, and a mysterious sixth that she suddenly realized was Orlanden en Selail.

Orlanden raised his free hand and pointed toward the west, spinning his dark bay daranval on her haunches to strike off in an easy jog trot. Alame fell in beside him, then Rekaré and Cenarth, both leading pack mules, then Katerin and Metkyi, the little mare between them. They jogged up the slope out of town and for some distance along the road, until they hit a straight, flat stretch along the top of a ridge. Then Orlanden urged his daranval into a brisk canter.

They jogged back down into a shallow draw, following the wide road alongside a creek, through brush and trees, carefully splashing through a partially iced-up ford before winding back up out of the draw. Once up top, they cantered again.

She eventually lost track of the number of times they climbed in and out of the little creek beds and alternated between jog and canter.

Finally, they walked their mounts while the horizon behind them began to lighten, a faint golden glow creeping into the sky. The western sky in front of them remained stubbornly dark purple-blue for the longest time before yielding to the glow.

The sun was barely over the horizon when Alame and Orlanden stopped in the middle of a large grove on the side of a ridge. Katerin sat dully on Mira, aware only of her fatigue as Alame and Orlanden whispered and pointed at what appeared to be two trails. Rekaré and Cenarth appeared to be as tired as she was, while Metkyi seemed changelessly alert as he watched Alame and Orlanden.

Alame nodded. Orlanden urged his daranval along the narrower trail, and Alame waved them ahead. The trail led to a narrow passage along a steep canyon wall just barely wide enough for one horse, daranval or mule. Katerin let the rope for the little daranval mare slip through her fingers until she held the knot at the end of it. She refused to look down, trusting that even a tired Mira remained sure-footed.

The trail ended on a small, forested ledge at the tip of a point overlooking a steeper canyon. Two large, heavy-timbered adjacent corrals took up most of the open space, with a huge, iced-over, wooden trough running down part of the center fence.

"We'll rest here," Alame said. "No fire. Animals in one corral. We'll move on in mid-afternoon. We won't see our friends for at least another day, and we should keep on moving in the dark as much as we can. Orelyets will push to catch up with us, don't worry about that."

Katerin was too tired to worry. She got Metkyi started with the little daranval before tending to Mira and helping with the mules. Then she lugged bedrolls into the cabin along with Rekaré and Cenarth while Alame and Orlanden organized food. By the time Metkyi joined them, the three of them had finished setting up bedrolls in the small cabin. Alame and Orlanden handed out oatcakes, jerky, and dried fruit. When they finished, Alame passed around a flask of fiery Larijian brandy. A sip was enough to relax Katerin's muscles and send her to the bedroll. Metkyi lingered up, scribbling in one of his books by the faint light of one of his small torches.

* * *

SHE STILL FELT tired when Metkyi shook her awake in the late afternoon. They ate more oatcakes, jerky, and fruit. She helped Rekaré tie down a load on the big black mule she had traded to Kwellet.

Then Katerin heard hoofbeats. Orlanden rode back, smiling.

"Your magic held, old man," he said to Alame. "Small parties on the trail, no one looked at our turning from what I can tell."

Alame snorted. "And just who's calling whom an old man, *old man?*"

"Compared to these youngsters, that's both of us," Orlanden said. "It looks good. We're still ahead of the caravan."

"Good. We should press on hard tonight, then ease back and let them catch up with us. By then any observers will have been taken care of."

They fell into a single file behind Orlanden on the narrow trail, Metkyi bringing up the rear. Once they were back at the road, without hesitation Orlanden picked up the jog and the group went into the formation they held the night before.

The sunset was marred by fast-moving clouds. They slowed after dark because there was not even the moon to light their way. Occasionally the clouds would break to let a moonbeam through, but it was otherwise a darker ride and, as the wind came up, full of shadows. Katerin's hands chilled in her heavy mittens when the wind rose in intensity.

When they finally stopped for this night's ride, this time in a camp down the creek from the trail, her stomach roiled suddenly. Katerin braced her hands on Mira's neck and breathed through her mouth. Her stomach settled. She slid carefully off of Mira and leaned against her.

"You all right?" Metkyi asked.

"Just tired, I think. The jerky might not have sat well."

"Want me to take care of Mira for you?"

She shook her head. "Go ahead and help with the bedrolls tonight. You've fussed with the daranval?"

"Oh yes," Metkyi said. "She's a nice little mare."

"Good. I'll do the rest of it."

But the work seemed longer and harder than before. Katerin trudged back to the cabin in the growing storm, grateful that this night Alame and Orlanden had ventured to light a small fire.

My monthlies are late. Maybe they're getting ready to start.

If so, though, they were starting without the preliminary cramping and headaches she was used to experiencing.

Maybe all this riding has taken care of that.

Once inside, she was tired enough not to object when Metkyi insisted she crawl inside their bedroll and eat there. Once she had eaten, she went to sleep, barely aware when Metkyi joined her after spending his time with his book, stroking her face gently.

If she dreamed this day, she didn't remember it.

* * *

"KATERIN!" Metkyi hissed. "We need to get going! *Now!*"

Katerin startled up. "What's wrong?"

"Orlanden's spotted Saubral on our trail. Mira started raising a fuss about midday, and it caught his attention. He went to check, and his daranval picked up the sign as well."

Good girl, Mira.

Katerin tried to reach out for Mira's mind, wondering why her mare hadn't contacted her, but got only a muddled impression of *danger, trouble, danger*. Mira was focusing on the danger and relaying what she was sensing to another daranval.

She jammed on her boots. Metkyi helped her secure the bedroll and slung it over his shoulder.

"Mira's tacked up," he said.

"Thanks." Katerin blinked at the snow as they emerged from the cabin. It had snowed hard during the morning and the snow was halfway up her calves; soft, loose, powdery snow, instead of heavy, wet stuff. And it was coming down at a steady rate.

She hurried over to Mira. The gray mare gave her an impatient nudge, then turned back to staring toward the trail. Katerin quickly checked the tack, felt the go bag of medical supplies fastened around her waist to make sure it was safe, and braced her bow, the chill of fear spreading through her as she remembered the attack that had sent her to Wickmasa.

She hung the bow from her saddle and mounted Mira. Once

up, she checked her sword and reached for the little daranval's lead, but Metkyi already had it in his hand. Katerin noted that his saddle and saddlebags were on the daranval and the little brown mare carried nothing but the saddle that had been on the daranval.

He means not to lose anything if he can avoid it.

That knowledge sent a chill through her.

"You keep track of your bow," Metkyi said. "I'll manage the daranval."

"You sure?"

"If I have to switch horses, I want to have her in my hand."

"Understood. I'll wait for you if you need to change."

Metkyi shook his head. "No. I can do a mounted transfer from horse to horse."

"Let's go!" Orlanden snapped, striking off down the brush-lined trail at a fast trot. They fell into a single file. Katerin tied herself into Mira's senses. It seemed to take longer and be harder to hook into Mira's mind.

—*There. Stinking buffalo dung stench of Saubral. Faint trod of Saubral houndrider trackers. Cold mineral reek of Shadowwalker.*

—*Strong Shadowwalker.*

At last they broke free of the thick brush, high on a canyon wall above a steep drop-off. The narrow trail pitched sharply downward. The gray light around them gave no clue as to what time of day it was, a flat light that blurred everything so that Katerin felt a quick tinge of vertigo until she focused on Mira again.

Orlanden picked up the pace to a fast canter, still a gait within the range of horse and mule ability but pushing it with the snow and footing. They had already dropped far enough in elevation that the snow was maybe about the depth of her ankle, but it was still slick, with mud underneath it.

Oh the Gods, if Metkyi has to try a transfer here—

Katerin focused on keeping her own balance steady on

Mira's back. The Saubral were gaining on them. Shadows grew. Sunset neared.

Oh my Goddess, please watch over us.

The trail flattened out and widened slightly. Hoofbeats gained on them, then Metkyi pulled beside her, riding the bay daranval mare.

"My mare's played out!" he shouted. "No choice!"

"Understood! They're close!"

"I know! I feel it too, through Rainin!"

Bonding's started. He knows her name.

Somehow the mules kept up with the daranvelii. Alame glanced back, and shouted something Katerin couldn't hear. The mules slowed, their leads dropped by Rekaré and Cenarth, and the other riders eased into the daranval fast gait.

Katerin and Metkyi dodged the mules and urged Mira and Rainin into the fast, floating gallop.

Ride. We must ride.

Katerin's gut tightened with fear. Even daranval speed might not be enough to save them. And with the mules went bedding, feed for the animals, and anything above emergency food.

The howls of the Saubral raiders rose on the canyon wall above them and ahead of them.

We're trapped.

Alame and Orlanden pushed their daranvelii into a faster, breakneck pace. Katerin clung tight to Mira, thrusting her heels down hard to help keep her legs steady on the mare's sides.

Run. We must run.

Howls from in front of them. Even closer howls above them. They were trapped.

Mira skidded to a halt. Katerin sat up, heart pounding, sick with fear, swallowing hard to wet her dry throat.

"Shield!" Alame barked. Mira plunged toward the others, responding to his command. Katerin clung tight as they spun to face the Saubral charging down the rocky hillside toward them, fanning out to form a semi-circle with the only escape a straight plunge over the edge of the cliff behind them.

Rekaré and Cenarth drew their swords while Metkyi lit a firebrand, his sword in his other hand. Rainin snorted at the fire but kept close to Mira. Katerin nocked an arrow and watched for the Saubral to come closer. Maybe she'd get the Shadowwalker.

One of the houndriders came within her range. Katerin breathed a prayer to the Goddess, took aim, and fired at the giant hound. The arrow caught flame en route and hit the hound dead center. A second shot put down the rider, setting off a chorus of howls from his companions.

"Good shot!" Metkyi bellowed, half-transformed into the Voice of Staul. Katerin shivered as she glanced over at him, glad he was with them and not with the Saubral. Amazingly, Rainin stood steady, not flinching as Metkyi transformed.

Where's the Shadowwalker?

Another arrow, not hers, not magicked, found a target in a hound and tracker coming at them from the other side. Orlanden cheered and brandished his bow before nocking another arrow.

Two archers. Maybe we can keep them back.

She fired again, twice quickly at a hound and tracker venturing closer than the others, and hit the hound but not the tracker.

Then chills ran all over her, and Mira half-reared, screaming defiantly. The Shadowwalker crested the slight rise above them. A *major* Shadowwalker, Katerin realized with a sinking fear. The Shadowwalker's magic crashed over her joined awareness with Mira like an avalanche, paralyzing Katerin's thoughts, tightening her chest so she couldn't breathe. Even Mira couldn't seem to hold solid against this Shadowwalker.

We're going to die here.

All those years, all those people protecting Rekaré, all those sacrifices in vain.

Then Alame leaned low over his daranval's neck and charged uphill, Aireii magic dancing in bright shades around him.

"For Delian!" he roared.

Next to Katerin, Rekaré cried out and Mira plunged forward without being cued. Rainin matched Mira's strides as she clawed her way uphill, while Metkyi—Katerin dared one glance, then looked away. She wasn't sure what was more frightening, the Shadowwalker or *their* Voice of Staul.

Alame slammed his daranval into the giant red stallion the Shadowwalker rode, screaming as he swung his sword. The Shadowwalker fell back, momentarily losing his balance as he tried to fend off Alame.

For one crazy moment Katerin thought Alame could knock the Shadowwalker onto the ground. Then Alame's daranval overbalanced and fell. Alame pulled the Shadowwalker off of his horse. They fell clear of horse and daranval, rolling free. Alame landed downhill from the Shadowwalker. He lunged at the Shadowwalker.

Katerin could barely restrain an enraged Mira from charging the Shadowwalker, unwilling to risk interfering with Alame. Rainin followed Mira's lead, snorting and squealing, lunging against Metkyi's hands on the reins, burning with the instinctive daranval hatred of Shadowwalkers.

Alame and the Shadowwalker broke apart, Alame on the uphill side. The Shadowwalker circled around, trying to move Alame. Blood oozed from Alame's chest and shoulder. Rekaré groaned softly from behind her, and Katerin risked a glance back. Rekaré, Cenarth and Orlanden held the remainder of the Saubral at bay, although the Saubral seemed more interested in the battle between Alame and their Shadowwalker.

The Shadowwalker feinted and Alame stumbled, recovering quickly, but not quickly enough.

He'll be down soon. Maybe I should let Mira go after the Shadowwalker. No. Too easy to get in Alame's way.

She wanted to nock an arrow, wanted to pull her sword, wanted to do *something*, but she had to hold Mira back. No hands free.

Alame and the Shadowwalker engaged again. Alame stabbed one hard thrust into the Shadowwalker's gut with both hands slashing high and hard before dancing back, sword in hand.

That's it. He's done it.

Exultation rushed over Katerin.

The Shadowwalker bellowed, half in pain, half in rage as his guts spilled out. Somehow managing to keep moving, he raised his sword high. Alame stepped back and to the side as the Shadowwalker brought his sword down two-fisted. And then, with an uncannily swift twist, the Shadowwalker thrust his sword into Alame's chest up to its hilt. He followed the blow with a mighty kick that sent Alame rolling down the canyon wall. The Shadowwalker bellowed in victory, shaking his fists above his head even as his guts spilled free.

Tears flooded Katerin's eyes and she released Mira, dropping bow and arrow to pull her sword, to kill the Shadowwalker or die herself, rage filling every piece of her being. Rainin followed Mira.

The Shadowwalker broke off his victorious shouts as Mira and Rainin lunged at him. He ducked underneath Mira's neck and staggered downhill toward his stallion. Mira and Rainin turned to follow.

And then Katerin was fighting Mira to a halt as best she could.

Rekaré stood between the Shadowwalker and the red stallion, her sword held high. The Shadowwalker, whose attention had been on the daranvelii behind him, tried to stop, and slipped.

Rekaré's sword neatly separated the Shadowwalker's head

from his body before he finished falling, sending it flying down the sloping hillside and over the cliff.

"Don't let those bastards get away!" she bellowed, her face seeming to take on an aspect of Nitel. "Make them pay!"

Their pursuit was short. They brought down the rest of the Saubral quickly. Katerin whirled Mira back toward Alame's crumpled body, not wanting to think of what she'd seen in Rekaré's face.

He's Aireii. He's of the House of Miteal. With the magic in his blood, if anyone could survive that, he could.

But she knew better. His daranval nudged forlornly at Alame's torso, trying to rouse him. Katerin checked pulse, checked breath, in spite of the contorted angle of the neck and the blood. Sometimes, just sometimes despite all odds, life still endured in these circumstances, and they did have Metkyi with them, as well as Rekaré. Between a priest of Staul and Aireii magic, maybe even a hopeless case could be reclaimed.

The hairs on her neck stood up as magic flowed. Alame's eyelids flickered briefly, staring straight up into hers. He struggled to lift one hand and she took it, shaking suddenly as magic of a strength she had never felt before poured into her.

"Daughter," Alame breathed. "Watch over her for me, my daughter."

"I—I," Katerin gasped, knowing somehow it was true, as his eyelids flickered one last time. She struggled for breath as her father's deathgift of a magic she hadn't the faintest idea of how to manage and control swarmed over her, her limbs trembling as she realized this power was her legacy.

He was my father. But how?

Someone knelt beside her. She looked up into the unfamiliar face of the Voice of Staul in full aspect, her new magic giving his strength a glory in crimson and black and purple that she had not been able to understand until now.

"Metkyi," she groaned. "Can *you* do anything?"

Metkyi elbowed her aside and took Alame's head in his hands. For a moment he held it firmly, then sighed and touched his forehead to Alame's, muttering something she couldn't understand. The fires of Staul blazed about him in shades of red and purple. Then he eased Alame's head to the ground and yanked the Shadowwalker's sword out of Alame's body. He held it high and chanted deep rolling phrases that sent tremors through Katerin's body.

Light flashed. The sword disappeared. He continued to hold his hands high, chanting.

Then he stopped. He took three deep breaths, and was Metkyi again, face pale and drawn as he closed Alame's eyelids.

"Walk in peace," he groaned. "Rest now, last prince of Miteal. You did your best."

Rekaré knelt beside her great-uncle. She bowed low over him, pressing her head to his body, shaking as if sobbing but no tears or sounds of tears coming forth.

Then she rocked onto her heels, tossed her head back like a wolf's, and screamed, pain, rage and sorrow all twined together into one voice. Her keening sent cold shivers through Katerin as she noted the greater resemblance to Nitel.

Rekaré drew her knife and hacked at her braid. Her hands faltered halfway through the first jagged cut.

Katerin took the knife. "I'll make it an even cut. Takes two hands."

Should I cut hair for him? she wondered. *No,* she decided. If it were even true that he was her father. No, she would not feel this power stirring within her if it wasn't so. *This will be my cutting hair.*

"Thank you," Rekaré gasped. She wiped her eyes, twice, as Katerin finished. Then she reached out her hand for both braid and knife. Katerin gave her the knife first, then the braid.

Rekaré stroked the braid, kissed it, then threw it onto Alame's body. Her body trembled as if she were sobbing, but no tears spilled from her eyes as she mouthed something Katerin could not hear. Then Rekaré stood and frowned at her companions, her face no longer shadowed by Nitel's visage.

"They will pay for this." Her voice was hoarse and raspy at first, steadying as she continued. "*They will pay*. Katerin, Metkyi. Find our mules. Orlanden, Cenarth. Build him a cairn. We go on. But not to Chellni."

The chill in Rekaré's voice froze Katerin. She *saw* the power spilling from Rekaré.

"My lady, we planned to go to Chellni," Orlanden said. "We'll have aid."

"No more time. More people won't do us any good. We go to Medvare-the-city from here." She glared at them. "*We go to Medvare*," she repeated. "For what I have to do, five is as good as five hundred. Maybe even better. *We go to Medvare*." Her voice trailed off into a choked sob.

The rage in her eyes kept them from arguing with her.

CHAPTER 31

They found the mules pawing through the snow for grass not far from where they had been turned loose. Metkyi's horse was not with them. He cast around in the snow until he finally came up with her bridle. He plunged down the hillside until he reached the cliff's edge, looked over, and shook his head. He struggled back up the hillside. Rainin nervously picked her way down to him. Katerin heard him softly praise Rainin, gently urge her around without slipping, and get her started back uphill. He fell to his knees. Rainin stopped, looking distressed. She hesitated, then carefully, precisely, backed up until he could grab her stirrup to help him stand. This time he held onto the saddle, and they climbed back up to the trail.

"She went over the cliff," he said, swinging back up on Rainin. They rode side-by-side down the trail. "She must have collapsed and rolled over. The pace we were keeping was too much for a horse, even a big-hearted horse like her—I think she was going down when I jumped to Rainin. Doesn't seem to affect *these* beasts, though." He popped the rope almost too sharply on a mule as he grabbed a bite of grass. "We better get

291

back to the others quickly. We need to find shelter—and take care of other things."

"Do you think Rekaré took any taint?"

"I don't think so," Metkyi said. "That was a clean kill. The Shadowwalker didn't touch her at all. I'm amazed she had the strength to kill him that easily. Neither you nor I could have lopped off his head like that. Not physical strength. He had too much magic."

"Maybe Alame's death gave her enough power. Alame shouldn't have had the effect on the Shadowwalker that he did." She hesitated to mention the look of Nitel on Rekaré's face.

"True. The power that Shadowwalker had!" Metkyi shivered slightly. "You and I are the only ones after Alame's death who might have had the strength to affect him. Not Rekaré."

"*I* wasn't strong enough." As the trail narrowed, Katerin urged Mira ahead, and turned her head back toward Metkyi, trusting Mira's surefootedness.

"Neither was I," Metkyi said. "So neither one of them should have been, either. He did say, *For Delian*. Alame recognized the Shadowwalker, and Delian was killed by a Shadowwalker near here. Vengeance. And he was Aireii, of the Miteal. Don't underestimate the power of the Goddess's kindred."

"So Rekaré is probably clear from Shadowwalker taint."

"She's clear," Metkyi said firmly.

Katerin nodded. "Her reaction makes me wonder."

"Grief," Metkyi said grimly. "Even before she rode with him for these past five years, he was still dear to her."

"But that much power?"

"I don't know." Metkyi frowned. "I saw something else in her face. And there's more." Metkyi urged Rainin up close to Katerin and Mira. "You now hold Alame's magic. Why would he choose you?"

"Metkyi," her voice caught. "I don't understand it. He called me *daughter*, before he went. But how can that be?"

Metkyi studied her carefully. "It could be. I hadn't seen it before, but it could be."

"Oh Gods, Metkyi, what does this mean?"

"If it's true, you're cousin to Alicira and Rekaré. What that means beyond the blood tie is what *they* will decide. No one else can say."

Katerin nodded, unable to find words.

They climbed a rise in the trail that Katerin hadn't remembered from the chaos of flight, and spotted Rekaré, Cenarth and Orlanden, gathered around a rock cairn on the edge of the cliff. Alame's daranval stood by the cairn, head lowered, his left foreleg bowed, not bearing weight.

"We're almost done," Orlanden said as he came to meet them. "But Rekaré thinks the daranval may be tainted."

"I'll check," Katerin said.

"Thank you."

Alame's daranval raised his head slightly, staring at Katerin with dull eyes. She noted the gashes on his neck from the Shadowwalker's red stallion and eyed his left foreleg. He'd taken an injury there.

He was a risk.

—*Black stallion with faint scent of Shadowwalker,* came from Mira.

Katerin looked at Metkyi and shook her head.

"Do you want help?" he asked.

"I need a cross-chant. The taint hasn't started to work on him, but I want the protection."

"I'll gladly do that," Metkyi said.

"No hope?" Cenarth asked. Rekaré stood silent and tall behind him.

"No hope."

"Then let it be done quickly."

Katerin took the black stallion's reins. He reluctantly limped away from Alame's cairn. Katerin's throat tightened as he stumbled along for two steps, and despite the risk of potential contamination, she ran a hand down the left foreleg.

A small fracture in the cannon bone, just below the knee. Her new awareness gave her a greater picture than she had ever had before.

We'd have needed to put him down anyway.

In some small way that made her feel better. She dropped the reins. No need to make him go further.

"Katerin?" Cenarth asked.

"He's injured," she said through the rising ache in her throat. "Broken cannon bone. It's not his fault he took on the taint, and I'm not going to make an honest daranval move any further when it hurts him." She fumbled in her medical pouch for a powder to dull the stallion's mind and blew it into his nostrils, whispering reassurances as he raised his head, eyes widening. Then he shuddered and lowered his head, heaving a deep sigh.

Metkyi handed Katerin a bone-handled knife with a short, sharp curved blade. She checked it on her own hair, cutting loose a small hank, more than was needed.

My way of cutting hair for both daranval and rider.

She blew another pinch of the powder into the stallion's nostrils to ensure he would not resist, before she carefully closed the small leather bag and tucked it away. Then she raised the stallion's head, chanting a soft magic to further dull his mind and his reactions. Metkyi joined her in the chant. As the stallion's eyes glazed and he swayed, she quickly slit his throat, still chanting, distantly noting that blood and not green goop oozed from his throat.

She eased the stallion's head down as his legs buckled. As she straightened both Mira and Rainin rumbled deep in their throats.

Katerin drew the protective circle, then let Metkyi call down the red fire from Staul to honor the stallion's sacrifice. His body was consumed immediately.

The ashes cooled quickly due to Metkyi's magic, and, still chanting, Metkyi and Katerin spread them over Alame's cairn. Then Metkyi rested his hands on Katerin's shoulders.

"I need to check you," he said. "Just in case."

She nodded, closing her eyes, opening herself to his influence.

His lips brushed against her forehead.

"You're clear."

"Let's go," Orlanden said. "We need to find a better place to spend the night."

They mounted and set off down the trail, dropping into the canyon until the snow thinned into a mix of snow and rain. They reached the creek at the bottom before they finally found a small, three-wall shelter with a tiny corral. Without speaking, they set up camp.

Katerin lingered with Mira for a couple of moments, leaning her head against her daranval. Too much had happened this day.

Alame's daughter? In truth?

A hand rested on her shoulder. Katerin turned to face Rekaré.

"Thank you for cutting my hair," Rekaré said.

Katerin shrugged, not wanting to say anything. Their eyes met. Rekaré's eyes widened, and she bent close to study Katerin.

"He gave *you* his magic," she whispered. "I didn't *think* I'd felt that leave us. I'd dreaded where it'd gone. But to take it you'd have to be—"

"He named me as daughter," Katerin groaned.

Rekaré put her hands on Katerin's shoulders again, pulling her closer. Katerin stared into Rekaré's blue-gray eyes, unable to look away as pale blue and gold lights played around them.

Aireii magic. I should be more afraid.

Her hands and arms tingled, a warm sensation arising first in her fingertips and then flowing inside, deep within her body. Rekaré's hands tightened, and she gave Katerin a little shake.

The tingling and warm snapped away and Katerin staggered to her right. She let out a deep sigh, unaware until that moment that she had been holding her breath.

"It's real." Rekaré traced spirals on Katerin's forehead and cheeks. "The magic speaks true. You're part Miteal. You're his daughter. But why didn't anyone notice?"

Katerin shook her head. "I don't know. I've been teased for looking Aireii-kin, for being so pale. But no one ever suggested my father was Aireii!"

"And no one ever suspected." Rekaré frowned. "It may have taken his deathgift for *me* to see it, much less anyone else. This changes so much. Why didn't he say anything?"

"I don't think he knew until we met. Though he did try to say something to me when he found out how old I was. I don't know why Terani never tried to contact him."

And why she never told me or anyone else who the father might have been.

Why? By the Gods, why had Terani remained silent? What would her new kinsfolk do? Katerin sagged against Mira. She couldn't stop trembling, couldn't stop the wetness coming to her eyes. It was too much to bear.

Father at last, and it's this.

"*Cousin,*" Rekaré murmured, her face softening. "Oh, cousin, I am so sorry. So sorry you had to find out this way, with his deathgift." She pulled Katerin into her arms. "Not a way anyone should find out about their heritage. I am so, so sorry."

Katerin gulped, her body still shaking. "I don't know what to do. Should I cut hair? I don't know what to do. I feel so strange."

"You are one of us," Rekaré said firmly. "You are kin."

"But the magic. I don't know what to do."

Rekaré gently eased Katerin away from her. "You know enough for now. You know how to feed the energy from it to me and to Metkyi. For now, that will do. Later, my mother and

Inharise can help you. Can train you. I just can't. Not now. I'm so sorry Katerin, but I have *so much* to do."

Katerin swallowed hard, feeling Rekaré's emotions and *knowing*, really knowing, the burden she bore.

"I will try," she whispered back to Rekaré. "I am of the Healing House. I do have some knowledge. I will do my best to help you, as a kinswoman of the Miteal should, though I know not what to do."

"That is all I ask." Rekaré gently brushed her fingertips across the raw edges of hair where Katerin had tested the knife. "And for now, this is enough hair for you to cut. There will be time later for full mourning."

"Will you tell the others?"

"If you want."

"Metkyi knows."

Rekaré nodded. "I'll tell Cenarth and Orlanden. Let's rest. And Katerin, there is one other thing you should know."

"What's that?" Something about Rekaré tightened Katerin's stomach.

"If I fail—" Rekaré's voice faltered slightly. "If I fail," she repeated, "then it will fall to you to take on Zauril. You will be the last of the House of Miteal. My mother." Her voice broke, then regained strength. "My mother can't do it."

She took one of Katerin's hands, and squeezed it tightly. "But I promise you this, Katerin, my new-found cousin, that I will do my best to not let it come to that."

"And for my part, I will do my best to ensure you don't fail," Katerin said.

Rekaré smiled faintly. "I was thinking I rode without kin. You don't know how much it eases my heart to know that kin still rides with me. The choice I had to make seems very far away, now. Maybe I won't—" She gave Katerin a quick hug.

They walked back together, Katerin wondering what Rekaré meant by *Maybe I won't.*

* * *

THE NEXT DAY they followed the creek bottom to the Chellana. As they drew near to the river, the snow turned to ice, then icy rain. It was sleeting when they reached the Chellana. Chunks of ice floated down the big river. Orlanden took the lead until they reached the main road, which descended from the ridges above the Chellana. He rode forward to check out the tracks on the road.

"No sign of a large party," he said.

Metkyi glanced downriver, frowning at the clouds hanging along the ridges lining the other side of the river. "Weather could have held them up."

"Weather or Saubral," Rekaré said. "How much further, Orlanden?"

"I know a small ranch where we can stay the night, just this side of the next town. Better than going to the roadhouse."

"Any shelter that's safe," Rekaré said.

"We might have to stay in the barn," Orlanden cautioned.

"Any shelter that's safe," Rekaré repeated.

Orlanden nodded, and they fell into line. Katerin wished for the shawl she left back in Wickmasa, to help her jacket repel the icy rain. But she hadn't brought it along, thinking that it would be more of a hindrance than a comfort on this fast, hard ride.

I could use it now.

She slumped deep into the minimal protection of her saturated jacket, shivering at the small drips of wet oozing in from the seams. She hadn't gotten a magicked jacket, figuring the cost to be too dear.

They trudged into the rancher's yard. Even Mira stood quietly, pinning her ears and tossing her head at the rancher's dogs swarming around her legs. Orlanden exchanged a few words with the rancher, then waved them forward.

"Our host's offered us a spot in the bunkhouse, and stabling for our mounts," he said.

"And a bite of warm food," the rancher added. "No room in the main house. Our winter hands have all moved inside, but we have biscuits and meat gravy tonight, and by the time you've eaten, the bunkhouse should be warm enough for comfort."

"Thank you," Rekaré said, throwing back her hood.

"Always a pleasure to do right by travelers with Orlanden en Selail," the rancher said. "You have further need, let me know."

Rekaré sighed and slid off of her daranval. Katerin took that as her cue to dismount, and followed Orlanden and the others to the barn. There, they stripped the tack and their supplies off the daranvelii and mules, and started to rub them dry. Two ranch hands helped them care for their animals, then carry their bags to the bunkhouse.

"Dinner's in the main house," the taller hand said.

Katerin cast a longing eye at their bedroll. Sleep sounded almost better than food, but warm food sounded better than the jerky and oatcakes that had been roiling her stomach the past few days.

Dinner proved well worth it. They sat to table with the rancher and his hands, plus two young children and the cook, who at her advanced age clearly was not the rancher's wife. A portrait of a woman who resembled the two children hung on the wall. The rancher noticed Katerin's study of the portrait.

"My wife," he said. "Died in the last plague."

"I'm sorry," Katerin said.

"We did what we could, including him," He nodded toward Orlanden.

"My friend, there wasn't much we could do. Even with help from a Miteal."

"Where *is* Alame en Miteal? Thought for sure he'd be riding with you, Orlanden. Always see you two together."

Orlanden shook his head slowly. "He rides no more, my friend. He passed on to the Dreamless Land."

"I'm sorry to hear it," the rancher said. "I still owe him a big debt for trying to help my lady. When did it happen?"

"Yesterday," Rekaré said sharply.

"Lady, I'm sorry to hear it." The rancher's voice faded and he stared at Rekaré, his eyes widening. "You—you're—*her*. His niece. The one the Saubral seek. You look like your mother."

"That is information you best not share with any," Orlanden cautioned.

The rancher bowed politely and deeply to Rekaré. "Lady, when I saw you, I recognized your Miteal kinship, though I knew not who you were. Now that I know, I and my people stand ready to help you."

"Thank you," Rekaré said. "Giving us shelter for the night is help enough."

"If there is more I can do?"

"Watch for a large party from Wixtnal. They've not come through yet?"

The rancher shook his head. "No. No large parties."

"Best to maintain a watch," Orlanden said. "We were attacked by Saubral and a Shadowwalker yesterday afternoon."

"And that's how the Miteal met his fate?"

"Yes. That Shadowwalker and his riders no longer roam these lands."

The rancher's lips tightened. "We'll watch for you tonight, and tomorrow send you on your way with any provisions you need."

"I thank you," Rekaré said.

"A pleasure, my lady," the rancher said.

Once dinner was finished, Katerin pled fatigue and fled to the bunkhouse. Metkyi came with her while Orlanden, Cenarth and Rekaré lingered in the main house.

"Are you all right?" he asked as they tucked into their bedroll, her back to his front.

"Just tired," she told him. Then, hesitatingly, she continued. "My monthlies are late, and I don't feel like they're coming on."

His arms tightened around her. "You've been taking your preventatives?"

She nodded. "And you?"

"Every morning," he breathed. "Those are supposed to work, for both of us. Except for when we were out after being chased by the Hunt. That—Oh. Katerin, what have we gotten ourselves into?"

"The Gods weren't supposed to have let it happen. Not that fast. I shouldn't even be feeling this now. It's too early."

"Not unless the Gods will it," he said. "Gods. Katerin. We should send you back to Wickmasa."

"No. I've not quickened yet. Until then, it's not a certainty. And I'm not going to leave now. I may be only half-Aireii, but Rekaré needs the power I carry." She shivered. "If she fails, it's now up to me."

"Damn the necessity," he whispered.

"We have no choice. We made our vows and pledges. It's against our honor to do anything else. Even more now than before."

"I *know* that. But still, damn our pledges and honor." Metkyi buried his head in the back of her neck. "I'm worried about you. Oh love, your power, your father, and now this."

"If it's meant to be, it will be. Don't tell the others, please. It's not real until the quickening."

"But still, I felt something when I checked you yesterday. That must have been the child. Your child. Our child." He paused. "*Our child*. Katerin, this isn't possible."

"I know," she whispered. "They tell us healers that the powders only help the Gods in their purposes. Not many Healers bear children, and I can't think of any who are celibate."

"As a Voice of Staul, I'm not supposed to be able to sire children." Metkyi stroked her cheek. "Oh Gods, Katerin, what have we gotten ourselves into?"

"I don't know. It scares me. My mother wasn't supposed to bear children, either. But here I am. Just like she was."

He kissed her. "Whatever comes, I'm with you. All the way. Understand?"

She nodded, and buried her head into his chest.

They said no more but lay there quietly, snuggling into sleep. Katerin barely roused when Metkyi left her to write in his journal.

* * *

THEY LEFT EARLY, after a sturdy hot breakfast. Katerin's stomach roiled at the thought of much more than a small serving of oatmeal and some ham. Metkyi quietly asked the cook to package up more ham and some biscuits. He passed them to her as they went out to the daranvelii.

"In case you get hungry further along."

"Thanks. But you didn't need to do that."

"If you're not eating much because your stomach's upset, that could explain some of the chills you're having."

"That, and the fact I was stupid enough to leave my shawl back at Wickmasa. It would have made a difference yesterday."

"Will today, for that matter," Metkyi muttered, glowering as a gust of wind blew icy rain in their faces. "Wonder if we can get one for you."

But there turned out to be no need to ask. The ranch hands produced heavy rain slickers for all of them, and wouldn't take payment when Rekaré tried to press it upon them. Katerin shrugged into hers before mounting Mira inside the barn, grateful for the covering the oilcloth material gave in addition to her jacket.

The storm eased by dusk. They found another rancher, and the pattern repeated itself with the offer of barn and a warm place to sleep, although this time there was no disclosure. The next few days blurred into riding and stopping at the small ranches and farms along the Chellana, steering wide to avoid the villages and towns, provisioning at their borders.

They saw no sign of Orelyets and the rest of the caravan, nor did they hear of any messenger that had been sent ahead.

It was nearing midday when Orlanden led them through a small town. The great dark ridge Metkyi had pointed out to Katerin back at Wixtnal now rose in front of them, the darkness caused by a thickness of trees she'd not seen before.

"The Dry Line." Metkyi pointed to where the thin stringers of pines and open meadows changed abruptly to thicker forests. "It marks the boundary of Medvara."

Orlanden pulled up, waiting for Rekaré.

"Chellni is over there," he said, nodding toward the village on the other riverbank. "This is the last ferry crossing until Medvare itself. Do we cross here, do we try to swim the river further down, or do we risk the ferry at Medvare-the-city?"

Rekaré shook her head. "I don't want to take the Medvare ferry. Even less do I want to swim the river. We cross here, but we don't stop."

"Understood." Orlanden rode forward to negotiate their passage.

Rekaré turned to them. "Tonight, we sleep in Medvara. We'll ride down the river for two, three more days. And then we'll be at Medvare-the-city itself."

Katerin shivered, and Metkyi took her hand, squeezing it gently. He angled Rainin so that he could bend over and speak to her privately. "It's not too late. You could stay in Chellni."

She shook her head.

Metkyi sighed, but said no more.

CHAPTER 32

For the next two days, they fought their way along the narrow, overgrown side trails that paralleled the main road. The rain in Medvara was no less icy than it had been further east, but it was damper and colder than east of the Dry Line.

We're not the only ones avoiding others, Katerin thought as they ducked off of the trail to let someone pass in the opposite direction. She was certain, at least twice, that other riders hid from them in the brush.

"I wouldn't travel alone around here like I do in Clenda," she murmured once to Metkyi, around midday of the second day in Medvara.

"You wouldn't want to." He shook his head. "It's a different land once you cross the Dry Line."

They stopped at a campsite near the Saktrin River, the river near the eastern boundary of Medvare-the-city, one that Orlanden knew that had shelters and a common well available for a small price. Other campers glowered at them as they rode through the area, looking for an open camp. They found a spot high above the water line, out of sight of the settlement on the other side of the river. When Katerin and Metkyi went for water at the common well, two other groups waited in the shadows of the trees around the well, not venturing close until the group before them had disappeared. One person filled buckets while the other stood watch.

"This doesn't feel right," she whispered to Metkyi.

"There's no trust in Medvara."

Katerin would have said more, but it was their turn at the well. She filled their buckets quickly while Metkyi stood watch, uneasily aware of the eyes on her back.

When they returned to camp, it didn't seem right to talk. She did her camp chores, then stood by the fire next to Metkyi.

Shortly after dark, a nearly toothless woman stomped by, demanding payment. While Rekaré and Katerin hung back deep in the shelter and Orlanden seemed to have faded into the brush, Metkyi and Cenarth negotiated for one night's stay.

When the woman had gone, Orlanden rejoined them. Both he and Rekaré appeared to be more relaxed and less tense than they had been before the crone had come by.

"We're here, my lady," Orlanden said to Rekaré. "What's our plan?"

"When I talked with my mother and my uncle, they both told me about my father's movement patterns. Mother's been gathering information on his movements for some years now. We ride upriver to the town of Saktrin. My mother told me it was a good place to make connections."

"It is."

"There, we gather more information to ensure Zauril's still following his old routines."

Orlanden cocked his head wryly at her. "What, you're not wanting to ride directly into Medvare-the-city and take Zauril on immediately?"

They all laughed at that, including Rekaré.

"No. They'd strip all of you away from me in a moment, and I'd choose to avoid losing my support, especially Katerin. I've lost too much already." Her voice trailed off.

"A wise choice," Orlanden agreed. "We gather information, and then what?"

"What we do next depends on what we learn," Rekaré said. "I'd prefer to confront Zauril away from the castle and his places of power. If we can find the right place, even if we're outnumbered, that gives me a magical chance."

"And if we can't catch Zauril away from the castle and the city?"

"Then we think about going into the city. To him. But that's a choice I'd sooner not make."

* * *

THIS PART of Medvara didn't look any better by the gray daylight. The trees and the brush were greener than Katerin was accustomed to seeing, and the trees were gray-barked giants in comparison to the redbark pines of Keldara and Clenda.

A land of gray and green.

The underbrush was thicker and taller than that of the eastern highlands of Clenda and Keldara, and the entire place felt damper and colder, water seeming to ooze out from the ground and plants as well as falling from the sky.

They headed upriver before dawn, following a broad trail that slowly opened up into shades of green and gray as morning dawned. The trail climbed to the top of a ridge to avoid following the Saktrin through a steep, short gorge. At the top of the ridge, they could see a short distance to the west before fog and clouds blocked their view. Katerin spotted the spires and buildings of a great city. She shivered, recognizing Medvare-the-city from the descriptions she'd heard and the sketches she'd seen in books. On the other side of Orlanden, Rekaré stared off at the city thoughtfully, chewing on her lower lip.

"Those spires are those of the house where your mother grew up, Rekaré, and your father too, Katerin," Orlanden said. "That's where I first met Alicira, a month before Zauril overthrew her grandfather and killed most of her family." He sighed. "Medvare-the-city, the crown jewel of Medvara. Or so it used to be."

"It's a grand-looking place," Katerin said.

Orlanden snorted. "It was grander years ago. See how the fogs lay low over the city? Zauril dares not use the magic that your family created and used. It won't respond to him. Instead, he uses coal and wood to power the machines. As long as Alicira lives and retains power through Rekaré, he can't use the magic."

"I thought it was just the yarn and the fabrics that she magicked and had control over," Metkyi said.

"She controls more," Orlanden said. "Much, much more."

Rekaré roused from her meditation. "If the Empire in Daran chooses to move against us, and my mother thinks they *will*—"

"Yes," Orlanden said. "*If* the Empire remembers you, would be best for all of us that Medvara's magic is revived and strong." He lifted his reins. "Meanwhile, my lady, we'd best be moving on."

"Yes," Rekaré said, a distant expression on her face. "We should."

* * *

THEY FOUND an inn at the edge of Saktrin. Once their animals were settled into the stable and they found their rooms, they gathered in Rekaré and Cenarth's room.

"Keep your voices low," Orlanden said. "I don't know how well your magics are going to work without drawing attention."

"I'm using a faint one," Rekaré said. "They'll hear us talking, but not clearly. You'll need to listen for anyone who might be skulking around out there."

"I'll try."

"So," Rekaré said. "This evening, we gather information. I have a couple of possible contacts. Cenarth and I will try to find my contacts. Katerin and Metkyi, survey the town. Orlanden—"

"I'm too well known to wander around. I'll remain here, perhaps take in what's being said in the tavern next door."

"Remember this is a garrison town," Rekaré continued. "I don't know if they'll be more on guard here than they would be elsewhere."

"More confrontational," Orlanden warned. "Cenarth, Metkyi, you'll need to be clearly bonded to Rekaré and Katerin to keep soldiers from them. The soldiers will respect your bonds if you're obvious about it. Medvara is more traditional than Keldara or Clenda about women's roles, so remember that."

"That will change," Rekaré muttered.

"We need to listen for any discussion of troop movements, or are we listening for discussions about Zauril?" Metkyi asked.

"Both," Rekaré said. "He comes here to review his troops. We need to get some idea of when his next review happens. Understood?"

They nodded agreement.

"Meet back here at ten bells."

"A bit early, my lady?" Orlanden asked.

"I'm not comfortable with any of us being out later. Not here. Even paired as we are."

Orlanden nodded. "Ten bells it is."

Katerin and Metkyi headed back to their room.

"You will be able to do this?" Metkyi asked Katerin as they changed out of their travel-stained clothing.

"As much as I'll ever be."

He gave her a tight-lipped smile. They took turns bathing, then Metkyi trimmed his beard while Katerin dressed.

She dug out the one good outfit she had packed, a gray woolen skirt with a high-collared white linen shirt and woven green vest with elaborate embroidery. Paired with a fresh set of leggings to wear underneath, she was warm and looked sufficiently feminine to match the Medvaran expectations for women's attire, if a little outdated.

Metkyi finished his trim and pulled on his clothes. Katerin brushed her hair and pinned it back with plain silver hairpins. He joined her in front of the mirror as she was finishing her final touches, and adjusted her necklace over her shirt. The necklace and chain tingled after he touched them. She smiled at his reflection in the mirror and his tight-lipped grimace softened into a true smile. He bent forward and kissed her cheek, then turned her for a deeper kiss.

She wished they could stay in instead of going out tonight. They hadn't had much quiet time since they left Wixtnal, and she could use a night's rest.

Metkyi seemed to sense her reluctance.

"You could stay in and I could go alone," he said.

Katerin shook her head. "It wouldn't be restful. I'd worry the whole time."

He laughed softly. "Ah, Katerin, Katerin. What are we going to do?"

"We'll have a good dinner. Walk about Saktrin, see what's going on, then eat. Look and act like a young newlywed couple from the country who're just traveling through. I don't look like a healer from Clenda, do I?"

Metkyi stepped back and carefully looked her over. "No. Do I look like a priest of Staul?" He spread his arms wide and minced in a circle, smirking.

Katerin couldn't stifle the giggle that burst from her lips as she surveyed his neatly fitted tan breeches, black linen shirt, and sweeping black coat. Newly polished knee-high black boots finished his ensemble, and the swoop of his carefully combed and braided hair twitched something inside her.

A handsome man. By all the Gods, how did I end up with one such as him?

"Of course not, unless you raise aspect!" she laughed. His clothes were a little old and slightly out of style, like hers. But nothing about them suggested that the wearer was from Clenda, although they looked like a couple from beyond the Dry Line.

"We need to have a story about who we are," Metkyi said, the lightness leaving his face. "We're part of a party passing through. Perhaps we should be from Nere."

"We'd need to explain why we ride daranvelii."

"We come from a trading cohort. We're passing through Medvara on our way to the coast, to check out supplies of dried fish. Nerean traders ride daranvelii."

Katerin gave him a quizzical look. "Dried fish?"

"Whale oil, then. Or we're headed for the Cooscol seaport to find an alternative spice route, and we also want to talk to the Cooscol about a new wine trade."

"Then why would we be coming through Medvara, and not going directly to Cooscol? Medvare-the-city is way north of Cooscol and Nere."

Metkyi grinned at her. "We're newly bonded, on our celebration tour. And our trading cohort back home in Nere gave us the task of checking out Chellni and Medvare-the-city as well as Cooscol before we came home. That would explain why we're going this way to Cooscol."

"Makes sense."

"And we *are* newly bonded." He took her into his arms once again. They kissed, then stood together for a few moments. Metkyi heaved a sigh. "Time for us to go."

* * *

IT DIDN'T TAKE LONG to investigate Saktrin's options. Two large, muddy streets ran parallel to each other for a few short blocks before they faded out on the edge of the village. Their inn was on the west side of the town, and the garrison buildings were on the east side of town. The food establishments and taverns on the east side of town were rough-appearing and not the sort of place that would appeal to out-of-town newlyweds.

They walked arm in arm back toward their inn, checking out what shops there were. Besides the obvious gambling, food and drink palaces, and whorehouses, they found a few cheap jewelry shops, blacksmiths, a dilapidated stable, two weapons shops, and several small general stores. It wasn't until they were almost back to their inn that they encountered the sort of shops that might be of interest to a couple. A tailor, a laundry that appeared to be of service to higher-ranking military officers, judging by the men they saw coming in and out, a larger general store, and some nicer-looking restaurants. A high level of nervous energy bounced around this part of Saktrin, and a lot of men seemed drunker than she would expect.

"It's almost like they're celebrating something," she said softly.

He nodded, keeping his eyes on one clot of soldiers who ogled her. "They're acting like they just got some good news, or got back from a tough campaign. But we've not heard anything about a Medvaran war, so something's up. Too many of them are in a celebration mode. If I didn't know better—"

She caught a flickering image of Rekaré in chains, and nodded.

"Yes. If we didn't know better, that's what I'd think it is. But I wonder what they're celebrating?"

"Maybe this is the place to find out." Metkyi nodded toward a sign advertising *The Victorious Chef—The Place to Celebrate!*

Katerin chuckled at the sign depicting an elegant-looking woman smiling indulgently at two dancing men.

"If it's not a brothel."

"I don't think it is." They stopped outside the door, eying the limited menu posted there.

"This work for you?"

Katerin sniffed at the enticing smells. "Doesn't smell too bad."

"Let's eat, then."

From the moment they walked in it was all Katerin could do to keep from walking back out. The restaurant was filled with Medvaran military officers far along on a drunk of epic quantities, shouting at each other while white-faced, trembling servers ran from table to table.

One of the servers spotted Katerin and Metkyi. But one of the officers also noticed them.

"What's that riff-raff doing in here?" He knocked his chair over as he rose.

The dining room fell silent as the server stopped in front of Katerin and Metkyi.

"I'm sorry," he whimpered. "But this is a private party. Just—leave. Please."

Katerin felt Metkyi bristle under her arm.

"We saw no notice," he said.

"Sorry. You must leave. Now. *Please.*"

But it was too late. The drunken officer shoved the server aside and pushed into Metkyi's face, almost sending Katerin sprawling.

"Just who do you think you are?" he blustered to Metkyi.

Katerin pulled on Metkyi's arm. "Let's go. Please," she whispered. Explosive tension radiated from both men. Metkyi quivered under her arm, ready to lash out. Then she felt his muscles relax, and she knew he was yielding to her wishes.

Not fast enough for the officer, though.

"Civilian outlanders!" He swung his fist at Metkyi.

Katerin saw a flash in his hand.

"He's got a knife!" she yelled, and feinted to one side, pushing Metkyi away from her. The other officers bellowed as Metkyi dodged under the officer's arm and whirled to face him, one of his knives sliding out into his hand as if by magic and not from the sheath Katerin knew was strapped to his forearm.

"Some of us outlanders know more about fighting than the mighty Medvaran army thinks we do," Metkyi sneered.

In return, the officer bellowed and dove again at Metkyi. Metkyi sidestepped, and Katerin was relieved to see him reverse his hand and smack the officer's head with his knuckles instead of driving the blade up to the hilt in the man's chest. The last thing they needed was trouble from the Medvaran army for killing an officer.

But still, he had to protect himself. And the officer now seemed aware that he was up against a fighter. He feinted, and Metkyi reacted mildly, not leaving the officer the opening he'd obviously expected for a second rush.

—*Whatever you do, don't raise aspect!* Katerin thought hard toward Metkyi, hoping that maybe he could pick up just a hint of her worry. His eyes never left the officer, but Katerin suddenly felt assurance rushing through her. He was not about to risk exposing any more of himself than necessary.

Not his first bar fight.

"Once we find that little witch, all you outlanders will be ours!" the officer snarled and jumped Metkyi, no feint this time. The two men clenched, and Metkyi grasped the officer's knife hand, dropping his knife and knocking the officer's knife free.

Katerin seized both knives and scrambled away as the men struggled. One of the other officers grabbed Katerin. She turned on him with her teeth bared, a knife in each hand. He laughed softly and backed away, holding his hands open so she could see he was unarmed. She remained tense but vigilant, ready to strike should he decide to reach for her again. She watched his eyes dart to the fighters, then back to her.

"Outlander wench's got a bite, huh?" he cackled.

"Stay back. Keep it fair."

He eyed her and backed off further. "Your man's no slouch in a fight. Military training?"

"No!" Katerin snapped.

She cautiously turned to watch, keeping one eye on this officer in case he decided to come after her again. Metkyi delivered a blow to his opponent's gut, followed by a punch to the jaw that sent the man sprawling. Katerin saw an opening and jumped to Metkyi's side, handing him his knife as he stood over the other man, who was curled up and moaning, slamming one hand on the ground.

"Apologize to my wife for upsetting her evening," Metkyi growled at him.

The officer snarled and tried to roll to his knees. Metkyi shoved him back down.

"Apologize!" he snapped.

The officer who'd spoken to Katerin stepped forward. "I apologize on his behalf. Norral's a bit hasty. At least this time he wasn't stupid enough to try to knife you outright, for both your sakes and his."

"I want to hear it from him."

"You'd best let him up, then." The other officer's tone was pleasant, but there was no question about the command in it.

"Not if he's going to take another swing at me."

"I'll stand parole for that. Norral, stand up, and leave the outlander man and his woman alone."

Metkyi warily backed off as Norral rose. When Norral would have dived at Metkyi, the other officer held him firm.

"This good man's shown you he's the better. Apologize to him and his goodwife, and let them go in peace."

"I was just having some fun," Norral grumbled. "Bastard don't fight fair."

"You think the Clendans and those other outlanders will fight fair in battle?" The officer shook his head. "Apologize, and I'll buy you another drink."

Norral straightened up. "Sorry," he grunted, then shambled toward the others.

The other officer caught the eye of one of the servers trembling on the side. "Whatever that one wants. On my tab," he called over to them. Then he turned to Katerin and Metkyi. "I'll escort you out, so there's no further trouble."

"We can take care of ourselves," Metkyi said stiffly.

The officer laughed. "I have no question about that. Norral's one of my best street fighters, and he's handy with his knife. You're quicker than he is." Even as he spoke, he had them headed to the door, his attention switching back and forth between Katerin and Metkyi and the other men now singing and yelling once again.

The officer looked Metkyi over once they were outside. "You're pretty quick in a fight. Interested in joining up with the army?"

"I am a Free Trader," Metkyi said. "I have no interest in fighting in any army."

"Free Trader, hmm?" the officer chuckled. "And just which cohort do you hie from?"

"The Open Cohort of Nere," Metkyi said proudly.

"Huh. So what brings a Nerean trader to Medvara? Not your usual run, is it? I've not seen you before, and a fighter such as you I'd remember."

"My wife and I are newly bonded, and on a tour to celebrate. We thought we'd check out Medvara on our way to Cooscol."

"Cooscol, hmm? Still certain you don't want to sign up with any army?"

Metkyi shook his head. "I'm a trader, not a fighter."

"Let me make a suggestion, then, Mr. Free Trader with a very lovely, and skilled in her own right newly bonded spouse. Leave Saktrin tomorrow. Norral will be looking for you. You embarrassed him and he doesn't take that well. Leave Medvara. You're going to see war soon enough, this spring, and you'll have to choose a side, like it or not. I'd sooner see you on the winning side."

"I'm a Trader. We don't fight."

"You *will* be fighting," the officer said. "We all will be, once Zauril captures his daughter. Remember this. When war comes to you, should you be interested, I've a slot for you in my company. Devral's my name, Captain Devral. I like the cut of your cloth, Free Trader," He let his words hang.

"Makri," Metkyi said, reluctantly.

"Makri, then. But for tonight, I'll tell you where to find dinner, in a place where you're not going to run into another batch of us. Though what you're doing in a garrison town is beyond me!"

"A choice of the people we're riding with. They said this was a good and quiet place, without the craziness of Medvare-the-city." Metkyi snorted. "Looks like a bunch of drunks spoiling for a fight."

The officer laughed. "That it is, tonight. We've had a spot of good news, so we're letting our boys play a little. You might want to warn your Trader friends about that. Traveling will not be very safe for a while, not unless you go heavily armed. If I were you I'd head for Cooscol as fast as you can, and stay put."

"We have obligations," Metkyi snapped. "Thanks for the warning. We'll be fine."

"It's your choice. But. For tonight. Go along this street, back toward the west. You'll find a dinner place more to your liking next to the Shepherd's Inn. And if you ever change your mind about joining an army, you can tell any Medvaran officer that Captain Devral of Zauril's Own Guard wants first grabs at you."

Katerin fought back any reaction she might have had as Captain Devral bowed low to her, taking her hand in his and lightly brushing the back of it with his lips.

"And as for you, lovely lady," Devral continued. "There's places for someone like you who's handy with a knife, should your man choose the right side. We can use both of you."

Katerin shook her head, still numb at the revelation that they'd stumbled into Zauril's Own.

"We appreciate the offer," Metkyi said, taking Katerin's hand. "And the advice for a place to eat. But as for employment," he bowed politely. "We're not looking."

"Keep it in mind," Captain Devral said, then went back inside.

Metkyi took Katerin's arm in his. They walked silently back to the Shepherd's Inn, stopping at a general store to pick up a half-loaf of bread, a chunk of cheese, and a length of dry sausage. They bought the last fruit pasties from a street vendor, and carried their food up to their room. Metkyi set their packages down on the table.

"By the gods, Katerin, just what is going on here?"

"I wish I knew. Officers of Zauril's Own having a drunken party. Talk of war and open recruitment. Gods, Rekaré was absolutely right to come here now. *If* what he was saying was correct, and not a ruse."

"Oh, I believe him." Metkyi sat down. "But what a way to get that information." He shook his head ruefully and dropped his hands on his thighs. "I don't think I'd make a good spy. That fight was too evenly matched for my liking. Norral was *good*, Katerin. I didn't see any way to back down."

"There wasn't one." She was shivering now, thinking about the possibilities. "What do we do? It's only seven bells now. We're supposed to meet at ten bells. I don't want to go back out there."

"Let's stay in until it's time to meet with Rekaré. We've got food, and as for things we can do until it's time to meet...." His arms wrapped more tightly around her.

"I just hope we've done enough," she murmured.

"We've gathered enough information. I think we'll do better service to Rekaré by staying out of sight." He began to unbutton her vest. "Meanwhile—"

CHAPTER 33

"*Y*ou did *what?*" Rekaré snapped.

Metkyi met Rekaré's gaze straight on.

"I got into a bar fight with an officer of Zauril's Own," he repeated. "Katerin and I wandered into a restaurant where the officers were celebrating. He took offense at our presence and attacked me before we could leave."

"You were to be discreet!"

"You saw the mood out there yourself, my dear," Cenarth said. "They're both celebrating and on edge, ready to pick fights with anyone. Remember, we had our own touchy moments."

"True," Rekaré conceded.

"It would be hard to avoid such encounters tonight," Orlanden added. "If I had any notion we would be walking into this mood in Saktrin, I'd have suggested we stay elsewhere."

"I was advised to leave town tomorrow, as the officer who fought me might be looking for me," Metkyi said.

"You didn't hurt him?" Rekaré asked.

Metkyi frowned at her. "You know I've better training than that! I did nothing more to Norral than he probably gets from his own mates. He'll have a sore jaw from walking into my fist.

However." His hand tightened harder on Katerin's. "His commanding officer took no little interest in us."

"And his commanding officer was?" Orlanden asked.

"A Captain Devral. He tried to recruit both of us."

"*Devral*, of all people," Orlanden growled, grimacing. "*He'll* remember you, Metkyi. Gods. What did you *do*?"

"Bested one of his best street fighters."

"And Katerin? How did Devral come to notice her?"

"She picked up our knives and nearly got into it with Devral when he tried to take them away from her."

Orlanden shook his head, an unwilling smile creeping across his face. "Gods, I'd have loved to have seen *that* encounter. But it's unfortunate that you both attracted his attention. Devral's got a memory as long as the Chellana. He's one reason *I'm* not walking the town. I'm surprised he didn't pick up on Katerin's Aireii connections. Some say he's got a piece of Zauril's magic hidden in him, as a protection for Zauril."

"I didn't sense anything like that," Metkyi said.

"Katerin?" Rekaré looked over at her.

Katerin shrugged and spread her hands. "That's a magic I don't know how to work."

"I could check," Rekaré said.

"What purpose would it serve?" Orlanden asked. "If we find him with Zauril, he'll die before he'll let you harm Zauril. Do you need to know more?"

"No," Rekaré conceded.

"So," Orlanden turned back to Metkyi. "Devral tried to recruit you?"

"Both of us." Metkyi repeated the conversation.

"Troops receiving good news," Rekaré frowned and glanced over at Cenarth. "It matches what we were told."

"And what I heard next door," Orlanden said. "Metkyi. What did you tell Devral about yourselves?"

"I identified myself as Makri, a Free Trader from Nere's

Open Cohort. I didn't identify Katerin." He glanced questioningly at Katerin and she shook her head. "She didn't identify herself, either. I told him we were newly bonded and on our celebration tour, to Cooscol by way of Medvara. He didn't question our story."

"And he told you to leave town?"

Metkyi nodded.

Orlanden frowned. "You need to move quickly if you want to catch Zauril off guard, Rekaré."

"I've thought of several options. We need to strike tomorrow. There's supposed to be a troop review on the Western Parade Grounds."

"That could work, if we found him at the right place with only a few guards," Orlanden said. "The whispers I heard hint that Zauril's not that well-liked by his own troops. If you take him down, and Devral with him, it's unlikely even Zauril's Own will avenge him."

"The road to the Western Parade Grounds. That's one of the locations my mother recommended we scout," Rekaré said.

"It's where Zauril ambushed your grandfather," Orlanden said. "It would be highly ironic for him to feel safe enough to take that route."

"Yes," Rekaré said. "That would be so, wouldn't it? The Gods work in mysterious ways."

Orlanden frowned at her. "The Gods, or magic?"

"As you said, it would be ironic that he finds that route to be safe." Rekaré swallowed hard. "We have to do something soon. I know why they're celebrating. He plans to attack Chellni. We know his routes. We need to strike tomorrow. Orlanden, for all his arrogance, I think he's afraid."

"Of what?"

"Of *me*. Of what alliances I've made. Attacking Chellni is a fool's game. He'll disrupt trade and bankrupt Medvara in the process. Now I know why my magic came to me this winter. If I waited to move until my birthday, we would already be in open war."

"I agree. But may I give you more advice?" Orlanden frowned at Rekaré.

"You are the one who knows Medvara best," Rekaré said.

"Keep our reservations at this inn and leave the mules in the stable. Light packs on the daranvelii. If anyone asks, we can say we're going to a small resort nearby."

"And then what?" Metkyi asked.

"We wait for our opening. If that works for you, my lady?" Orlanden raised one eyebrow in question at Rekaré.

"It works quite well for me," Rekaré said.

The five of them against Zauril's Own. Katerin shivered.

"Early in the morning, then," Orlanden said. "And dress warmly. We might be waiting for quite some time."

Tomorrow, Katerin thought in a daze. *Tomorrow I encounter my fate.*

Metkyi's hand on hers was slight comfort as they went quietly to their room.

Tomorrow. If it all comes together. Tomorrow.

It was all she could do to remain steady and calm as she prepared for bed. Even with Metkyi holding her tightly, it took some time before Katerin eased into a troubled sleep, filled with dreams of her mother.

* * *

DREAD WAS NOT an emotion that lingered after spending a cold, wet morning staked out in the woods alongside the road to the Western Parade Grounds. Boredom came quickly enough as they watched. Katerin and Metkyi alternately sat or knelt on their rain slickers while a light drizzle turned everything damp around them. Katerin reviewed sword-fighting strategies in her head to pass the time.

I'm glad for the Swordmaster drills during the winters at the Healing House now.

She hoped that would be enough to hold off fighters until Rekaré unleashed whatever magic she planned to use against Zauril. She hoped—Gods, she just hoped to survive this day.

Metkyi picked up her hand and held it. Just the slight contact settled Katerin's nerves. He was here. She wasn't alone. She had a Voice of Staul at her side.

Rekaré, Cenarth and Orlanden sat on the other side of the road. They had established signals. Rekaré's sense of Zauril's presence might give them some warning of his approach.

A hawk's cry from Rekaré's location startled Katerin.

The signal.

She and Metkyi quietly slid onto Mira and Rainin.

Then they heard shouting and a jingle of tack. Devral's troop had passed once, going toward Medvare-the-city, and had returned with Norral in the lead rather than Devral. By Metkyi's whispered count, the troop was short not only by Devral but by at least five other riders.

And now, Devral rode in the lead of a small troop, eyes darting from side-to-side, hand on his sword. Behind him came his riders, two-by-two, with their last rider following. In their midst, Zauril rode a reddish-golden stallion just a few shades darker than Rekaré's golden mare. Zauril looked just like the paintings that dominated everything in Saktrin, a tall, sallow man with hollow cheeks, wearing an ornamental helmet.

The magic Katerin had inherited from Alame rose within her, triggered by the sight of Zauril. Her perspective changed. Zauril wore an aspect of Nitel, old and faded, nothing left to him but skin and bone, gray-green slimy growths oozing around and into his body. The reek of corruption emanated from him.

A tremor vibrated through Metkyi's body. "He abuses his

power," Metkyi whispered. "He abused his gift. This is where Makri got it."

Blue light exploded in front of the troop. Rekaré, as strongly colored with the aspect of Dovré as Zauril was with the perversion of Nitel, charged into the road. Katerin urged Mira forward, words she didn't know coming from her lips as she pulled her sword. The world around her shifted form and substance, just like it had during the battle with Makri.

—Rekaré must strike Zauril first, Alame's ghostly voice whispered inside her head. *—Devral must be yours. He protects Zauril. Let me help you just this time, to know the magic.*

—Yes, she answered.

The unfamiliar magic crashed over her.

Devral charged toward Rekaré while his subordinates clustered around Zauril. Cenarth blocked Devral, his daranval's heavier weight sending Devral's horse staggering toward Katerin and Metkyi. Rekaré's eyes focused solely on Zauril. Blue-edged, red-gold lights flickered up and down her sword, twin to the lights on Katerin's blade.

"This is your time to *die*, father!" Rekaré shouted. Then she and Basnen charged the group shielding Zauril.

Zauril yelled something Katerin couldn't hear and urged his daranval toward Rekaré. The golden mare and Zauril's stallion collided. The fight exploded around them, Cenarth, Orlanden, Katerin and Metkyi matched against Zauril's guard while Zauril and Rekaré grappled together, still mounted, magic swirling around them.

Metkyi brought down one rider, making the numbers even. Devral reined around, cursing. Katerin blocked his way. His eyes widened in recognition as he focused on her.

"Free Traders of Nere, my—" he growled, swinging at Katerin.

Mira struck, seizing Devral's upraised arm with her teeth and pulling him off his horse.

"Go help Rekaré!" Katerin shouted at Metkyi. "We'll take care of Devral!"

"But you—"

"*Rekaré!*" Katerin screamed. She had little time to think of anything else as Devral rose from the ground, swinging his sword high. She let the unfamiliar magic guide her strokes.

Gods, I wish I'd practiced mounted fighting a dismounted opponent!

But she had Mira. Even though Katerin didn't know all the moves, Mira did. Katerin focused on swordwork, letting Mira do what she knew. Devral knocked Katerin off-balance. She grabbed at Mira's mane with one hand, almost falling off the other side. Mira grabbed Devral's shoulder and smacked his leg with a hoof while Katerin struggled to regain her balance.

Devral whirled and slashed Mira's throat with one quick blow. Mira staggered sideways, then collapsed.

No! No!

Katerin fought for breath, her new magic suddenly gone, struggling to get free as Mira's collapse trapped her in the mud. Devral screeched a victory yell and pinioned Katerin with his knees, raising his sword to strike.

Her necklace tingled and Devral's blow went awry. Metkyi bellowed, and yanked Devral away from her. Katerin gulped for breath, trying to separate from the dying embers of Mira's awareness. She wrenched her leg free and rested her hand on Mira for a moment, knowing there was no time to save her, no time but for a quick farewell.

—By all the Gods, my dearest partner. He'll pay!

Somehow, somewhere, she felt one last twinge of Mira.

—Katerin rising and fighting.

—Yes. Yes.

Katerin staggered up. Metkyi and Devral. She circled around behind Devral.

For Mira. I'll make you pay!

Devral pressed Metkyi hard, and nearly got him in the shoulder.

Hold it, hold it, hold it.

She saw her opening and swung, catching Devral in the leg. Devral's weight slackened, like he was going to go down. Then, with a speed Katerin did not think possible, Devral drove his sword straight and deep into Metkyi's chest, yelling in mixed pain and triumph as Metkyi's eyes widened and he sagged forward.

No. No. Not both of them!

The necklace suddenly burned around her throat as the world seemed to go silent around her. Katerin struck Devral hard in the back. Power flowed and surged over her and through her, throbbing through the necklace as Devral writhed on her blade, darkness seething from him.

He's possessed. Like Makri.

She struggled to hold Devral down, whipsawed by the magics pulsing through her. The magic battering her was worse than anything she'd faced until now, worse even than when she had killed the Makri wolf. The necklace burned hot.

Hold steady. Hold.

A touch like Metkyi's brushed her shoulders, then moved in her, flowing into her hands. The voice was not unlike Dovré's as it resonated deep inside her, cooling the fire in her necklace.

Hold steady, my child.

She knew it suddenly to be Staul of the Balance, using her as his agent.

Devral screamed as the power flowed through her hands and into the sword, a bright red fire consuming him and withering his body into ashes. And then Staul was gone from her, one soft touch on her cheek like Metkyi's.

Metkyi.

She dropped her sword and ran to him.

"*No!*" She gathered Metkyi in her arms, wanting to do something but knowing from the look on his face, the glazing of his eyes that it was too late, too late, *too late.* "Metkyi, my love, my dearest—"

"Katerin—" he managed to gasp, blood running out of his mouth. "Katerin. My Katerin."

Katerin lowered her head to his, struggling, trying to seize any magic she could pull down, even that of Staul's.

A nose brushed against her back, and she startled, and then the awareness of a young and strong daranval swarmed over her.

Rainin. If there's any hope. Rainin.

Katerin grabbed at Rainin's mind, but it was too young, too untrained to do any more but give her enough power to probe Metkyi's failing body and see that there was nothing she could do to save him.

"Oh Metkyi," she sobbed. "Oh *Gods,* Metkyi. Metkyi."

"Katerin," he whispered. "Oh the gifts you've given me. Oh Katerin." He brushed her cheek with his trembling fingers, and his glazing eyes came clear. "Our child," he gasped. "Our daughter. Witmara. Daughter of the promise. Witmara. Not a child of the village. Promise. *Promise.*"

"I will not raise our child to be a daughter of the village," Katerin croaked. "I would never do that to a child of mine. Of ours. Oh Metkyi, Metkyi." Sobs overwhelmed her.

His eyes widened. "Mira's here. For me." The pain faded from his voice, replaced by soft awe as his eyes grew duller. "The Gods are here, too, Katerin. Both of them. They're here. Can't you see them? And Alame too."

Katerin shook her head.

"*My Lord Staul,*" Metkyi whispered. "*Lady Dovré.* I come. I come. But oh, Katerin, Katerin, *my dearest Katerin.*"

Fresh blood poured out of his mouth and his body stiffened, then slackened in her arms as he gagged, then stopped breathing.

"Metkyi, oh Metkyi," Katerin groaned. She rested her forehead on his face, careless of Metkyi's blood smearing over her as she let the sobs take her.

A soft nose prodded her back once again. Katerin raised her head, still keening, as Rainin's awareness flooded over her. For a brief moment, she saw two shadowy figures in front of her. Mira, with Metkyi astride her, waiting for Katerin to acknowledge them. Just past them, Alame stood with a fiery sword raised high in triumph. And beyond them, she saw the everlasting shapeless glory of the Goddess, with Staul beside her.

Too much, too bright.

Then the Gods' arms enfolded Mira and Metkyi, and all five of them were gone, Alame taking a moment longer to fade. Katerin blinked. Mira's still form lying a few strides away became clear. She eased Metkyi down and gently closed his eyelids. That simple action brought her back to the world.

A troop of soldiers thundered down on them as Zauril staggered back from Rekaré, seeming to age years in mere moments. Rekaré bellowed. With a single swift motion, she struck hard at Zauril's neck, the same blow she'd used to kill the Shadowwalker. Zauril's head went flying across the road and rolled down it for a few strides, coming to a halt just short of the troop.

The troop halted, the captain staring down at the head of his fallen leader, a surprised expression on his face. Rekaré strode over and seized Zauril's head by his long, graying hair. She lifted it high, brandishing both it and her sword at the captain.

"Thus do I avenge the wrongs done to my family!" she screamed. "I am Rekaré ea Miteal, daughter of Alicira ea Miteal, granddaughter of Alexran en Miteal and great-granddaughter of Richenax en Miteal! I claim Medvara as mine by right!" She bared her teeth at the captain. "Do you dispute my claim?"

Nitel's visage blurred Rekaré's features, the blue aura around her shifting swiftly to purple.

She has an affinity for Nitel. Gods help us. Nitel rides her.

Cenarth moved to Rekaré's right side, his sword at the ready, while Orlanden took her left. Katerin clung to Rainin's neck, as yet unable to move, wanting to join the others but not able to do more as Rekaré glared at the troop captain.

Tension simmered between Rekaré and the captain as she stood unafraid, Zauril's head dangling from her left hand while her right hand clutched the sword, her clothing stained with blood. The power came back over Katerin, and she saw magic swirling away from the captain, from the rest of the troop. The captain sagged as magic ebbed away from him.

That's how Zauril did it. Magical control.

Katerin looked at Rekaré. Magic and power simmered there, ready to explode out but held in restraint. But Katerin saw Rekaré moving her lips, whispering a spell, and the malignant face of Zauril murmuring in her ear as Nitel's visage came clearer in Rekaré's face.

She could do the same thing that Zauril did. She's his daughter and she's called up Nitel. Nitel gave her the strength for those killing blows.

Fear tightened through her. Katerin tried to use what little magic and strength she had left to touch Rekaré. The balance of the world seemed to swing as the power surged within Rekaré. The face of Zauril grew exultant and Rekaré's face became that of Nitel's.

—*No.* Katerin extended her hand toward Rekaré, summoning up magic what she could. —*Not your path. You can't.*

A greater power filled her. Katerin straightened up and focused on Zauril's shadow, words coming to her lips that she didn't understand. With each word, Zauril's visage faded, until with one last shriek he was gone.

Rekaré/Nitel turned her terrible gaze upon Katerin, scowling.

—*No.* Katerin stared into Rekaré's pitiless, cold eyes. —*Not your path. Not like your father. Not your path. Not your way.*

Rekaré reeled back from Katerin, Nitel's visage fading. But she was still wrapped in the terrible, pitiless chill of Nitel. Katerin pushed her.

My mother used Karnoi and Cirdel to banish Nitel. If I have to, can I use Staul and Dovré?

The choice would mean the dreamless sleep for her—*and what of my child?* Katerin shivered. Prepared for one last spell.

This is my fate, at last.

Cenarth turned to Rekaré. Power emanated from him, different from Rekaré and Katerin's, a power of earth and growing things. The strength of horses and daranvelii radiated from him as his face burned with a golden-brown light.

He took her hand, the hand with the sword.

"No, love," was all he said.

Rekaré turned her gaze from Katerin. For a moment she seemed to resist Cenarth. Then she took a deep breath, shuddering as the terrible, pitiless cold dropped away from her and her features became her own again, a golden-brown warmth tinged with blue rising to meet his.

She dropped the sword and lifted his hand to her lips. "You're right. Thank you, my dearest, for bringing me back. *Thank you.*"

It is done.

With a sigh, Katerin released the bindings she had been about to invoke. She dropped to her knees and leaned against Rainin's forelegs, momentarily unable to move any further. She barely felt the little mare's soft nuzzle against her cheek.

The captain's face sagged. "At last the world comes right. The Miteal have returned to us." He flashed a hand sign to his troop, and slid off of his horse, dropping to his knees in the mud and bowing deep to Rekaré as he offered his sword to her.

"We give our swords to you, Lady Rekaré," he said.

The others followed his lead.

"Your name," Rekaré demanded.

"Senjal, my lady."

"Captain Senjal." Rekaré took Senjal's sword. "I hereby name you the Captain of my personal Guard." She raised her voice. "Do you all swear loyalty to me as your ruler, and will you be my protectors?"

"We do, Lady Rekaré!" they shouted back.

Rekaré offered the sword back to Senjal. "Rise, Captain Senjal. We have work to do. Kindly send two of your men to tell the army there is a new leader in Medvara. We have much to do to make Medvara right again." Rekaré turned, and her eyes widened as she took in the scene of Mira's body, Metkyi lying prone. "We have casualties and wounded."

"Not wounded," Katerin croaked. "Rekaré, they're dead."

Shock flitted across Rekaré's face. "I'm sorry, Katerin," she said. She turned back to Captain Senjal. "We have dead to honor." She looked down at Zauril's head. "And we have *this* to deal with."

"What should we do with my lor—his body?" Senjal steeled himself visibly for Rekaré's next statement.

"He was a ruler of Medvara. Usurper, yes, but still a ruler. And my," she gulped and swallowed, looking down for a moment before looking back up at the captain. "My father. Treat his remains fairly, but with no mourning."

Senjal nodded sharply. "It will be done as you say."

"Do the same for these others, except for the man of my party. He was a priest of Staul. He served me for many years. His lady will direct you until one of Staul's own can come." She nodded at Katerin.

"And the daranval?"

"The lady was the daranval's rider. She is a Voice of Dovré. Give her assistance for what she needs."

Rekaré continued speaking, but Katerin heard no more. Rainin nudged Katerin back to her feet. She wanted to wail over Metkyi's body, but Mira needed to be honored.

A wave of strength came to her from Rainin, and Katerin dropped her head quickly on the little mare's neck, sending thanks for the help. She fumbled for her belt knife, and limped over to Mira's body. Slowly, she cut the saddle girth and bridle straps. Other hands helped her pull them off.

"Tie the saddlebags on the bay daranval," she directed one of the men.

She knelt beside Mira.

You served me well, my dearest daranval.

Katerin blinked back the wetness filling her eyes. Slowly, she gathered a fistful of mane in her left hand and cut the hair free, tucking it into one of her pockets, and did the same for the tail. Slowly, she fumbled for her blue glimmer dust and drew the ritual circle around Mira's body. Slowly, she called down the cool fire that consumed Mira's body, ignoring the startled gasps from the men around her. When it was done, someone gave her a bag, and she collected what she could of the ashes from the mud.

Now Metkyi. Katerin turned back to him. Someone had pulled Devral's sword from Metkyi's body and straightened his limbs. Katerin knelt beside him and slowly, jaggedly, cut his braid free, setting it on his chest. Then she reached up with shaking hands to hack at her own braid.

Someone took braid and knife from her hands. Katerin opened her mouth to protest, and looked up to see Rekaré.

"You helped me with my uncle. Your father," Rekaré said. "Let me help you. Now is your time to cut hair."

Katerin sank down onto her knees and let Rekaré make the cut, closing her eyes as she felt the knife tug against her hair, pulling her head back slightly. Tears oozed past her eyelids and she didn't have the strength to wipe them away while her head rocked with Rekaré's quick cuts.

"I tried to keep it straight," Rekaré said finally.

"Thank you," Katerin whispered. She held up her hand for

the knife and her braid, still keeping her eyes closed as she tucked them away.

If I don't see it, maybe it's not real.

She reached out her hand again, eyes still closed, and took Metkyi's braid. His body was cooler than it had been, and she wanted to find a way to warm him back into life.

Instead she brought his braid to her cheek. She'd helped him plait it just this morning. The texture of the hair against her face still held a whisper of life, his scent rising from it. Katerin allowed herself to fold up, resting her head on her knees as she began to sob again, holding the braid. Shivers wracked her body.

Someone tried to take her away from Metkyi.

"No. I stay with him. I go when he goes."

A voice barked orders. The hands went away.

Someone else draped a cloak around her shoulders. Yet another person poked at her hand with a flask, and she took a draw of it, grateful when the taste was simply water and not liquor. She was aware of the presence of others around her, working quietly, but whether they were friends or strangers she didn't know and couldn't care. As she warmed slightly, Katerin reached for Metkyi's hand and held it to her cheek.

A wagon rolled up next to them. Hands gently eased Metkyi's out of her own, then lifted him onto the wagon. Katerin would have walked alongside, except that the same hands guided her to the front of the wagon and urged her onto the seat. Someone put Rainin's rope into her free hand. Katerin's hand closed tight around it, welcoming the painful sensation of the brittle horsehair. The sharp prickle was the only thing she could feel at this moment. It felt good to focus on that and not on the other, deeper ache that permeated her body.

She rode with her eyes half-closed, enduring the jostles. They stopped. She opened her eyes. They were back in Saktrin, outside of an ornate building she hadn't noticed earlier. Men in brown robes gathered around the wagon.

Gentle hands took Rainin's lead and Metkyi's braid. They guided her behind the men who carried Metkyi's body. When they entered the building, they tried to take her in a different direction from Metkyi. She screamed at them. The gentle hands yielded.

They took her to the room where they were preparing Metkyi's body. She pushed in and undressed him. Someone took the outer clothing from her.

"His hair?" one asked Katerin.

"Mine," she said. "Bondmate's claim."

The man nodded. She would have helped with the washing of his body, but they led her to a stool. She dully watched. The men handled Metkyi with a gentle respect, touching him as softly as if he were still alive and likely to cry out if they pressed too hard.

Then only his face remained to be cleaned. The man who had spoken to her started to wash Metkyi's face, then paused. He offered Katerin the sponge. She dipped it in the basin of bloody water before she gently washed his face, working until all traces of blood and dirt were gone, silent tears running down her cheeks.

The man offered her a basin of clean water, soap, and a towel. She washed her hands. The acolytes dressed Metkyi in priest's robes, then adjusted his necklace so that it sat properly on top of his robes. The men picked up the board that his body lay upon. A set of double doors that Katerin had not noticed before opened. The men carried Metkyi's body into a chapel and set it on a bier.

Someone guided her to a chair placed beside the bier, where she could look at Metkyi's face. Others lit torches. A chant picked up around her, until she could stand it no more and began her own counterpoint, a mourning chant of Dovré's that wove in and out with the chants of Staul.

It stopped. One-by-one the men bowed low to Katerin, until only one remained.

"It is time for you to rest now," he said to Katerin.

"I want to stay with him."

"He lies in state for three days. You may sit with him as much as you like, but you need to care for yourself, you need to tend to your hurts, you need to rest. The Gods rode you hard today, and you have suffered great loss. Take care of yourself, and you may return to him." His voice brooked no argument.

Katerin yielded. She allowed him to lead her to a suite. Two female attendants helped Katerin change out of her clothing and eased her into a deep, warm bath. She would have fallen asleep save that they kept gently prodding at her.

Once out of the bath, they helped her dress for bed. With polite bows, they left her alone.

No Mira to touch her mind.

No Metkyi to warm her body.

Alone.

Katerin pulled a pillow to her chest.

She cried herself to sleep.

CHAPTER 34

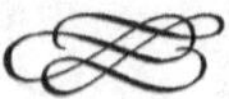

The next three days came in bits and pieces.

"Your daranval's trying to tear down her stall," someone whispered to Katerin about midway through the first morning.

Dread clutched at Katerin's gut. Rainin and Metkyi had been close to bonding.

No, not her too!

She rushed out of the chapel and heard the pounding of Rainin's hooves against the stall walls clear across the barnyard as she hurried to the stable.

"Shh, shh, little one," she called.

The pounding stopped, followed by a frantic whinny. Rainin pressed close to the stall door as Katerin fumbled with the latch. No sooner had Katerin pushed the door open than the little mare pressed her head against Katerin's chest. Katerin held Rainin's head in both hands, alternately stroking each cheek.

—Katerin, Metkyi, Rainin and Mira.

Images of the four of them kept coming at Katerin. She kept soothing Rainin until the barrage of images ceased.

Poor confused little thing. I'm all she has left.

Katerin rubbed Rainin's ears. She looked around the stall. She saw hoofprints on the wall but no significant damage. She checked Rainin's legs and feet. No harm done. Rainin's hay was untouched, so Katerin checked her for colic. Nothing.

Katerin groaned. Rainin had been sufficiently bonded to Metkyi that she needed another human bondmate, and soon. Once daranvelii started to bond, they either needed that human bond or the services of a skilled Horsemaster like Kwellet to soothe them if something happened to their human, to tide them over until they found a bondmate.

It has to be me.

She didn't trust anyone else here to do the right thing by Rainin.

Ideally, she'd have longer to recover from Mira's death. Ideally, she'd have a choice of several unbonded daranvelii. Ideally, she'd not be handling a baby barely broken to saddle. Rainin had been intended to be sold as a lightly handled daranval of good breeding, to someone with the time and skill to bond with her and finish her training.

I'm not a trainer.

But Rainin couldn't wait. Katerin rested her head against Rainin's. The mare pressed against her.

—*Katerin,* Katerin thought at Rainin.

—*Rainin* came back, then —*RaininandKaterin, Katerin riding Rainin.*

Tears seeped from Katerin's eyes. Rainin was nothing like Mira had been. Touching Rainin's mind, deliberately seeking out that contact brought back memories of Mira, Mira's images of buffalo dung when she was annoyed or angry or disgusted with something, Mira's bravery and boldness and beauty.

Mira, oh Mira. Katerin sobbed into Rainin's forehead.

—*MiraandKaterin,* then —*Rainin and Metkyi,* then —*KaterinandMetkyi,* came from Rainin. Then —*RaininandKaterin* came strongly. Katerin lifted her head, laughing softly through her tears at the little mare's insistence.

—*KaterinandRainin*, she sent back. They stood for some time, communing wordlessly.

At last, she gave Rainin a last scratch, promising to return later today. Rainin sent her a contented —*RaininandKaterin* as she turned to her hay.

Katerin's heart was lighter as she returned to her position. The connection with Rainin helped sustain her as the acolytes of Staul processed in and out of the chapel to pray at Metkyi's side. Not all who came were acolytes of Staul, but those who weren't of Staul were among the very few.

In the afternoon the sun came out, so she visited Rainin again. Katerin took the little mare for a short ride.

She scampered back into the chapel just as the rain started up again. It seemed stuffy and confining after the short spell outside, but the rain pounding hard on the chapel roof fit Katerin's mood as she stared at Metkyi.

Gods, if I can't have him back, then I just want this to be over!

That evening, Rekaré and Cenarth paid their respects, Rekaré garbed in finer clothing than Katerin had ever seen her wear. She rested a hand on Katerin's shoulder before leaving, not saying a word.

The second day went much as the first had, with only one chance to escape to Rainin. Katerin was beginning to fade. She hadn't thought that this long vigil would be as grueling as it was. The constant chanting, the whispers, the incense that choked her nose didn't take away the deep hole in her heart. It was easy to brood about the short time she had with Metkyi, to think back and realize that *he'd known* something like this was going to happen.

Was it why he allowed himself that much abandon in their relationship? Thinking back about the little things, the short moments brought on tears.

"Katerin." She startled. Senai, face tired and thin, stood next to her, Eldoran at her side and Yevtin slightly back.

"You're all right?" Eldoran asked.

"As much as I can be," Katerin said.

"We're here for the ceremony," Eldoran said. "Staying in Medvare-the-city. Just got in. Rekaré told us."

"Thank you," Katerin whispered.

"We'll be back tomorrow," Eldoran said. "We have rooms for you, too, after the ceremony."

"Thank you," Katerin repeated.

Senai hugged her, and then they were gone.

* * *

THE BURIAL CEREMONY was as grim and difficult as Katerin had feared. Metkyi's status among those of Staul, the means of his death, and Rekaré's orders about the funeral, trebled the pomposity of the ceremony.

She shut everyone and everything out as she followed Metkyi's bier on its solemn procession to his pyre, bolstered only by Rainin's presence next to her. It was the only way she could tolerate the wailing chants, the cloying incense, and the heavy ceremonial dress she wore. It had sigils of the Goddess worked into it, white, gold and red, with a matching cloak. It fit as if someone had designed it specifically for her.

She lost track of the crowd. Some were professional mourners, others were from the army, but there were more present than she expected. Katerin was ready to drop by the time they reached the small, tree-lined meadow where the final ceremony would take place. She thought there would be a few words said, then the pyre, and they would be done.

But it was more complicated than she had expected.

First of all came Orelyets, as tired and as grim-looking as

Senai and the others had been the night before. He spoke of Metkyi's youth and of his calling to Staul.

Next came the head priest of Staul. He recited the details of Metkyi's training, his honors within the brotherhood of Staul, the powers he'd gained and the other priests he'd helped, honored and trained. Lastly, he sang the souls that Metkyi had helped along the path to the Otherworld, including Alame's.

How would he know who Metkyi guided?

Katerin wondered wearily. Then she remembered the notebooks Metkyi kept, the careful scribing even when they'd been traveling. Someone must have read them.

Last came Rekaré. "Metkyi of Wickmasa and I were friends. He was tied to me to give me strength when I was twelve. Then, when I was thirteen, after my party was waylaid by Saubral on our way here, he gave me the counsel to make the choices I needed to make."

Tears overwhelmed Katerin at this point, and she lost track of Rekaré's words for a few moments.

"His death gave his bondmate, my cousin, the needed opportunity to kill Devral and remove the spells and protection that kept Zauril alive. Without that," Rekaré's voice trailed away, and her eyes met Katerin's. Then she drew a deep breath. "Without that," she repeated, "I might not be standing here. I honor and respect this man and the pledges of honor he kept for me. And I ask you to remember him with honor as well."

Rekaré bowed, first to Metkyi's body, then to Katerin, and then was gone. The head priest proclaimed the final blessings.

Katerin managed to keep herself upright and mutter the responses the head priest had taught her that morning. The head priest handed her the torch, and she unsteadily lit the pyre. The flames hesitated for a moment, then took off. They stood around it until Metkyi and the wood were consumed.

Katerin yearned to leap up on Rainin's back as they returned to the temple of Staul, but she couldn't do that with her fancy dress. She trudged along with her hand on Rainin's withers, aimlessly going wherever they were pointed.

Back at the temple, the female attendants helped Katerin out of the ornate dress and back into her own clothing.

The head attendant bowed low when they were finished. "We are to escort you back outside. Your friends will take you and your daranval to the place you will now be staying."

"Thank you."

She let them lead her out.

Eldoran waited, holding Rainin's lead, a mule loaded with Katerin and Metkyi's bags on his other side.

"Where do we go?" she asked Eldoran.

"The palace," Eldoran said. "Rekaré insisted. Your place is there as Alame's daughter."

"I just want to leave this city. This country. This place."

"In time. We have a coronation to go through first. Rekaré wants us there, especially you as her heir."

Katerin groaned softly. "I'm done with all this."

"Just a little bit more. Then you can go back to the Healing House. Even as a Miteal, you're still one of us."

"I can't go back," Katerin said dully.

"Siljaren's at Wickmasa. She can stay there until Hinet's ready. They'll understand."

"I can't go back to the Healing House," Katerin repeated. "Siljaren's lost Alame. I owe her duty as his daughter and, and Eldoran, I'm with child."

Eldoran reined to a stop. "You're *what?*"

"I'm with child," Katerin repeated. "I'm not far enough along to have quickened, but I've definitely missed a cycle. Metkyi felt it. At the end. He had a sight. It's a girl. He named the child."

Eldoran shook his head. "Katerin, Katerin."

"I'm not raising her as a child of the village. I promised Metkyi." Her voice dropped to a whisper.

"We'll find a way, Katerin."

"I just want all this to be over with," Katerin whispered. "I just want to rest."

"We'll get you some time to rest as soon as we get to the Leader's House."

"Thank you."

Katerin followed Eldoran's lead, detached once again from the world around her. They passed through the gates, and Eldoran hurried Katerin along the grounds until they had reached the stables.

Senai and Yevtin waited for them. Eldoran spoke with Senai as Katerin eased off of Rainin and fumbled with her bags. Senai gently started to steer her away from Rainin.

"I need to tell Rainin I'll be back." Katerin gave Rainin a soft scratch.

—*Katerin visiting happy Rainin in stall.*

—*Rainin waiting for Katerin in stall, Rainin eating.*

Katerin laughed softly, resting her head for a moment on Rainin's neck. The little mare's happy moods couldn't help but make her laugh. Then she gave Rainin one last pat and went with Senai.

Senai led her to a set of rooms the likes of which Katerin had never seen before. Ornate, overstuffed furniture in shades of red, white and gold cluttered the room; not just one or two stuffed chairs but four, two loveseats, and much more furniture. The wallpaper repeated the curlicue designs on the wooden frames of the furniture.

Katerin closed her eyes, then opened them slowly.

"I know," Senai said. "It takes some getting used to. I spent last night staring at the walls, it was so bright. Do you want to bathe?"

"Yes. Then sleep. I'm tired."

"Need help?" Senai led her into a chamber with a readied, steaming bath in a tub large enough for four people.

Katerin shook her head wearily.

"Mind if I join you?"

Katerin shook her head again. She stripped and sank into the hot water, letting herself float for a few moments, starting to ease off into sleep.

Senai kicked her. "Hey. You'd best not dawdle too long. I don't want to drag you out of the tub."

"You won't have to do that." Katerin slowly began to wash. She clambered herself out of the tub, dried off, and found a flannel nightgown hanging from a hook.

"Mine? Or yours?" she asked Senai.

"Yours. Mine's on my bed. I'm going down to dinner. You sure you don't want to come?"

"I'm not hungry, Senai. I haven't been hungry." Katerin's voice trailed off.

"You look all in. Go to bed. I'll bring up some soup. How many cycles have you missed?"

"Just the one," Katerin said slowly. "It hasn't been that long, Senai."

"Rest. I'll bring you some food. We've plenty of time. Rekaré is waiting until her mother gets here for the coronation."

"That could take a while."

"The last I heard, it was going to be seven days." Senai led her into yet another room. "Here's your bed. I'm in the next room."

"I'm going to get lost in here," Katerin muttered. "How many rooms?"

"Sitting room, bathroom, and three bedrooms. Same for Yevtin and Eldoran's."

"This makes every other place I've been look like a hovel." Katerin stared at the massive bed.

"It does. Go ahead. Get on in."

Somehow, she found the strength to crawl into the high bed. She collapsed swiftly into sleep once she relaxed into the soft feather mattress, rousing only when Senai brought her soup.

The next morning, she would have slept even longer, except

for a wistful query from Rainin. Katerin drug herself out of bed, and found a small pastry to nibble on as she looked for her clothes. She found them hanging from a peg in the bathroom. On her way out through the sitting room, she stopped suddenly as she saw the bags stacked neatly in a pile. Her things. Metkyi's things. She took one step toward them, then fled.

It took several wrong turns before she found the exit from the palace, and then further looking around before she found the right stable. Katerin spent most of the morning grooming and working with Rainin.

Finally, she staggered back inside. A faint scent of food wafted down the corridors. Hunger was her first reaction, followed by a churning in her gut. Katerin's nose twitched, and she decided to return to her rooms instead.

Senai was gone. Someone had been through and made the beds. More pastries sat on a plate on the larger table. Katerin looked away from them. She reluctantly fumbled through her own bags, looking for a change of clothes.

I should unpack.

But the bags she kept looking at were not her own, but Metkyi's. Finally, she pulled his saddlebags off of the pile and sat down on the floor next to the bags. If his journals had not been taken, they'd be here.

The left saddlebag carried traveling staples, much like her own. Flatbread, dried fruit and nuts, extra gloves, a scarf. Katerin instinctively raised the scarf to her nose, drawing in the remnants of Metkyi's scent, tears brimming in her eyes. She wrapped it around her neck.

She looked in the other side. A smaller bag held Metkyi's writing kit. And a familiar, black-covered book. Katerin pulled that out. She opened it. Tucked inside the front cover were several neatly folded and sealed papers with names on them, one name hers.

Katerin blinked. Carefully setting the book aside, she broke the seal on her letter.

My dearest Katerin—the opening line read, in Metkyi's neat handwriting.

Tears fuzzed her vision.

She wasn't sure how long she had been crying when Senai shook her.

"Katerin. Katerin. What's wrong?"

Katerin shook her head, unable to speak. Senai held her until her sobs ebbed. Then she left the room. Katerin curled her knees to her chest and wiped her eyes on the sleeve of her sweater. She forced herself to read the letter.

My dearest Katerin.

If you're reading this, then I am dead. I hoped we could avoid this fate, but the odds are far too high against us, especially since you are of the house of Miteal. I would do what I can to ensure your survival and that of our daughter. To do that means I must die, in order for my lord Staul to protect you if need be.

Tears started flowing again, but this time Katerin disciplined herself to wipe her eyes and keep reading, forcing back the sobs. Senai returned with a cup of water and Katerin drank it absently, her eyes fixed on the letter.

Too much power, concentrated in two people. The relationships of Staul and Dovré can never last for very long because of this. Add in your growing power from your father, and it is unlikely that we could survive for long without someone trying to use us.

But I can tell you this. Our daughter has the potential to be great. She will be our legacy to the world, greater than anything you or I could do separately. I wish I could see her, but even the limited glimpses Staul has shown me give me hope.

If you are reading this, I can't be present for our daughter. But I can do this. I have left papers with Myrieke, Orelyets, and Imnari naming you as my heir. This gives you a significant share in our family's trade income. This should be enough to provide for both you and our child until her majority, along with whatever the Healing House will give you. This frees you from the need to travel the healing circuit, and it frees you from your new-discovered relatives, should you choose not to stay in Medvara.

Katerin's eyes misted over again. She shook her head and buried it on her knees. Senai rubbed her back.

Katerin raised her head. She had to finish the letter.

Know that I love you, and will love you, from beyond the end of time. If there were any other way, I would do my best to find it. Since I can't, I will do what I can to watch and protect you from now until you join me.

Have faith, my dearest. Have courage. I love you.

The letter fell from Katerin's fingers. She dropped her head on her knees again. Paper rustled as Senai picked up the letter.

"Katerin, may I?"

"Yes," Katerin groaned.

More rustling of paper. Then Senai gasped. "Katerin, this means—"

"I know," Katerin said. "But I'd trade every gold piece of that fortune to have his living arms around me right now."

Senai hugged her again. "If there's anything I can do, I will do it."

"Thank you," Katerin whispered. "Thank you. I just want to get out of this place. I want to go back to Wickmasa. I don't want any part of Medvara."

"Seven days," Senai said.

"Help me bear it," Katerin pleaded. "Just help me get through this."

"I will," Senai promised. "We all will."

CHAPTER 35

Katerin spent the next days sorting through Metkyi's bags, working with Rainin, and reading Metkyi's journal. When she wasn't with Rainin, she kept to her rooms. Eldoran and Yevtin visited often, and Senai was a frequent but silent companion. Rekaré visited when she could dodge matters of state.

Orelyets stopped by her rooms before going back to the Trading Fair.

"We'll wait for you in Chellni," he said tersely, after reading his letter from Metkyi. His face twisted in one of his rare attempts at a smile. "There's always a home for you in our clan. You did right by Metkyi."

"Thank you," Katerin said.

"I'll teach you the watchwords that can always get you help from a caravan. You'll be staying in Wickmasa?"

"As far as I know."

"Is the child going to be yours or ours?"

"No," Katerin said firmly. "The child will not be one of the village. I will raise Metkyi's daughter."

"Good." Orelyets patted her shoulder again, as if she were a timid caravan mount needing reassurance, and shuffled out.

Katerin sorted out the pieces of Metkyi's life that were with her. When she tired of this task, she curled up on one of the loveseats and read Metkyi's journal. He used an elaborate code, but she could puzzle out the references to Rekaré and Cenarth, as well as encounters with Heinmyets, Alicira and Inharise.

Makri had most probably been jealous of his brother's close ties to power, she decided. But Metkyi had not sought out power. His abilities drew people to him, and yet, he'd been a very lonely man, unlike his more gregarious brother.

She was getting to know Metkyi even better. She already knew he was different, but after reading his journal, all she could wish for was that they had a full winter together, or even longer.

Not meant to be.

* * *

It was the afternoon of the fifth day since Metkyi's funeral, a rainy, miserable day, as far too many winter days in Medvara seemed to be. Katerin had ventured out in mid-morning to ride Rainin in the indoor school. They worked until Katerin was chilled. The damp cold went directly to her bones.

I'll be glad to go back to the other side of the Dry Line.

She ate, and changed into dry clothing. Now Katerin curled up in front of the fireplace with a blanket over her and a hot cup of berry tea on the low, round marble table next to the loveseat. Metkyi's journal was open on her lap as she gazed into the flames. Then someone knocked on the main door.

Katerin raised a brow. By now, those who wanted to see her simply came in.

"Come in," she called, closing the journal.

Alicira ea Miteal entered quietly. She still wore traveling

clothes, except for her slippers. Katerin sprang up from the loveseat.

"Sit down, my lady, you must be tired from the ride."

Alicira shook her head. "I've done enough sitting for five people." She smiled wryly. "I found out I'm not too old and frail to ride a vigorous pace from Keldara to Medvara. I'll stand, thank you, but *you* need to be sitting. You look tired."

"At least let me get you some tea, or something."

"*Sit,*" Alicira commanded, and in that moment Katerin glimpsed the ruler in the woman. Then Alicira softened. "I'm well taken care of. Rekaré's plied me with tea, and I've been told to rest enough times that I'm tired of it. *You*, though. You're all right?"

"As well as can be expected, my lady." Katerin sank back down on the loveseat.

"No need to be so formal, cousin!" She strode over to the fire. "My backside appreciates a good fire. I can use *this* much more than a seat, thank you very much!"

"You're welcome." Katerin still felt nervous. What could Alicira want from her? She studied the leader with a healer's eye. Alicira still looked tired and wan. But the strain that had underlain her every move in Wickmasa was gone.

She doesn't need to protect Rekaré from Zauril anymore. That makes a difference.

"Your father," Alicira started to say, then stopped.

"I didn't know," Katerin said. "And I don't know how to use his magic."

"Magic you can learn. It will come to you. Your training at the Healing House will be of use."

"What does this mean for me, my lady? I mean, no one knows if this is really true or not, except for maybe the magic."

Alicira made a rude noise and waved one hand. "Drop the *my lady*, will you? We're cousins. That changes everything. I should have known. *He* should have known. Now that I look at you, you do have a faint look of him. And you aided Rekaré. Wielded magic that only those born to *the house of Miteal* could have done."

"I am not used to being Aireii. I don't know the language; I don't know the magic."

"You will learn."

"But is there a place for me?"

"Until Rekaré and Cenarth have a child, you're her heir. I can't inherit now. The deal I made to keep my magic years ago. There's none other of the Miteal left alive. Zauril was thorough in his murders."

"Lady, I know nothing of the house of Miteal. Of the Aireii. Of ruling. I'd be a poor successor."

"You would learn," Alicira said.

"I don't want to stay in Medvara."

"Medvara is the last place you should be. The danger from Daran remembering they have colonies here is too great for any heir of Rekaré's to stay here. No. You would not remain in Medvara."

Katerin sighed with relief. "I'm just a simple healer, my la—Alicira. And I have duties and obligations."

Alicira cocked a brow at her. "I'm not here to persuade you to stay in Medvara. Rather, I would thank you, not only for the aid you gave Rekaré but for all you did to help Alame."

Katerin shrugged. "It was what any healer would have done."

"Maybe." Alicira sounded unconvinced. "However, that leaves me with a greater need."

"What's that?"

"Siljaren. She traveled with Alame, but she was also my healer. Now that Alame's dead, that will change. She's never been fond of the traveling Clendan mountain life."

"Lady, you could get someone from the Healing House to attend you."

"I *could*. But I have my own preferences. What are *your* plans?"

"I have responsibilities to Wickmasa which go above that of a healer. Metkyi made me his heir."

"He thought well of you."

"I carry his child."

"That I had been told. However. You have new duties to Medvara. Perhaps we can combine the training you will need along with my need for a healer."

"I have responsibilities to Wickmasa as well as to Medvara."

"Why? Because you're bearing Metkyi's child?" Alicira shook her head. "You'd really bring up a child there? It's a nice village, but it's a *village*. They didn't understand Metkyi, nor will they understand you or your daughter, now that it's known you're Miteal and the heir to Medvara. *She* will be an heir, as well."

"I think they would still want to know his daughter."

"I'm sure they would. Ah, that's warm enough! *Now* I'm ready to sit down." Alicira turned one of the overstuffed chairs to face Katerin.

"Alicira, this is all so new to me. And I'm not so sure I'd make a good Miteal."

"Come live with Heinmyets, Inharise and me. Not just as healer but as student. Raise your child with us."

"There's still the matter of Wickmasa. Not only do I owe them a contract for the remainder of the winter, but I have a kinswoman's duty to them now for Metkyi's daughter."

"Understandable." Alicira started pacing. Katerin watched her warily, remembering Alicira's collapse at the meeting in Wickmasa.

"Wickmasa can still be your base," Alicira continued. "But. Katerin Healer, no, Katerin *ea Miteal*, I need someone of your ability to care for my family. For you to be a kinswoman makes this possibility even sweeter." She stopped and faced Katerin. "My daughter Cirenna is frail, and spends most of her time in

Dera. I don't expect her to last longer than a couple more years. Cenarth and Rekaré will be Heinmyets's heirs when it comes time."

"A lot rests on those two," Katerin said in a low voice.

"Yes. I need someone I can trust as healer and possible regent for Rekaré's heir, either here or in Keldara, should the worst happen. My hope is that they have enough children for one to follow Heinmyets, and that Heinmyets lives long enough for that heir to come to adulthood. It could happen. His family is long-lived."

"But my child?"

"Your child will also be an heir to Rekaré. And after that— ah, best not to tempt the Gods!"

Katerin rested her chin on her knees. "My daughter will be due toward the end of the summer. Who would attend *me*, if I am *your* healer?"

"Someone from the Healing House. We'd pay generously for a season's contract."

"But what of my things and Metkyi's? He would want our child to have them. I can't see dragging that behind us."

"We visit Wickmasa often enough. Keep what you want in storage. Myrieke is an excellent custodian. That way, your daughter would know *all* her kinfolk."

Katerin released her knees and sat up. "I'd still need time in Wickmasa before I could join you. I can't commit until spring. And I don't know what training in magic will do to a baby."

"That would be no problem. Zauril left Medvara a mess. Rekaré has many things to fix before she can restore the magic here. She needs my help to get that started. Contacting old friends who've gone into hiding under Zauril, fixing twisted magics, negotiating new alliances. There's a lot to be done that my presence will make easier for her to accomplish. I need to be here through the winter. In spring, I'll come back to Clenda. We won't be training until the baby is weaned. You best be tempering what magics you practice, soon enough. Pregnancy and magic," she sighed. "I know that challenge well enough. You'll lose even your healing magics in a month or two."

Katerin stared into the fire again. Healer to Alicira.

Can I live up to this?

"I never thought of myself as good at magic."

"You're better than you think. And besides being my cousin, you're the healer I want by my side. Someone unafraid to face the Hunt."

"I had enough fear for five people."

"Nonetheless, you did it, *Banisher of Shadows*. That takes no little talent. The best magicians always have that self-doubt."

"Last summer I was still the fatherless daughter of Terani the God-Killer, with debt still owed for keeping her alive as well as for my training. An ordinary healer. And now, pregnant, a bastard daughter of the House of Miteal, an heir to Medvara, so much. So fast."

"You'll get used to it. You've walked a hard road, like I have."

"But why us?"

"We are the tools of the Gods." Alicira frowned into the fire, twisting her fingers around themselves. "The best I can tell you, Katerin, is that somehow we were chosen to further the struggles for power between the Seven Crowned Gods."

"But why do they struggle?"

"That's one thing for which the Gods seem to think we don't need an answer. I just know that the Goddess sometimes chooses to ride me. These days I am grateful that she mostly chooses to leave me alone."

"I think Metkyi knew why they struggle. I've been reading his journals. Trying to understand."

"You may find you're better off not knowing," Alicira said. "I think Rekaré knows. These days, she has more strength and power than I thought she would ever have come into. Her choice is not one I could have made."

"She possesses a lot of power because of both you and her father."

"Yes. And the price she pays now, and will pay," Alicira shook her head. "I could not have done it. Cannot do it."

Katerin had nothing more to say.

At last, Alicira stirred. She rose, and bowed low. "I would stay. It's peaceful here with you, my new-found cousin, but I have duties." She grimaced. "These days I find I have little taste for the trappings of Medvaran courtly etiquette. But, for Rekaré's sake, I can endure it for a winter."

"Let me see you out."

"No, no, I'm perfectly capable of taking care of myself." Alicira stopped before she opened the door. "We'll be seeing each other at the coronation. After that, I'll see you in the spring."

"In the spring," Katerin repeated.

She dug out Metkyi's journal again, fingering idly through it. He had only filled about half of this book.

I wonder how many more there are back in the lodge?

She glanced at the last few pages, smiling as she read what he had written after she told him she was with child.

I should continue this journal, as a record for our daughter.

She got his writing kit.

Here begins the record of Katerin Healer ea Miteal, bondmate of Metkyi and mother-to-be of his daughter, she wrote.

Looking up from those words, she could almost swear she saw Metkyi's face smiling out at her from the flames. She studied the flames for a few moments longer.

"I hope I've made the right choice," she said to the fire. "At least one where the Gods leave me alone for a while."

The flames laughed back at her.

—What makes you think the gods are done with you, Banisher of Shadows? she heard Dovré laugh, deep inside her head.

—When there is need, you will be called, Staul's voice added.

May that be a long, long time in the making.

The only response was another laugh.

—*When there is need, you will be called,* the Goddess repeated.

—*Until then,* Katerin agreed, too tired to argue with both Gods. *Until then,* she promised herself.

And, with luck, that time would never come again, as long as she lived.

THE END

RETURN TO WICKMASA

This was not the return to Wickmasa that Katerin had envisioned.

Of course, neither she nor Metkyi had dared to speak of what would happen after they got Rekaré to Medvara and done...whatever it would take to help Rekaré succeed. *If* they achieved their goal of toppling Zauril and replacing him with Rekaré.

But when Katerin had allowed herself to imagine the return, it didn't look like this. She had visualized her and Metkyi returning on a cold but sunny day. Snow crunched under her daranval Mira's hooves, with everything dazzling bright and white, in contrast to the rain and gray-green gloom of Medvara. They would ride in the middle of Orelyets' trade caravan, laded with goods from a successful Midwinter Fair at Chellni. Her newly-discovered father, Alame, would have ridden ahead looking for his beloved Siljaren, who had remained behind in Wickmasa as healer in place of Katerin. The Gods would be quiet for once, content to leave their dedicated ones alone for a season.

The reality was nothing like that. The small troop that

included Katerin rode the wide trail winding down the canyon wall to the village, huddled in their heavy winter parkas. Icy snow pellets pounded the riders, snowing so hard that she couldn't make out anything more than two horse lengths ahead. She kept a snug contact on her reins to help support Rainin, who was still sufficiently green-broke to worry about maintaining her balance on the ice-crusted snow with a rider. It was only due to Orelyets's knowledge of the trail that kept Katerin confident that they were indeed not that far from Wickmasa.

And she had lost so much in the span of a month.

No Metkyi. No Mira. No Alame.

All three dead.

Instead of Mira, Katerin rode Rainin in the place of honor between Heinmyets and Inharise. What remained of Alame lay under a cairn in the canyon walls above the great Chellana River. Metkyi's ashes rested in a cedar bentwood box tucked into one of Katerin's saddlebags. Another small bentwood box held Mira's ashes.

Katerin hadn't decided what to do with those yet. Her stomach roiled in dread of what would happen when they reached Wickmasa, tension adding to the already sour gut of pregnancy. She did not look forward to telling Siljaren the details of Alame's death, much less tell Metkyi's sister Twana about her brother's death.

And yet she was the survivor. The one who had to speak to those left behind. She had to talk, to share the fate of their loved ones.

Gods, Metkyi. I wish you were here.

Sometimes thinking about him could evoke a sense of his presence. Not now. The heavy, clammy sensation of Metkyi's patron, the God Staul, rose instead.

—*Now is not the time to speak to your lost beloved.*

Staul's tone carried a warning. Katerin bit her lip. Ever since their stop at Nixyin, Staul had blocked her attempts to reach to Metkyi's spirit for comfort. And Dovré was silent.

—*Must I always be alone?* she cried to the God.

Staul did not answer. Neither did Dovré.

Katerin blinked back tears. No time for this, not in these conditions, as the snowstorm intensified. She could barely see Orelyets riding in front of them, and their pace slowed even more. Rainin tossed her head impatiently, mouthing at the bit and trying to pull more rein free.

"Enough," Katerin said, squeezing the reins to keep her grip secure and the contact where it should be. Rainin relented and she eased her hand slightly. "Steady, girl. It won't be long."

She stifled a shiver as the wind whistling around them took a malign tone. Gods swirled about them in the gusts, Gods who shouldn't be there even in the faint traces she sensed.

Karnoi and Cirdel.

—*Beware, Banisher of Shadows. The fate of Terani the God-Killer may yet be yours,* a presence that reminded Katerin of Cirdel snarled.

Katerin shuddered. *That* threat, from *those* Gods, was all too real.

Dovré, do not abandon me now!

Surely the Goddess would rouse from her silence and rise to protect her. Katerin closed her eyes for a moment and transferred both reins to her left hand. Her right hand fumbled under her heavy jacket to grasp the Eye of Dovré that hung around her neck on a braided leather cord.

—*Protect me, oh Goddess, from the shards of Karnoi and Cirdel.*

The smoothly polished rutilated quartz stone warmed in her palm even through her thick leather gloves.

—*I am here. I cannot speak when you try to reach for your lost beloved. But protect you and your child—yes. I will do that.*

The faint touch of the Goddess ruffled Katerin's hair, as if it were free and not covered by the heavy parka's fur hood she had pulled over her head.

—*Do not fear,* Dovré whispered. —*They are but shadows. We ride with you.*

"Are you well?" Heinmyets asked, words muffled through his own scarf.

"Just Gods whispering to me," Katerin said.

"We are with you." He urged Elantai, closer, and patted her hand. Then Elantai jumped a half-step sideways as Rainin flicked her ears back and tossed her head at him to express her discomfort at his closeness.

"Steady, girl," Katerin said to Rainin. She sent Rainin images of them walking calmly next to the big stallion.

Rainin sent back grumpy feelings about —*slipping in snow and ice and wanting space, tired, hungry, want to be home.*

Katerin swallowed hard and reached forward to pat Rainin's neck reassuringly, missing Mira and her images of buffalo dung when she was unhappy. She kept *those* feelings buried deep away from Rainin, though, thinking about —*warm food, shelter, hay, soon* instead.

"It's been a long ride for a young daranval," Inharise said, from Katerin's other side. "She's done well."

"She's just crabby and tired," Katerin said.

"Not far to go," Inharise said.

Katerin nodded, her throat tightening as she began to recognize landmarks. They passed the trail leading to the meadow shrine dedicated to Staul and Dovré. A few twists down the path further, and they passed by the place where she and Mira had rescued Metkyi from Karnoi and Cirdel's pursuit. With every turn her throat cranked even more shut in anticipation of the news she needed to share.

At last they leveled out. Down in the narrow canyon the winds lessened, snow falling steadily but softly, no wind-driven pellets here.

Metkyi would have made note of that.

He had always recorded the weather in his role as the priest of Staul.

Her heart sank even more as she saw who stood in front of those who waited, wearing their ceremonial robes and hats in spite of the storm, dreading the explanations ahead of her. Of course they would be there. She had known that. But all the same, seeing all of those she would need to talk to lined up and waiting, knowing she would soon need to explain what had happened—if Rainin was not so tired and fatigued, she would have almost ridden on in hopes of avoiding this.

Stop that. It is your duty.

But gods, she was *so tired.* And seeing all of those waiting just added to the waves of fatigue crashing over her. Imnari, the Eldest of Wickmasa, the woman who led the village. Twana, shaman of the God Artel, Metkyi's sister. Next to Twana, Siljaren, legendary healer and beloved of Katerin's father Alame —the sight of Siljaren twisted Katerin's gut even more. They would already know the news—*all* of it, thanks to messages that had been sent on ahead by messenger bird and couriers. But news from paper and scroll was one thing—news from the ones who had been there would be another.

Twana began to chant Artel the Judge's mourning song as they approached, Siljaren picking up a counterpoint melody of Dovré's a few notes later. Others within those waiting began the mourning songs of their patrons. Katerin wanted to join those singing for Dovré but her throat was too tight and choked, even as others of their party began to sing in response.

They halted before Imnari, Twana, and Siljaren. The three women bowed in respect to Heinmyets and Inharise. Katerin half-nodded, half-bowed back to them.

"My lady Katerin, you have no need to bow to us," Imnari said, just the faintest whisper of reproof in her voice.

"I am no more than Katerin Healer," Katerin whispered hoarsely, tension making her unable to speak louder.

"Katerin Healer who is also the lady Katerin ea Miteal, daughter of Alame the last prince of the Miteal family," Imnari corrected. "Katerin the Banisher of Shadows, beloved of Metkyi priest of Staul. You have grown, Katerin. You have become greater than just Katerin Healer. You have earned this honor."

"You also speak for Medvara to the Two Nations as Rekaré's heir," Heinmyets added. "You have earned your honors, Katerin."

Katerin nodded, throat tight again. "I am sorry. I'm just a Healer. I'm not good with protocol."

"Do not be nervous." Heinmyets's voice softened, and he leaned close, speaking low so that only she and Inharise could hear him. "We remember that this is all still new to you. We would not honor you so if you did not deserve it, for all you have done for Rekaré. For Medvara."

She nodded again, unable to answer.

Heinmyets straightened up in his saddle. "We request an overnight stay in Wickmasa, Eldest Imnari."

"But of course, Leader Heinmyets. Why would I object?"

"Thank you. I always prefer to ask, especially when I would ask a greater favor of Wickmasa."

"Which is?"

"I would beg that Wickmasa allow us the time of Katerin Healer for a few days more before she returns to her contracted Healer duties. She bears messages to my Court in Dera from Medvara, but we will send her back to you as quickly as possible."

"If Siljaren is amenable," Katerin croaked.

"I know my duty," Siljaren answered, sounding as if her throat was as tight and hard and choked as Katerin's.

"We are more than willing to grant this favor, Leader," Imnari said brusquely. "So shall we get in out of this weather?"

"Yes," Inharise said.

"I'll go to my lodge with Siljaren," Katerin told them.

Imnari frowned. "There are things we should know."

"Katerin is exhausted," Inharise said. "As are we all. Tomorrow will be better for the telling."

Yes. Yes. If I could just tell Siljaren tonight...

"The families should know," Imnari said.

"I can tell the clan about Metkyi tonight," Orelyets said. "Presenting Katerin as the mother to a new clan member can wait until she returns from Dera."

"I'll join Siljaren and Katerin," Twana said. "I can help Katerin settle in tonight—at least beyond what Davni and Colerei will do."

Katerin could only nod in response. Twana was not just Metkyi's sister but a friend and fellow speaker for the Gods. All the same—she would have to speak of two of the three deaths tonight if Twana came to her lodge, when what she really wanted to do was curl up in front of the fire and not talk at all.

At least Mira's death is only mine to mourn.

But it was only fair that Twana should know what happened to Metkyi as soon as possible, as his closest blood kin.

"Go, Katerin. Rest," Imnari said, her stern face softening. "We will speak in the morning."

"Thank you," Katerin said.

Imnari stepped back as Katerin urged Rainin ahead. Siljaren and Twana walked next to them as they headed for Katerin's lodge on the edge of the village, near the river.

* * *

Katerin's assistants Davni and Colerei were watching for their arrival. No sooner had Katerin slid off of Rainin than both girls were there, hugging her. Rainin startled back, and Katerin had to break away to calm the excited mare as she snorted, eyes wide and white-rimmed.

"She's still a baby," Katerin murmured to Davni and Colerei. "And she's tired. I'd best put her away."

"The shelter is ready." Davni hurried ahead as Katerin led Rainin to the lean-to shed which had been Mira's. "Fresh bedding, I laid in hay for Rainin, and I brushed out Mira's blankets for Rainin as well. Unless you have something else?"

Katerin shook her head. She led Rainin into the shed and eased the hackamore off of Rainin's head.

"Not yet," she said when the impatient mare would have rushed for her hay. She made Rainin back two steps and wait. "Let's unsaddle you first." She pulled off her saddlebags, then the saddle.

"May I brush her?" Davni asked, a brush from Katerin's saddlebags already in her right hand.

"Let her meet you first," Katerin advised. "But quickly!" she added as Rainin stretched her head toward the hay. "She's starving, and still young enough that she gets crabby when she hungers."

Davni offered the back of her left hand to Rainin to smell. The mare sniffed Davni's hand, blew out slowly, nudged Davni, then moved past her for the hay. Rainin grabbed a great mouthful from the rack and dropped it on the ground, burying her nose in her food.

"She doesn't have much silver in her mane," Davni said as she began brushing. "Not like Mira did. Does that mean she's not a powerful a daranval as Mira was?"

"Mira was older and stronger," Katerin said. "Rainin is young and coming into her strength. As her magic grows, her mane and tail will become more silver." She reached into a saddlebag for a hoof pick and started to remove the magical boots that protected Rainin's feet, frowning at the condition of the first boot.

Need to put new boots on her when we ride out tomorrow.

Luckily, the boots she had purchased for Mira at the beginning of winter would also fit Rainin.

Rainin raised her head as she finished the big mouthful of hay and blew out a long, slow breath, eying Davni. Then she turned her head and shoved Davni hard with her muzzle before turning back to the hayrack. Davni staggered back two steps, giggling.

"Rainin!" Katerin scolded, slapping the daranval mare's shoulder. She sent disapproving thoughts. "Don't let her push you like that, Davni. She tests boundaries. Tell her no the next time she tries and push her head away."

"I'm sorry. But it was funny!"

Rainin turned her head toward Katerin, ears forward, eyes soft, lower lip sagging, doing her best to look innocent. Katerin shook a finger at Rainin. Then, yielding to Rainin's *who me?* expression, she scratched the mare's poll. Rainin sent approving feelings back to Katerin, mixed with an image of Davni.

Katerin finished pulling the hoof boots and put the hoof pick away. Then she ran her fingers through Rainin's fur, pulling off a glove to feel between Rainin's forelegs to ensure she wasn't too hot and sweaty.

"She's in good shape," Davni said. "Blanket her tonight? Or will you bring her inside like you did—" her voice caught. "Like you did Mira?" she finally gulped.

Katerin shook her head. "I am not bringing Rainin inside. She's young and strong. Blanketing will be enough."

Davni nodded and went to the walled-off area where she had placed Katerin's tack. She pulled out a blanket and together they spread it over Rainin's back, fastening it closed with big safety pins at her chest and under her belly, then strapping a surcingle around Rainin's abdomen just behind her forelegs to keep the blanket secure. Katerin checked the water in the wooden bucket, looked at the hay supply, then scratched Rainin's forehead. Davni waited to help Katerin with the gate that had been added to the shelter in Katerin's absence. Together they pulled it closed, Katerin blinking away wetness that threatened to blur her vision.

Mira didn't need a gate.

Before she could grab the saddlebags, Davni scooped them up.

"Davni—" she began.

Davni shook her head. "You've had a long ride and a hard time. Colerei has prepared a roast and fresh bread for you and Siljaren. Rest."

Katerin was too tired to argue. She followed Davni into the lodge, entering on the side which had been her personal quarters. As the mat and skin door fell shut behind her, she stopped short, looking around. She had not lived in this lodge for many days before leaving for Medvara. But even though her things were here, they all seemed unfamiliar. Even her Blue Starry Robe clan mask that hung on the far side of the room, over her shrine, seemed shadowed and alien.

"Not—here," she said in a choked voice to Davni. "I'll make my bed on the other side. Tell Siljaren she can sleep here."

Davni turned toward Katerin. "But—" She cut off her objection as she studied Katerin. "As you wish, Katerin Healer," she said, and picked up the saddlebags before she pushed back the hide that covered the doorway between the two rooms of Katerin's lodge. "We will leave you here with Siljaren, but we will be back in the morning. Rest well."

Katerin took a deep, shuddering breath as Davni left her alone, looking around her. Metkyi had moved in with her during the last days before they left for Medvara. His things still were mixed with hers. His trunks next to hers, one of his jackets hanging on the wall, and the rocks and bones he collected scattered about the room.

I'll need to sort all that when I return from Dera.

Some things she would keep, others she would destroy, and the rest—mostly clothing and tools, especially Metkyi's traveling goods—would go to the village to be distributed to those who needed such things.

She caught a glimpse of herself in the mirror and flinched. While she wasn't as pale as her Aireii kin, still her dust-brown skin was a faint gray-brown shade paler than her natural healthy color. The skin on her face was drawn tight over her high cheekbones. Only her dark hair and brown eyes still looked familiar, tokens of her mother's people. She turned away from the mirror.

She moved toward the shrine instead, but found no peace there. Metkyi's heartstone, a double-lobed gray stone with green chips, lay shattered in three pieces. Katerin whirled away and started for the other room. Siljaren pushed back the door and stood just inside it before Katerin reached the opening.

"Are you certain you want to sleep on the healing side of your lodge?" she asked.

"Yes, Siljaren, the memories—I'd prefer you sleep on this side if you don't want to be in the other with me."

Siljaren gulped. "I haven't been able to sleep on the healing side since you left. Too many memories of sleeping there with Alame...." Wetness formed in Siljaren's eyes.

Katerin tool the older woman into her arms. Siljaren hugged Katerin fiercely, bursting into sobs. Katerin held her close, teardrops oozing from her eyes but not the same deep cries as Siljaren's. She had cried herself out at Metkyi's death, at his mourning, during the nights alone in Medvara.

Siljaren's tears eased, and she straightened up. "When did you find out you were Alame's daughter?"

"At his death, when he passed on his magic to me," Katerin whispered. "He tried to tell me before then, but someone or something always interrupted."

Siljaren pulled her close again. "He suspected but wasn't certain."

"I wish I'd known before then," Katerin gulped, her tears beginning anew. "I had no idea—and now I'm heir to Medvara, at least until Rekaré bears her own heirs."

"And you've lost Metkyi and Mira as well. The Gods are cruel."

"I carry Metkyi's child."

"At least you have that. While I—"

"You called me daughter," Katerin whispered.

Would that it were true.

Her mother had always been distant, more concerned about Katerin's magic skills and her dedication to Dovré instead of the Twin Gods Terani served.

"A slip of the tongue, only. I can't usurp Terani's place."

"Why not? She chose to battle Nitel in spite of the concerns about the impact on her daughter. Once she discovered I was called to serve Dovré, she had no use for me. Besides, she has died."

She no longer needed to send tribute to the witches to keep Terani safe in the dreamless sleep.

"Foolish of her to not see your potential." Siljaren shook her head. "You truly would not mind?"

"I would be honored to have you call me daughter, Heartmother," she said.

"*Heartsdaughter,*" Siljaren murmured. "Welcome home, however long it may be that you remain here. Come. Sit. You must be exhausted—" She took Katerin by the hand, leading her to the doorway. "Colerei has food ready and Davni has already left. Twana is waiting—should I send her away?"

Katerin shook her head. "I need to tell her about Metkyi. About the child."

"You need not do everything before riding to Dera," Siljaren chided as she and Katerin entered the healing side of the lodge.

"I owe it to her. To you. We three are bound together now."

Twana rose as Katerin and Siljaren joined her around the iron stove in the middle of the lodge. Colerei fussed over the food on the table. The rich scent of venison roast made Katerin both hungry and nauseated.

"Thank you, Colerei," she said. "My stomach has been cranky of late."

"Travel food isn't always the best." Colerei frowned at Katerin.

"Especially when one is pregnant," Katerin said, deciding not to delay sharing the news with Colerei and Twana any further.

"Pregnant?" Both Twana and Colerei startled.

Katerin nodded. "Senai Healer and Eldoran Healer have both confirmed it."

Twana's expression brightened. "So something of Metkyi still remains with us. That is a blessing for all."

"Yes." Katerin sank down on one of the tripod-backed chairs, fumbling with her boots. Colerei hurried over to help her. "Colerei, that's not necessary!"

"You've ridden long and hard after a loss," Colerei said. "Let me do this for you."

Katerin yielded. The warmth from the stove made her sleepy. She fumbled with her coat. Twana and Siljaren helped her remove her outer clothing. When Katerin would have gotten up to get her food, Colerei shook her head. She dished up a small portion of meat, root vegetables, and fresh bread and brought it back to Katerin. It was still warm, so Katerin set it down to cool. Siljaren fussed around the stove, putting a pot of water on to boil before going over to Katerin's medicine case to mix a tea.

"There's a tea I give to mothers early in their pregnancy," she said. "Unless you have something already prepared?"

"I do." Katerin leaned her head against the fur lining the chair back. It was one of Metkyi's and still exuded a faint whiff of his scent. "You'll find the mixture I use on the third shelf, fourth compartment from the left."

"Mmhmm." Siljaren opened the front of the case. She extracted a jar from that compartment and sniffed. "Very similar to mine."

"I'll be back in the morning to make you a good breakfast before you leave for Dera," Colerei said. "Don't you dare leave without a good meal!" She pulled on her coat and set her hat securely on her head. "I will be here at first light."

"Thank you, Colerei," Katerin said.

Siljaren brought Katerin her tea, then dished up her own food. Twana followed. Katerin sipped her tea slowly, letting it settle her stomach before setting it down and picking up her food.

When she had finished she put her plate down. "How much do you want to know tonight?" she asked them.

"Whatever you can bear to share," Siljaren said. Twana nodded.

Katerin drew a deep breath. "I'll start with my father's death," she said.

*   *   *

She shared the bare bones of what had happened. Neither Siljaren nor Twana pressed Katerin for more when she was finished.

"I will be your sister," Twana said. "But it grows late, and you must sleep. Take care and rest well, beloved of my brother. I hope you will call me Heartsister."

"I will," Katerin promised. "I just—I wish that Metkyi's heartstone had not broken."

"It was when it broke that I knew the worst had happened," Twana said. "Siljaren rushed to tell me."

"It is a token I hoped to cherish," Katerin said.

"Perhaps I can do something," Twana said. "If I may…?"

Katerin nodded. Twana picked up one of the oil lamps and went into the other room. She returned with the three pieces of the heartstone.

"Three pieces," she mused as she sat on the hide rug next to Katerin's chair. "I would not have expected it to break into three. Two, perhaps."

"It might represent Katerin, Metkyi, and the child to be," Siljaren said, sitting next to Twana.

"Very possible." Twana turned the pieces in her hand. "Or it could represent the three of us. You and Katerin have lost Alame. Katerin and I have lost Metkyi. Katerin has lost Alame, Metkyi, and Mira. Three losses, three divisions." She fitted the pieces together. "This should not be so difficult a challenge as I feared. The stone broke cleanly and there are no chips missing. Well within my power as Artel's shaman."

"I have no idea of what we would do," Katerin said.

"Nor do I," Siljaren said.

A brief smile flitted across Twana's lips. "Ah, but as an acolyte of Artel the Judge, this falls into one of the things I can do, if the God so chooses to grant it. The three of us are tied together. The three of us can unite this stone." She handed one outside piece to Siljaren and the middle to Katerin.

"What do we do?" Siljaren asked.

"Let me speak to the God." Twana straightened up, crossing her legs and resting her hands on her knees.

She placed her piece of the stone in front of her and closed her eyes, chanting atonal syllables that Katerin didn't recognize as words. Twana fell silent, then leaned forward, eyes still closed, and picked up her piece, lifting it high. An orange-yellow glow radiated from her hands into the stone. Twana opened her eyes and her lips moved but no sound came out.

She lowered the stone. "Katerin. Match your centerpiece to

mine, and state how you share in this loss. Let your Goddess guide your words."

Katerin carefully fitted her piece to Twana's, pressing hard. She closed her eyes.

—Lady Dovré, what would you have me say?

Tingles ran up and down her body as the Goddess's awareness overshadowed Katerin. She coughed, then the Goddess began to speak through her. Katerin had no idea what she was going to say.

"Twana, you are the sister of my lost beloved. In the three of us Wickmasa had representatives of Staul, Dovré, and Artel. That threefold bond is now broken. Let the three of us vow to renew this bond, two of us for Dovré and one for Artel."

Heat pulsed through Katerin and the rock chunk pulled hard against her fingers. She tightened her grasp as a loud CRACK! echoed through the lodge.

"I believe that's done the job," Twana said, her voice oddly deep. "Now. Katerin, keep your fingers on the stone. Siljaren. Match your end piece to Katerin's center, and state how you share in this loss. Let the Goddess speak through you."

Siljaren fitted her piece to Katerin's. A yearning rose within Katerin.

If only it were this easy to heal from the extent of our losses!

"Katerin, you are the daughter of my lost beloved," Siljaren said, her voice a deeper contralto than usual. "We are both healers of Wickmasa, and we both vowed with your lost beloved and with Twana to protect this village. As your Heartmother, I vow to keep you and the child you carry safe throughout your pregnancy and beyond. Twana, as sister to my Heartsdaughter's lost beloved, I will take you also as Heartsdaughter. I have lost my dearest beloved, but have gained two Heartsdaughters. Together we three will protect Wickmasa and the Two Nations."

Once again the loud CRACK! resonated throughout the lodge.

"Check it, Katerin," Twana said.

Katerin turned the stone in her fingers. Thin silver lines ran through the spaces between the segments that had broken apart, showing where the breaks had been. Other than that, she could not feel any weakness or crumbling from the stone. Wordlessly, she showed it to both Twana and Siljaren.

"It is done," Twana said.

"Good." Siljaren wrapped one arm around Katerin, and gestured for Twana to slide closer. She enveloped them both in a tight hug. "My loss still aches. But I have two Heartsdaughters now." She choked and a sob broke free. "Oh Gods, why couldn't Alame see this? Why couldn't he have cherished Katerin openly as his daughter?"

Katerin blinked back tears, lowering her head.

"Oh Gods, Katerin. Gods. It must have been awful in Medvare-the-city, all by yourself," Siljaren said.

She couldn't respond other than to try and fail to gulp back a new wave of tears. Twana and Siljaren held her until this spate of sobbing faded.

"You don't know how horrible it was to be so alone," Katerin finally whispered. "No daranval, at least not until I bonded to Rainin because her bond to Metkyi was gone. No Metkyi. And to know that Alame was my father, and—" She choked again.

"You have a Heartsister here, now," Twana said, rubbing her back.

"And a Heartmother," Siljaren added. "You have us. A family."

"A family," Katerin repeated. She wiped away her tears. "I don't—I've not had any family beyond what the Healing House had to offer. When Orelyets told me there would always be a place in the clan for me—what does that mean?"

"Family," Twana said. "A place where you will always find help, and support."

"You will no longer need to be a traveling Healer," Siljaren said.

"Not that I could be one with a child," Katerin said. "But what will that mean? What will I do? Alicira wants—" she hesitated. Should she be the one to tell this to Siljaren?

"I no longer want to be Alicira's personal healer," Siljaren said softly. "It also makes more sense that you would be her Healer—you are blood kin, and your child will need to know about that part of their life."

"Her life," Katerin said. She gulped. "Metkyi told me—in Medvare—after he passed. But the Gods won't let me talk to his spirit anymore!"

"Sweet sister, it is necessary for both of you to constrain your contacts. Metkyi must learn his role on the Other Side and you—you must focus on your child," Twana said.

"Is that you speaking or Artel speaking?" Katerin whispered.

"Both of us," Twana said. She rose and kissed Katerin's forehead. "I will let you rest now. Would it be of help if I rode with you to Dera? I can tell you stories about Metkyi as a boy."

"Please," Katerin said. She swallowed back more tears. "If you can bear it."

"I want to do it," Twana said. "It—it would be a relief and a pleasure for me. I will tell Orelyets and Imnari tonight."

"Thank you."

Twana left. Siljaren loaded another chunk of wood into the stove before settling onto another chair.

"Davni made up your bed in here," she said. "Would you mind if I slept in here as well? I will be alone after you go tomorrow."

"I would like that, yes," Katerin said. She rose and went to her bags, seeking the cap she wore at night. "I am going to bed now. It's been a long, hard ride, and I still have four days to Dera —plus who knows how long there."

"That is fine. I will sleep as well."

Katerin settled into her bedroll, carrying Metkyi's mended

heartstone with her. She held it in one hand. It warmed with the contact, and she thought she sensed Metkyi's presence nearby.

Tired as she was, it took a while to fall asleep. Katerin kept expecting the touch of Mira's thoughts. She reached out to Rainin, but the young mare lay sprawled on her side, sound asleep. Katerin closed her eyes and listened to the crack and pop from the firewood in the stove. To herself, she admitted that she hoped that one of her ghosts might reach for her.

But there was no sound in the lodge except for Siljaren's even, quiet breaths and the crackle of the fire. Quiet. Peaceful. Finally.

Only she didn't think she was ready for quiet and peaceful after all.

Be careful what you wish for.

Not that any of this was what Katerin Healer had even imagined as possible, before she came to Wickmasa. And here she was again, in the village that had changed her life.

Just for the remainder of my contract with the village. And then...

Parenthood. Traveling with the Three Leaders. Katerin rolled onto her back and looked up through the darkness. Her old life was almost gone, would be gone when her contract with Wickmasa expired in the spring.

Walk with us, oh Goddess. Keep us safe. Help me to remain Katerin Healer as long as possible.

She saw no glows, no manifestations of Dovré. But a gentle touch radiated from Metkyi's heartstone, sending a reassuring warmth through Katerin that felt like someone holding her tight.

Leave tomorrow to its own worries.

Katerin wasn't certain if it were Dovré or Metkyi's shade speaking to her. It didn't matter. The voice soothed her racing mind and she finally felt like she could sleep. She exhaled, turned onto her right side, and closed her eyes, relaxing into the warmth.

THE END

CROWN ANNIVERSARY

"Are you *certain* you want to attend the Anniversary?" Seijina frowned at Betsona as she wheeled the wicker and metal-framed chair to where Betsona clung to the bedframe. "You don't look well."

"I don't *feel* well." Betsona eased herself into the wheelchair's seat, wincing as her lower back started spasming. So it was to be one of *those* days. "A pillow for my lower back, please."

The other woman slipped the bolster behind Betsona, lips pressed tight in disapproval. "We shouldn't have come this year."

"I *have* to be here this year." Betsona adjusted the bolster. *Ah. There.*

Her back hurt less, now that she had the pillow in place. She wheeled over to her vanity and picked up a tiny bottle that nested nicely inside her palm, unstoppering it and letting one drop of the potion within fall under her tongue. Then she replaced the stopper and tucked the bottle into her bodice. Hopefully she wouldn't need any more pain drops tonight, but if she did…the bottle was handy.

"It's only the first anniversary of Chatain's crowning. Why should you reveal your weakness?"

"Chatain of all people knows my weaknesses better than most." Betsona forced herself to face her uneven features in the mirror. The withered right arm and matching hunched shoulder. The distorted scar across her face. The way her spine curved so that she could never sit straight up. The golden skin that spoke of her non-Aireii mother, lightly covered with white powder to minimize the difference in shade from the ruling Aireii for Court purposes. "If I don't attend, he wins."

"What do you gain from this exercise in futility besides fatigue and pain that leaves you abed for five or six days?"

"I remind Chatain of his failure, and that despite his delusions, he is not all-powerful."

Betsona reached out with her good left hand to pick up the copper tiara with inlaid turquoise stones from the vanity and placed it on her head. Copper and turquoise clashed with her bright red hair, but the copper was enough to mark her as a daughter of the late Emperor Dunaran, albeit one without political standing. One of the coppers of Dunaran's descent, not even bronze, much less gold or silver.

And yet it would have been different if our father had lived even two more seasons.

The golden crown would have been on her head.

I just needed more time to work on Father.

Seijina scowled as she tweaked the tiara's position, straightening it. "My lady—"

"Best not to speak that title out loud. I don't like it from your lips anyway, beloved." She fumbled for the green scarf on the vanity and draped it around her shoulders. Then she took a deep breath and picked up the silver, seven-pointed star brooch with a brilliant dark blue topaz set in the center, carefully using both hands to pin the shawl into place.

Now she looked at herself again.

Does my rage show?

The topaz and silver blazed brilliantly, revealing only a tiny portion of the magic it bore, but otherwise…there was no indication of her mood. She placed her good hand over the brooch for a moment. Her half-brother Chatain, the new Emperor, would be on edge for this first celebration of his crowning. No reason to give him more reason to react. When she dropped her hand the topaz and silver still glowed, but not as brightly.

Behind her Seijina simmered with tight-lipped anger. Betsona reached for Seijina.

"Don't be angry, dearest."

Seijina's hand tightened on hers. "Someone has to be. It should be you being feted tonight, not him—"

"Hush! You dare not even whisper that."

"But it is true," Seijina whispered. "And you know it. Using *those* colors this night of all nights. Here you are, fussing about me using a title, when nearly everything you're wearing proclaims your position!"

"And you are mirroring my colors," Betsona pointed out. Seijina wore a shapeless pale ankle-length, turquoise-shaded dress with copper accents given form by a blue belt and silver buckle. "That's not discreet. If you're going to scold me for showing who I am, then what about your choice?"

"No sense only one of us getting into trouble now, is there? If Chatain banishes you to an even more isolated exile, then at least I can go along."

"I am the one who should bear the brunt of his wrath, not you." A wave of pain washed over Betsona, and she braced against it. The drop hadn't taken effect yet. "I cannot claim the tiara that should be mine, but Chatain knows better than to deny me this much, on *this* night."

Had it only been one year since their father died and Chatain started his vendetta against all perceived threats to his reign as Emperor? She would not miss this first crown anniversary short of being on her deathbed, and at age twenty-three, even with her health, she was nowhere near dying. Even if she felt like she'd been dragged through a thorny brush arbor backwards and every joint ached.

Their surviving siblings would be present. She wanted to remind him—and *them*— that his magic could fail.

That his control over magitech was not as solid as he bragged it was.

That she still lived. That she was not vulnerable.

That their father had gifted *her* the Star of Elithtra before he died. That had Chatain not crippled her in that garden accident where magitech when wild, he might well be the one bending the knee to her.

For a moment Betsona let herself consider how different it was for her distant cousins in far-off Varen over the sea. Where Rekaré ruled as Leader in the rebel colony of Medvara. Where Alicira had gone native, become a Leader in one of the barbarian nations. If they were in Varen, she might well be the one who ruled, not Chatain.

But this was not Varen, and she had to make do with what options were available to her in a land under her brother's rule.

She took another deep breath as a welcome warm fuzziness oozed through her back, blunting the sharpness of her pain.

Finally.

"I am ready. Let us go to the Hall."

Seijina silently wheeled Betsona out of her chambers and down the dark hallway. She grimly clutched the seat as Seijina wrestled the chair down the steep ramp that allowed her access to the rest of the imperial chambers. At least she only had to endure this farce of a court in Daraelen once a year, now that Chatain had exiled her to the house in the distant city of Adalane.

Once down the ramp and out of the private royal quarters, they joined the line of nobles waiting to be escorted to their seats in the great Presentation Hall. A year ago, Betsona might have demanded a position ahead of everyone else in the line.

But this was behavior that Chatain would expect from her, so no. She would not yield to his expectations.

Faraln, a younger half-brother, swooped by, his golden skin heavily powdered in an attempt to make him look more Aireii instead of a half-breed like her. He grimaced as he saw Betsona and averted his eyes, pushing forward to be at the head of the line.

She bit back a smile as the majordomo's assistant sent him back. Now it was her turn to look away as he approached her, hoping to cut into the line. Typical for Faraln.

"Cousin!" Their distant relative Larien en Ralsem smoothly intercepted Faraln before he reached Betsona. "Seijina. May I have the favor of joining you lovely ladies?"

Faraln scowled and tried to shove past Larien. He turned his back on Faraln, moving side to side to block him as Faraln tried to get closer to Betsona to plead his case.

"But of course." She liked *this* cousin and didn't see enough of Larien, isolated as he was in the Ourigny Islands as part of Chatain's navy. He bent to kiss her cheek, then carefully hug her before turning to Seijina and formally kissing her hand. "How have things been in the islands?" she asked.

"Oh, the usual state of affairs. Busy. Perhaps we could speak after this?"

"I would love to," she said. "Provided we both survive this event."

"If anyone survives it will be you," Larien said.

"We shall see."

"Humph!" Faraln snorted from behind Larien. "I should be joining you, *sister*, not this cousin and this—this jumped-up *servant* you've made yours."

"I need Seijina's assistance thanks to our dear brother's actions sixteen years ago." She let her voice carry a sharp needle of magic to emphasize her point, not daring to use too much and exhaust her strength.

He dares to attack Seijina!

"I—I—" Faraln flinched back. "Of course not. How could we ever forget that?"

"You seemed to. I suppose I should forgive since you were only three years old at the time. But. I am your sister now?" Betsona raised her brows. "That was not what I heard from your lips a year ago at Chatain's Coronation. Or am I only imagining that you were amongst those who told Chatain that Adalane was the perfect place for me?"

"But-but—you *are* interested in the arts!"

"The arts take many forms," Betsona said smoothly. "Perhaps you should pay more attention to some of Adalane's plays. May I suggest *The Betrayal of Elithtra* as one you might benefit from studying?"

"Well! I—" Faraln spotted someone in the line behind them and marched away.

"Playing with fire, cousin," Larien said.

Seijina snorted. "Is anything new?"

"He's an ass. I'm surprised he's survived until now."

"Oh, his days are short, believe me." Larien leaned close to whisper. "Chatain is going to send him to the Ourignies. He doesn't know it yet. While he's supposed to command a ship, I can guarantee that his attitude will lead to him taking a few swims with the Goddess Terat. If not worse."

Betsona stifled a chuckle as they moved ahead. "I am glad to see you are well and have not changed, cousin."

Larien shrugged. "Easy enough to do in the Islands. I'm in the right place for now. No one pays attention to me. So far." He coughed. "How are you finding Adalane?"

"Well, I'm seeing a lot of plays these days, and I am cultivating a circle of playwrights."

He raised an eyebrow. "Perhaps we will see a play about the events of sixteen years ago?"

"Now that *would* be playing with fire," Betsona murmured as they approached the head of the line. "Do you see ships traveling to Varen very often?"

"Only some of the Sorcerer-Captains," Larien said. "There's been more of that since Rekaré became Leader in Medvara. Smuggling, in both directions. Very discreet, of course. It's something we can discuss over a glass of wine."

"I look forward to speaking further," Betsona said as Seijina rolled her chair to the head of the line.

The majordomo bowed to them, then turned to the hall. "Lord Captain Larien en Ralsem, second in command of the fleet at Ourigny Prime."

Betsona raised her brows at that. "You have risen high, cousin," she said softly to Larien.

"Less impressive than it sounds," he said. "Ostwen is the one in charge." Instead of following his escort to his assigned place in the melee of attendees, he stepped aside, waiting for Betsona.

"Betsona ea Ralsem ei Vespla," the majordomo announced.

Ei Vespla. Though the epithet was new since Chatain's ascension, it still struck a sour note deep within her soul. Daughter of Vespla the concubine. She couldn't just be Betsona ea Ralsem, she had to have the qualifier *ei Vespla*. It hadn't been that way when their father was alive. Then it had been an honor to be Vespla's daughter.

As Seijina rolled Betsona's chair forward, she fancied that everyone in the room stared at her. Or was it just her imagination? Betsona raised her chin high. She *was* a Ralsem and the Emperor's daughter, even if her mother had been one of his slave concubines. The magic of the Ralsems—and before them, the Miteals—pulsed through her veins, just like it did Chatain's.

Larien processed next to Betsona as a young slave boy decked in the Emperor's blue and silver led her to a space in the lesser rank of Darani nobles. The young boy tried to guide Larien away, but he shook his head and took his seat next to Betsona as Seijina stood behind her chair.

"You risk your position," she breathed softly to him.

"Ostwen won't let it happen," he whispered back. "That would leave him at the mercy of the incompetents who don't understand the tech part of magitech."

Faraln marched by them, sneering as the slave led him to a position in the first rank. Betsona frowned as her magic flared slightly, sharp prickles of defensive magic needling up and down her forearms.

He carries more magic than he used to.

He hadn't damped it like he should around Chatain. She glanced at Larien to see if he had noticed. But his focus was on the stage at the front of the Hall, where Chatain would appear.

Perhaps Faraln will not make it to the Ourignies.

That would not break her heart. He had tormented her when they were both younger, whenever he thought their father would not notice. Surprising that he had survived this long into Chatain's reign. She hadn't imagined Chatain would have possessed enough patience to tolerate Faraln's boorishness.

Unless Chatain's position is more precarious than I thought.

Now that was something to consider.

The announcements ceased. The low murmur of voices around them stilled as the majordomo marched down the center aisle, followed by five small slave boys decked in the brightly brocaded blue and silver uniforms of the Emperor's staff. They lined up below the stage, facing the crowd, arms crossed behind their backs.

No Guards. Betsona glanced carefully around. *Does Chatain grow so confident?*

She hadn't felt anyone else's magic stir besides Faraln's since they entered the Hall. Chatain must have worked a dampening spell to counter those who hadn't leashed their magic. It was one reason why she had calmed the Star of Elithtra. Better she be the one to quiet its spells rather than Chatain.

So why was she feeling Faraln's magic? That dampening spell should have shut him down as well.

The majordomo thumped his staff four times. "All rise for Chatain en Ralsem, Glorious Emperor of Daran, Conqueror of Ternar, Rightful Ruler of the Colonies in Varen, Master of Magitech, Master Sorcerer, Bearer of the Ruby Crown."

Seijina and Larien helped Betsona struggle to her feet. They held her steady as a column of chained and half-naked golden-skinned men and women trudged down the center aisle in ranks four across, whip-bearing guards marching beside every other rank. The first rank went to hands and knees in front of the stage. Two more ranks formed behind them. The next two ranks climbed on top of their cohorts. One in the fourth rank reluctantly held back until a guard lashed her into submission. The final rank climbed to the very top, their backs level with the top of the stage.

Betsona bit her lower lip, shuddering. Her mother had been golden-skinned like these people. Had Vespla endured such a humiliation before Dunaran had taken her to his bed, after his original conquest of Ternar? She swallowed hard, wanting to be sick.

No. You must stay strong.

Gods, the outrage. And the Ternarese were hardly rebels. They had been vassals to Dunaran ever since the battle where her mother was captured.

Chatain strikes at you through this. They were loyal to you—and they paid for it.

She lifted her chin high, tightening her lips. She dared not let him see her anger and hurt.

"Cha-tain. Cha-tain. Cha-tain." The five small slave boys began the chant, thrusting their fisted right arms high, taken up by the crowd. Betsona mouthed the words. At least her withered right arm excused her from the salute.

"CHA-TAIN. CHA-TAIN. CHA-TAIN." The volume escalated with each repeat until she wanted to press her hands against her ears to block out the din.

A heavy warmth pushed against Betsona—Chatain was projecting his full magical presence. Her half-brother processed down the aisle, robed in blue and silver, the Ruby Crown glowing bright on his head. Betsona glanced down quickly, in time to cover the Star of Elithtra to calm it yet again as Chatain walked by. He glanced at her, frowning as the Star's magic flared before she could damp it further.

Not good.

And yet could she blame the Star for recognizing the Crown? She bowed her head submissively. Chatain half-smiled and looked away.

The oppressive warmth faded as he approached the chained captives. Chatain stepped on the first rank, using them as human stairs. Betsona squinched her eyes hard shut to avoid seeing it.

Gods.

This was worse than his crowning. She shuddered.

Seijina squeezed her shoulder. "It's done," she whispered.

Betsona opened her eyes as her brother turned to face the crowd.

"CHA-TAIN. CHA-TAIN. CHA- TAIN."

He raised his hands high, shaking them in rhythm with each syllable of his names. Then he closed them. A tightness briefly shuttered Betsona's throat as the room fell silent, cut off in mid-cry. Chatain dropped his hands, and the tightness went away.

"My people. I greet you on this first anniversary of my ascension to the Crown, praise be to the Lady Nitel."

"Praise be to the Lady Nitel," the crowd echoed.

Betsona's lips formed the words but she did not give voice to them, tamping back her anger. That wrathful Goddess was no patron of hers. She should never have become the patron of Daran.

Chatain pointed to the ranks of chained captives, still forming a human stair. "Behold the fruits of our latest victory. These are the former leaders of Ternar, now part of our realm and our servants."

Ternar.

Her mother's people had been granted autonomy at Betsona's birth, in reward for Vespla's production of a powerful sorceress for Dunaran. Betsona tightened her lips, biting back another surge of rage. Was it her imagination that Chatain smirked in her direction?

"Now we have retaken Ternar. Next—we not only recapture our colony in Medvara, but we subjugate all of Varen!"

That will not happen.

The crowd roared around her but she could not join in.

"But I could not do it without your support." Chatain glowered directly at Betsona. "I continue to sort through my royal kin to determine who is and is not worthy to be considered a potential heir—until I can sire a likely prospect."

Something *shifted* in the corner of her eye. Power stirred. Betsona tuned out Chatain's next words, trying to figure out who dared to work magic here. She had to be careful, because Chatain would use any excuse to cull her and this would be the perfect setting for him to do so...*Faraln!* Like her his mother had been Ternarese. But his mother had not held the stature with Dunaran that Vespla had. There were other siblings here, all with greater standing than Faraln—enough to stir his ambition. Why would he risk it today?

His exile to the Ourigny Islands.

She shifted position to watch him. A faint shimmer rose around Faraln, edged with magenta and purple. The colors of the Twin Gods, Karnoi and Cirdel.

He means to strike at Chatain.

Betsona drew herself up as straight and tall as she could. If he acted and she responded...she needed something to make her look favorable in Chatain's eyes. Faraln would not hesitate should she be so foolish as to attack Chatain here. She could do no less.

"I challenge you, false brother!" Faraln screamed, the shimmer about him coalescing into a ball made up of worm-like magenta and purple strands that sinuously twisted around each other. He raised his hands high to fling it at Chatain. Those around him backed away as quickly as they could in the throng of people in that first rank.

Chatain startled and lifted his hands to cast a spell, but Betsona was faster.

Fire, she thought at the Star of Elithtra.

Blue flame licked out from the topaz to burst the ball. Faraln screamed as the magenta and purple strands whipped around him, tightening. They changed shade to blue and silver, binding Faraln tightly.

Chatain growled and pointed his right index finger at Faraln. Orange flame lashed out from his fingertip. It set Faraln on fire, starting at his feet and surging up his body, until his screams finally ceased and his corpse fell to the floor, still burning.

Murmurs rose around her.

"Chatain is strong in magic to strike like that," she heard over and over.

Betsona knew better. This was one of the devices she had designed, a flamethrower triggered by magic to shoot directly at an intended target, not quite perfected before her father died and she had been exiled from the labs. She had wondered what had become of it.

Chatain lowered his hands. He glared at Betsona as she let her lips twitch up in a knowing smirk. She met his stare without flinching.

"And that is the fate of those who challenge us," he said

finally. "Our thanks to the lady Betsona for her quick action." But the anger in his glare belied his words.

Betsona inclined her head slightly in acknowledgement. "I exist to serve you, Lord Chatain." She couldn't keep a mocking tone out of her voice.

Once again I have proven myself better at magitech than you!

He flinched as if he had read her thoughts, his glower deepening, tossing a quick magical projectile at her. She blocked and muted it, using the Star to raise a personal shield to deflect such low-level attacks.

Really, brother?

Her lips tightened. He looked away, but the grimace and sour expression told her that between her and Faraln, his first crown anniversary had been tarnished.

She swayed and Seijina grabbed her tight as her knees buckled, easing her back into the chair. Wielding the Star alone drew too much of her energy.

Someday you will falter beyond easy recovery, brother. I live to see that day.

Oh Gods, she hoped to live that long.

NEWSLETTER

Like this story and want to know what's coming out next, or what deals Joyce is offering on her book?

Check out Joyce's monthly newsletter at

https://joycespublishingnewsfromwideopenspaces.kit.com/a65eaa89cd

And get a free download snippet from the Martiniere Multiverse!

BOOKS AND PUBLICATIONS

The Cost of Power

The Martiniere Legacy

People of the Martiniere Legacy

Broken Angel: The Lost Years of Gabriel Martiniere: A Martiniere Legacy Novel

Justine Fixes Everything: Reflections on Mortality

The Martiniere Multiverse

A Different Life: What If?
A Different Life: Now. Always. Forever.
A Very Multiversal Christmas Miracle

Goddess's Honor titles currently available (chronological order):

The Goddess's Choice: A Goddess's Honor Short Story
Beyond Honor and Other Stories: Goddess's Honor Book One
Exile's Honor: A Goddess's Honor Novelette
Birth of Sorrow: A Goddess's Honor Short Story
Pledges of Honor: Goddess's Honor Book Two
Return to Wickmasa: A Goddess's Honor Short Story
Crown Anniversary: A Goddess's Honor Short Story
Challenges of Honor: Goddess's Honor Book Three
Cleaning House: A Goddess's Honor Outtake Story
Unexpected Alliances: A Goddess's Honor Rough Draft Outtake Story
Choices of Honor: Goddess's Honor Book Four
Judgment of Honor: Goddess's Honor Book Five

Netwalk Sequence Author Preferred 2022 Editions

Life in the Shadows: Book One
Netwalk: Book Two
Netwalker Uprising: Book Three
Netwalk's Children: Book Four
Learning in Space: Book Five
Netwalking Space: Book Six

Bright Star Fair Witches

Becoming Solo: A Bright Star Fair Witches Novella

Non-Series Titles currently available:

Alien Savvy: A Western SF Novella
Klone's Stronghold
Beating the Apocalypse
Bearing Witness
Fabulist and Fantastical Worlds: A Short Story Collection
Federation Cowboy
Vision of Alliance

Vella Titles:

Falcon of the Martinieres (part of *Justine Fixes Everything*)
Bearing Witness
Beating the Apocalypse
A Different Life—What If? An Alternative Martiniere Legacy Novel
Becoming Solo
A Different Life—Linda's Story: An Alternative Martiniere Legacy Novel
Federation Cowboy

Audiobooks Available:

Alien Savvy: A Western SF Novella

Released from other publishers:

"Queen of the Snows," in *Once Upon A Winter: A Folk and Fairy Tale Anthology*, edited by H. L. Macfarlane

"My Man Left Me, My Dog Hates Me, and There Goes My Truck," in *Black-Eyed Peas on New Year's Day: An Anthology of Hope*, edited by Shannon Page

"Lost Loves," in *All Worlds Wayfarer*

"The Wisdom of Robins," in *Whimsical Beasts: A Campcon Anthology*, edited by Joyce Reynolds-Ward

"The Cow at the End of the World," in *Well...It's Your Cow,* edited by Frog Jones

"To Plant or Pull Up Stakes," in *Pulling Up Stakes: A Campcon Anthology*, edited by Joyce Reynolds-Ward

"The Notice," in *Children of a Different Sky*, edited by Alma Alexander

ABOUT THE AUTHOR

The work of Joyce Reynolds-Ward includes themes of high-stakes family and political conflict, digital sentience, personal agency and control, realistic strong women, and (whenever possible) horses. She is the author of *The Netwalk Sequence* series, the *Goddess's Honor* series, *The Martiniere Legacy* series, *The People of the Martiniere Legacy* series, and the recently published *The Cost of Power* trilogy as well as standalones *Klone's Stronghold, Alien Savvy, Beating the Apocalypse,* and *Federation Cowboy.* Joyce is a Self-Published Fantasy BlogOff Semifinalist, a Writers of the Future SemiFinalist, and an Anthology Builder Finalist. She is a member of the Science Fiction and Fantasy Writers Association and a member of Soroptimists International.

9 780989 847353